Praise for *The Finkler Question*

'Like all of [Jacobson's] work, *The Finkler Question* has a kind of energy that you have to look at through your fingers, like an eclipse. As the brightness of his brilliance is hard to look at, so is the darkness of his humor. I don't know a funnier writer alive' Jonathan Safran Foer, *Los Angeles Times*

'Every page is thick with [wit]: dark humour, bittersweet humour, black humour, irony, comic timing, comic subtlety, comic cynicism, knowing humour, unknowing humour . . . *The Finkler Question* is further proof, if any was needed, of Jacobson's mastery of humour' *The Times*

'Wonderful . . . Jacobson is seriously on form' *Evening Standard*

'Sentence by sentence, there are few writers who exhibit the same unawed respect for language or such a relentless commitment to re-examining even the most seemingly unobjectionable of received wisdoms' *Daily Telegraph*

'A richly satisfying read' *Sunday Times*

'Jacobson cunningly crafts sublime pathos from comedy and vice versa. As such, he is the literary equivalent of Tony Hancock, illuminating the conflict, anger, love and dependence created by friendship while wincing at the ignominy and absurdity of the characters' predicament. Jacobson's prose is a seamless roll of blissfully melancholic interludes. Almost every page has a quotable, memorable line' *Independent on Sunday*

'Wonderful. A blistering portrayal of a funny man who at last confronts the darkness of the world' Beryl Bainbridge

'A striking novel and a subtle one . . . *The Finkler Question* has all the qualities we expect from Mr. Jacobson—especially a mordant wit, sometimes as acrid as it is exuberant' *Wall Street Journal*

'A riotous morass of jokes and worries about Jewish identity, though it is by no means too myopic to be enjoyed by the wider world. It helps that Mr. Jacobson's comic sensibility suggests Woody Allen's, that his powers of cultural observation are so keen, and that influences as surprising as Lewis Carroll shape this book. Mr. Jacobson stages a Mad Seder that brings Carroll's Mad Tea Party to mind' *New York Times*

'Brilliantly, painfully comic, *The Finkler Question* is a revelation even in the land that gave birth to Philip Roth' *Boston Globe*

'*The Finkler Question* tackles an uncomfortable issue [Jewish identity] with satire that is so biting, so pointed, that it pulls you along for 300 pages and leaves a battlefield of sacred cows in its wake . . . It's a must read, no matter what your background' National Public Radio

'A clever, canny, textured, subtle, and humane novel exploring the friendship of three ageing male friends . . . Although *The Finkler Question* is by no means a straightforward comic novel, it once again demonstrates Jacobson's mastery of the form' *Daily Beast*

'An enjoyable novel . . . as politically timely as it is comically well-timed' *Sydney Morning Herald*

'An incomparable marvel' *West Australian*

THE FINKLER QUESTION

An award-winning novelist and critic, **HOWARD JACOBSON** was born in Manchester and read English at Cambridge under F. R. Leavis. He taught at the University of Sydney, Selwyn College, Cambridge, and finally Wolverhampton Polytechnic – the inspiration for his first novel, *Coming From Behind*. Other novels include *The Mighty Walzer* (winner of the Bollinger Everyman Wodehouse Prize), *Kalooki Nights* (longlisted for the Man Booker Prize) and, most recently, the highly acclaimed *The Act of Love*. Howard Jacobson writes a weekly column for the *Independent* and has written and presented several documentaries for television. He lives in London.

BY THE SAME AUTHOR

Fiction

Coming From Behind
Peeping Tom
Redback
The Very Model of a Man
No More Mister Nice Guy
The Mighty Walzer
Who's Sorry Now?
The Making of Henry
Kalooki Nights
The Act of Love

Non-fiction

Shakespeare's Magnanimity (with Wilbur Sanders)
In the Land of Oz
Roots Schmoots: Journeys Among Jews
Seriously Funny: From the Ridiculous to the Sublime

THE FINKLER QUESTION

Howard Jacobson

BLOOMSBURY

LONDON · BERLIN · NEW YORK · SYDNEY

First published in Great Britain 2010
This paperback edition published 2011

Copyright © 2010 by Howard Jacobson

The moral right of the author has been asserted

Bloomsbury Publishing, London, Berlin, New York and Sydney

Bloomsbury Publishing Plc
50 Bedford Square
London WC1B 3DP

www.bloomsbury.com

Bloomsbury Publishing, London, New York and Berlin
A CIP catalogue record for this book is available from the British Library

ISBN 978 1 4088 0993 8
10 9 8 7 6 5

Export ISBN 978 1 4088 1846 6
10 9 8 7 6 5 4 3 2 1

Typeset by Hewer Text UK Ltd, Edinburgh
Printed in Great Britain by Clays Ltd, St Ives plc

MIX
Paper from
responsible sources
FSC® C018072

To the memory of three dear friends, great givers of laughter

Terry Collits (1940–2009)

Tony Errington (1944–2009)

Graham Rees (1944–2009)

Who now will set the table on a roar?

PART ONE

ONE

I

He should have seen it coming.

His life had been one mishap after another. So he should have been prepared for this one.

He was a man who saw things coming. Not shadowy premon-itions before and after sleep, but real and present dangers in the daylit world. Lamp posts and trees reared up at him, splintering his shins. Speeding cars lost control and rode on to the footpath leaving him lying in a pile of torn tissue and mangled bones. Sharp objects dropped from scaffolding and pierced his skull.

Women worst of all. When a woman of the sort Julian Treslove found beautiful crossed his path it wasn't his body that took the force but his mind. She shattered his calm.

True, he had no calm, but she shattered whatever calm there was to look forward to in the future. She *was* the future.

People who see what's coming have faulty chronology, that is all. Treslove's clocks were all wrong. He no sooner saw the woman than he saw the aftermath of her – his marriage proposal and her acceptance, the home they would set up together, the drawn rich silk curtains leaking purple light, the bed sheets billowing like clouds, the wisp of aromatic smoke winding from the chimney – only for every wrack of it – its lattice of crimson roof tiles, its gables and dormer windows, his happiness, his future – to come crashing down on him in the moment of her walking past.

3

She didn't leave him for another man, or tell him she was sick of him and of their life together, she passed away in a perfected dream of tragic love – consumptive, wet-eyelashed, and as often as not singing her goodbyes to him in phrases borrowed from popular Italian opera.

There was no child. Children spoilt the story.

Between the rearing lamp posts and the falling masonry he would sometimes catch himself rehearsing his last words to her – also as often as not borrowed from the popular Italian operas – as though time had concertinaed, his heart had smashed, and she was dying even before he had met her.

There was something exquisite to Treslove in the presentiment of a woman he loved expiring in his arms. On occasions he died in hers, but her dying in his was better. It was how he knew he was in love: no presentiment of her expiry, no proposal.

That was the poetry of his life. In reality it had all been women accusing him of stifling their creativity and walking out on him.

In reality there had even been children.

But beyond the reality something beckoned.

On a school holiday in Barcelona he paid a gypsy fortune-teller to read his hand.

'I see a woman,' she told him.

Treslove was excited. 'Is she beautiful?'

'To me, no,' the gypsy told him. 'But to you . . . maybe. I also see danger.'

Treslove was more excited still. 'How will I know when I have met her?'

'You will know.'

'Does she have a name?'

'As a rule, names are extra,' the gypsy said, bending back his thumb. 'But I will make an exception for you because you are young. I see a Juno – do you know a Juno?'

4

She pronounced it 'Huno'. But only when she remembered.

Treslove closed one eye. Juno? Did he know a Juno? Did *anyone* know a Juno? No, sorry, no, he didn't. But he knew a June.

'No, no, bigger than June.' She seemed annoyed with him for not being able to do bigger than June. 'Judy . . . Julie . . . Judith. Do you know a Judith?'

Hudith.

Treslove shook his head. But he liked the sound of it – Julian and Judith. Hulian and Hudith Treslove.

'Well, she's waiting for you, this Julie or Judith or Juno . . . I do still see a Juno.'

Treslove closed his other eye. Juno, Juno . . .

'How long will she wait?' he asked.

'As long as it takes you to find her.'

Treslove imagined himself looking, searching the seven seas. 'You said you see danger. How is she dangerous?'

He saw her rearing up at him, with a knife to his throat – *Addio, mio bello, addio.*

'I did not say it was she who was dangerous. Only that I saw danger. It might be you who is dangerous to her. Or some other person who is dangerous to both of you.'

'So should I avoid her?' Treslove asked.

She shuddered a fortune-teller's shudder. 'You cannot avoid her.'

She was beautiful herself. At least in Treslove's eyes. Emaciated and tragic with gold hooped earrings and a trace, he thought, of a West Midlands accent. But for the accent he would have been in love with her.

She didn't tell him anything he didn't already know. Someone, something, was in store for him.

Something of more moment than a mishap.

He was framed for calamity and sadness but was always somewhere else when either struck. Once, a tree fell and

5

crushed a person walking just a half a yard behind him. Treslove heard the cry and wondered whether it was his own. He missed a berserk gunman on the London Underground by the length of a single carriage. He wasn't even interviewed by the police. And a girl he had loved with a schoolboy's hopeless longing – the daughter of one of his father's friends, an angel with skin as fine as late-summer rose petals and eyes that seemed forever wet – died of leukaemia in her fourteenth year while Treslove was in Barcelona having his fortune told. His family did not call him back for her final hours or even for the funeral. They did not want to spoil his holiday, they told him, but the truth was they did not trust his fortitude. People who knew Treslove thought twice about inviting him to a death-bed or a burial.

So life was still all his to lose. He was, at forty-nine, in good physical shape, had not suffered a bruise since falling against his mother's knee in infancy, and was yet to be made a widower. To his knowledge, not a woman he had loved or known sexually had died, few having stayed long enough with him anyway for their dying to make a moving finale to anything that could be called a grand affair. It gave him a preternaturally youthful look – this unconsummated expectation of tragic event. The look which people born again into their faith sometimes acquire.

2

It was a warm late-summer's evening, the moon high and skittish. Treslove was returning from a melancholy dinner with a couple of old friends, one his own age, one much older, both recently made widowers. For all the hazards of the streets, he had decided to walk a little around a part of London he knew well, mulling over the sadness of the night in retrospect, before taking a cab home.

A cab, not a Tube, though he lived only a hundred yards from a Tube station. A man as fearful as Treslove of what might befall him above ground was hardly going to venture beneath it. Not after the close shave with the gunman.

'How unutterably sad,' he said, not quite aloud. He meant the death of his friends' wives and the death of women generally. But he was also thinking of the men who had been left alone, himself included. It is terrible to lose a woman you have loved, but it is no less a loss to have no woman to take into your arms and cradle before tragedy strikes . . .

'Without that, what am I for?' he asked himself, for he was a man who did not function well on his own.

He passed the BBC, an institution for which he had once worked and cherished idealistic hopes but which he now hated to an irrational degree. Had it been rational he would have taken steps not to pass the building as often as he did. Under his breath he cursed it feebly – 'Shitheap,' he said.

A nursery malediction.

That was exactly what he hated about the BBC: it had infantilised him. 'Auntie', the nation called the Corporation, fondly. But aunties are equivocal figures of affection, wicked and unreliable, pretending love only so long as they are short of love themselves, and then off. The BBC, Treslove believed, made addicts of those who listened to it, reducing them to a state of inane dependence. As it did those it employed. Only worse in the case of those it employed – handcuffing them in promotions and conceit, disabling them from any other life. Treslove himself a case in point. Though not promoted, only disabled.

There were cranes up around the building, as high and unsteady as the moon. That would be a shapely fate, he thought: as in my beginning, so in my end – a BBC crane dashing my brains out. The *shitheap*. He could hear the tearing of his skull, like the earth's skin opening in a disaster movie. But then life was a disaster movie in which lovely women died, one after another. He quickened his pace. A tree reared up at him. Swerving, he almost walked into a fallen road mender's sign. DANGER. His shins ached with the imagined collision. Tonight even his soul shook with apprehension.

It's never where you look for it, he told himself. It always comes from somewhere else. Whereupon a dark shadow materialised from a doorway into an assailant, took him by the neck, pushed him face first against a shop window, told him not to shout or struggle, and relieved him of his watch, his wallet, his fountain pen and his mobile phone.

It was only when he had stopped shaking and was able to check his pockets and find them emptied that he could be certain that what had happened had happened in reality.

No wallet, no mobile phone.

In his jacket pocket no fountain pen.

On his wrist no watch.

And in himself no fight, no instinct for preservation, no *amour de soi*, no whatever the word is for the glue that holds a man together and teaches him to live in the present.

But then when had he ever had that?

He'd been a modular, bits-and-pieces man at university, not studying anything recognisable as a subject but fitting components of different arts-related disciplines, not to say indisciplines, together like Lego pieces. Archaeology, Concrete Poetry, Media and Communications, Festival and Theatre Administration, Comparative Religion, Stage Set and Design, the Russian Short Story, Politics and Gender. On finishing his studies – and it was never entirely clear when and whether he *had* finished his studies, on account of no one at the university being certain how many modules made a totality – Treslove found himself with a degree so unspecific that all he could do with it was accept a graduate traineeship at the BBC. For its part – *her* part – all the BBC could do with Treslove when she

8

got him was shunt him into producing late-night arts programmes for Radio 3.

He felt himself to be a stunted shrub in a rainforest of towering trees. All around him other trainees rose to startling eminence within weeks of their arriving. They shot up, because there was no other direction you could go but up, unless you were Treslove who stayed where he was because no one knew he was there. They became programme controllers, heads of stations, acquisitors, multi-platform executives, director generals even. No one ever left. No one was ever fired. The Corporation looked after its own with more fierce loyalty than a family of mafiosi. As a consequence everyone knew one another intimately – except Treslove who knew no one – and spoke the same language – except Treslove, who spoke a language of loss and sorrow nobody understood.

'Cheer up,' people would say to him in the canteen. But all that did was make him want to cry. Such a sad expression, 'Cheer up'. Not only did it concede the improbability that he ever would cheer up, it accepted that there could be nothing much to cheer up for if cheering up was all there was to look forward to.

He was reprimanded on an official letterhead by someone from the Creative Board – he didn't recognise the complainant's name – for addressing too many morbid issues and playing too much mournful music on his programme. 'That's the province of Radio 3,' the letter concluded. He wrote back saying his programme *was* on Radio 3. He received no reply.

After more than a dozen years roaming the ghostly corridors of Broadcasting House in the dead of night, knowing that no one was listening to anything he produced – for who, at three o'clock in the morning, wanted to hear live poets discussing dead poets, who might just as well have been dead poets discussing live poets? – he resigned. 'Would anyone notice if my programmes weren't aired?' he wrote in his letter of resignation. 'Would anyone be aware of my absence if I just stopped turning up?' Again he received no reply.

Auntie wasn't listening either.

He answered an advertisement in a newspaper for an assistant director of a newly launched arts festival on the south coast. 'Newly launched' meant a school library which had no books in it, only computers, three visiting speakers and no audience. It reminded him of the BBC. The actual director rewrote all his letters in simpler English and did the same with his conversation. They fell out over the wording of a brochure.

'Why say exhilarating when you can say sexy?' she asked him.

'Because an arts festival isn't sexy.'

'And you want to know why that is? Because you insist on using words like exhilarating.'

'What's wrong with it?'

'It's indirect language.'

'There's nothing indirect about exhilaration.'

'There is the way you say it.'

'Could we try for a compromise with exuberance?' he asked, without any.

'Could we try for a compromise with you getting another job?'

They had been sleeping together. There was nothing else to do. They coupled on the gymnasium floor when no one turned up to their festival. She wore Birkenstocks even during lovemaking. He only realised he loved her when she sacked him.

Her name was Julie and he only noticed that when she sacked him, too.

Hulie.

Thereafter he gave up on a career in the arts and filled a succession of unsuitable vacancies and equally unsuitable women, falling in love whenever he took up a new job, and falling out of love – or more correctly being fallen out of love with – every time he moved on. He drove a removal van, falling in love with the first woman whose house he emptied, delivered milk in an electric float, falling in love with the cashier who paid him every Friday night, worked as an assistant to an Italian carpenter who replaced sash windows in Victorian houses and replaced Julian Treslove in the affections of the cashier, managed a shoe department in a famous London store, falling in love with the woman who managed soft furnishings on the floor above, finally finding semi-permanent and ill-paid occupation with a theatrical agency specialising in providing doubles of famous people for parties, conferences and corporate events. Treslove didn't look like anybody famous in particular, but looked like many famous people in general, and so was in demand if not by virtue of verisimilitude, at least by virtue of versatility.

And the soft-furnishings woman? She left him when he became the double of no one in particular. 'I don't like not knowing who you're meant to be,' she told him. 'It reflects badly on us both.'

'You choose,' he said.

'I don't want to choose. I want to know. I crave certainty. I need to know you're going to be there through thick and thin. I work with fluff all day. When I come home I want something solid. It's a rock I need, not a chameleon.'

She had red hair and angry skin. She heated up so quickly Treslove had always been frightened to get too near to her.

'I am a rock,' he insisted, from a distance. 'I will be with you to the end.'

'Well, you're right about that at least,' she told him. 'This *is* the end. I'm leaving you.'

'Just because I'm in demand?'

'Because you're not in demand with me.'

'Please don't leave. If I wasn't a rock before, I'll be a rock from now on.'

'You won't. It isn't in your nature.'

'Don't I look after you when you're ill?'

'You do. You're marvellous to me when I'm ill. It's when I'm well that you're no use.'

He begged her not to go. Took his chance and threw his arms around her, weeping into her neck.

'Some rock,' she said.

Her name was June.

Demand is a relative concept. He wasn't so much in demand as a lookalike for everybody and nobody that there weren't many vacant hours in which to think about all that had befallen him, or rather all that hadn't, about women and the sadness he felt for them, about his loneliness, and about that absence in him for which he didn't have the word. His incompletion, his untogetherness, his beginning waiting for an end, or was it his end waiting for a beginning, his story waiting for a plot.

It was exactly 11.30 p.m. when the attack occurred. Treslove knew that because something had made him look at his watch the moment before. Maybe the foreknowledge that he would never look at it again. But with the brightness of the street lamps and the number of commercial properties lit up — a hairdresser's was still open and a dim sum restaurant and a newsagent's having a refit — it could have been afternoon. The streets were not deserted. At least a dozen people might have come to Treslove's rescue, but none did. Perhaps the effrontery of the assault — just a hundred yards from Regent Street, almost within cursing distance of the BBC — perplexed whoever saw it. Perhaps they thought the participants were playing or had become embroiled in a domestic row on the way home from a restaurant or the theatre. They could — there was the strange part — have been taken for a couple.

That was what Treslove found most galling. Not the interruption to one of his luxuriating, vicariously widowed reveries. Not the shocking suddenness of the attack, a hand seizing him by the back of his neck and shoving him so hard into the window of Guivier's violin shop that the instruments twanged and vibrated behind the shattering pane, unless the music he heard was the sound of his nose breaking. And not even the theft of his watch, his wallet, his fountain pen and his mobile phone, sentimental as his attachment to the first of those was, and inconvenient as would be the loss of the second, third and fourth. No, what upset him beyond all these was the fact that the person who had robbed, assaulted and, yes, terrified him – a person against whom he put up not a whisper of a struggle – was . . . a woman.

3

Until the assault, Treslove's evening had been sweetly painful but not depressing. Though they complained of being without compass or purpose on their own, the three men – the two widowers and Treslove, who counted as an honorary third – enjoyed one another's company, argued about the economy and world affairs, remembered jokes and anecdotes from the past, and almost managed to convince themselves they'd gone back to a time before they had wives to lose. It was a dream, briefly, their falling in love, the children they'd fathered – Treslove had inadvertently fathered two that he knew of – and the separations that had devastated them. No one they loved had left them because they had loved no one yet. Loss was a thing of the future.

Then again, who were they fooling?

After dinner, Libor Sevcik, at whose apartment between Broadcasting House and Regent's Park they dined, sat at the piano and played the Schubert Impromptus Opus 90 his wife Malkie had loved to play. Treslove thought he would die with grief for his friend. He didn't know how Libor had survived Malkie's death. They had been married for more than half a century. Libor was now approaching his ninetieth year. What could there be left for him to live for?

Malkie's music, maybe. Libor had never once sat at the piano while she was alive – the piano stool was sacred to her, he would as soon sit on it as burst in on her in the lavatory – but many a time he had stood behind her while she played, in the early days accompanying her on the fiddle, but later, at her quiet insistence ('Tempo, Libor, tempo!'), standing behind her without his fiddle, marvelling at her expertise, at the smell of aloes and frankincense (all the perfumes of Arabia) that rose from her hair, and at the beauty of her neck. A neck more graceful, he had told her the day they had met, than a swan's. Because of his accent, Malkie had thought he had said her neck was more graceful than a svontz, which had reminded her of a Yiddish word her father often used, meaning penis. Could Libor really have meant that her neck was more graceful than a penis?

Had she not married Libor, or so the family mythology had it, Malkie Hofmannsthal would in all likelihood have gone on to be a successful concert pianist. Horowitz heard her play Schubert in a drawing room in Chelsea and commended her. She played the pieces as they should be played, he said, as though Schubert were inventing as he went along – emotional improvisations with a bracing undernote of intellectuality. Her family regretted her marriage for many reasons, not the least of them being Libor's lack of intellectuality and breeding, his low journalistic tone, and the company he kept, but mostly they regretted it on account of the musical future she threw away.

'Why can't you marry Horowitz if you have to marry someone?' they asked her.

'He is twice my age,' Malkie told them. 'You might as well ask why I don't marry Schubert.'

'So who said a husband can't be twice your age? Musicians live for ever. And if you do outlive him, well . . .'

'He doesn't make me laugh,' she said. 'Libor makes me laugh.'

She could have added that Horowitz was already married to Toscanini's daughter.

And that Schubert had died of syphilis.

She never once regretted her decision. Not when she heard Horowitz play at Carnegie Hall – her parents had paid for her to go to America to forget Libor and bought her front-row seats so that Horowitz shouldn't miss her – not when Libor won a measure of renown as a show-business journalist, travelling to Cannes and Monte Carlo and Hollywood without her, not when he fell into one of his Czech depressions, not even when Marlene Dietrich, unable to figure out the time anywhere in the world but where she was, would ring their London apartment from the Chateau Marmont at three thirty in the morning, call Libor 'my darling', and sob down the phone.

'I find my entire fulfilment in you,' Malkie told Libor. There was a rumour that Marlene Dietrich had told him the same, but he still chose Malkie whose neck was more graceful than a svontz.

'You must go on playing,' he insisted, buying her a Steinway upright with gilded candelabra at an auction in south London.

'I will,' she said. 'I will play every day. But only when you're here.'

When he could afford it he bought her a Bechstein concert grand in an ebonised case. She wanted a Blüthner but he wouldn't have anything in their apartment manufactured behind the Iron Curtain.

In their later years she had made him promise her he would

not die before her, so incapable was she of surviving an hour without him – a promise he had solemnly kept.

'Laugh at me,' he told Treslove, 'but I got down on one knee to make her that promise, exactly as I did the day I proposed to her. That is the only reason I am staying alive now.'

Unable to find words, Treslove got down on one knee himself and kissed Libor's hand.

'We did discuss throwing ourselves off Bitchy 'Ead together if one of us got seriously sick,' Libor said, 'but Malkie thought I was too light to hit the sea at the same time she did and she didn't fancy the idea of hanging around in the water waiting.'

'Bitchy 'Ead?' Treslove wondered.

'Yes. We even drove there for a day out. Daring each other. Lovely spot. Great spiralling downs with seagulls circling and dead bunches of flowers tied to barbed-wire fences – one with its price ticket still on, I remember – and there was a plaque with a quotation from Psalms about God being mightier than the thunder of many waters and lots of little wooden crosses planted in the grass. It was probably the crosses that decided us against.'

Treslove didn't understand what Libor was talking about. Barbed-wire fences? Had he and Malkie driven on a suicide pact to Treblinka?

Seagulls, though . . . And crosses . . . Search him.

Malkie and Libor did nothing about it anyway. Malkie was the one who got seriously sick and they did not a damned thing about it.

Three months after her death, Libor ventured bravely into the eye of his despair and hired a tutor, who smelt of old letters, cigarettes and Guinness, to teach him to play the impromptus which Malkie had interpreted as though Schubert were in the room with them (inventing as he went), and these he played over and over again with four of his favourite photographs of Malkie on the piano in front of him. His inspiration, his instructress, his companion, his judge. In one of them she looked unbearably young, leaning laughing over the pier at Brighton, the sun in her face. In another she wore her wedding dress. In all of them she had eyes only for Libor.

Julian Treslove wept openly the moment the music began. Had he been married to Malkie he didn't doubt he would have wept over her beauty every morning he woke to find her in his bed. And then, when he woke to find her in his bed no more, he couldn't imagine what he'd have done ... Thrown himself off Bitchy 'Ead – why not?

How do you go on living knowing that you will never again – not ever, ever – see the person you have loved? How do you survive a single hour, a single minute, a single second of that knowledge? How do you hold yourself together?

He wanted to ask Libor that. 'How did you get through the first night of being alone, Libor? Did you sleep? Have you slept since? Or is sleep all that's left to you?'

But he couldn't. Perhaps he didn't want to hear the answer.

Though once Libor did say, 'Just when you think you've overcome the grief, you realise you are left with the loneliness.'

Treslove tried to imagine a loneliness greater than his own. 'Just when you get over the loneliness,' he thought, 'you realise you are left with the grief.'

But then he and Libor were different men.

He was shocked when Libor let him into a secret. At the end they had used bad language to each other. Really bad language.

'You and Malkie?'

'Me and Malkie. We talked vulgar. It was our defence against pathos.'

Treslove couldn't bear the thought. Why did anyone want a defence against pathos?

Libor and Malkie were of the same generation as his parents, both long deceased. He had loved his parents without

17

being close to them. They would have said the same about him. The watch of which he would be divested later that evening was a gift from his ever-anxious mother. 'Jewels for my Jules', it was inscribed. But she never called him Jules in life. The sense of being properly put together which he had lost, likewise, was an inheritance from his father, a man who stood so straight he created a sort of architectural silence around himself. You could hang a plumb line from him, Treslove remembered. But he didn't believe his parents were the reason for the tears he shed in Libor's company. What moved him was this proof of the destructibility of things; everything exacted its price in the end, and perhaps happiness exacted it even more cruelly than its opposite.

Was it better then – measuring the loss – not to know happiness at all? Better to go through life waiting for what never came, because that way you had less to mourn?

Could that be why Treslove so often found himself alone? Was he protecting himself against the companioned happiness he longed for because he dreaded how he would feel when it was taken from him?

Or was the loss he dreaded precisely the happiness he craved?

Thinking about the causes of his tears only made him cry the more.

The third member of the group, Sam Finkler, did not, throughout Libor's playing, shed a single tear. The shockingly premature death of his own wife – by horrible coincidence in the very same month that Libor was made a widower – had left him almost more angry than sorrowful. Tyler had never told Sam he was her 'entire fulfilment'. He had loved her deeply all the same, with an expectant and even watchful devotion – which did not preclude other devotions on the side – as though he hoped she would vouchsafe her true feelings for him one day. But she never did. Sam sat by her bedside throughout her last night. Once she beckoned to him to come closer. He did as she bade him, putting his ear to her poor dry mouth; but if she meant to say something tender to him she did not succeed. A gasp of pain was all he heard. A sound that could just as easily have come from his own throat.

Theirs, too, had been a loving if sometimes fractious marriage, and a more fruitful one, if you count children, than Libor and Malkie's, but Tyler had always struck Sam as withheld or secretive somehow. Perhaps faithless, he didn't know. He might not have minded had he known. He didn't know that either. He was never given the opportunity to find out. And now her secrets were, as they say, buried with her. There were tears in Sam Finkler, but he was as watchful of them as he had been of his wife. Were he to weep he wanted to be certain he wept out of love, not anger. So it was preferable – at least until he grew better acquainted with his grief – not to weep at all.

And anyway, Treslove had tears enough for all of them.

Julian Treslove and Sam Finkler had been at school together. More rivals than friends, but rivalry too can last a lifetime. Finkler was the cleverer. Samuel, he insisted on being called then. 'My name's Samuel, not Sam. Sam's a private investigator's name. Samuel was a prophet.'

Samuel Ezra Finkler – how could he be anything but cleverer with a name like that?

It was to Finkler that Treslove had gone running in high excitement after he'd had his future told on holiday in Barcelona. Treslove and Finkler were sharing a room. 'Do you know anyone called Juno?' Treslove asked.

'J'you know Juno?' Finkler replied, making inexplicable J noises between his teeth.

Treslove didn't get it.

'J'you know Juno? Is that what you're asking me?'

Treslove still didn't get it. So Finkler wrote it down. *D'Jew know Jewno?*

Treslove shrugged. 'Is that supposed to be funny?'

'It is to me,' Finkler said. 'But please yourself.'

'Is it funny for a Jew to write the word Jew? Is that what's funny?'

'Forget it,' Finkler said. 'You wouldn't understand.'

'Why wouldn't I understand? If I wrote *Non-Jew don't know what Jew know* I'd be able to tell you what's funny about it.'

'There's nothing funny about it.'

'Exactly. Non-Jews don't find it hilarious to see the word Non-Jew. We aren't amazed by the written fact of our identity.'

'And d'Jew know why that is?' Finkler asked.

'Go fuck yourself,' Treslove told him.

'And that's Non-Jew humour, is it?'

Before he met Finkler, Treslove had never met a Jew. Not knowingly at least. He supposed a Jew would be like the word Jew – small and dark and beetling. A secret person. But Finkler was almost orange in colour and spilled out of his clothes. He had extravagant features, a prominent jaw, long arms and big feet for which he had trouble finding wide enough shoes, even at fifteen. (Treslove noticed feet; his were dainty like a dancer's.) What is more – and everything was more on Finkler – he had a towering manner that made him look taller than he actually was, and delivered verdicts on people and events with such assurance that he almost spat them out of his mouth. 'Say it, don't spray it,' other boys sometimes said to him, though they took their lives in their hands when they did. If this was what all Jews looked like, Treslove thought, then Finkler, which sounded like Sprinkler, was a better name for them than Jew. So that was what he called them privately – *Finklers*.

He would have liked to tell his friend this. It took away the stigma, he thought. The minute you talked about the *Finkler Question*, say, or the *Finklerish Conspiracy*, you sucked out the toxins. But he was never quite able to get around to explaining this to Finkler himself.

They were both the sons of uppity shopkeepers. Treslove's father sold cigars and smoking accoutrements, Finkler's pharmaceuticals. Sam Finkler's father was famous for dispensing pills which reinvigorated people apparently at death's door. They took his pills and their hair grew back, their backs straightened, their biceps swelled. Finkler senior was himself a walking miracle, a one-time stomach cancer patient now become the living proof of what his pills were capable of achieving. He would invite customers to his pharmacy, no matter what their ailments, to punch him in the stomach. Right where his cancer had once been. 'Harder,' he'd say. 'Punch me harder. No, no good, I still don't feel a thing.'

And then when they marvelled at his strength he would produce his box of pills. 'Three a day, with meals, and you too will never feel pain again.'

For all the circus hocus-pocus he was a religious man who wore a black fedora, was an active member of his synagogue, and prayed to God to keep him alive.

Julian Treslove knew he would never be clever in a Finklerish way. *D'Jew know Jewno* . . . He'd never be able to come up with anything like that. His brain worked at a different temperature. It took him longer to make his mind up and no sooner did he make his mind up than he wanted to change it again. But he was, he believed, and perhaps for that reason, the more boldly imaginative of the two. He would come to school balancing his night's dreams like an acrobat bearing a human pyramid on his shoulders. Most of them were about being left alone in vast echoing rooms, or standing over empty graves, or watching houses burn. 'What do you think that was about?' he'd ask his friend. 'Search me,' was Finkler's invariable reply. As though he had more important things to think about. Finkler never dreamed. On principle, it sometimes seemed to Treslove, Finkler never dreamed.

Unless he was just too tall to dream.

So Treslove had to figure out his own dreams for himself.

They were about being in the wrong place at the wrong time. They were about being too late, unless they were about being too early. They were about waiting for an axe to fall, a bomb to drop, a dangerous woman to dabble her fingers in his heart. Julie, Judith, Juno . . .

Huno.

He also dreamed about misplacing things and never being able to find them despite the most desperate searches in unlikely places – behind skirting boards, inside his father's violin, between the pages of a book even when what he was looking for was bigger than the book. Sometimes the sensation of having misplaced something precious lasted throughout the day.

Libor, more than three times their age when they met him, had turned up out of the blue – he really did look, in his maroon velvet suit and matching bow tie, as though he'd pushed open the wrong door, like Treslove in his dreams – to teach them European history, though mainly what he wanted to talk to them about was communist oppression (from which he'd had the foresight to flee in 1948, just before it sunk its claws into his country), Hussite Bohemia and the part played by windows in Czech history. Julian Treslove thought he had said 'widows' and became agitated.

'Widows in Czech history, sir?'

'Windows, chlapec, windows!'

He had been a journalist of sorts in his own country, a well-connected film critic and gossip columnist, and then again, as Egon Slick, a showbusiness commentator in Hollywood, squiring beautiful actresses around the bars of Sunset Boulevard, and writing about them for the glamour-starved English press, yet now here he was teaching the absurdities of Czech history to English schoolboys in a north London Grammar School. If anything could be more existentially absurd than Czech history, it was his own.

It was for Malkie that he'd relinquished Hollywood. She

never accompanied him on his assignments, preferring to keep the home fires burning. 'I like waiting for you,' she told him. 'I love the anticipation of your return.' But he could tell the anticipation was wearing thin. And there were material cares he didn't feel he could leave her to go on handling on her own. He broke a contract and argued with his editor. He wanted time to write the stories of where he'd been and who he'd met. Teaching gave him that time.

Pacific Palisades to Highgate, Garbo to Finkler – the trajectory of his career made him laugh disrespectfully during his own classes, which endeared him to his pupils. Morning after morning he delivered the same lesson – a denunciation of Hitler and Stalin followed by the First and – 'if you're well behaved' – the Second Defenestration of Prague. Some days he'd ask one of the boys to give his lesson for him since they all knew it so well. When no questions about the First, the Second or indeed Any Subsequent Defenestrations of Prague appeared on their examination papers, the class complained to Libor. 'Don't look to me to prepare you for *examinations*,' he told them, curling his already curly lip. 'There are plenty of teachers who can help you get good marks. The point of me is to give you a taste of the wider world.'

Libor would have liked to tell them about Hollywood but Hollywood wasn't on the syllabus. Prague and its defenestrations he could slip in, the stars and their indiscretions he could not.

He didn't last long. Teachers who wear bow ties and talk about the wider world seldom do. Six months later he was working for the Czech Department at the World Service by day, and writing biographies of some of Hollywood's loveliest women by night.

Malkie didn't mind. Malkie adored him and found him funny. Funny was better than absurd. Her finding him funny kept him sane, 'And you can't say that about many Czechs,' he joked.

He continued to see the two boys when he had time. Their innocence diverted him; he had never known boyish innocence himself. He would take them out to bars they could not afford to go to on their own, mixing them drinks they had never before heard of let alone tasted, describing in considerable detail his erotic exploits – he actually used the word erotic, snagging his tongue on it as though the salaciousness of the syllables themselves was enough to arouse him – and telling them about the Bohemia from which he had luckily escaped and expected never to see again.

Of the nations of the free world, only England and America were worth living in, in Libor's view. He loved England and shopped as he imagined the English shopped, buying scented tea and Gentleman's Relish at Fortnum & Mason and his shirts and blazers in Jermyn Street, where he also indulged in a shave and hot towels soaked in limes as many mornings as he could manage. Israel, too, he spoke up for, as a Finkler himself, though that was more about needling people with the fact of its existence, Treslove thought, than wanting to live there. Whenever Libor said the word Israel he sounded the 'r' as though there were three of them and let the 'l' fall away to suggest that the place belonged to the Almighty and he couldn't bring himself fully to pronounce it. Finklers were like that with language, Treslove understood. When they weren't playing with it they were ascribing holy properties to it. Or the opposite. Sam Finkler would eventually spit out Israel-associated words like Zionist and Tel Aviv and Knesset as though they were curses.

One day Libor told them a secret. He was married. And had been for more than twenty years. To a woman who looked like Ava Gardner. A woman so beautiful that he did not dare bring home his friends to meet her in case they were blinded by what they saw. Treslove wondered why, since he hadn't told them about her before, he was telling them about her now. 'Because I think you're ready,' was his answer.

'Ready to go blind?'

'Ready to risk it.'

The real reason was that Malkie had nieces the same age as Treslove and Finkler, girls who had trouble finding boyfriends. Nothing came of the matchmaking – even Treslove couldn't fall in love with Malkie's nieces who bore not the slightest physical resemblance to her, though he did, of course, fall in love with Malkie, despite her being old enough to be his mother. Libor had not exaggerated. Malkie looked so like Ava Gardner that the boys canvassed the possibility between them that she *was* Ava Gardner.

The friendship faded a little after that. Having shown the boys his wife, Libor had little else to impress them with. And the boys for their part had Ava Gardners of their own to find.

Shortly afterwards the first of the biographies was published, quickly followed by another. Juicy and amusing and slightly fatalistic. Libor became famous all over again. Indeed more famous than he had been before, because a number of the women he was writing about were now dead and it was thought they had confided more of their secrets to Libor than to any other man. In several of the photographs, which showed Libor dancing with them cheek to cheek, you could almost see them spilling their souls to him. It was because he was funny that they could trust him.

For several years Sam and Julian kept in touch with Libor's progress only through these biographies. Julian envied him. Sam less so. Word of Hollywood rarely penetrated the deserted late-night corridors of Broadcasting House which were home – if a hell can be called a home – to Julian Treslove. And because he considered Libor's career to be the inverse of his own, he was continuously, if secretly, seduced by it.

Sam Finkler, or Samuel Finkler as he still was then, had not done a modular degree at a seaside university. He knew better, he said, which side his bread was buttered. Finklerish of him,

Treslove thought admiringly, wishing he had the instincts for knowing on which side his own bread was buttered.

'So what's it going to be?' he asked. 'Medicine? Law? Accountancy?'

'Do you know what that's called?' Finkler asked him.

'What what's called?'

'The thing you're doing.'

'Taking an interest?'

'Stereotyping. You've just stereotyped me.'

'You said you knew which side your bread was buttered. Isn't that stereotyping yourself?'

'I am allowed to stereotype myself,' Finkler told him.

'Ah,' Treslove said. As always he wondered if he would ever get to the bottom of what Finklers were permitted to say about themselves that non-Finklers were not.

Unstereotypically – to think which was a further form of mental stereotyping, Treslove realised – Finkler studied moral philosophy at Oxford. Though this didn't appear an especially wise career move at the time, and his five further years at Oxford teaching rhetoric and logic to small classes seemed less wise still, Finkler justified his reputation for shrewdness in Treslove's eyes by publishing first one and then another, and then another and then another, of the self-help practical philosophy books that made his fortune. *The Existentialist in the Kitchen* was the first of them. *The Little Book of Household Stoicism* was the second. Thereafter Treslove stopped buying them.

It was at Oxford that Finkler dropped the name Samuel in favour of Sam. Was that because he now wanted people to think he was a private investigator? Treslove wondered. Sam the Man. It crossed his mind that what his friend didn't want to be thought was a Finkler, but then it would have made more sense to change the Finkler not the Samuel. Perhaps he just wanted to sound like a person who was easy to get on with. Which he wasn't.

In fact, Treslove's intuition that Finkler no longer wanted to be thought a Finkler was the right one. His father had died, in great pain at the last, miracle pills or no miracle pills. And it had been his father who had kept him to the Finkler mark. His mother had never quite understood any of it and understood less now she was on her own. So that was it for Finkler. Enough now with the irrational belief systems. What Treslove couldn't have understood was that the Finkler name still meant something even if the Finkler idea didn't. By staying Finkler, Finkler kept alive the backward sentiment of his faith. By ditching Samuel he forswore the Finkler future.

On the back of the success of his series of practical wisdom guides he had gone on – his big feet and verbal sprinkling and, in Treslove's view, all-round unprepossessingness of person notwithstanding – to become a well-known television personality, making programmes showing how Schopenhauer could help people with their love lives, Hegel with their holiday arrangements, Wittgenstein with memorising pin numbers. (And Finklers with their physical disadvantages, Treslove thought, turning off the television in irritation.)

'I know what you all think of me,' Finkler pretended to apologise in company when his success became difficult for those who knew and loved him to accept, 'but I have to earn money fast in preparation for when Tyler leaves and takes me for all I've got.' Hoping she would say she loved him too much to dream of leaving him, but she never did. Which might have been because she did little else but dream of leaving him.

Whereas Finkler, if Treslove's supposition was correct, was too tall to dream of anything.

Though their lives had gone in different directions, they had never lost contact with each other or with each other's families – in so far as Treslove could be said to have a family – or with Libor who, first at the height of his fame, and then as it dimmed and his wife's illness became his preoccupation, would suddenly remember their existence and invite them to a party, a house-warming, or even the premiere of a film. The first time Julian Treslove went to Libor's grand apartment in Portland Place and heard Malkie play Schubert's Impromptu Opus 90 No. 3 he wept like a baby.

Since then, bereavement had ironed out the differences in their ages and careers and rekindled their affection. Bereavement – heartless bereavement – was the reason they were seeing more of one another than they had in thirty years.

With their women gone, they could become young men again.

For 'gone', in Treslove's sense, read gone as in packed their bags, or found someone less emotionally demanding, or just not yet crossed his path on the dangerous streets and destroyed his peace of mind.

4

After dinner, Julian had walked alone to the gates of Regent's Park and looked inside. Finkler had offered him a lift but he refused it. He didn't want to sink into the leather of Sam's big black Mercedes and feel envy heat up his rump. He hated cars but resented Sam his Mercedes and his driver for nights when he knew he would be drunk – where was the sense in that? Did he want a Mercedes? No. Did he want a driver for nights when he knew he would be drunk? No. What he wanted was a wife and Sam no longer had one of those. So what did Sam have that he hadn't? Nothing.

Except maybe self-respect.

And that also needed explaining. How could you make programmes associating Blaise Pascal and French kissing and still have self-respect? Answer – you couldn't.

And yet he did.

Maybe it wasn't self-respect at all. Maybe self didn't enter into it, maybe it was actually a freedom from self, or at least from self in the Treslove sense of self – a timid awareness of one's small place in a universe ringed by a barbed-wire fence of rights and limits. What Sam had, like his father the show-man pharmaceutical chemist before him, was a sort of obliviousness to failure, a grandstanding cheek, which Treslove could only presume was part and parcel of the Finkler heritage. If you were a Finkler you just found it in your genes, along with other Finkler attributes it was not polite to talk about.

They barged in, anyway, these Finklers – Libor, too – where non-Finklers were hesitant to tread. That evening, for example, when they weren't listening to music, they had discussed the Middle East, Treslove staying out of it because he believed he had no right to an opinion on a subject which wasn't, at least in the way it was to Sam and Libor, any business of his. But did they truly know more than he did – and if they did, how come they disagreed about every aspect of the subject – or were they simply unabashed by their own ignorance?

'Here we go,' Finkler would say whenever the question of Israel arose, 'Holocaust, Holocaust,' even though Treslove was certain that Libor had never mentioned the Holocaust.

It was always possible, Treslove conceded, that Jews didn't have to mention the Holocaust in order to have mentioned the Holocaust. Perhaps they were able by a glance to thought-transfer the Holocaust to one another. But Libor didn't *look* as though he were thought-transferring Holocausts.

And Libor, in his turn, would say, 'Here we go, here we go, more of the self-hating Jew stuff,' even though Treslove had never met a Jew, in fact never met anybody, who hated himself less than Finkler did.

Thereafter they went at it as though examining and shred-ding each other's evidence for the first time, whereas Treslove, who knew nothing, knew they'd been saying the same things for decades. Or at least since Finkler had gone to Oxford. At school, Finkler had been so ardent a Zionist that when the Six Day War broke out he tried to enlist in the Israeli air force, though he was only seven at the time.

'You've misremembered what I told you,' Finkler corrected Treslove when he reminded him of that. 'It was the Palestinian air force I tried to enlist for.'

'The Palestinians don't have an air force,' Treslove replied.

'Precisely,' Finkler said.

Libor's position with regard to Israel with three 'r's and no 'l' − Isrrrae − was what Treslove had heard described as the lifeboat pos-ition. 'No, I've never been there and don't ever want to go there,' he said, 'but even at my age the time might not be far away when I have nowhere else *to* go. That is history's lesson.'

Finkler did not allow himself to use the word Israel at all. There was no Israel, there was only Palestine. Treslove had even heard him, on occasions, refer to it as Canaan. Israelis, however, there had to be, to distinguish the doers from the done-to. But whereas Libor pronounced Israel as a holy utterance, like the cough of God, Finkler put a seasick 'y' between the 'a' and the 'e' − Israyelis − as though the word denoted one of the illnesses for which his father had prescribed his famous pill.

'History's lesson!' he snorted. 'History's lesson is that the Israyelis have never fought an enemy yet that wasn't made stronger by the fight. History's lesson is that bullies ultimately defeat themselves.'

'Then why not just wait for that to happen?' Treslove tentatively put in. He could never quite get whether Finkler resented Israel for winning or for being about to lose.

Though he detested his fellow Jews for their clannishness about Israel, Finkler couldn't hide his disdain for Treslove for so much as daring, as an outsider, to have a view. 'Because of the blood that will be spilled while we sit and do nothing,' he said, spraying Treslove with his contempt. And then, to Libor, 'And because as a Jew I am ashamed.'

'Look at him,' Libor said, 'parading his shame to a Gentile world that has far better things to think about, does it not, Julian?'

'Well,' Treslove began, but that was as much of what the Gentile world thought as either of them cared to hear.

'By what right do you describe me as "parading" anything?' Finkler wanted to know.

But Libor persisted blindly. 'Don't they love you enough for the books you write them? Must they love you for your conscience as well?'

'I am not seeking anyone's love. I am seeking justice.'

'Justice? And you call yourself a philosopher! What you are seeking is the warm glow of self-righteousness that comes with saying the word. Listen to me – I used to be your teacher and I'm old enough to be your father – shame is a private matter. One keeps it to oneself.'

'Ah, yes, the family argument.'

'And what's wrong with the family argument?'

'When a member of your family acts erroneously, Libor, is it not your duty to tell him?'

'Tell him, yes. Boycott him, no. What man would boycott his own family?'

And so on until the needs of men who lacked the consolations of female company – another glass of port, another unnecessary visit to the lavatory, an after-dinner snooze – reclaimed them.

Watching from the sidelines, Treslove was enviously baffled by their Finklerishness. Such confidence, such certainty of right, whether or not Libor was correct in thinking that all Finkler wanted was for non-Finklers to approve of him.

Whatever Sam Finkler wanted, his effect on Julian Treslove was always to put him out of sorts and make him feel excluded from something. And false to a self he wasn't sure he had. It had been the same at school. Finkler made him feel like someone he wasn't. Clownish, somehow. Explain that.

Treslove was considered good-looking in a way that was hard to describe; he resembled good-looking people. Symmetry was part of it. He had a symmetrical face. And neatness. He had neat features. And he dressed well, in the manner of who was it again? Whereas Finkler – whose father had invited customers to punch him in the belly – had allowed himself to put on weight, often let his own belly hang out of his shirt, spat at the camera, waddled slightly on his big feet when he went on one of those pointless television walks down the street where the laundry van knocked down Roland Barthes or through the field where Hobbes had an allotment, and when he sat down seemed to collapse into his own bulk like a merchant in a spice souk. And yet he, Treslove, felt the clown!

Did philosophy have something to do with it? Every few years Treslove decided it was time he tried philosophy again. Rather than start at the beginning with Socrates or jump straight into epistemology, he would go out and buy what promised to be a clear introduction to the subject – by someone like Roger Scruton or Bryan Magee, though not, for obvious reasons, by Sam Finkler. These attempts at self-education always worked well at first. The subject wasn't after all difficult. He could follow it easily. But then, at more or less the same moment, he would encounter a concept or a line of reasoning he couldn't follow no matter how many hours he spent trying to decipher it. A phrase such as 'the idea derived from evolution that ontogenesis recapitulates phylogenesis' for example, not impossibly intricate in itself but somehow resistant to effort, as though it triggered something obdurate and even delinquent in his mind. Or the promise to look at an argument from three points of view, each of which had five salient features, the first of which had four distinguishable aspects. It was like discovering that a supposedly sane person with whom one had been enjoying a perfectly normal conversation was in fact quite mad. Or, if not mad, sadistic.

Did Finkler ever encounter the same resistance? Treslove asked him once. No, was the answer. To Finkler it all made perfect sense. And the people who read him found that he too made perfect sense. How else was one to account for there being so many of them?

It was only when he waved goodbye that it occurred to Treslove that his old friend wanted company. Libor was right – Finkler *was* seeking love. A man without a wife can be lonely in a big black Mercedes, no matter how many readers he has.

Treslove looked up at the moon and let his head spin. He loved these warm high evenings, solitary and excluded. He took hold of the bars as though he meant to tear the gates down, but he did nothing violent, just listened to the park breathe. Anyone watching might have taken him for an inmate of an institution, a prisoner or a madman, desperate to get out. But there was another interpretation of his demeanour: he could have been desperate to get in.

In the end he needed the gate to keep him upright, so intoxicated was he, not by Libor's wine, though it had been plentiful enough for three grieving men, but by the sensuousness of the park's deep exhalations. He opened his mouth as a lover might, and let the soft foliaged air penetrate his throat.

How long since he had opened his mouth for a lover proper? Really opened it, he meant, opened it to gasp for air, to yell out in gratitude, to howl in joy and dread. Had he run out of women? He was a lover not a womaniser, so it wasn't as though he had exhausted every suitable candidate for his affection. But they seemed not to be there any more, or had suddenly become pity-proof, the sort of women who in the past had touched his heart. He saw the beauty of the girls

33

who tripped past him on the street, admired the strength in their limbs, understood the appeal, to other men, of their reckless impressionability, but they no longer had the lamp-post effect on him. He couldn't picture them dying in his arms. Couldn't weep for them. And where he couldn't weep, he couldn't love.

Couldn't even desire.

For Treslove, melancholy was intrinsic to longing. Was that so unusual? he wondered. Was he the only man who held tightly to a woman so he wouldn't lose her? He didn't mean to other men. In the main he didn't worry much about other men. That is not to say he had always seen them off – he was still scarred by the indolent manner in which the Italian who repaired sash windows had stolen from him – but he wasn't jealous. Envy he was capable of, yes – he'd been envious and was envious still of Libor's life lived mono-erotically (*elotic-shrly* was how Libor said it, knitting its syllables with his twisted Czech teeth) – but jealousy no. Death was his only serious rival.

'I have a Mimi Complex,' he told his friends at university. They thought he was joking or being cute about himself, but he wasn't. He wrote a paper on the subject for the World Literature in Translation module he'd taken after fluffing Environmental Decision Making – the pretext being the Henri Murger novel from which the opera *La Bohème* was adapted. His tutor gave him A for interpretation and D– for immaturity.

'You'll grow out of it,' he said when Treslove questioned the mark.

Treslove's mark was upgraded to A++. All marks were upgraded if students questioned them. And since every student did question them, Treslove wondered why tutors didn't just dish out regulation A++s and save time. But he never did grow out of his Mimi Complex. At forty-nine he still had it bad. Didn't all opera lovers?

And perhaps – like all lovers of Pre-Raphaelite painting, and all readers of Edgar Allan Poe – an Ophelia Complex too. The death betimes of a beautiful woman – what more poetic subject is there?

Whenever Julian passed a willow or a brook, or best of all a willow growing aslant a brook – which wasn't all that often in London – he saw Ophelia in the water, her clothes spread wide and mermaidlike, singing her melodious lay. Too much of water had she right enough – has any woman ever been more drowned in art? – but he was quick to add his tears to her inundation.

It was as though a compact had been enjoined upon him by the gods (he couldn't say God, he didn't believe in God), to possess a woman so wholly and exclusively, to encircle her in his arms so completely, that death could find no way in to seize her. He made love in that spirit, in the days when he made love at all. Desperately, ceaselessly, as though to wear down and drive away whichever spirits of malevolence had designs upon the woman in his arms. Embraced by Treslove, a woman could consider herself for ever immune from harm. Dog-tired, but safe.

How they slept when he had done with them, the women Treslove had adored. Sometimes, as he kept vigil over them, he thought they would never wake.

It was a mystery to him, therefore, why they always left him or made it impossible for him not to leave them. It was the disappointment of his life. Framed to be another Orpheus who would retrieve his loved one from Hades, who would, at the last, look back over a lifetime of devotion to her, shedding tears of unbearable sorrow when she faded for the final time in his arms – 'My love, my only love!' – here he was instead, passing himself off as someone he wasn't, a universal lookalike who didn't feel as others felt, reduced to swallowing the fragrances of parks and weeping for losses which, in all decency, were not his to suffer.

So that was something else he might have envied Libor – his bereavement.

5

He stayed at the park gates maybe half an hour, then strode back with measured steps towards the West End, passing the BBC – his old dead beat – and Nash's church where he had once fallen in love with a woman he had watched lighting a candle and crossing herself. In grief, he'd presumed. In chiaroscuro. Crepuscular, like the light. Or like himself. Inconsolable. So he'd consoled her.

'It'll be all right,' he told her. 'I'll protect you.'

She had fine cheekbones and almost transparent skin. You could see the light through her.

After a fortnight of intense consolation, she asked him, 'Why do you keep telling me it'll be all right? There isn't anything wrong.'

He shook his head. 'I saw you lighting a candle. Come here.'

'I like candles. They're pretty.'

He ran his hands through her hair. 'You like their flicker. You like their transience. I understand.'

'There's something you should know about me,' she said. 'I'm a bit of an arsonist. Not serious. I wasn't going to burn down the church. But I am turned on by flame.'

He laughed and kissed her face. 'Hush,' he said. 'Hush, my love.'

In the morning he woke to twin realisations. The first was that she had left him. The second was that his sheets were on fire.

Rather than walk along Regent Street he turned left at the church, stepping inside the columns, brushing its smooth animal roundness with his shoulder, and found himself among the small wholesale fashion shops of Riding House and Little Titchfield Streets, surprised as always at the speed with which, in London, one cultural or commercial activity gave way to another. His father had owned a cigarette and cigar shop here – *Bernard Treslove: Smokes* – so he knew the area and felt fondly towards it. For him it would always smell of cigars, as his father did. The windows of cheap jewellery and gaudy handbags and pashminas made him think of romance. He doubled back on himself, in no hurry to get home, then paused, as he always paused when he was here, outside J. P. Guivier & Co. – the oldest violin dealer and restorer in the country. Though his father played the violin, Treslove did not. His father had dissuaded him. 'It will only make you upset,' he said. 'Forget all that.'

'Forget all what?'

Bernard Treslove, bald, browned, straight as a plumb line, blew cigar smoke in his son's face and patted his head affectionately. 'Music.'

'So I can't have a cello, either?' J. P. Guivier sold beautiful cellos.

'The cello will make you even sadder. Go and play football.'

What Julian did was go and read romantic novels and listen to nineteenth-century operas instead. Which also didn't please his father, for all that the books which Treslove read, like the operas he listened to, were on his father's shelves.

After this exchange, Bernard Treslove went into his own room to play the violin. As though he didn't want to set a bad example to his family. Was it only Treslove's fancy that his father wept into his violin as he played?

So Julian Treslove played no instrument, though every time he passed J. P. Guivier's window he wished he did. He could, of course, have taken up music any time he wanted to after his father died. Look at Libor who had learnt to play the piano in his eighties.

But then Libor had someone to play it for, no matter that she was no longer with him. Whereas he . . .

* * *

It was as he was looking at the violins, lost in these tristful reflections, that he was attacked, a hand seizing him by his neck without warning, as a valuable cat out on the tiles might be grabbed by a cat snatcher. Treslove flinched and dropped his head into his shoulders, exactly as a cat might. Only he didn't claw or screech or otherwise put up a fight. He knew the people of the street – the beggars, the homeless, the dispossessed. Imaginatively, he was one of them. To him, too, the roads and pavements of the city were things of menace.

Years before, between jobs, and in pursuit of a beautiful unshaven nose-ringed charity worker with whom he believed he was destined to be happy – or unhappy: it didn't matter which, so long as it was destined – he had donated his services to the homeless and made representations on their behalf. He could hardly argue when they made representations for themselves. So he fell limp and allowed himself to be flung into the window and emptied.

Allowed?

The word dignified his own role in this. It was all over too quickly for him to have a say in the matter. He was grabbed, thrown, eviscerated.

By a woman.

But that wasn't the half of it.

It was what – reliving the event in the moments afterwards – he believed she had said to him. He could easily have been wrong. The attack had been too sudden and too brief for him to know what words had been exchanged, if any. He couldn't be sure whether or not he had uttered a syllable himself: Had he really accepted it all in silence, without even a 'Get off me!' or a 'How dare you?' or even a 'Help'? And the words he thought she had spoken to him might have been no more than the noise of his nose breaking on the pane or his cartilages exploding or his heart leaping from his chest. Nonetheless, a collection of jumbled sounds persisted and began to form and re-form themselves in his head . . .

'Your jewels,' he fancied he'd heard her say.

A strange request, from a woman to a man, unless it had once been made of her and she was now revisiting it upon him in a spirit of bitter, vengeful irony. 'Your jewels – now you know how it feels to be a woman!'

Treslove had taken a module entitled Patriarchy and Politics at university. In the course of that he often heard the sentence, 'Now you know how it feels to be a woman.'

But what if he'd manufactured this out of some obscure masculinist guilt and what she had actually said was 'You're Jules' – employing his mother's fond nickname for him?

This, too, took some explaining since he hardly needed telling who he was.

It could have been her way of marking him, letting him know that she knew his identity – 'You're Jules and don't suppose that I will ever forget it.'

But something else would surely have followed from that. Something else of course did, or had, in that she comprehensively relieved him of his valuables. Wouldn't she, though, for her satisfaction to be complete, have wanted him to know who she was in return? 'You're Jules, I'm Juliette – remember me now, you little prick!'

The more he thought about it, the less sure he was that 'Your' or 'You're' was quite the sound she'd made. It was more truncated. More a 'You' than a 'Your'. And more accusatory in tone. More 'You Jules' than 'You're Jules'.

'You Jules', as in 'You Jules, you!'

But what did that mean?

He had the feeling, further, that she hadn't pronounced any 's'. He strained his retrospective hearing to catch an 's' but it eluded him. 'You Jule' was more what she had said. Or 'You jewel'.

But is it consonant with calling someone a jewel that you smash his face in and rob him blind?

Treslove thought not.

Which returned him to 'You Jule!'

Also inexplicable.

Unless what she had said as she was emptying his pockets was, 'You Ju!'

TWO

I

'What's your favourite colour?'

'Mozart.'

'And your star sign?'

'My eyesight?'

'Star sign. *Star*.'

'Oh, Jane Russell.'

So had begun Libor's first date of his widowhood.

Date! That was some joke – he ninety, she not half that, maybe not a third of that. Date! But what other word was there?

She did not appear to recognise the name Jane Russell. Libor wondered where the problem lay – in the accent he had not quite lost or the hearing he had not quite kept. It was beyond his comprehension that Jane Russell could simply be forgotten.

'R–u–s–s–e–l–l,' he spelt out. 'J–a–n–e. Beautiful, big . . .' He did the thing men do, or used to do, weighing the fullness of a woman's breasts in front of him, like a merchant dealing in sacks of flour.

The girl, the young woman, the child, looked away. She had no chest to speak of herself, Libor realised, and must therefore have been affronted by his mercantile gesture. Though if she'd had a chest she might have been more affronted still. The things you had to remember with a woman you hadn't been married to for half a century! The feelings you had to take into account!

A great sadness overcame him. He wanted to be laughing with Malkie over it. 'And then I . . .'

'Libor – you didn't!'

'I did, I did.'

He saw her put her hand to her mouth – the rings he had bought her, the fullness of her lips, the shake of her black hair – and wanted her back or wanted it to be over. His date, his awkwardness, his sorrow, everything.

His date was called Emily. A nice name, he thought. Just a pity she worked for the World Service. In fact, the World Service was the reason friends had introduced them. Not to canoodle over the goulash and dumplings – Austro-Hungarian food was his idea: old world gluttony that would soak up any gaps in conversation – but to talk about the institution they had in common, maybe how it had changed since Libor had been there, maybe to discover she had worked with the children of whom Libor had known the parents.

'Only if she's not one of those smug leftists,' Libor had said.

'Libor!'

'I can say it,' he said. 'I'm Czech. I've seen what leftists do. And they're all smug leftists at the BBC. Especially the women. Jewish women the worst. It's their preferred channel of apostasy. Half the girls Malkie grew up with disappeared into the BBC. They lost their sense of the ridiculous and she lost them.'

He could say 'Jewish women the worst', too. He was one of the allowed.

Fortunately, Emily wasn't a Jewish leftist. Unfortunately she wasn't anything else. Except depressed. Two years before, her boyfriend Hugh had killed himself. Thrown himself under a bus while she was waiting for him to collect her. At the Aldwych. That was the other reason friends had connected them – not, of course, with a view to anything romantic, but in the hope that they would briefly cheer each other up. But of the two – Emily and Hugh – Libor felt more of a connection to Hugh, dead under a bus.

'What bands do you like?' she asked him, after a longer dumpling-filled silence than she could bear.

Libor pondered the question.

The girl laughed, as at her own absurdity. She twirled a lifeless lock of hair around a finger that had an Elastoplast on it. 'What bands did you *used* to like,' she corrected herself, then blushed as though she knew the second question was more absurd than the first.

Libor turned his ear to her and nodded. 'I'm not in principle keen on banning anything,' he said.

She stared at him.

Oh, God, he remembered in time, she will want me to be against fox hunting and runways and animal experiments and electric light bulbs. But there was no point starting out – not that they were going anywhere – with a lie.

'Four-wheel drives,' he said. 'Dropped aitches – mine are cultural – talk radio, socialism, trainers, Russia, but definitely not fur coats. If you'd seen Malkie in her chinchilla . . .'

She went on staring at him. He feared she was going to cry.

'No, bands,' she said at last. '*Bands.*'

Deciding against saying the Czech Philharmonic, Libor sighed and showed her his hands. The flesh, disfigured with liver spots, was loose enough for her to slide her fingers under. It would peel clean away, like the skin on a lightly roasted chicken. His knuckles were swollen, his fingernails yellow and bent over at the ends.

Then he ran his hands over his baldness and inclined his head. He had always been a balding man. Balding had suited him. But he was plucked clean by time now. The patina of extreme old age was on him. He wanted her to see her own reflection in his pate, measure all the time she had left in the dull mirror of his antiquity.

He could tell she couldn't figure out what he was showing her. When he presented his bald head to Malkie she would polish it with her sleeve.

It used to excite her. Not just the head but the act of polishing it.

They had furnished their apartment in the style of Biedermeier. Libor's taste not Malkie's (though Malkie had Biedermeier blood in her veins), but she had humoured the aspiring European petit bourgeois in him. 'Reminds me of our escritoire,' she would tell him. 'It responds in the same way to a good buffing.'

It amused him to be her furniture. 'You can open my drawers whenever you like,' he would say. And she would laugh and cuff him with her sleeve. At the end they had talked dirty to each other. It was their defence against pathos.

'I'm sorry,' he told the girl, folding his napkin. 'This isn't fair to you.'

He signalled to the waiter before remembering his manners. 'You don't want a dessert do you, Emily?' he asked. He was pleased he could recall her name.

She shook her head.

He paid the bill.

She was as relieved as he was when they parted.

2

'I could use the company but I can't go through the pain of getting it,' he told Treslove on the phone.

It was a week after they had dined together. Treslove hadn't told Libor about the attack. Why worry him? Why make Libor afraid of his own neighbourhood?

Not that Libor was the one who needed protecting. Treslove marvelled at his courage – dressing himself up, going out on a date, making small talk. He pictured him in his David Niven outfit, fine white polo neck jumper worn under a blue blazer with faux military buttons. Most men Libor's age wore lovat jackets, the colour of sick, and trousers that were too short for them. This had always bemused and worried Treslove. At a certain age men began to shrink, and yet it was precisely at that age that their trousers became too short for them. Explain that.

But not Libor. Or at least not Libor when he was got up to meet a friend, or a woman. He was still the Mittel European dandy. Only on the telephone did he sound his age. It was as though the telephone filtered out everything that wasn't of the voice alone – the comedy, the bravado, the dancing hands. An old torn tissue-paper larynx was all that was left. Treslove knew to picture Libor in the flesh when he spoke to him on the phone, spruce in his polo neck, but the sound still depressed him. He heard a dead man speaking.

'I bet it wasn't as painful as you're pretending,' he said.

'You weren't there. On top of that it wasn't decent.'

'Why, what did you do?'

'I mean proper.'

'Why, what did you do?'

'I mean it was wrong of me to agree to meet her. I was there under false pretences. I don't want to be with another woman. I can't look at another woman without making the comparison.'

When Malkie was alive Libor carried her photograph in his wallet. Now that she was gone, he had her on his mobile phone. While he rarely used his phone as a phone – he found it hard to read the keyboard – he consulted her image a hundred times a day, flipping and unflipping the lid in the middle of a conversation. A ghost that never left him, gifted by technology. Gifted by Finkler, to be precise, since he was the one who had set it up for him.

Libor had showed the screen to Treslove, Malkie not as she was at the end of her life, but as she had looked at the beginning of her time with Libor. Her eyes smiling and wicked, appreciative, adoring, and slightly blurred, as though seen through a mist – unless that was a mist clouding Treslove's vision.

Treslove imagined Libor opening his phone and looking at Malkie under the table, even as his date asked him his star sign and his favourite band.

'I bet the girl had a ball with you,' Treslove said.

'Trust me, she didn't. I have sent her flowers to apologise.'

'Libor, that will just make her think you want to go on.'

'Ech, you English! You see a flower and you think you've been proposed to. Trust me, she won't. I enclosed a hand-written note.'

'You weren't rude to her.'

'Of course not. I just wanted her to see how shaky my handwriting was.'

'She may have taken that as proof she excited you.'

'She won't have. I told her I was impotent.'

'Did you have to be so personal?'

'That was to stop it being personal. I didn't say *she* had made me impotent.'

Treslove was embarrassed by potency talk. And not just because he'd recently been divested of his manliness by a woman. He had not been brought up, as Finkler men evidently were, to discuss matters of a sexual nature with someone with whom he was not having sex.

'Anyway –' he said.

But Libor didn't detect his embarrassment. 'I am not in fact impotent,' he went on, 'though I'm reminded of a time when I was. It was Malkie's doing. Did I ever tell you she met Horowitz?'

Treslove wondered what was coming. 'You didn't,' he said tentatively, not wanting to be thought to be leading Libor on.

'Well, she did. Twice in fact. Once in London and once in New York. At Carnegie Hall. He invited her backstage. "Maestro", she called him. "Thank you, Maestro," she said and he kissed her hand. His own hands, she told me, were icy cold. I've always been jealous of that.'

'His icy hands?'

'No, her calling him Maestro. Do you think that's strange?'

Treslove thought about it. 'No,' he said. 'I don't. A man doesn't want the woman he loves calling other men Maestro.'

'But why not? He *was* a maestro. It's funny. I wasn't in competition with him. I'm no maestro. But for three months after I couldn't do it. Couldn't get it up. Couldn't rise to the challenge.'

'Yes, that is funny,' Treslove said.

Sometimes even a Finkler as reverend and aged as Libor could make him feel like a Benedictine monk.

'The power of words,' Libor went on. '*Maestro* – she calls him *Maestro* and I might as well not have a pecker. But listen, do you want to go out somewhere to eat tonight?'

Twice in one week! It wasn't that long ago that they hadn't seen each other twice in a year. And even now that widowerhood had rebonded them they were not seeing each other twice in a month. Were things as bad as that for Libor?

'I can't,' Treslove said. He was unable to tell his friend the truth: that the reason he couldn't come out was that he had a black eye, maybe a broken nose and was still unsteady on his legs. 'I have things I must do.'

'What things?' Nearing ninety, you could ask such questions.

'*Things*, Libor.'

'I know you. You never say "things" if you really have things to do. You always name them. Something's the matter.'

'You're right, I don't have things to do. And that's what's the matter.'

'Then let's go eat.'

'Can't face it, Libor. Sorry. *I need to be alone.*'

The reference was to the title of Libor's most famous show-business book. An unofficial biography of Greta Garbo with whom Libor was once rumoured to have had an affair.

'With Garbo?' Libor exclaimed when Treslove once asked him whether it was true. 'Impossible. She was gone sixty when I met her. And she looked German.'

'So?'

'So sixty was too old for me. Sixty is still too old for me.'

'That's not what I was querying. I was querying her looking German.'

'Julian, I stared deep into her eyes. As I'm staring into yours now. Trust me – they were the eyes of a Teuton. It was like looking into the wastes of the frozen North.'

'Libor, you come from a cold place yourself.'

'Prague is hot. Only the pavements and the Vltava are cold.'

'Even so, I don't see why that should have been a problem. Come on – Greta Garbo!'

'Only a problem had I been contemplating an affair with her. Or she with me.'

'You absolutely could not contemplate having an affair with someone who looked German?'

'I could contemplate it. I couldn't do it.'

'Not even Marlene Dietrich?'

'Especially not her.'

'Why not?'

Libor had hesitated, scrutinising his old pupil's face. 'Some things you don't do,' he said. 'And besides, I was in love with Malkie.'

Treslove had made a mental note. *Some things you don't do.* Would he ever get to the bottom of the things Finklers did and didn't do? Such conversational indelicacy one moment, such scrupulousness as to the ethno-erotic niceties the next.

Over the phone, this time, Libor ignored the allusion. 'One day you will regret needing to be alone, Julian, when you have no choice.'

'I regret it now.'

'Then come out and play. It's you or someone who wants to know my star sign.'

'Libor, *I* want to know your star sign. Just not tonight.'

He felt guilty. You don't refuse the desperation of a lonely impotent old man.

But he had his own impotence to nurse.

3

Finkler, who did not dream, had a dream.

He dreamed that he was punching his father in the stomach.

His mother screamed for him to stop. But his father only laughed and shouted, 'Harder!'

'*Los the boy allein*,' he told his wife. Which was cod Yiddish for 'Leave the boy alone'.

In life, when his father spoke to him in cod Yiddish, Finkler turned his back on him. Why his father, English university-educated and normally softly spoken – a man of learning and unshakeable religious conviction – had to make this spectacle of himself in his shop, throwing his hands around and yelling in a peasant tongue, Finkler couldn't understand. Other people loved his father for these shows of Jewish excitability, but Finkler didn't. He had to walk away.

But in the dream he didn't walk away. In the dream he summoned all his strength and threw punch after punch into his father's stomach.

What woke him was his father's stomach opening. When Finkler saw the cancer swimming towards him in a sea of blood he could not go on dreaming.

He, too, was surprised when Libor rang. Like Treslove, he found it upsetting that Libor needed company twice in the same week. But he was able to be more accommodating than his friend. Perhaps because he too needed company twice in the same week.

'Come over,' he said. 'I'll order in Chinese.'

'You speak Chinese now?'

'Funny guy, Libor. Be here at eight.'

'You sure you're up for it?'

'I'm a philosopher, I'm not sure about anything. But come. Just don't bring the Sanhedrin with you.'

The Sanhedrin were the judges of the ancient land of Israel. Finkler wasn't in the mood for Israyel talk. Not with Libor.

'Not a word, I promise,' Libor said. 'On condition that none of your Nazi friends will be there to steal my chicken in black bean sauce. You will remember that I like chicken in black bean sauce?'

'I don't have Nazi friends, Libor.'

'Whatever you call them.'

Finkler sighed. 'There'll be just the two of us. Come at eight. I'll have chicken with cashew nuts.'

'Black bean sauce.'

'Whatever.'

He set two places, antique horn chopsticks for each of them. One of his last gifts to his wife, hitherto unused. It was risky but he risked it.

'These are beautiful,' Libor noted with tenderness, widower to widower.

'It's either part with them, which I can't bear to do, or use them. There's no point in making a mausoleum of unused things. Tyler would have said use them.'

'Harder to do with dresses,' Libor said.

Finkler laughed a laughless laugh.

'What is it about a dress a woman never got to wear?' Libor asked. 'You'd think it would be those that carry the memory of her shape and warmth, that still have her perfume on them, that you couldn't bear to touch. But the unworn ones are harder.'

'Well, isn't it obvious?' Finkler said. 'When you look at a dress Malkie never wore you see her alive and unworn in it herself.'

Libor appeared unconvinced. 'That feels too backward-looking to me.'

'We're allowed to look back.'

'Oh, I know that. I do nothing else. Since Malkie went I feel as though my head has been put on backwards. It's your explanation of the sadness of unused things I find too back-ward-looking. When I see an unworn dress, and Malkie had so many – saving them up for special occasions that never came, some with their labels still on as though she might yet take them back to the store – I see the future time that was stolen from her. I look forwards into the life she didn't have, the Malkie she didn't get to be, not the Malkie she was.'

Finkler listened. Malkie was eighty when she died. How much more life could Libor imagine for her? Tyler never made it to fifty. So why couldn't he feel what Libor felt? Though convinced he was gifted with an unenvious nature – what, when all was said and done, did he have to envy? – he was envious nonetheless, not of the longer life Malkie enjoyed, but of Libor's range of grief. He could not, as Libor did, throw his sorrow into the future. He did not miss the Tyler who never got to be, only the Tyler who was.

He measured his husbandly worth against the older man's. With mirth, it's true, but also meaning it, Libor had always claimed to be the perfect husband, refusing the bed of some of the most beautiful women in Hollywood. 'Not because I'm handsome did they want me, you understand, but because I made them laugh. The more beautiful the woman, the more she needs to laugh. That's why Jewish guys have always done so well. But for me they were easy to resist. Because I had Malkie who was more beautiful than all of them. And who made *me* laugh.'

Who knew the truth of it?

Libor told how Marilyn Monroe, desperate for laughter but notoriously confused by international time zones – in Libor's stories all beautiful women never knew what time it was – would ring him in the dead of night. Malkie always took the phone. It was on her side of the bed. 'Marilyn for you,' she would say in a bored, sleepy voice, waking her husband. Fucking Marilyn again.

She never doubted his fidelity because she was so secure in it. So did that fidelity – a fidelity with no pains or deprivations in it, Libor insisted, a fidelity filled to the brim with sensual delight – explain Libor's exemption from remorse? Guilt had become Finkler's medium when he thought about his wife, and guilt existed only in the past. Guilt-free, assuming he told the truth, Libor was able to sorrow over the future he and Malkie, though aged, didn't have. At any age there is future one doesn't have. Never enough life when you are happy, that was the thing. Never so much bliss that you can't take a little more. Sadness for sadness, Finkler did not know which was the more estimable, if sadness can be esteemed – feeling cheated of more of the happiness you'd enjoyed, or never having had it in the first place. But it looked better to be Libor.

And that, maybe, because it was better to have been married to Malkie. Finkler tried to dismiss this thought but could not: it takes two to create fidelity, and while he wouldn't go so far as to say Tyler was not worthy of his, she certainly hadn't made it easy. Was this why he didn't feel robbed of a future life with Tyler? Because he couldn't be sure he had one to look forward to? And whose fault was that?

'Do you ever wonder,' he mused as they ate, 'whether you're doing it all right?'

'Grieving?'

'No. Well, yes, but not just grieving. Everything. Do you ever wake in the morning and ask yourself if you've lived the best life you could have lived? Not morally. Or not only morally. Just squeezed the most out of your opportunities.'

'I'm surprised to hear that question from you, of all people,' Libor said. 'I remember you as a bright pupil, right enough. But there are many bright pupils and I would never have guessed you would achieve what you have.'

'You're telling me I have made a little go a long way.'

'Not at all, not at all. But to my eye you have fulfilled yourself more than most men. You're a household name –'

Finkler, pleased, waved the compliment away. Who cared about being a household name? The flush of satisfaction in his cheeks was probably not satisfaction at all, just embarrassment. *Household name* – for God's sake. *Household name!* How many households, he wondered, were naming him this very moment? How many households did it take to make a household name?

'Only think of Julian,' Libor continued, 'and how disappointing his life must appear to him.'

Finkler did as he was told and thought about it. The two spots of colour in his cheeks, previously the size of ten pence pieces, grew into two blazing suns.

'Yes, Julian. But then he has always been in waiting, hasn't he? I never waited for anything. I took. I had the Jewish thing. Like you. I had to make it quick, while there was time. But that only means that what I am capable of doing I have done, whereas Julian, well, his time might yet come.'

'And does that scare you?'

'Scare me how?'

'Scare you to think he might overhaul you in the end. You were close friends, after all. Close friends don't get over their dread of being beaten in the final straight. It's never over till it's over with a friend.'

'Who are you afraid might overtake you, Libor?'

'Ah, with me it really is over. My rivals are all long dead.'

'Well, Julian's not exactly breathing down my neck, is he?'

Libor surveyed him narrowly, like an old red-eyed crow watching something easy to get its beak into.

'He's not now likely to make it as a household name, you mean? No. But there are other yardsticks of success.'

'God, I don't doubt that.' He paused to ponder Libor's words. Other yardsticks, other yardsticks . . . But couldn't think of any.

Libor wondered if he'd gone too far. He remembered how touchy he had been about success at Finkler's age. He decided to change the subject, re-examining the chopsticks Finkler had bought his wife. 'These really are lovely,' he said.

'She talked about collecting them, but never did. She often discussed collecting things but never got round to it. What's the point? she'd ask. I took that as a personal affront. That our life together wasn't worth collecting for. Could she have known what was going to happen to her, do you think? Did she *want* it to happen to her?'

Libor looked away. He was suddenly sorry he had come. He couldn't take another man's wife-sorrows on top of his own. 'We can't know those things,' he said. 'We can know only what we feel. And since we're the ones who are left, only our feelings matter. Better we discuss Isrrrrae.' He put a fourth 'r' in the word to irritate his friend out of pathos.

'Libor, you promised.'

'Anti-Semites, then. Did I make a promise not to discuss your friends the anti-Semites?'

The comedic Jewish intonation was meant as a further irritant to Finkler. Libor knew that Finkler hated Jewishisms. *Mauscheln*, he called it, the hated secret language of the Jews, the Yiddishising that drove German Jews mad in the days when they thought the Germans would love them the more for playing down their Jewishness. The lost provincial over-expressiveness of his father.

'I don't have friends who are anti-Semites,' Finkler said.

Libor screwed up his face until he resembled a medieval devil. All he lacked were the horns. 'Yes, you do. The Jewish ones.'

'Oh, here we go, here we go. Any Jew who isn't your kind

54

of Jew is an anti-Semite. It's a nonsense, Libor, to talk of Jewish anti-Semites. It's more than a nonsense, it's a wickedness.'

'Don't get *kochedik* with me for speaking the truth. How can it be a nonsense when we invented anti-Semitism?'

'I know how this goes, Libor. Out of our own self-hatred . . .'

'You think there's no such thing? What do you say to St Paul, itching with a Jewishness he couldn't scratch away until he'd turned half the world against it?'

'I say thank you, Paul, for widening the argument.'

'You call that widening? Strait is the gate, remember.'

'That's Jesus, not Paul.'

'That's Jesus as reported by Jews already systematically Paulised. He couldn't take us on in the flesh so he extolled the spirit. You're doing the same in your own way. You're ashamed of your Jewish flesh. Have *rachmones* on yourself. Just because you're a Jew doesn't mean you're a monster.'

'I don't think I'm a monster. I don't even think *you're* a monster. I'm ashamed of Jewish, no, Israyeli actions—'

'There you are then.'

'It's not peculiar to Jews to dislike what some Jews do.'

'No, but it's peculiar to Jews to be *ashamed* of it. It's our *shtick*. Nobody does it better. We know the weak spots. We've been doing it so long we know exactly where to stick the sword.'

'You admit then there are weak spots?'

And they were away.

After Libor left, Finkler went into the bedroom and opened his late wife's wardrobe. He had not removed her clothes. There they hung, rail after rail of them, the narrative of their life together, her lean and hungry social sharpness, his pride in her appearance, the heads that turned when they entered a room, she like a weapon at his side.

He tried for sadness. Was there something she hadn't worn,

that would break his heart for the life she had not lived? He couldn't find a thing. When Tyler bought a dress she wore it. Everything was for now. If she bought three dresses in a day she contrived to wear three dresses in a day. To garden in, if she had to. What was there to wait for?

He breathed in her aroma, then closed the wardrobe doors, lay down on her side of the bed and wept.

But the tears were not as he wanted them to be. They were not Libor's tears. He couldn't forget himself in them.

After ten minutes he rose, went to his computer and logged on to online poker. In poker he could do what he couldn't do in grief – he could forget himself.

In winning he could forget himself even more.

4

In Treslove's dream a young girl is running towards him. She bends, in her running, barely slowing down, to take off her shoes. She is a schoolgirl in school uniform, a pleated skirt, a white blouse, a blue jumper, an untied tie. Her shoes impede her. She bends in her running to take them off so that she can run faster, freer, in her grey school socks.

It is an analytic dream. In it, Treslove questions its meaning. The dream's meaning and the reason he is dreaming it, but also the meaning of the thing itself. Why does the girl affect him as she does? Is it the girl's vulnerability, or the very opposite, her strength and resolution? Does he worry for her feet, shoeless on the hard pavement? Is he curious about the reason for her hurry? Jealous perhaps because she is heedless of him and running to someone else? Does he want to be the object of her hurry?

He has dreamed this dream all his life and no longer knows if it has its origins in something he once saw. But it is as real to him as reality and he welcomes its recurrence, though he does not summon it before he goes to sleep and does not always remember it with clarity when he wakes. The debate as to its status takes place entirely within the dream. Sometimes, though, when he sees a schoolgirl running, or bending to tie or untie a shoelace, he has a dim recollection of knowing her from somewhere else.

It is possible he dreamed this dream the night he was mugged. His sleep was deep enough for him to have dreamed it twice.

He was a man who ordinarily woke to a sense of loss. He could not remember a single morning of his life when he had woken to a sense of possession. When there was nothing palpable he could reproach himself for having lost, he found the futility he needed in world affairs or sport. A plane had crashed – it didn't matter where. An eminent and worthy person had been disgraced – it didn't matter how. The English cricket team had been trounced – it didn't matter by whom. Since he didn't follow or give a fig for sport, it was nothing short of extraordinary that his abiding sense of underachievement should have found a way to associate itself with the national cricket team's. He did the same with tennis, with footballers, with boxers, with snooker players even. When a fly and twitchy south Londoner called Jimmy White went into the final session of the World Snooker Championship seven frames ahead with eight to play and still managed to end the night a loser, Treslove retired to his bed a beaten man and woke broken-hearted. Did he care about snooker? No. Did he admire Jimmy White and want him to win? No. Yet in White's humiliating capitulation to the gods of failure Treslove was somehow able to locate his own. Not impossibly, White himself passed the day following his immeasurable loss laughing and joking with friends, buying everyone he knew drinks, in far better spirits than Treslove did.

Strange, then, that the morning after his humiliating

mugging Treslove had woken to an alien sensation of near-cheerfulness. Was this what had all along been missing from his life – a palpable loss to justify his hitherto groundless sensation of it, the theft of actual possessions as opposed to the constantly nagging consciousness of something having gone missing? An objective correlative, as T. S. Eliot called it in a stupid essay on Hamlet (Treslove had earned a B- upgraded to an A++ for his essay on T. S. Eliot's), as though all Hamlet had ever needed to explain his feeling like a rogue and peasant slave was someone to divest him of his valuables.

He and Finkler had quoted *Hamlet* endlessly to each other at school. It was the only work of literature they had both liked at the same time. Finkler was not a literary man. Literature was insufficiently susceptible to rationality for his taste. And lacked practical application. But *Hamlet* worked for him. Not knowing that Finkler wanted to kill his father, Treslove hadn't understood why. He liked it himself, not because he wanted to kill his mother, but on account of Ophelia, the patron saint of watery women. Whatever their separate motivation, they entwined the play around their friendship. 'There are more things in heaven and earth, Samuel, than are dreamt of in your philosophy,' Treslove used to say when Finkler wouldn't go to a party with him because he didn't believe in getting pissed. 'Come on, it'll be a laugh.' But Finkler, of course, was bound to tell him that he had of late, wherefore he knew not, lost all his mirth.

After which he usually changed his mind and went to the party.

Speaking for himself, all these years later, Treslove wasn't sure he had any native mirth to regain. He hadn't been amused for a long time. And he wasn't exactly amused now. But without doubt he felt more purposeful this minute than he had in years. How this could be, he didn't know. He would have expected himself to want to stay in bed and never rise again. Mugged by a woman! For a man whose life had been one absurd disgrace after another, this surely was the crowning ignominy. And yet it wasn't.

And this despite the unpleasant physical after-effects of the attack. His knees and elbows smarted. There was nasty bruising around his eyes. It pained him to breathe through his nostrils. But there was air out there and he was eager to breathe it.

He got up and opened his curtains and then closed them again. There was nothing to see. He lived in a small flat in an area of London which people who couldn't afford to live in Hampstead called Hampstead, but as it wasn't Hampstead he had no view of the Heath. Finkler had Heath. Heath from every window. He – Finkler – had not the slightest interest in Heath but he had bought a house with a view of it from every window, just because he could. Treslove checked this near re-descent into consciousness of loss. A view of the Heath wasn't everything. Tyler Finkler had enjoyed a different view of the Heath from every window and what good had any of them done her?

During breakfast there was a light nosebleed. He normally liked to take an early walk to the shops but he couldn't risk being seen by someone he knew. Nosebleeding – like grief, as Treslove recalled Libor saying – is something you do in the privacy of your own home.

He remembered what, in his humiliation and exhaustion, he had forgotten the night before – to cancel his credit cards and report his mobile phone lost. If the woman who had robbed him had been on his phone all night to Buenos Aires, or had flown to Buenos Aires on one of his cards and been on the phone all morning from there to London, he would already be insolvent. But strangely, nothing had been spent. Perhaps she was still deciding where to go. Unless theft was not her motive.

Had she wanted simply to complicate his life she couldn't have chosen a more efficient method. He was on his house phone for the rest of the morning, waiting for real people who spoke a language he could understand to answer, having to prove he was who he said he was though why he would have been worrying about the loss of his cards if he wasn't who he said he was he didn't know. The loss of his mobile was more serious; it seemed he would have to have a new number just when he had finally got round to memorising the old one. Or maybe not. It depended on the plan he was on. He hadn't known he was on a plan.

Yet not once did he turn tetchy or ask to speak to a supervisor. If further proof was needed that actual as opposed to imaginary loss had done wonders for his temper, this was it. Not once did he ask for someone's name or threaten to get them sacked. Not once did he mention the ombudsman.

There was no mail for him. Though he had the emotional strength to open envelopes, as was not always the case with him in the morning, there was relief in there being nothing to open today. No mail meant no engagements, for he accepted engagements by no other means, no matter that they came directly from his agents. Agree by phone to show up God knows where looking like God knows whom and there was a fair chance it would be a wild goose chase. Only actual mail meant actual business. And about actual business he was conscientiously professional, never refusing a gig on the superstitious assumption that the first gig he refused would be his last. There were plenty of lookalikes out there clamouring for work. London was choked with other people's doubles. Everyone looked like someone else. Fall out of sight and you'd soon be out of mind. As at the BBC. But he'd have had to refuse today given how he looked. Unless he was asked to turn up to someone's party as Robert De Niro in *Raging Bull*.

Besides, he had things he needed some mental space to think about. Such as why he had been attacked. Not only to what end, if neither his credit cards nor his mobile phone had been used, but why *him*? There was an existential form this question could take: Why me, O Lord? And there was a practical one: Why me rather than somebody else?

Was it because he looked an easy victim? An inadequately put-together man with a modular degree who was sure to offer no resistance? A nobody in particular who just happened to be at the window of J. P. Guivier when the woman – deranged, drunk or drugged – just happened to be passing? A lookalike for a man against whom she had a grievance, whoever she was?

Or did she know him for himself and wreak a vengeance she had long been planning? Was there a woman out there who hated him that much?

Mentally, he went through the list. The disappointees, the wronged (he didn't know how he had wronged them, only that they looked and felt and sounded wronged), the upset, the insulted, the abused (he didn't know how he had abused them etc.), the discontented, the never satisfied or appeased, the unhappy. But then they had all been unhappy. Unhappy when he found them and unhappier when they left. So many unhappy women out there. Such a sea of female misery.

But none of it his doing, for Christ's sake.

Had he ever raised a hand to a woman to explain why a woman should want to raise a hand to him? No. Not ever.

Well, once . . . nearly.

The fly incident.

They'd been away for a long romantic weekend, he and Joia – Joia whose voice had the quality of organza tearing and whose nervous system was visible through her skin, a tracery of fine blue lines like rivers on an atlas – three fretful days in Paris during which they hadn't been able to find a single place to eat. In Paris! They'd passed and looked into restaurants, of course, on some occasions even taken a seat, but whichever he fancied, she didn't – on nutritional or dietetic or humanitarian or simply feel-wrong grounds – and whichever she did, he didn't, either because he couldn't afford it or the waiter had insulted him or the menu made greater demands of his French than he could bear Joia – Hoia – to witness. For three days they walked the length and breadth of the greatest eating city on earth, squabbling, ashamed and famished, and then when they returned to Treslove's flat in sullen silence they found upwards of ten thousand flies in their death throes – *mouchoirs*, no, *mouches*: how come he remembered that word alone of all the French he knew; what a pity *mouches* had not been on a single menu – a mass suicide of flies in its final stages, flies dying on the bed, on the windows and the windowsills, in the dressing-table drawers, in Joia's shoes even. She had screamed in horror. It was possible he had screamed in horror too. But if he did, he stopped. And Joia, whose organza screams would have harrowed hell, did not. Treslove had seen enough films in which a man slapped a hysterical woman to bring her to her senses to know that that was how you brought a hysterical woman to her senses. But he only made as if to slap her.

The making as if to slap her – the frozen gesture of a slap – was as bad, though, as if he'd slapped her in earnest, and maybe even worse since it signalled intentionality rather than temporary loss of sanity of which hunger was a contributory cause.

He didn't deny, to himself at least, that the sight of all those flies dying like . . . well, like flies – *tombant commes des mouches* – had a no less deranging effect on him than it had on Joia, and that his almost-slap was as much to calm his nerves as hers. But it is expected of a man to know what to do when the unforeseen happens, and his not knowing what to do counted as much against him as the almost-slap.

'Hit the flies if you must hit someone,' Joia cried, her voice quavering as though on a high wire of silk, 'but don't you ever, ever, ever, ever think of hitting me.'

For a moment it occurred to Treslove that there were more evers multiplying in his bedroom than there were flies dying.

He closed his eyes against the pain and when he opened them Joia was gone. He shut the door of his bedroom and went to sleep on his couch. The following day the flies were dead. Not a one twitched. He swept them up and filled the bin with them. No sooner had he finished than Joia's brother came around to collect her things. 'But not the shoes with the flies in,' he told Treslove, as though Treslove was a man who out of malice put flies in women's shoes. 'Those my sister says you can keep to remember her by.'

Treslove remembered her all right, and knew it was not she who had attacked him. Joia's bones could not have carried the weight of his assailant. Nor could her voice have ever dropped so low. Besides, he would have known if she was in the vicinity. He would have heard her nerves twanging blocks away.

And the contact would have destroyed his mind.

Then there was *the face-painting incident*.

Treslove remembered it only to forget it. He might have woken to an alien sensation of near–cheerfulness, but he wasn't up to recalling *the face-painting incident*.

After four days of lying around in a fair bit of pain he rang his doctor. He had a private doctor – one of the perks of his having no wife or similar to put a strain on his finances – which meant he was able to get an appointment that afternoon instead of the following month by which time the pain would have subsided or he would be dead. He wound a scarf around his throat, pulled his trilby down over his eyes, and scurried down the lane. Twenty years before he had been a patient of Dr Gerald Lattimore's father, Charles Lattimore, who had keeled over in his surgery just minutes after seeing Treslove. And more than twenty years before that Dr Gerald Lattimore's grandfather, Dr James Lattimore, had been killed in a car crash while returning from delivering Treslove. Whenever Treslove visited Dr Gerald Lattimore he remembered Dr

Charles Lattimore's and Dr James Lattimore's deaths and imagined that Gerald Lattimore must remember them, too.

Does he blame me? Treslove wondered. Or worse, does he dread my visits in case the same thing happens to him? Doctors read the genes the way fortune-tellers read the tea leaves; they believe in rational coincidence.

Whatever Dr Gerald Lattimore dreaded or remembered, he always handled Treslove more roughly than Treslove believed was necessary.

'How painful is that?' he asked pinching Treslove's nose.

'Bloody painful.'

'I still think nothing's broken. Take some paracetamol. What did you do?'

'Walked into a tree.'

'You'd be surprised how many of my patients walk into trees.'

'I'm not in the slightest bit surprised. Hampstead's full of trees.'

'This isn't Hampstead.'

'And we're all preoccupied these days. We don't have the mental space to notice where we're going.'

'What's preoccupying you?'

'Everything. Life. Loss. Happiness.'

'Do you want to see someone about it?'

'I'm seeing you.'

'Happiness isn't my field. You depressed?'

'Strangely not.' Treslove looked up at Lattimore's ceiling fan, a rickety contraption with thin blades which rattled and wheezed as it slowly turned. One day that's going to come off and hit a patient, Treslove thought. Or a doctor. 'God is good to me,' he said, as though that was who he'd been looking at in the fan, 'all things considered.'

'Take your scarf off a minute,' Lattimore said suddenly. 'Let me see your neck.'

For a doctor, Lattimore was, much like his fan, insubstantially put together. Treslove remembered his father and imagined his grandfather as men of bulk and authority. The third Dr Lattimore looked too young to have completed his studies. His wrists were as narrow as a girl's. And the skin between his fingers pink, as though the air had not got to him yet. But Treslove still did as he was told.

'And did the tree also make those marks on your neck?' the doctor asked him.

'OK, a woman scratched me.'

'Those don't look like scratches.'

'OK, a woman manhandled me.'

'A woman manhandled you! What did you do to her?'

'You mean did I manhandle her back? Of course not.'

'No, what did you do to *make* her manhandle you?'

Culpability.

From before Treslove could remember, first the first Dr Lattimore, by implication, and second the second Dr Lattimore, by looks and stern words, had punished him with culpability. It didn't matter what ailment he turned up with – tonsillitis, shortness of breath, low blood pressure, high cholesterol – it was always somehow Treslove's fault; simply being born, Treslove's fault. And now a suspected fractured nose. Also his fault.

'I am innocent of any responsibility for this,' he said, sitting down again and hanging his head, as though to suggest a beaten dog. 'I was mugged. Unusual, I know, for a grown man to be beaten up and then to have his pockets emptied by a woman. But I was. I'd say it's my age.' He thought twice about what he said next but he said it anyway. 'You might not know that your grandfather delivered me. I have been in the hands of Lattimores from the beginning. It might be time now for a third-generation Lattimore to recommend me sheltered accommodation.'

'I don't want to disabuse you but if you think you'll be safe in sheltered accommodation you're mistaken. There are women there who'd rob you as soon as look at you.'

'What about an old folks' home?'

'The same, I'm afraid.'

'Do I look that soft a target?'

Lattimore looked him up and down. The answer was clearly yes. But he found a tactful way of putting it. 'It's not about you,' he said, 'it's about the women. They're getting stronger by the day. That's medical progress for you. I have patients in their eighties I wouldn't want to tangle with. I'd say you're safer out in the world where at least you can run.'

'I doubt it. The word must be out by now. And they'll be able to smell the fear on me anyway. Every woman mugger in London. Even some who have never before given a thought to armed robbery.'

'You sound cheerful about the prospect.'

'I'm not. I'm just trying not to let it get me down.'

'Very sensible. I hope they've caught this one at least.'

'Who? The police? I didn't notify the police.'

'Don't you think you should have?'

'So that they can ask me what I did to provoke her? No. They'll accuse me of propositioning or abusing her. Or they'll warn me against going out at night on my own. Either way they'll end up laughing. It's thought to be amusing – a man copping a broken nose from a woman. It's the stuff of seaside cartoons.'

'It's not broken. And I'm not laughing.'

'You are. Inside you are.'

'Well, I hope you are, inside, as well. Best medicine, you know.'

And strangely, Treslove was. Laughing inside.

But he wasn't expecting it to last.

And he wasn't convinced his nose wasn't broken.

There was something else Treslove had wanted to bring up, because he needed to bring it up with somebody, but in the laughter had thought better of it. And Lattimore, he decided, wasn't the man for it either. Wrong type. Wrong build. Wrong persuasion.

What the woman had said to him.

Treslove wasn't exactly on secure ground about this, even with himself. Maybe he had only imagined that she had called him what she'd called him. Maybe she had, after all, only asked him for his jewels, referring possibly, and in a spirit of violently affronted ribaldry, to his family jewels. I'll have your manhood, she could have been saying. I'll have your balls. Which indeed she had.

Then again, why not just leave it at her identifying him, for her own private satisfaction, as 'You Jules?'

Trouble was – how did she know his name? And why did she want, of all people's balls, *his* balls?

None of it made any sense.

Unless she knew him. But he'd been through this. Other than Joia (and Joia was ruled out), and Joanna whose face he'd painted (and Joanna was ruled out because Treslove wouldn't allow himself to think of her), what woman who knew him would want to attack him? What bodily as opposed to psychic harm had he ever done a woman?

No matter how often he revolved it in his mind, he came out at the same place. No to jewels, no to jewel, no to Jules, no to Jule, and yes to Ju.

You Ju . . .

A solution that created more mysteries than it cleared up. For if the woman wasn't known to him, or he to her, what was she doing making such a mistake as to his – he was damned if he knew what to call it – his ethnicity, his belief system (he would have said his faith but Finkler was a Finkler and Finkler *had* no faith)? His spiritual physiognomy, then.

You Ju.

Julian Treslove – a Ju?

Was it simply a case, therefore, of mistaken identity? Could she, in confusion, have followed him from Libor's, where she'd been waiting for Sam Finkler, not him? He looked nothing like Sam Finkler – indeed, Sam Finkler was one of the few people he *didn't* look like – but if she was simply obeying orders or carrying out a contract, she might not have been adequately apprised of the appearance of the person she'd been hired to get.

And in the confusion he had not had the presence of mind to say, 'Me no Ju, Finkler he Ju.'

But then who would be out to get Sam Finkler? Who other than Julian Treslove, that is? He was a harmless, if wealthy and voluble, philosopher. People liked him. They read his books. They watched his television programmes. He had sought and earned their love. There were some troubles with fellow-Finklers he gathered, especially of the sort who, like Libor, called Israel Isrrrae, but no fellow Finkler, let him be the most Zionistical of Zionists, would surely attack him and abuse him on the grounds of their common ancestry.

And why a woman? Unless it was a woman Finkler had hurt personally – there were certainly a number of those – but a woman Finkler had hurt personally would surely know the difference between Finkler and Treslove up close. And she had got up very close.

He had smelt her body odour. She must have smelt his. And he and Finkler . . . well . . .

None of it made the slightest sense.

And here was something else that made not the slightest sense, except that it made, if anything, only too much. What if the woman hadn't been addressing him by his name – *You* or *You're Jules . . . You Jule . . . You Ju* – but had been apprising him of hers – not *You're* or *Your Jules*, but *Your Juno, Your Judith*, or *Your June*? His, in the sense that a Spanish fortune-teller with a Halesowen accent had once promised him a Juno or a Judith or a June. And warned him of danger into the bargain.

He didn't, of course, believe in fortune-telling. He doubted he would even have remembered the fortune-teller had he not fallen in love with her. Treslove never forgot a woman he fell in love with. He never forgot being made a fool of either, not least as the one often followed hard upon the other. And then there was Sam's smart-arsed D'Jew know Jewno joke, designed to show him that when it came to lingusitic virtuosity a non-Finkler didn't hold a candle to a Finkler. D'Jew know Jewno was as a scar that had never healed.

But what he remembered aside, the only way a fortune-teller could have known the name of the woman who would mug him thirty years later was by her being the woman who would mug him thirty years later, and what likelihood was there of that? Nonsense, all of it. But the idea of something foreordained can shake the soul of the most rational of men, and Treslove was not the most rational of men.

None of it might have had meaning, but then again all of it might have had meaning, even if it was only the meaning of extreme coincidence. She could have been calling him *You Jules* or *You Ju* or whoever *and* telling him that she was his Judith or whoever. Jules and Judith Treslove – Hules and Hudith Treslove – why the fuck not?

Knocked him senseless for his credit card and phone and then used neither. Therefore knocked him senseless for himself.

No, none of it made the slightest sense.

But the conundrum added to his unexpected (all things considered) breeziness. Had he been more familiar with the state he might have gone further and declared himself – to use the word that had pissed off the woman who had fucked him in her Birkenstocks (for her, too, he had never forgotten) – exhilarated.

Like a man on the edge of a discovery.

For the same reason that he didn't tell the police, Treslove didn't tell either of his sons.

In their case they would not even have bothered to ask what he had done to provoke the woman. Though the sons of different mothers they were similar in their view of him and took his provocativeness for granted. This being what you get as a father when you walk out on your children's mothers.

In fact, Treslove hadn't walked out on anyone, if by 'walking out' some callous act of desertion was implied. He lacked the resolution, call it the independence of soul, for that. Either he drifted away, as a matter of tact – for Treslove knew when he wasn't wanted – or women deserted him, whether on account of flies, or for another man, or simply for a life which, however lonely, was preferable to one more hour with him.

He bored them into hating him, he knew that. Though he had promised no woman an exciting life when he met her, he gave the impression of glamour and sophistication, of being unlike other men, of being deep and curious – an arts producer, for a while, an assistant director of festivals, and even when he was merely driving a milk float or selling shoes, artistic by temperament – all of which combined to make women think they had been assured an adventure, of the mind at least. In their disappointment, they took his devotion to them to be a sort of entrapment; they talked about dolls' houses and women's prisons, they called him a jailer, a collector, a sentimental psychopath – well, maybe he was a sentimental psychopath, but that should have been for him to say, not them – a stifler of dreams, a suffocator of hopes, a bloodsucker.

As a man who loved women to death, Treslove didn't see how he could also be a stifler of their dreams. Prior to his leaving the BBC, Treslove had asked one of his presenters – a woman who dressed in a red beret and fishnet stockings, like a pantomime French spy – to marry him. In some corner of himself he saw it as a favour. Who else was ever going to ask Jocelyn for her hand? But he was in love with her too. A woman's inability to be stylish no matter how hard she tried always moved Julian Treslove. Which meant that he was moved by most of the women he worked near in the BBC. Beneath their painfully frenetic striving to dress new wave or challengingly out of vogue – *nouvelle vague,* or *ancienne vogue* – he saw a grubby slip-strap spinsterliness leading into an interminable old age and then into a cold and unvisited grave. So 'Marry me,' he said, out of the kindness of his heart.

They were eating a late, late Indian meal after a late, late recording. They were the only people in the restaurant, the chef had gone home and the waiter was hovering.

Perhaps the hour and the surroundings gave his proposal a desper-ation – a desperation for them both – he didn't intend. Perhaps he shouldn't have made it sound quite so much like a favour.

'Marry you, you old ghoul!' Jocelyn told him, laughing under her French beret, her matching red lips twisted into a grimace. 'I'd die in your bed.'

'You'll die out of it,' Treslove said, hurt and enraged by the violence of the rejection. But meaning what he said. Where else was Jocelyn going to get a better offer?

'There you are,' she snorted, pointing as at some ectoplasmic manifestation of Treslove's true nature. 'That's the ghoulishness I was talking about.'

Afterwards, on a late-night bus, she patted his hand and said she hadn't meant to be unkind. She didn't think of him in that way, that was all.

'In what way?' Treslove asked.

'As anything other than a friend.'

'Well find another friend,' he told her. Which – yes, yes, he knew – only proved her point a second time.

So where would be the sense in looking for sympathy from his sons, both of whom were the sons of women who would have said about Treslove exactly what Jocelyn said?

And as for bringing up any of the you Ju me Judith business, he'd have died first.

They were in their early twenties and not marrying men themselves. Not marrying men by temperament, that is, whatever their age. Rodolfo, Ralph to his friends, ran a sandwich bar in the City – much in the spirit that his father had driven a milk float and replaced sash windows, Treslove surmised, and, he imagined, out of similar professional frustrations, though with added gender issues. His son had a pigtail and wore an apron to prepare the fillings. It was not discussed. What was Treslove going to say – 'Stick to women, my son, and you'll have the fine time I've had'? Good luck to him, he thought. But he understood so little of it he might have been talking about a Martian. Alfredo – Alf to his friends, though his friends were few and far between – played the piano in palm court hotels in Eastbourne, Torquay and Bath. Music had skipped a generation. What his father forbade, Treslove, from a distance, encouraged. But there was little joy for him in Alfredo's musicality. The boy – the man now – played introvertedly, for nobody's pleasure but his own. This made him ideally suited to playing during afternoon tea or dinner in large dining rooms where no one wanted to hear any music except occasionally for 'Happy Birthday to You', and not even that in places where the diners knew how sarcastically Alfredo played it.

Gender problems again? Treslove thought not. He had sired a man who could take women or leave them alone, that was all. Another Martian.

And anyway there was no history between them of Treslove talking about what concerned him. There were advantages in having sons he hadn't brought up. He didn't have to blame himself for what had become of them, for one. And he wasn't the first person they came to when they were in trouble. But he sometimes missed the intimacy he imagined real fathers enjoying with their sons.

Finkler, for example, had two sons plus a daughter, all at one end or another of their university trajectories, campus kids like their father, and Treslove supposed they had got into a huddle when Tyler Finkler died and supported one another. Perhaps Finkler had been able to cry with his boys, maybe even cry into their necks. Treslove's own father had cried into his neck, just once; the occasion was burnt into his brain, not fancifully, no, not fancifully – so hot had been his father's tears, so desperate had been his grip on Treslove's head, both hands clawing at his hair, so inconsolable his father's grief, so loud the sorrow, that Treslove thought his brain would combust.

He wished no such terrible experience on his own sons. There was nowhere to go after it for Treslove and his father. They were fused from that moment and either had to go through what was left of their lives together melded in that fashion, like two drowning swimmers holding each other down in molten grief, or they had to look away and try not to share a moment of intimacy ever again. Without its ever being discussed, they chose the latter route.

But between weeping like a broken god into your children's necks and roughly shaking them by their hands as a stranger might, there must, Treslove thought, be intermediate territory. He hadn't found it. Rodolfo and Alfredo were his sons, they even sometimes remembered to call him Father, but any suggestion of intimacy terrified all three of them. There was some taboo on it, as on incest. Well, it was explicable and probably right. You can't not bring your children up and then expect them to give you their shoulders to cry on.

He wasn't sure, either, that he wanted to confide a moment of shame and weakness, let alone wild supposition and superstition, to them. Could it be that they admired him

– their remote, handsome father who could be mistaken for Brad Pitt and brought home money for the privilege? He didn't know. But on the off chance that they did, he wasn't prepared to jeopardise that admiration by telling them he'd been rolled by a woman in the middle of town in what was, effectively, broad daylight. He didn't have much of a grasp of family life but he guessed that a son doesn't want to hear that about his father.

The good thing was that he only rarely spoke to them at the best of times, so they wouldn't be attaching any significance to his silence. Whatever *they* knew about family life they knew that a father was someone from whom one rarely hears.

Instead, after giving himself time to mull it over – Treslove was not a precipitate man when it came to doing anything other than proposing marriage – he resolved to invite Finkler out for afternoon tea, a tradition that went back to their schooldays. Scones and jam on Haverstock Hill. Finkler owed him a show after failing to turn up the last time they'd arranged a meeting. Busy man, Finkler. Sam the Man. And he owed Finkler a warning if somebody really was out to get him, preposterous as that sounded when he rehearsed saying it.

And besides, Finkler was a Finkler and Treslove was on Finkler business.

6

'It's possible somebody's out to get you,' he said, deciding to come right out with it, while pouring the tea.

For some reason he always poured when he was with Finkler. In over thirty years of taking tea together he could not remember a single occasion on which Finkler had either poured the tea or paid for it.

He didn't mention this to Finkler. Couldn't. Not without being accused of stereotyping him.

They were at Fortnum & Mason, which Treslove liked because it served old-fashioned rarebits and relishes, and Finkler liked because he could rely on being recognised there.

'Out to get me? Out to get me critically? There's nothing new in that. They've always all been out to get me.'

This was Finkler's fantasy – that they'd all always been out to get him critically. In fact no one had been out to get him critically, except Treslove who didn't count, and maybe the mugger who'd got Treslove instead. Though her motives were surely not of the artistic or philosophic sort.

'I don't mean out to get you in that way,' Treslove said.

'So in what way do you mean?'

'Out to get you in the out to get you sense.' He pointed an imaginary pistol at Finkler's gingery temples. 'You know –'

'Out to *kill* me?'

'No, not kill. Out to rough you up a bit. Out to steal your wallet and your watch. And I only said *it's possible*.'

'Oh, well, as long as you think it's only *possible*. Anything's possible, for God's sake. What makes you think that this is?'

Treslove told him what had happened. Not the ignominious details. Just the bare bones. Strolling along in dark. Oblivious. Crack! Head into pane of Guivier's. Wallet, watch and credit cards gone. All over before you could say –

'Christ!'

'Quite.'

'And?'

'And what?'

'And where do I come in?'

Self, self, self, Treslove thought. '*And* it's possible she had followed me from Libor's.'

'Hang on. *She*? What makes you so sure it was a she?'

'I think I know the difference between a she and a he.'

'In the dark? With your nose up against a windowpane?'

'Sam, you know when a woman's assaulting you.'

'Why? How many times *has* a woman assaulted you?'

75

'That's not the point. Never. But you know it when it's happening.'

'You felt her up?'

'Of course I didn't feel her up. There wasn't time to feel her up.'

'Otherwise you would have?'

'I have to tell you it didn't cross my mind. It was too shocking for desire.'

'So she didn't feel you up?'

'Sam, she mugged me. She emptied my pockets.'

'Was she armed?'

'Not that I know of.'

'Know of or knew of?'

'What's the difference?'

'You could know now that she wasn't though you thought then that she was.'

'I don't think that I thought then that she was. But I might have.'

'You let an unarmed woman empty your pockets?'

'I had no choice. I was afraid.'

'Of a woman?'

'Of the dark. Of the suddenness –'

'Of *a woman*.'

'OK, of a woman. But I didn't know she was a woman at first.'

'Did she speak?'

A waitress, bringing Finkler more hot water, interrupted Treslove's answer. Finkler always asked for more hot water no matter how much hot water had already been brought. It was his way of asserting power, Treslove thought. No doubt Nietzsche, too, ordered more hot water than he needed.

'That's sweet of you,' Finkler told the waitress, smiling up at her.

Did he want her to love him or be afraid of him? Treslove wondered. Finkler's lazy imperiousness fascinated him. He had only ever wanted a woman to love him. Which might have been where he'd gone wrong.

'So let me see if I've got this right,' Finkler said, waiting for Treslove to pour the hot water into the teapot. 'This woman, this *unarmed* woman, attacks you, and you think it was me she thought she was attacking, because *it's possible* she followed you from Libor's – who, incidentally, isn't looking well, I thought.'

'I thought he looked fine, all things considered. I had a sandwich with him the other day, as you were meant to. He looked fine then too. You worry me more. Are you getting out?'

'I've seen him myself and he didn't look fine to me. But what's this "out" concept? What's the virtue in out? Isn't out where there are women waiting to attack me?'

'You can't live in your head.'

'That's good coming from you. I don't live in my head. I play poker on the internet. That's nowhere near my head.'

'I suppose you win money.'

'Of course. Last week I won three thousand pounds.'

'Jesus!'

'Yeah, Jesus. So you needn't worry about me. But Libor is rubbing at the pain. He is holding on to Malkie so tight she'll take him with her.'

'That's what he wants.'

'Well, I know you find it touching but it's sickly. He should get rid of that piano.'

'And play poker on the internet?'

'Why not? A big win would cheer him up.'

'What about a big loss? No one wins for ever – someone you've written a book about must have said that. Isn't there a famous philosophic wager? Hume, was it?'

Finkler looked at him steadily. Don't presume, the look seemed to say. Don't presume on my apparent grieflessness. Just because I haven't gone the Libor route of turning my life into a shrine doesn't mean I'm callous. You don't know what I feel.

Or Treslove may just have invented it.

'I suspect you're thinking of Pascal,' Finkler said, finally. 'Only he said the opposite. He said you might as well wager on God because that way, even if He doesn't exist, you've nothing to lose. Whereas if you wager against God and He does exist . . .'

'You're in the shit.'

'I wish I'd said that.'

'You will, Finkler.'

Finkler smiled at the room. 'Anyway,' he said, 'so there you are coming out of Libor's place ever so slightly the worse for wear when this muggerette, mistaking you for me, follows you several hundred yards to where it's actually lighter – which makes no sense – and duffs you up. What exactly about the incident links her to me? Or me to you? We don't exactly look alike, Julian. You're half my size, you've got twice as much hair –'

'Three times as much hair.'

'I'm in a car, you're on foot . . . what would have led her to make that mistake?'

'Search me . . . Because she had never seen either of us before?'

'And saw you and thought he looks as though he's got a fat wallet, and what happened happened. I still don't know why you think she was after me.'

'Maybe she knew you'd won three thousand pounds playing poker. Or maybe she was a fan. Maybe a Pascal reader. You know what fans are like.'

'And maybe she wasn't.' Finkler called for more hot water.

'Look,' Treslove said, shifting in his chair, as though not wanting the whole of Fortnum & Mason to hear, 'it was what she said.'

'What did she say?'

'Or at least what I think she said.'

Finkler opened wide his arms Finklerishly. Infinite patience beginning to run out, the gesture denoted. Finkler reminded Treslove of God when he did that. God despairing of His people from a mountain top. Treslove was envious. It was what God gave the Finklers as the mark of His covenant with them – the ability to shrug like Him. Something on which, as a non-Finkler, Treslove had missed out.

'What she said or what you think she said – spit it out, Julian.'

So he spat it out. '*You Jew*. She said *You Jew*.'

'You've made that up.'

'Why would I make it up?'

'Because you're a bitter twisted man. I don't know why you'd make it up. Because you were hearing your own thoughts. You'd just left me and Libor. *You Jews*, you were probably thinking. *You fucking Jews*. The sentence was in your mouth so you transferred it to hers.'

'She didn't say *You fucking Jews*. She said *You Jew*.'

'*You Jew?*'

Now he heard it on someone else's lips, Treslove couldn't be sure he was sure. 'I think.'

'You *think*? What could she have said that sounded like *You Jew?*'

'I've already been through that. *You Jules*, but then how would she know my name?'

'It was on the credit cards she'd stolen from you – doh!'

'Don't doh me. You know I hate being dohed.'

Finkler patted his arm. 'It was on the credit cards she'd stolen from you – no doh.'

'My cards have my initials. J. J. Treslove. No reference to any Julian and certainly not to any Jules. Let's call a spade a spade, Sam – she called me a Jew.'

'And you think the only Jew in London she could have confused you for is me?'

'We'd just been together.'

'Coincidence. The woman is probably a serial anti-Semite.

79

No doubt she calls everyone she robs a Jew. It's a generic word among you Gentiles for anyone you don't much care for. At school they called it Jewing (you probably called it Jewing yourself) – taking what's not yours. It's what you see when you see a Jew – a thief or a skinflint. Could be she was Jewing you back. *I Jew You* – could she have said that? *I Jew You*, in the spirit of tit for tat.'

'She said *You Jew*.'

'So she got it wrong. It was dark.'

'It was light.'

'You told me it was dark.'

'I was setting the scene.'

'Misleadingly.'

'Poetically. It was dark in the sense of being late, and light in the sense of being lit by street lamps.'

'Light enough for you patently not to be a Jew?'

'As light as it is here. Do I look a Jew?'

Finkler laughed one of his big television laughs. Treslove knew for a fact that Finkler never laughed in reality – it had been one of Tyler's complaints when she was alive that she had married a man who had no laughter in him – but on television, when he wanted to denote responsiveness, he roared. Treslove marvelled that a single one of Finkler's however many hundreds of thousand viewers swallowed it.

'Let's ask the room,' Finkler said. And for a terrible moment Treslove thought he just might. *Hands up which of you think this man is, or could be mistaken for, a Jew.* It would be a way of getting everyone who hadn't already registered Finkler to notice he was there.

Treslove coloured and put his head down, thinking as he did so that it was precisely this diffidence that put the seal of non-Jewishness on him. Who had ever met a shy Jew?

'So there you have it,' he said when he at last found the courage to raise his head. 'You tell me. What would Wittgenstein advise?'

'That you get your head out of your arse. And out of mine and Libor's. Look – you got mugged. It isn't nice. And you were already in an emotional state. It's probably not healthy, the three of us meeting the way we do. Not for you anyway. We have reason. We are in mourning. You aren't. And if you are, you shouldn't be. It's fucking morbid, Julian. You can't be us. You shouldn't want to be us.'

'I don't want to be you.'

'Somewhere you do. I don't mean to be cruel but there has always been some part of us you have wanted.'

'*Us?* Since when were you and Libor *us?*'

'That's an insensitive question. You know very well since when.Now that's not enough for you. Now you want another part of us. Now you want to be a Jew.'

Treslove almost choked on his tea. 'Who said I want to be a Jew?'

'You did. What is all this about otherwise? Look, you're not the only one. Lots of people want to be Jews.'

'Well, *you* don't.'

'Don't start that. You sound like Libor.'

'Sam – Samuel – read my lips. I. Do. Not. Want. To. Be. A. Jew. OK? Nothing against them but I like being what I am.'

'Do you remember saying how much you wished my father had been your father?'

'I was fourteen at the time. And I liked the fact that he invited me to punch him in the stomach. I was frightened to touch my own father on the shoulder. But this had nothing to do with being Jewish.'

'So what are you?'

'I beg your pardon?'

'You said you like being what you are, so what are you?'

'What am I?' Treslove stared at the ceiling. It felt like a trick question.

'Exactly. You don't know what you are so you want to be

81

a Jew. Next you'll be wearing fringes and telling me you've volunteered to fly Israeli jets against Hamas. This, Julian, I repeat, is not healthy. Take a break. You should be on the town. "Out" as you call it. Get yourself a bird. Take her on holiday. Forget about the other stuff. Buy a new wallet and get on with your life. I promise you it wasn't a woman who stole your old one, however much you wish it had been. And whoever it was still more certainly didn't confuse you with me or call you a Jew.'

Treslove seemed almost crestfallen in the face of so much philosophic certainty.

THREE

I

'Hi, Brad.'

The speaker was a strong-jawed woman in a waterfall of blonde curls and a limp Regency dress that showed her breasts off to impressive effect. This was the third time that evening that Treslove – on his first night back working as a lookalike – had been taken for Brad Pitt. In fact, he'd been hired to look like Colin Firth in the part of Mr Darcy. It was a lavish birthday party in a loft in Covent Garden for a fifty-year-old lady of means whose name really was Jane Austen, so who else could he have been hired to look like? Everyone was in costume. Treslove, in tight breeches, a white hero shirt and silk cravat, affected a sulky manner. How then he could be taken for Brad Pitt he didn't know. Unless Brad Pitt had been in a *Pride and Prejudice* production he'd missed.

But then everyone was drunk and vague. And the woman who had accosted him was drunk, vague and American. Even before she opened her mouth Treslove had deduced all that from her demeanour. She looked too amazed by life to be English. Her curls were too curly. Her lips were too big. Her teeth too white and even, like one big arc of tooth with regular vertical markings. And her breasts had too much elevation and attack in them to be English. Had Jane Austen's heroines had breasts like these they would not have worried about ending up without a husband.

'Guess again,' Treslove said, flushed from the encounter. She was not his kind of woman. She would too obviously outlive him to be his kind of woman, but he found her forwardness arousing. And he too was growing vague.

'Dustin Hoffman,' she said, inspecting his face. 'No, I guess you're too young for Dustin Hoffman. Adam Sandler? No, you're too old. Oh, I know, Billy Crystal.'

He didn't say *Why would Billy Crystal be at a Jane Austen party?*

She took him back to her hotel in the Haymarket. Her suggestion. She was lewd in the taxi, sliding her hand up into his hero shirt and down into his tight Mr Darcy breeches. Calling him Billy, which it occurred to her, as they swung past Eros, rhymed with willy. Strange how impure Americans could be, Treslove thought, for a people puritanical to their souls. Prim and pornographic all at once.

But he was in no position to be judgemental.

Gratitude and a sense of relief overwhelmed him. He was still in the game; he was still a player. In fact, he'd never been a player but he knew what he meant.

He slid his tongue behind her dazzling panorama of teeth, trying without success to distinguish one tooth from another. He had the same trouble with her breasts. They didn't divide. They constituted a bosom, singular.

She was so perfect she needed only one of everything.

She was a television producer, over in London for a few days to discuss a joint venture with Channel 4. He was relieved it wasn't the BBC. He wasn't sure he could sleep with anyone with BBC connections. Not if he was to manage a decent erection for any length of time.

In the event he didn't manage a decent erection for any length of time because she bounced up and down on him in a flurry of nipple and curl which embarrassed him into prematurity.

'Wow!' she said.

'It's the dress,' he told her. 'I shouldn't have asked you to keep the dress on. Too many hot associations.'

'Such as?'

'Such as *Northanger Abbey* and *Mansfield Park.*'

'I can take it off.'

'No. Keep it on and give me twenty minutes.'

They talked about their favourite Jane Austen characters. Kimberley — of course she was called Kimberley — liked Emma. That was who she was being. Emma Woodhouse, handsome, clever, rich, 'And with her tits out,' she laughed, putting them back in. Or, rather, Treslove thought, putting *it* back in.

Taking it back out again, he said he found some of Jane Austen's heroines a touch effervescent for his taste — not Emma, of course not Emma — preferring Anne Elliot, no, loving, really *loving* Anne Elliot. Why? Not sure, but he thought something to do with her running out of time to be happy.

'Drinking in the last-chance saloon,' Kimberley said, showing she understood the nuances of Georgian England.

'Yes, yes, something like that. It's the idea of her faded beauty I love. Fading as you read.'

'You love faded beauty!'

'No, God no, not as a rule. I don't mean in life.'

'I should hope not.'

'God no.'

'I'm relieved to hear that.'

'It's the fairy-story quality,' he said, pausing to graze purposefully on her breast. 'Jane Austen waves her wand and conjures a happy ending at the eleventh hour, but in life it would have been a tragedy.'

She nodded, not listening. 'And now time for you to wave *your* wand,' she said, looking at her watch. She had given him exactly twenty minutes. She no more did approximations than she did tragedy.

'Wow!' she said again five minutes later.

It was the jolliest night of sex Treslove had ever had. A

surprise to him because he didn't do jolly. When he left her in the morning she handed him her card – in case he was ever in LA, but be careful to give her warning, her husband wouldn't be that enthusiastic about finding Billy Crystal on the doorstep in his Regency breeches. She slapped his behind as he left.

Treslove felt like a prostitute.

So what about that prematurity? Treslove, in his street clothes, stopped for coffee in Piccadilly to think it through. Bounce had never done the business for Treslove. Bounce, if anything, had always been detrimental to business. So what, on this occasion, had? The dress undoubtedly had had something to do with it – Anne Elliot straddling him and shaking her head from side to side like a Swedish porn star. But the dress alone could not explain the alacrity of his appreciation, nor his repeating it at twenty-minute intervals, not for the entire night but for more of it than was gentlemanly to brag about. Which left only the mugging. He would not have sworn to this in a court of law but he had a feeling he'd been half thinking about the woman who had attacked him while Kimberley rose and swelled and wowed! above him. They were a similar build, he fancied. So was he thinking about her or seeing her? He couldn't have sworn which of those either.

But there was a problem with this. The attack had certainly not stimulated him sexually at the time. Why would it have? He was not that kind of a man. A fractured nose was bloody painful, *end of*, as his sons said. Nor had it remotely stimulated him in the days following. And it wasn't doing anything for him sitting thinking of it now. But something was. Recollection of the night before, naturally. It had been a night to be pleased with and proud of. It hadn't only broken a long drought, it had been a one-night stand to rival the best of them and Treslove was not

86

by nature a one-night-stand man. Yet still some further consciousness of excitation or erotic disturbance nagged away at him.

Then he got it. Billy Crystal. Kimberley had taken him for Brad Pitt initially, but when she'd looked more closely into his face she had seen someone else. Dustin Hoffman . . . Adam Sandler . . . Billy Crystal. He had stopped her there, but had she continued the list would in all likelihood, given where it was heading, have included David Schwimmer, Jerry Seinfeld, Jerry Springer, Ben Stiller, David Duchovny, Kevin Kline, Jeff Goldblum, Woody Allen, Groucho Fucking Marx . . . did he have to go on?

Finklers.

Fucking Finklers every one.

He had read somewhere that every actor in Hollywood was a Finkler by birth, whether or not they kept their Finkler names. And Kimberley – Kimberley for God's sake; what was her name originally: Esther? – Kimberley had mistaken him for all of them.

By mistaken he didn't mean he couldn't have meant; *she* couldn't have meant – mistaken *in appearance*. Even to Kimberley's blurred vision he could not have physically resembled Jerry Seinfeld or Jeff Goldblum. He was the wrong size. He was the wrong temperature. He was the wrong speed. The resemblance he bore to these men must, in that case, have been of another order. It must have been a matter of spirit and essence. *Essentially* he was like them. *Spiritually* he was like them.

He couldn't have said whether taking him for a Finkler in essence pressed Kimberley's button – no reason it should have done, if they were all Finklers where she came from – but what if it pressed his?

Two such misidentifications in two weeks. Never mind what Finkler himself thought. Finkler was possessive of his Finklerishness. 'Ours is not a club you can just join,' he had explained to Treslove in the days when he insisted on being called Samuel.

'I wasn't thinking of joining,' Treslove had told him then.

'No,' Finkler had replied, already losing interest. 'I never said you were.'

So Finkler was not what could be called an uninterested party.

Whereas two women without an axe to grind – two weeks, two women, two identical misidentifications!

Treslove bit his knuckles, ordered more coffee and allowed his life – his lying life, was it? – to pass before him.

2

Finkler had asked for it.

That was Tyler Finkler's view at the time and it was Julian Treslove's too. Sam had it coming.

Tyler Finkler had the better case. Her husband was fucking other women. Or if he wasn't fucking other women he might as well have been fucking other women for the amount of attention he was showing her.

Treslove's case was simply that Finkler had it coming because he was Finkler. But he also saw that a woman as beautiful as Tyler shouldn't have to suffer.

Tyler Finkler. The *late* Tyler Finkler. Remembering her over a second coffee, Treslove sighed a deep sigh.

'Sam's on an all-consuming project,' he had said at the time. 'He's an ambitious man. He was an ambitious boy.'

'My husband was a boy!'

Treslove had smiled weakly. Finkler had not in fact been much of a boy but it didn't feel right saying so to Finkler's angry wife.

They were lying on Treslove's bed in that suburb he insisted on calling Hampstead. They should not have been lying on Treslove's bed in any suburb. They both knew that. But Finkler had asked for it.

Tyler had rung Treslove originally to enquire whether it was all right to come over and watch the first programme of her husband's new series on Treslove's television. 'Of course,' he had said, 'but won't you be watching it with Sam?'

'Samuel is watching it with the crew, otherwise known as his mistress.'

Tyler was the only person who still called Sam Samuel. It gave her power over him, the power of someone who knew an important person before he became important. Sometimes she went further and called him Shmuelly to remind him of his origins when he appeared to be in danger of forgetting them.

'Oh,' Treslove said.

'And the worst thing is that she isn't even the fucking director. She's just the production assistant.'

'Ah,' Treslove said, wondering if Tyler would have been watching it with Sam had Sam, more conventionally, been fucking the director. You never knew quite where you were with Finklers – men or women – when it came to matters that bore on humiliation and prestige. Non-Finklers judged all infidelities equally, but in his experience Finklers were prepared to make allowances if the third party happened to be someone important. Prince Philip, Bill Clinton, the Pope even. He hoped he wasn't stereotyping them, thinking that.

'Will you be bringing the children?' Treslove asked.

'The children? The *children* are away at school. They'll soon be at university. At least pretend to take an interest, Julian.'

'I don't do children,' he explained. 'I don't even do my own.'

'Well, you don't have to worry. We won't be doing any children ourselves. My body's past all that.'

'Oh,' said Treslove.

This was the first inkling he had that he and his friend's wife would not be watching much television that evening. 'Ha,' he said to himself, showering, as though he were the victim of whatever was going to happen, rather than an active partner in it. But there was never the remotest possibility that he would be able to resist Tyler, no matter that she was using him only to get her own back on her husband.

Though she wasn't the sort of woman he normally fell for, he had fallen for her anyway the first time Sam had introduced her as his wife. He had not seen his friend for a while and did not know he was going out with anyone in particular, let alone that there had been a marriage. But that was Finkler's way. He would lift the hem of his life infinitesimally, just enough to make Treslove feel intrigued and excluded, before lowering it again.

The newly married Mrs Finkler was not in fact beautiful, but she was as good as beautiful, dark and angular, with features on which a careless man could cut himself, and pitiless sarcastic eyes. Though there was little meat on her bones she was somehow able to suggest sumptuous occasions. Whenever Treslove met her she was dressed as for a state banquet, where she would eat little, talk with assurance, dance gracefully with whoever she had to, and win admiring glances from the whole room. She was the sort of woman a successful man needs. Competent, worldly, coolly elegant – so long as the man doesn't forget her in his success. The word *humid* came to Treslove's mind when he thought about Tyler Finkler. Which was surprising given that she was on the surface arid. But Treslove was imagining what she would be like below the surface, when he entered her dark womanly mysteriousness. She was somewhere he had never been and probably ought not to think of going. She was the eternal Finkler woman. Hence there never being the remotest possibility of his refusing her when she offered. He had to discover what it would be like to penetrate the moist dark womanly mysteriousness of a *Finkleress*.

They put the television on but didn't watch a frame of Sam's programme. 'He's such a liar,' she said, stepping out of a dress she could have worn to see her husband get a knighthood. 'Where's his philosophy when I don't have his dinner ready on time? Where's his philosophy when he should be keeping his dick in his pants?'

Treslove said nothing. It was odd having his friend's face on his television at the same time as he had his friend's wife in his arms. Not that Tyler was ever actually *in* his arms. She liked to be made love to from a distance as though it wasn't really happening. Much of the time she lay facing away from Treslove, working on his penis with her hand behind her back, as though fastening a complicated brassiere, or struggling with a jar that wouldn't open, while she traduced her husband in running commentary. She preferred the light on and saw no sensual virtue in silence. Only when he entered her – briefly, because she told him she did not welcome extended intercourse – did Treslove find the warm dark Finkleress *humidity* he had anticipated. And it exceeded all his imaginings.

He lay on his back and felt the tears well in his eyes. He told her he loved her.

'Don't be ridiculous,' she said. 'You don't even know me. That was Sam you were doing it to.'

He sat up. 'It most certainly was not.'

'I don't mind. It suits me. We might even do it again. And if it turns you on to be doing your friend – doing him or doing him over, let's not finesse here – it's fine by me.'

Treslove propped himself up on his elbow to look at her but she was turned away from him again. He reached out to stroke her hair.

'Don't do that,' she said.

'What you don't understand,' he said, 'is that this is the first time for me.'

'The first time you've had sex?' She didn't actually sound all that surprised.

'The first time' – it sounded tasteless now he had to put it into words – 'the first time . . . you know . . .'

'The first time you've done the dirty on Samuel? I shouldn't worry about that. He wouldn't hesitate to do it to you. Probably already has. He sees it as a *droit de philosophe*. Being a thinker he thinks he has a right to fuck whoever takes his fancy.'

'I didn't mean that. I meant that you're my first . . .'

He could hear his hesitancy irritating her. The bed chilled around her. 'First what? Spit it out. Married woman? Mother? Wife of a television presenter? Woman without a degree?'

'Don't you have a degree?'

'First what, Julian?'

He swallowed the word a couple of times but needed to hear himself say it. Saying it was almost as sweet in its unholiness as doing it. 'Jew,' he finally got out. But that wasn't quite the word he was after either. 'Jewess,' he said, taking a long time to finish it, letting the heated hiss of all those *ssss* linger on his lips.

She turned round as though for the first time she needed to see what he looked like, her eyes dancing with mockery. 'Jewess? You think I'm actually a *Jewess*?'

'Aren't you?'

'That's the nicest question you could have asked me. But where did you get the idea from that I'm the real deal?'

Treslove couldn't think of what to say, there was so much. 'Everything,' was all he could come up with in the end. He remembered attending one of the Finkler boys' bar mitzvahs but as he wasn't sure which he remained silent on the subject.

'Well, your everything is a nothing,' she said.

He was bitterly upset. Not a Jewess, Tyler? Then what *was* that dark humidity he had entered?

She hung her bottom lip at him. (And *that*, wasn't that

92

Jewish?) 'Do you honestly think,' she went on, 'that Samuel would have married someone Jewish?'

'Well, I hadn't thought he wouldn't.'

'Then how little you know him. It's the Gentiles he's out to conquer. Always has been. You must know that. He's done Jewish. He was born Jewish. They can't reject him. So why waste time on them? He'd have married me in a church had I asked him. He was the tiniest bit furious with me when I didn't.'

'So why didn't you?'

She laughed. A dry rattle from a parched throat. 'I'm another version of him, that's why. We were each out to conquer the other's universe. He wanted the goyim to love him. I wanted the Jews to love me. And I liked the idea of having Jewish children. I thought they'd do better at school. And boy, have they done better!'

(Her pride in them – wasn't *that* Jewish as well?)

Treslove was perplexed. 'Can you have Jewish children if you're not Jewish yourself?'

'Not in the eyes of the Orthodox. Not easily, anyway. But we had a liberal wedding. And I had to convert even for that. Two years I put in, learning how to run a Jewish home, how to be a Jewish mother. Ask me anything you need to know about Judaism and I can tell you. How to kosher a chicken, how to light the Shabbes candles, what to do in a mikva. Do you want me to tell you how a good Jewish woman knows her period is over? I am possessed of more Jewishkeit than all the *echt* Jewish women in Hampstead rolled together.'

Treslove absented himself, mentally rolling together all the *echt* Jewish women in Hampstead. But what he asked was, 'What's a mikva?'

'A ritual bath. You go there to cleanse yourself for your Jewish husband who will die if he encounters a drop of your blood.'

'Sam wanted you to do that?'

'Not Samuel, me. Samuel couldn't have given a monkey's. He thought it was barbaric, worrying about menstrual blood which in point of fact he quite likes, the sicko. I went to the mikva for me. I found it calming. I'm the Jew of the two of us even if I was born a Catholic. I'm the Jewish princess you read about in the fairy stories, only I'm not Jewish. The irony being –'

'That he's out fucking shiksas?'

'Too obvious. I'm still the shiksa to him. If he wants the forbidden he can get it at home. The irony is that he's out fucking Jews. That lump of lard Ronit Kravitz, his production assistant. I wouldn't put it past him to be converting her.'

'I thought you said she's already Jewish.'

'Converting her to Christianity, you fool.'

Treslove fell silent. There was so much he didn't understand. And so much to be upset about. He felt he'd been given a prize he had long coveted, only to have it snatched away from him again before he'd even found a place for it on his mantelpiece. Tyler Finkler, not a Finkler! Therefore the deep damp dark mysteriousness of a Finkler woman was still, strictly speaking – and this was a strict concept or it was nothing – unknown to him.

She began to dress. 'I hope I haven't disappointed you,' she said.

'Disappointed me? Hardly. Will you be coming for the second programme?'

'You have a think about it.'

'What's there to think about?'

'Oh, you know,' she said.

She didn't kiss him when she left.

But she popped her head back around his door. 'A word from the wise. Just don't let them catch you saying "Jew*ess*",' she warned him, imitating the languorous snakiness he had imparted to the word. 'They don't like it.'

Always something they didn't like.

But he did as she suggested, and had a think.

He thought about the betrayal of his friend and wondered why he wasn't guiltier. Wondered whether following Finkler into his wife's vagina was a pleasure in itself. Not the only pleasure, but a significant contribution to it. Wondered whether Finkler had in effect koshered his wife from the inside regardless of her origins, so that he, Treslove, could believe he had as good as had a Jewess – *ess, ess, ess* – (which word he mustn't for some reason let them catch him saying) after all. Or not. And if not, did he have to go back to the very beginning of wondering what it would be like?

And was still wondering about these and similar mysteries of the religio-erotic life after Tyler Finkler's tragic death.

3

Normally a heavy sleeper, Treslove began to lie awake night after night, revolving the attack in his mind.

What had happened? How would he tell it to the police, supposing that he *was* going to tell it to the police, which he wasn't? He had spent the evening with two old friends, Libor Sevcik and Sam Finkler, both recently made widowers – no, officer, I am not myself married – discussing grief, music and the politics of the Middle East. He had left Libor's apartment at about 11 p.m., spent a little time looking into the park, smelling foliage – do I always do that? no, only sometimes when I am upset – and then had ambled back past Broadcasting House, may its name be damned, may its foundations crumble – only joking – to a part of London where his father had owned a famous cigar shop – no, officer, I had not been drinking inordinately – when without any warning . . .

Without any warning, that was the shocking thing, without the slightest apprehension of danger or unease on his part, and he normally so finely attuned to hazard.

Unless . . .

Unless he had, after all, as he had turned into Mortimer Street, seen a figure lurking in the shadows on the opposite side of the road, seen it half emerge from a passageway, still in shadow, a large, looming, but possibly, very possibly, womanly figure . . .

In which case – the question was conditional: if he *had* seen him, it, her – why had he not minded himself more, why had he turned to Guivier's window, presenting his defenceless neck to whatever harm anyone, man or woman, might choose to do him . . .

Culpability.

Culpability again.

But did it matter what he'd seen or hadn't seen?

For some reason it did. If he'd seen her and invited her to attack him – or at least *permitted* her to attack him – that surely explained, or part explained, what she had said. He knew it was not morally or intellectually acceptable to accuse Jews of inviting their own destruction, but was there a proneness to disaster in these people which the woman had recognised? Had he, in other words, played the Finkler?

And if he had, *why* had he?

One question always led to another with Treslove. Let's say he had played the Finkler, and let's say the woman had observed it – did that justify her attacking him?

Whatever explanation could be found for his actions, what pos-sible explanation could be found for hers? Was a man no longer free to play the Finkler when the fancy took him? Let's say he had been standing staring into the window of J. P. Guivier looking like Horowitz, or Mahler, or Shylock, say, or Fagin, or Billy Crystal, or David Schwimmer, or Jerry Seinfeld, or Jerry Springer, or Ben Stiller, or David Duchovny, or Kevin Kline, or Jeff Goldblum, or Woody Allen, or Groucho Fucking Marx, was that any reason for her to attack him?

Was being a Finkler an open invitation to assault?

So far he had taken it personally – you do when someone calls you by your name, or something very like, and gets you to empty your pockets – but what if this was a random anti-Semitic attack that just happened to have gone wrong only in the sense that he wasn't a Semite? How many more of these incidents were taking place? How many real Finklers were being attacked in the streets of the capital every night? Round the corner from the BBC, for Christ's sake!

He wondered who to ask. Finkler himself was not the man to tell him. And he didn't want to frighten Libor by asking him how many Jews got beaten up outside his door most evenings. Not expecting to find anything post-thirteenth-century Chelmno, he looked up 'Anti-Semitic Incidents' on the internet and was surprised to find upwards of a hundred pages. Not all of them round the corner from the BBC, it was true, but still far more in parts of the world that called themselves civilised than he would ever have imagined. One well-maintained site gave him the option to choose by country. He started from far away –

VENEZUELA:

And read that in Caracas about fifteen armed men had tied up a security guard and forced their way into a synagogue, defacing its administrative offices with anti-Semitic graffiti and throwing Torah scrolls to the ground in a rampage that lasted nearly five hours. Graffiti left at the scene included the phrases 'Damn the Jews', 'Jews out', 'Israeli assassins' and a picture of a devil.

The devil detail intrigued him. It meant that these fifteen men had not gone out on the razzle, found themselves outside a synagogue and forced their way in on a whim. For who goes out on a razzle with a picture of the devil in his pocket?

ARGENTINA:

And read that in Buenos Aires a crowd celebrating Israel's anniversary was attacked by a gang of youths armed with clubs and knives. Three weeks earlier, on Holocaust Memorial Day – here we go, Holocaust, Holocaust – an ancient Jewish cemetery was defaced with swastikas.

CANADA:

Canada? Yes, Canada.

And read that in the course of Canada's now annual Israeli Apartheid Week events held on campuses throughout the country security officers roughed up Jewish hecklers, one of them warning a Jewish student to 'shut the fuck up or I'll saw your head off'.

Was that a home-grown Canadian deterrent, he wondered, sawing Jews' heads off?

Then tried closer to home.

FRANCE:

And read that in Fontenay-sous-Bois a man wearing a Star of David necklace was stabbed in the head and neck.

In Nice, 'Death to Jews' was spray-painted on the walls of a primary school. So death to Jews of all ages.

In Bischheim, three Molotov cocktails were thrown at a synagogue.

In Creteil, two sixteen-year-old Jews were beaten in front of a kosher restaurant by a gang that shouted 'Palestine will win, dirty Jews!'

GERMANY:

What, they were still doing it in fucking Germany?

And didn't bother to read what they were still doing in fucking Germany.

ENGLAND:

England his England. And read that in Manchester a thirty-one-year-old Jew was beaten by several men who shouted 'for Gaza' as they attacked him, leaving him with a black eye and several bruises.

In Birmingham, a twelve-year-old schoolgirl fled a mob of children no older than she was chanting 'Death to Jews'.

And in London, just around the corner from the BBC, a

forty-nine-year-old blue-eyed Gentile with orderly features was robbed of his valuables and called a Ju.

He rang Finkler after all to say how nice it had been to see him and did he know that in Caracas and in Buenos Aires and in Toronto – yes, Toronto! – and in Fontenay-sous-Bois and in London, but Finkler stopped him there . . .

'I'm not saying it makes pleasant listening,' he said, 'but it's not exactly Kristallnacht, is it?'

An hour later, after thinking about it, Treslove rang again. 'Kristallnacht didn't happen out of nowhere,' he said, though he had only a vague idea of what Kristallnacht did happen out of.

'Ring me when a Jew gets murdered for being a Jew on Oxford Street,' Finkler said.

4

Though it wasn't Kristallnacht, the unprovoked attack on him for being a Jew had become in Treslove's imagination little short of an atrocity. He admitted to himself that he was over-excited. The night with Kimberley, her misattribution of Jewish characteristics to him, as a consequence of which, he was bound to consider, he might just have had – at forty-nine! – the best sex of his life (well, at least they had both smiled during it), and the sense of history swirling around him, all made him an unreliable witness to his own life.

Did he any longer remember what actually had happened?

He decided to revisit the scene of the crime, re-run the evening's events, not starting with dinner at Libor's – he didn't want to involve Libor, he had kept the whole thing from Libor, Libor had troubles enough – but at the gates to Regent's Park. It had turned chillier in the weeks since the mugging, so he was not able to dress as he had on the night in question. Muffled up, he looked bulkier, but otherwise his assailant – Judith, as he now called her – had she too returned to the scene of the crime, would have recognised him.

He had no choice but to name her Judith. Something to do with the Canadian security man threatening to saw the Jewish student's head off. It was Judith who beheaded Holofernes. True, she was Jewish herself, but her action had a similar whiff of vengeful Middle Eastern violence about it. Where Treslove came from – call it Hampstead, to save time – people left even their enemies' heads on their shoulders.

To be on the safe side he had left his phone and his credit cards at home.

So what was he doing – inviting her to rough him up again? Come on, Judith, do your worst. *Hoping* she would rough him up again? (Only this time she would find him, forewarned and forearmed, a tougher proposition.) Or just wanting to confront her, the Jew-hater, eyeball to eyeball, and let fate decide the rest?

No to any one of those, but maybe yes, in an investigative way, to all of them.

Somewhere at the back of his disordered mind, too, was forming the resolution to apprehend her, if she so much as showed her face, and effect a citizen's arrest.

He clung to the park gates and looked in, breathing the foliage. He could not be light-headed again to will, could not make himself innocent of a knowledge which now crowded out all other thoughts. But had he been innocent a fortnight earlier? Or had he been looking for trouble?

There'd been Finkler talk at Libor's, he remembered that. He remembered the old sensation of exclusion, envying the men their animal warmth even as they'd argued routinely on *the* Finkler question of the hour, each of them saying 'Oh, here we go' every time the other spoke, as though mutual mistrust was stamped into Finklers like the name of a seaside resort into rock — *Here we go, here we go* — just as mutual love appeared to be. So he had their musk on him. Anyone who didn't especially care for that particular smell would have detected it on him. He suddenly wondered whether it was a mistake not to call on Libor and share a glass of wine with him. Could he hope to reproduce the other evening without having had proximity at least to Libor first?

He doubled back on himself and rang the bell. No one answered. Libor was out, then, maybe on another date, making himself discuss star signs with a girl too young to have heard of Jane Russell. Unless he was lying up there collapsed across the Bechstein with an emptied bottle of aspirin on the keyboard and a piano-wire noose around his throat, as he, Treslove, would be, had Malkie been his wife and left him all alone in the world.

His eyes filled with tears, hearing the Schubert in his head. Why hadn't his father let him play? What had he been afraid of in his son? Morbidity? Finkler's word. What was so wrong with morbidity?

He trod his way gingerly past the dangers, spiritual and actual, of Broadcasting House and rounded Nash's church again. He wasn't sure he could remember exactly the route he had taken on the night of the assault, but knew he had dawdled among the wholesale clothes showrooms where his father's cigar shop had been, so he tried up Riding House Street and then back down Mortimer Street towards J. P. Guivier, only he had to make sure he approached the violin shop from the right direction, which necessitated — he thought — returning the way he'd come and staying a little longer on Regent Street before cutting in again. Once off Regent Street he reminded himself to take more notice of shapes in doorways than was his customary practice. He also thought it a good idea to make himself appear more than usually vulnerable, though anyone who knew him would not have noticed any difference either in his gait or general air of agitation.

The streets were about as busy as they had been a fortnight earlier. The same hairdresser's and dim sum restaurant were open for late business. The same newsagent's was still undergoing renovation. But for the nip in the air the nights were identical. Treslove approached J. P. Guivier with his heart in his mouth. Foolish, he knew. The woman who attacked him must have better things to do than wait in the shadows on the off chance he'd return. And for what? She already had his only valuables.

But since none of it had added up then, there was no reason why it should add up now. What if she regretted what she had done and wanted to give him his valuables back? Or perhaps the mugging was just a taster of what she really had in store in him. A knife in his heart, maybe. A pistol at his head. A saw at his throat. Payback for some imaginary wrong he had done her. Or payback for some real wrong she had suffered at the hands of Finkler with whom she had confused him.

That possibility was truly frightening – not the being mistaken for Sam Finkler, though that was insult enough, but the being held responsible for something Finkler had done. Treslove didn't put it past Finkler to hurt a woman and drive her to the edge of madness. He imagined dying for Finkler, lying bleeding on the pavement, unattended, for a crime he had not and could never have committed. His legs went weak under him with the bitter irony of it. An ironical end to his life was not an abstract supposition for Treslove: he apprehended it as he apprehended a looming lamp-post or a falling tree.

And saw himself kicked out of the way by passers-by, like a Jew's dog on the streets of Caracas, or Buenos Aires, or Fontenay-sous-Bois, or Toronto.

He stood before the window of J. P. Guivier admiring the

instruments in their cases and the resins, a new satisfying arrangement of which had appeared – packaged like expensive chocolates – since he'd last looked. A hand tapped him on the shoulder – 'Judith!' he cried in shock – and the blood left his body.

FOUR

I

At around about this time – give or take half an hour – in a restaurant close by – give or take a quarter of a mile – Treslove's sons were settling the bill for dinner. They were in the company of their mothers. This was not the first time the two women had met, though they had known nothing of each other's existence in the months they were carrying Ralph and Alf respectively, or indeed in the years immediately following their sons' delivery.

Treslove was no Finkler. He could not lose his heart to more than one woman at a time. He loved too absorbedly for that. But he always knew when he was about to be thrown over and was quick to make provision, where he could, to love absorbedly again. As a consequence of which there was sometimes a brief overlap of new and old. On principle he didn't mention this to either of the overlapping parties – neither the one who had still not quite left him, nor the one who had not quite taken her place. Women were already hurt enough, in his view; there was no reason to hurt them further. In this, again, he saw himself as different to Finkler who evidently did not bother to conceal his mistresses from his wife. Treslove envied Finkler his mistresses but accepted they were beyond him. Even wives were beyond Treslove. Girlfriends were all he had ever managed. But there was still propriety in keeping overlapping girlfriends apart.

By the same reasoning he would have kept his sons apart, too, had he not confused the day of his right to have Rodolfo

(Treslove didn't hold with anglicising their names) with the day of his right to have Alfredo. The boys were six and seven, though Treslove couldn't be expected always to be precise in the matter of which was what. He didn't see enough of them for that, and in their absence found it easier to conflate them. Was that so serious? They were equally objects of devotion to him. That he merged their names and ages only went to show how very much and without favouritism he loved them both.

A surprise to each other on the day they met at their father's apartment, but infinitely preferring playing with someone roughly their own age to kicking a ball around a desolate park with Treslove – who tired easily, was always looking some-where else, and when he did remember they were there asked too many soulful questions about the state of their mothers' health – Alf and Ralph begged their father to confuse his visit-ing rights again.

The boys talked excitedly of their new half-brothers when they returned home, and soon Treslove was in receipt of unkind letters from his old girlfriends – in the case of Rodolfo's mother, reproaching him for a retrospective infidelity she wanted it to be clear she was hurt by only in the abstract, and in the case of Alfredo's, informing him his visiting rights were suspended until he heard otherwise from her lawyers. But eventually the wishes of the boys prevailed over the indolent malice (as Treslove called it) of their mothers, and in time the latter thought that they too might find a bristling sort of comfort in each other's company, not to say an answer to the question of why not just one woman but two had consented to have a baby by a man they didn't give a fig for. An inac-curate account, Treslove believed when it was relayed to him, given that consent on the one side implies request on the other, and he had never in his life requested any woman to have his baby. Why would he? The curtain always came down on Treslove's fantasy of happiness with him crying 'Mimi!' or 'Violetta!' and kissing the cold dead lips a last goodbye that would leave him inconsolable for ever. He couldn't have done that with a child there. A child turned a tragic opera into an *opera buffa* and necessitated at least another act, for which Treslove lacked both the stamina and imagination.

The women were taken aback, when they first met, by how alike not just the boys but they were.

'I could understand him going for a dark woman with large breasts and rounded thighs and a fiery Latin temperament,' Josephine said, 'but what could he possibly have thought he was seeing in you that he hadn't already got from me? We're both scrawny Anglo-Saxon cows.'

She was unamused but tried for laughter – an exhalation of sour breath, like a gasp, that frilled her narrow lips.

'That's assuming you have his defections in the right chronological order,' Janice replied. Her lips, too, were scalloped like the hem of a lace undergarment and seemed to move sideways rather than up and down.

Neither was sure which of them was on the scene first, and the ages of the boys didn't help, since Treslove was not exactly a clean finisher with women and sometimes visited an old girlfriend when he was with a new. But they both agreed he was a man who needed to be given his marching orders – 'Chop, chop,' in Janice words – and that they were equally lucky to be rid of him.

Treslove had met Josephine at the BBC and been sorry for her. The best-looking women at the BBC were the Jewesses but he didn't have the courage in those days to approach a Jewess. And it was partly because Josephine had neither the coloration nor the confidence of the BBC Jewesses that he felt sorry for her – though only partly. For all that she was, as she admitted, scrawny, she had the broad legs of a much larger woman which she drew attention to by wearing spidery patterned stockings. She was fond of lacy see-through blouses through which Treslove saw that she wore the brassiere of a woman twice her breast size together with at least one slip, something he believed was called a chemise, and something he recalled his mother referring to as a liberty bodice. Sitting opposite her at an awards ceremony – she was the recipient of a Sony Radio Academy Award for a programme she had made about the male menopause – Treslove, who was not the recipient of an award for anything, counted five straps on each of her shoulders. She blushed when she accepted her award – making a brief speech about unpacking a raft of ideas, which was how people at the BBC described having a thought – just as she blushed whenever Treslove accosted her in the corridor or the canteen, her skin remaining blotchy for hours after-wards. Treslove understood the shame that went with blushing and invited her to hide herself from the world by burying her face in his shoulder.

'It's humiliation that makes us human,' he whispered into her dead hair.

'Who's humiliated?'

He did the decent thing. 'I am,' he said.

She had his baby, aggressively, without telling him. Other than for his neat, even features, he was the last man she would have wanted for a father of her child. Why in that case she wanted his child she didn't know. Why did she want any child? Couldn't face the abortion was as good an explanation as any. And there were many women she knew who were bringing up children on their own. It was in the air at the time – single-mother chic. She might have tried lesbianism out of similar motives, only she could no more go the final yard of that than have an abortion.

Spite probably explained it as much as anything. She had Treslove's baby to punish him.

Treslove fell for Janice in anticipation of the raging Josephine's rejection of him, unless it was the other way round. The women were right to notice their resemblance. All Treslove's women resembled one another a bit, soliciting his pity by their neurasthenic paleness, by their being somehow out of time, not just in the dancing sense, though they were all bad dancers, but in the language and fashion sense as well, not a one of them knowing how to use language that was current or to put together two items of clothing that matched. It wasn't that he didn't notice and admire robust, fluent women who dressed well, it was simply that he didn't see how he could make life better for them.

Or they for him, given that a robust woman held out small promise of a premature expiry.

Janice owned one pair of boots which she wore in all seasons, repairing them with Sellotape when they threatened to fall apart. Over the boots she wore a filmy gypsy skirt of no colour that Treslove could distinguish and over that a grey-and-blue cardigan the sleeves of which she wore long, as though to protect her fingertips from the cold. In all weathers, Janice's extremities were cold, like those of an orphan child, as Treslove imagined, in a Victorian novel. She was not in the employ of the BBC, though it seemed to Treslove that she would have fitted in remarkably well with the BBC women he knew, and might even have cut a dash among them. An art historian who had written voluminously on the spiritual void in Malevich and Rothko, she appeared regularly on the sort of unremarked and barely funded arts programmes that Treslove worked through the night to produce. Her speciality was the absence of something in male artists, an absence which she was gentler on than was the fashion at the time. Treslove felt an erotic sorrow for her well up inside him the minute she walked shivering into his studio and put headphones on. They appeared to squeeze the last of the lifeblood from her temples.

'If you think I'm going to let you fuck me on our first date,' she said, letting him fuck her on their first date, 'you've got another think coming.'

Her explanation for that later was that what they'd been on wasn't a date.

So he asked her out on a date. She turned up wearing long

Edwardian opera gloves which she'd bought at a jumble sale, and wouldn't let him fuck her.

'Then let's go out not on a date,' he said.

She told him you couldn't plan not being on a date, because then it was a date.

'Let's neither go on a date nor not go on a date,' he suggested. 'Let's just fuck.'

She slapped his face. 'What kind of woman do you think I am?' she said.

One of the pearl buttons on the opera gloves cut Treslove's cheek. The gloves were so dirty he feared septic poisoning.

They stopped seeing each other after that, which meant he was free to fuck her.

'Give it to me,' she told him between gasps for air, as though reading words on the ceiling.

He pitied her to his soul.

But that didn't stop him giving it to her.

And perhaps she pitied him. Of Treslove's girlfriends of this period Janice was possibly the only one who felt anything that could be described as affection for him, though not to the extent of enjoying his company. 'You're not a bad man exactly,' she told him once. 'I don't mean you're not bad-looking or not bad in bed, I mean you're not malevolent. There's something missing from you, but it isn't goodness. I don't think you wish anyone harm per se. Not even women.' So it was possible she at least had his baby because she thought it would be not a bad thing to have. Per se.

But she told him she wanted to bring the child up on her own, which he told her was all right with him, but why.

'It would be just too hard going any other way,' she said. 'No offence intended.'

'None taken,' Treslove told her, deeply hurt yet relieved. He would miss her chilled extremities but not a baby.

What annoyed the two women most when they made each other's acquaintance and met each other's sons – in whom

109

they separately noted Treslove's unremarkable, not to say nondescript handsomeness – was the discovery that they had both so far capitulated to Treslove's influence as to call their children Rodolfo and Alfredo. In those days Treslove alternated playing records of *La Bohème* with records of *La Traviata*. Without knowing that they knew either opera both women in fact knew them backwards, particularly the love duets and the heartbreaking finales when Treslove as Rodolfo or Alfredo would call out their names, 'Mimi!' or 'Violetta!', sometimes confusing the operas, but always with the desperate plaintiveness of a man who believed that without them – Mimi or Violetta – his own life was over.

'He taught me to hate those bastard operas,' Josephine told Janice, 'and I wouldn't mind but I wasn't ever even going to tell him about Alfredo, so why did I call him Alfredo? Can you explain that to me?'

'Well I know why I called Rodolfo Rodolfo. Paradoxical as it may sound, it was to get Julian out of my system. It was all so deathly, I thought that if I substituted a new life for all that dying we'd be the better for it.'

'Oh God, I know what you mean. Do you think he was capable of being with a living woman?'

'No. Nor a living child. That's why I kept Rodolfo from him. I was frightened he'd play operas to him in his cot and fill his little head with nerve-worn women with cold hands.'

'Me the same,' Josephine said, thinking that, as the son of Janice, Rodolfo had no choice but to have his little head filled with nerve-worn women with cold hands.

'They're always the worst, the romantics, don't you think?'

'Absolutely. You want to swat them off you. Like leeches.'

'Except that you can't just swat a leech, can you? You have to burn them off.'

'Yes. Or pour alcohol on them. But you know what I mean. They're always telling you how desperately in love with you they are while looking for the next woman.'

'Yes, they always have their cases packed, mentally.'

'Exactly. Though I packed first.'

'Me too.'

'Christ, and those operas! When I think of all that dying on the record player . . .'

'I know. "Oh God, to die so young!" I don't just hear it, I can smell the sickbeds. Still. To this day. I sometimes think he's exerting his consumptive influence from afar.'

'Puccini?'

'No, Julian. But in fact it's Verdi. Yours is Puccini.'

'How does he do it?'

'Puccini?'

'No, Julian.'

'Frisk me.'

So once every two or three years they would meet, using the pretext of Alf's or Ralph's birthday, or some other anniversary they were able to concoct, such as their leaving Treslove, and never mind who left him first. And the custom continued even when the boys had grown up and left home.

Tonight, in line with their current practice, they had avoided all mention of Treslove who occupied more of their conversational space than he merited at the best of times, but who had in addition become something of an embarrassment to them now that he was doing what he was doing for a living. He remained Alf's and Ralph's father, no matter how much water had flowed under the bridge, and they would have liked to be able to say that their sons' father had done more with his life than become a celebrity double.

But as they were gathering their coats, Josephine took Rodolfo, Janice's boy, aside. 'Heard from your papa recently?' she asked. It appeared to be a question she was unable to ask her own son.

He shook his head.

'What about you?' Janice asked Alfredo.

'Well,' said Alfredo, 'it's funny you should mention him . . .'

And they had to ask the waiter if he minded their sitting down again.

2

'So who's Judith?'

Had Treslove's legs given way under him, as they threatened to do, it was unlikely Libor Sevcik would have had the strength to pull him up.

'Libor!'

'Did I frighten you?'

'What does it look like?'

'I asked the wrong question. *How come* I frightened you?'

Treslove made to look at his watch before remembering he no longer had a watch to look at. 'It's the dead of night, Libor,' he said, as though reading from his empty wrist.

'I don't sleep,' Libor told him. 'You know I don't sleep.'

'I didn't know you walked the streets.'

'Well, I don't as rule. Only if it's bad. Tonight was bad. Last night too was bad. But I didn't know you walked the streets either. Why didn't you ring my bell, we could have strolled together?'

'I'm not strolling.'

'Who's Judith?'

'Don't ask me. I don't know any Judith.'

'You called her name.'

'Judith? You're mistaken. I might have said Jesus. You gave me a shock.'

'If you weren't strolling and you weren't expecting Judith, what *were* you doing – choosing a cello?'

'I always look in this window.'

'So do I. Malkie brought me here to get my fiddle valued. It's one of our Stations of the Cross.'

'You believe in the cross?'

'No, but I believe in suffering.'

Treslove touched his friend's shoulder. Libor looked smaller tonight than he remembered him, as though the streets diminished him. Unless it was being without Malkie that did it.

'And did they give you a good valuation on your fiddle?' he asked. It was that or weep.

'Not so good that it was worth parting with. But I promised Malkie I would no longer insist on our playing duets. My fiddling was the only part of me she didn't adore, and she didn't want there to be any part of me she didn't adore.'

'Were you really no good?'

'I thought I was very good, but I wasn't in Malkie's class, despite my being related to Heifetz on my mother's side.'

'You're related to Heifetz? Jesus!'

'You mean Judith!'

'You never told me you were related to Heifetz.'

'You never asked.'

'I didn't know Heifetz was Czech.'

'He wasn't. He was Lithuanian. My mother's family came originally from that porous Polish–Czech border area known as Suwalki. Every country has occupied it. The Red Army gave it to the Germans so that they could kill the Jews there. Then they took it back to kill any that were left. I'm Heifetz's fourth or fifth cousin but my mother always made out we were half-brothers. She rang me from Prague when she read that Heifetz was playing at the Albert Hall and made me solemnly promise I would go backstage to introduce myself. I tried, but this is a long time ago, I didn't have the connections then that I had later and I hadn't yet learned how to manage without them. His flunkeys gave me a signed photograph and ordered me to leave. "So what did he say?" my mother asked me the next day. "He sent his love," I told her. Sometimes it does no harm to lie. "And did he look well?" Marvellous. "And his playing?" Superb. "And he remembered everybody?" By name. To you he blew a kiss.'

And standing there outside J. P. Guivier's at eleven o'clock on a London night he made the kiss, the lugubrious Baltic kiss that Heifetz would have blown his mother had Libor only been able to get to him.

Jews, Treslove thought, admiringly. Jews and music. Jews and families. Jews and their loyalties. (Finkler excepted.)

'But you,' Libor said, taking Treslove's arm, 'what really brings you to this window if it isn't Judith? I haven't heard from you for days. You don't ring, you don't write, you don't knock. You tell me you're too agitated to come out. And here you are a hundred yards from my door. You have, I hope, some explanation for this uncharacteristic behaviour.'

And suddenly Treslove, who loved it when Libor linked his arm in the street, feeling it made a clever little wizened European Jew of him, knew he had to spill the beans.

'Let's find a cafe,' he suggested.

'No, let's go back to my place,' Libor said.

'No, let's find a cafe. We might see her.'

'*Her*? Who's *her*? This Judith woman?'

Rather than tell him all at once, Treslove agreed to go home with Libor.

It was Libor's view that Treslove was overwrought – had been for some time – and probably needed a holiday. They could go away together to somewhere warm. Rimini, maybe. Or Palermo.

'That's what Sam said.'

'That you and I should go to Rimini or that you and he should go to Rimini? Why don't we all go?'

'No, that I was overwrought. In fact, he thought I needed to see less of you both, not more. Too much death, was his diagnosis. Too many widowers in my life. And this guy's a philosopher, don't forget.'

'Then do as he says. I'll miss you, but take his advice. I have friends in Hollywood I could introduce you to. Or at least the great-great-grandchildren of friends.'

'Why is it so difficult for people to believe that what happened, happened?'

'Because women don't mug men, that's why. Me a woman might have had a shot at. Me you can blow over. But you – you're still young and strong. That's A. B, women don't make a practice of attacking men in the street and calling them Jew, especially, C, when they're not Jewish. C's good. C clinches it.'

'Well, that's what she did and that's what she said.'

'That's what you think she said.'

Treslove settled down into the plush discomfort of Libor's Biedermeier sofa.

'Just what if?' he asked, taking hold of the wooden arm, anxious not to put his hands on the fabric, so exquisitely taut was it.

'What if what?'

'What if she was right?'

'That you're . . . ?'

'Yes.'

'But you're not.'

'We *think* I'm not.'

'And did you ever before think you were?'

'No . . . Well, yes. I was a musical boy. I listened to operas and wanted to play the violin.'

'That doesn't make you Jewish. Wagner listened to operas and wanted to play the violin. Hitler loved opera and wanted to play the violin. When Mussolini visited Hitler in the Alps they played the Bach double violin concerto together. "And now let's kill some Jews," Hitler said when they'd finished. You don't have to be Jewish to like music.'

'Is that true?'

'That you don't have to be Jewish to like music? Of course it's true.'

'No, about Hitler and Mussolini.'

'Who cares if it's true. You can't libel a dead Fascist. Listen, if you were what this imaginary woman said you were, and you'd have wanted to play the violin, you'd have played the violin. Nothing would have stopped you.'

'I obeyed my father. Doesn't that prove something? I respected his wishes.'

'Obeying your father doesn't make you a Jew. Obeying your mother would make you more of one. While your father's not wanting you to play the violin almost certainly makes him not a Jew. If there's one thing all Jewish fathers agree on —'

'Sam would say that's stereotyping. And you leave out the possibility that my father didn't want me to play the violin for the reason that he didn't want me to be like him.'

'He was a violinist?'

'Yes. Like you. See?'

'And why wouldn't he have wanted you to be like him? Was he that bad a violinist?'

'Libor, I'm trying to be serious. He might have had his reasons.'

'I'm sorry. But in what way would he have wanted you to be different from him? Was he unhappy? Did he suffer?'

Treslove thought about it. 'Yes,' he said. 'He took things hard. My mother's death broke his heart. But there was something broken-hearted about him before that. As though he knew what was coming and had been preparing himself for it all his life. He could have been protecting me from deep feelings, saving me from something he feared in himself, something undesirable, dangerous even.'

'The Jews aren't the only broken-hearted people in the world, Julian.'

Treslove looked disappointed to hear it. He blew out his cheeks, breathing hard, and shook his head, appearing to be disagreeing with himself as much as with Libor.

'Let me tell you something,' he said. 'In all the time I was growing up I didn't once hear the word Jew. Don't you think that's strange? Nor, in all the time I was growing up, did I meet a Jew in my father's company, in my father's shop, or in my parents' home. Every other word I heard. Every other kind of person I met. Hottentots I met in my father's shop. Tongans I met. But never a Jew. Not until I met Sam did I even know what a Jew looked like. And when I brought him home my father told me he didn't think he made a suitable friend. "That Finkler," he used to ask me, "that *Finkler*, are you still kicking about with him?" Explain that.'

'Easy. He was an anti-Semite.'

'If he'd been an anti-Semite, Libor, Jew would have been the *only* word I heard.'

'And your mother? If you are, then it has to be through her.'

'Jesus Christ, Libor, I was a Gentile five minutes ago, now you're telling me I can only be Jewish through the right channels. Will you be checking to see if I'm circumcised next? I don't know about my mother. I can only tell you she didn't look Jewish.'

'Julian, *you* don't look Jewish. Forgive me, I don't mean it as an insult, but you are the least Jewish-looking person I have ever met, and I have met Swedish cowboys and Eskimo stuntmen and Prussian film directors and Polish Nazis working as set builders in Alaska. I would stake my life on it that no Jewish gene has been near the gene of a member of your family for ten thousand years and ten thousand years ago there weren't any Jews. Be grateful. A man can live a good and happy life and not be Jewish.' He paused. 'Look at Sam Finkler.'

They both laughed wildly and wickedly at this.

'Cruel,' Treslove said, taking another drink and banging his chest. 'But that only serves my argument. These things are not to be decided superficially. You can be called Finkler and fall short of the mark; or you can be called Treslove —'

'Which is not exactly a Jewish name —'

'Exactly, and yet still come up to scratch. Wouldn't it have made sense, if my father didn't want me to know we were

Jews, or for anyone else to know we were Jews for that matter, to have changed our name to the least Jewish one he could find? Treslove, for Christ's sake. It screams "Not Jewish" at you. I rest my case.'

'I'll tell how you can rest your case, Mr Perry Mason. You can rest your case by stopping these ridiculous speculations and asking somebody. Ask an uncle, ask one of your father's friends, ask anyone who knew your family. This is a mystery that is solvable with a phone call.'

'No one knew my family. We kept ourselves to ourselves. I have no uncles. My father had no brothers or sisters, my mother neither. It was what attracted them to each other. They told me about it. Two orphans, as good as. Two babes in the wood. You tell me what that's a metaphor for.'

Libor shook his head and topped up their whiskies. 'It's a metaphor for your not wanting to know the truth because you prefer to make it up. OK, make it up. You're Jewish. *Trog es gezunterhait.*' And he raised his glass.

He sat down and crossed his little feet. He had changed into a pair of *ancien régime* slippers which bore his initials, woven in gold thread. A present from Malkie, Treslove surmised. Wasn't everything a present from Malkie? In these slippers Libor looked even more wispy and transparent, fading away. And yet to Treslove he was enviably secure. At home. Himself. In love still with the only woman he had ever loved. On his mantelpiece photographs of the two of them being married by a rabbi, Malkie veiled, Libor in a skullcap. Deep rooted, ancient, knowledgeable about themselves. Musical because music spoke to the romance of their origins.

Looking again in admiration at Libor's slippers he saw that the initials on one read *LS* while on the other they read *ES*. That was right of course; Libor had changed his own name, in his Hollywood years, from Libor Sevcik to Egon Slick. It was what Jews did, wasn't it, what Jews had to do? So why wasn't Libor/Egon more sympathetic to Teitelbaum/Treslove?

He swirled his whisky round in his glass. Bohemian Crystal. His father too had favoured crystal whisky glasses but they had been somehow different. More formal. Probably more expensive. Colder to the lip. That, essentially, was what the difference amounted to — temperature. Libor and Malkie — even poor Malkie dead — were somehow warmed by their submersion in a heated past. In comparison, Treslove felt that he had been brought up to play on the surface of life, like those vegetables that grow above ground, where it is chill.

Libor was smiling at him. 'Now you're a Jew, come to dinner,' he said. 'Come to dinner next week — not with Sam — and I'll introduce you to some people who would be pleased to meet you.'

'You make it sound sinister. *Some* people. Which people? Watchmen of the Jewish faith who will scrutinise my credentials? I have no credentials. And why wouldn't they have been pleased to meet me before I was Jewish?'

'That's good, Julian. Getting touchy is a good sign. You can't be Jewish if you can't do touchy.'

'I'll tell you what. I'll come if I can bring the woman who attacked me. She's my credentials.'

Libor shrugged. 'Bring her. Find her and bring her.'

He made the possibility sound so remote he could have been talking about Treslove finding God.

Something that worried Treslove ever so slightly as he lay on his bed, struggling for the thread that would wind him into sleep: Libor's story about Heifetz at the Royal Albert Hall . . . Wasn't it, in its — he didn't have the word: its preciousness, its preciosity, its oh-so-Jewish cultural-vulturalness — wasn't it a bit uncomfortably close to Libor's story about Malkie and Horowitz at the Carnegie?

They could conceivably both be true, but then again, the echo, once one heard it, was disconcerting.

True or not true, as family mythologies went, these were

enviably top-drawer. It wasn't Elvis Presley whom Malkie had called Maestro. It was Horowitz. As Egon Slick, Libor had put in half a lifetime rubbing shoulders with the vulgarly famous, and yet when the chips were down, when it was necessary to impress, he pulled his cards, without blushing, from another deck. It wasn't Liza Minnelli or Madonna he was claiming as his cousin – it was Heifetz. You had to place a high value on intellectual ritziness to want Horowitz and Heifetz at your party. And who did intellectually ritzy as Finklers did intellectually ritzy?

Yes, you had to hand it to them . . . they were brazen, they had cheek, but it was cheek predicated on a refined musical education.

Finding his thread, Treslove drifted into a deep sleep.

3

Although there had been little commerce between the Finklers and the Tresloves – not counting the commerce between Tyler Finkler and Julian Treslove – the Finkler boys and the Treslove boys had on occasions met, and certainly Alfredo and Rodolfo knew of Finkler well enough through his books and television to enjoy thinking of him as their famous uncle Sam. Whether Sam had any interest in thinking of them as his charming nephews Alf and Ralph was another matter. It was Treslove's suspicion that he didn't know either of them from Adam.

In this, as in so many other matters related and indeed unrelated to Finkler, Treslove was wrong. It was Treslove who didn't know either of his sons from Adam.

Finkler, as it happened, was well aware of his old friend's sons and felt warmly disposed to them, not impossibly because he was Treslove's rival in fatherhood and unclehood as well as in everything else, and wanted to be seen to be making up to the boys for what their real father hadn't given them. Making up to them and giving them a higher standard to judge by. Alf was the one he knew better, on account of an incident at the Grand Hotel in Eastbourne – the gist of it being that Finkler had calculated on the Grand being a reliably romantic and discreet place to take a woman for a Friday night and Saturday morning – seagulls outside the windows and the other guests being too old to be able to place him or to do anything about it if they had – but he hadn't calculated on finding Alf playing the piano during dinner.

This was two years before Tyler's death, two years before her illness had been diagnosed even, so his misbehaviour was not of the utterly unforgivable sort. Had he only known it, Tyler was herself misbehaving at the time, with Treslove as it happened, so that too, weighing one thing against another, took fractionally from his criminality. Even so, to go over to the piano to ask the pianist to play 'Stars Fell on Alabama' for Ronit Kravitz and to discover he was talking to Treslove's son Alfredo was a misfortune Finkler would rather have avoided.

He didn't register Alfredo immediately – where you don't expect to find people you don't know well it is easy not to recognise them – but Alfredo, having the advantage of seeing him frequently on television, recognised Finkler at once.

'Uncle Sam,' he said. 'Wow!'

Finkler thought about saying 'Do I know you?' but doubted he could put the words together with any conviction.

'Ahem!' he said instead, deciding to accept that he'd been caught red-handed and to play the naughty uncle about it. Given the incontrovertibility of Ronit Kravitz's décolletage, there was certainly no point in saying he was in Eastbourne for a business meeting

Alfredo looked across at the table Finkler had vacated and said, 'Auntie Tyler couldn't be with you tonight then?'

On the spot, Finkler realised that he had never liked Alfredo. He wouldn't have sworn that he had ever truly liked

Alfredo's father either, but school friends are school friends. Alfredo closely resembled his father, but had turned himself into an older version of him, wearing round gold-rimmed glasses which he probably didn't need and plastering his hair into a kind of greasy cowl that gave him the air of a 1920s Berlin gigolo. Only without the sex appeal.

'I was going to ask you to play a tune for my companion,' Finkler said, 'but in the circumstances –'

'Oh, no, I'll play it,' Alfredo said. 'I'm here for that. What would she like – "Happy Birthday to You"?'

For some reason Finkler was unable to ask for the song he had been sent to ask for. Had he forgotten it in the embarrassment of being found out, or was he punishing Ronit for being the cause of that embarrassment?

'"My Yiddishe Mama",' he said. 'If you know that.'

'Play it all the time,' Alfredo said.

And he did, more derisively than Finkler had ever heard it played, with crude honky-tonk syncopations followed by absurdly drawn-out slow passages, almost like a funeral march, as though it was a mockery of motherhood, not a celebration of it.

'That's not "Stars Fell on Alabama",' Ronit Kravitz said. Other than her décolletage, which was bigger than she was, there was little to observe on Ronit Kravitz's person. Under the table she wore high-heeled shoes with diamantés on them, but these were not visible. And though her hair was a beautiful blue-black, catching light from the chandeliers, it too, like every eye, fell into the boundless golden chasm which she carried before her as a proud disabled person carries an infirmity. The Manawatu Gorge was how Finkler thought of it when he wasn't in love with her, as he wasn't in love with her now.

'It's his interpretation,' he said. 'I'll hum it to you the way you like it later.'

It was a lesson he just seemed unable to learn: that the

company of preposterously sexy women always makes a man look a fool. Too long the legs, too high the skirt, too exposed the breasts, and it's laughter you inspire as the consort, not envy. For a moment he longed to be at home with Tyler, until he remembered that she was showing too much of everything these days as well. And she was a mother.

He didn't once wink at Alfredo across the dining room, or take him aside at the end of the evening and slip a fifty-pound note into the top pocket of his dinner jacket with a request to, you know, keep this between them. As a practical philosopher, Finkler was hot on the etiquette of treachery and falsehood. It was not appropriate, he thought, to strike up male collusion with the child of an old friend, let alone embroil him in an older generation's way of doing adultery, laughable or otherwise. He'd said 'Ahem'. That would have to suffice. But they did run into each other in the men's lavatory.

'Another night at the Copacabana knocked on the head,' Alfredo said, wearily zipping himself up and replastering his hair in the mirror. That done, he popped on a perky pork-pie hat which at a stroke took away all suggestion of Berlin and made Finkler think of Bermondsey.

His father's boy, all right, Finkler thought, capable of looking like everyone and no one.

'You don't like your job?'

'Like it?! You should try playing the piano to people who are here to eat. Or die. Or both. They're too busy listening to their own stomachs to hear a note I play. They wouldn't know if I was giving them Chopsticks or Chopin. I make background noise. Do you know what I do to entertain myself while I'm playing? I make up stories about the diners. This one's screwing that one, that one's screwing this one – which is hard to do in a joint like this, I can tell you, where most of them won't have had sex since before I was born.'

Finkler didn't point out that he was an exception to this rule. 'You hide your discontent well,' he lied.

'Do I? That's because I vanish. I'm somewhere else. In my head I'm playing at Caesar's Palace.'

'Well, you hide that well, too.'

'It's a job.'

'We all settle for just a job,' Finkler told him, as though to camera.

'Is that how you see what you do?'

'Mostly, yes.'

'How sad for you, then, as well.'

'As well as for you, you mean?'

'Yes, as well as for me, but I'm young. There's time for anything to happen to me. I might make it to Caesar's Palace yet. I meant how sad as well for Dad.'

'Is he unhappy?'

'What do you think? You've known him like for ever. Does he look a satisfied man to you?'

'No, but he never did.'

'Didn't he? Never – ha! That figures. I can't imagine him young. He's like a man who's always been old.'

'Well, there you are,' Finkler said, 'I think of him as a man who's always been young. All to do with when one meets a person, I guess.'

Under his pert pork-pie hat, Alfredo rolled his eyes, as though to say *Don't go deep on me, Uncle Sam*.

What he actually said was, 'We don't hit it off especially – I think he secretly prefers my half-brother – but I'm sorry for him, doing that stupid doubling thing, especially if it all feels to him the way it all feels to me.'

'Oh, come on, at your age the glass is half full.'

'No, it's at your age that the glass is half full. At my age we don't want half a glass, full or empty. In fact we don't want a glass, end of. We want a tankard and we want it overflowing. We are the have-everything generation, remember.'

'No, *we're* the have-everything generation.'

'Well we're the pissed generation then.'

Finkler smiled at him and felt a new book coming on. *The Glass Half Empty: Schopenhauer for Teen Binge Drinkers*.

It wasn't a cynical calculation. Quite unexpectedly, he experienced a vicarious paternal rush for the boy. Perhaps it was a resurfacing of something he had felt for Treslove all those years ago. Perhaps it was usurpation ecstasy – the joy that comes with being a father to someone else's children – the mirror image of the joyous role Treslove was enjoying that very hour – being a husband to someone else's wife, even if that wife insisted on turning away from him and fiddling with his penis behind her back, as though having trouble with the fastening of a complicated brassiere.

Before they left the lavatory together Finkler handed Alfredo his card. 'Give me a ring sometime when you're in town,' he said. 'You're not stuck down here all the time, are you?'

'Shit no. I'd die.'

'Then call me. We can talk about your father . . . or not.'

'Right. Or – I do the Savoy and Claridge's some weeks – you could always pop in and say hello . . .'

With a floozie, the little bastard means, Finkler thought. That's how he'll always see me. Out on the razzle with the Manawatu Gorge. And he'll never let me forget it.

In his mind's eye Finkler saw himself meeting Alfredo in lavatories for the next fifty years – until Alfredo was far older than he was now and he, Finkler, had become a bent old man – passing him wads of unused notes in Manila envelopes.

They shook hands and laughed. Each a little wary and a little flattered.

This boy is an opportunist, Finkler thought, but never mind.

He thinks I think there's some advantage to me in knowing him, Alfredo thought, and maybe there is. But there's some advantage to him in knowing me as well. He might learn how to choose himself a less tacky piece of skirt.

So began a somehow compelling but mutually irritating friendship between two men of unequal age and interests.

Alfredo had never discussed any of this with his mother or half-brother. He was a man who liked secrets. But here, when he sat down again after dinner with them, was a secret he couldn't keep.

'Dad's been mugged. Did you know that?'

'Everyone gets mugged,' Rodolfo said. 'This is London.'

'No but this was a mugging with a difference. This was a mega-mugging.'

'God, is he hurt?' Janice wondered.

'Well here's the thing. Apparently he says no but Uncle Sam thinks yes.'

'You've seen Uncle Sam?'

'Ran into him in a bar. That's how I know about it.'

'Your father would make a fuss about it if he'd been hurt,' Josephine put in. 'He makes a fuss if he cuts his finger.'

'It's not that kind of hurt. Sam says it's shaken him badly but he won't accept it. He's in denial, Sam reckons.'

'He's always been in denial,' Josephine said. 'He's in denial that he's a bastard.'

'What does Sam think he's in denial about?' Janice asked.

'Hard to say. His identity or whatever.'

Josephine snorted. 'Tell me something new.'

'It's weirder than that. It seems he was mugged by a woman.'

'A woman?' Rodolfo couldn't contain his amusement. 'I knew he was a wimp, but a woman – !'

'Sounds like some sort of wish-fulfilment,' Janice said.

'Yeah, mine,' Josephine laughed. 'I only wish I could tell you it was me that did it.'

'Josephine!' Janice admonished her.

'Come off it. Don't tell me you wouldn't want to mug him if you saw him coming down the street looking like Leonardo

DiCaprio's grandfather and dodging the cracks or whatever he does now?'

'Why don't you come off the fence and tell us what you really think of Dad?' Rodolfo said, still amused at the idea of his father cowering before a woman.

'You mean admit I love him?' She put her fingers down her throat.

'Sam says it's bollocks, anyway,' Alfredo said. 'His theory is that Dad's stressed out.'

'By what?' Janice wanted to know.

'By what happened to Auntie Tyler and the wife of another of his friends. Too much dying for him to handle, Uncle Sam reckons.'

'That's your father all over,' Josephine said. 'Greedy little grave robber. Why can't he allow other men to mourn their own wives? Why must he always get in on the act?'

'Sam said he was very fond of both women.'

'Yeah — I'll bet. Especially when they snuffed it.'

Ignoring this, Janice said, 'So Sam thinks this mugger materialised from Julian's grief . . .'

'Grief!'

'No, it's an intriguing thought. Maybe this is what a ghost is — the embodiment of what's upsetting you. But why as a mugger, I wonder? Why the violence?'

'This conversation is getting beyond me,' Rodolfo said. 'Can't we go back to Dad being bashed by some bag lady?'

'Guilt's my guess,' Josephine said, ignoring him. 'He'd probably been shafting them both. Or worse, singing Puccini arias to them.'

'Yours were Verdi,' Janice reminded her.

'Anyway,' Alfredo went on, 'Sam suggested we send him away for a bit.'

'To the loony bin?'

'Arrange a holiday for him. You know how reluctant he is to make plans to go away. Frightened of trains, frightened of planes, frightened to be somewhere he doesn't know the local word for paracetamol. It would be best, Uncle Sam said, for us actually to go with him. Anyone want to go on holiday with Dad?'

'Not me,' Rodolfo said.

'Not me,' Janice said.

'Not if he was the last man on the planet,' Josephine said. 'Let Sam Finkler go with him if he thinks it's such a good idea.'

'So that's a no then, is it?' Alfredo laughed.

It was only as they were getting up to leave again, having agreed that the boys should at least give him a call and maybe take him out for lunch, that Alfredo remembered something else Uncle Sam had told him. 'And, *and* . . . he's decided he's a Jew.'

'Uncle Sam? Isn't Uncle Sam already a Jew?'

'No, Dad. *Dad*'s decided he's a Jew.'

'Dad's decided he's a Jew? Dad, a Jew?'

All four sat down again.

'Yep.'

'How do you mean decided?' Rodolfo wanted to know. 'You can't just get up one morning and *decide* you're a Jew — or can you?'

'I've worked with a lot of people at BH who got up one morning and decided they were *not* a Jew,' Josephine said.

'But it can't work the other way, surely?'

'Search me,' said Alfredo. 'But I don't think Dad's planning to become a Jew. If I understood Uncle Sam he's got this bee in his bonnet that he already *is* a Jew.'

'Christ,' Rodolfo said, 'what does that make us?'

'Not Jewish,' Josephine said. 'Don't worry about it. Jews don't trust their women in the sack, so you can only be Jewish through the vagina. And I don't have a Jewish vagina.'

'Nor me,' Janice said. 'Nor mine.'

Alfredo and Rodolfo exchanged vomit faces with each other. But Rodolfo was perplexed as well as nauseated. 'I don't get how that works. If you can't trust your women why would you want them to be the ones that make you Jewish?'

'Well, you wouldn't be a Jew at all if you relied on your father and he was a bloody big Arab with gold teeth.'

'Do Jewish women sleep with Arabs?'

'Darling, Jewish women sleep with anybody.'

'Hush it,' Janice said, signalling the waiters with a mute revolution of her head. They were, don't forget – her eyes warned them – in a Lebanese restaurant.

'Interesting, though,' Rodolfo said. 'If I discover I'm half Jewish will I suddenly become half clever?'

Janice ruffled her son's hair. 'You don't need *him* to make you half clever,' she said.

'Half rich, then?'

FIVE

I

You don't say 'Find her and bring her' to an obsessive man.

But Treslove was damned if he was going to give the 'her' in question another minute of his time. One day you just have to say no to a compulsion. He put on a coat and took it off again. Enough was enough. He knew what he thought. He knew what he had heard. *You Jew.* Not *You Bloody Jew* or *You Dirty Jew* or *You Lovely Jew. Just You Jew.* And it was the oddity of that, all things considered, that proved that she had said it. Why would he make up anything so strange? *You Jew,* unvarnished – *You pure unvarnished Jew* – supported no theory or assumption. It answered to no necessity that Treslove recognised in himself. It provided nothing, solved nothing, assuaged nothing.

Treslove knew the argument against. He had made it up out of need. So show him the need?

Its very arbitrariness was the proof of its authenticity. His psychology was innocent of seeking or finding the slightest gratification from it. But that still left the mugger. Would she have called him *Jew* just for the fun of it? No, she had called him *Jew* because she'd seen a Jew. Why she needed to tell him what she'd seen was a different question. She didn't, all things considered, have to say anything. She could have taken his valuables and left without a word. He wasn't exactly putting up a fight. Or looking for a thank-you. Most muggers, he assumed, didn't identify their victims while they were mugging them. *You Protestant, You Chinaman.* Why bother? The

Protestant and the Chinaman could be relied on to know what they were without a mugger telling them. So *You Jew* was either an expression of irrepressible rage or it was intended to be informative. *I've taken your watch, your wallet, your fountain pen, your mobile phone and your self-respect – your jewels, in short – but in return I give you something: just in case you didn't know it, and I have a sneaking little feeling (don't ask me why) that you might not have known it, you're a Jew.*

Bye.

Treslove was not willing to accept that he had encountered a person with a screw loose, or that he had just happened to be in the wrong place at the wrong time. He'd been subject to enough accident. His whole life had been an accident. His birth was an accident – his parents had told him that, 'You weren't planned, Julian, but you were a nice surprise.' His own sons the same. Only he'd never told them they were a nice surprise. Doing a modular degree had been an accident; in another age he'd have read classics or theology. The BBC was an accident. A malign accident. The women he'd loved were all accidents. If life didn't have a thread of meaning to it, why live it? Some men find God where they least expect to. Some discover their purpose in social action or self-sacrifice. Treslove had been in waiting for as long as he could remember. Very well then. My fate cries out, he thought.

Two nights later he was dining with fellow Jews at Libor's place.

2

Half a year before his wife died, Sam Finkler accepted an invitation to be a castaway on *Desert Island Discs*.

It would be cruel to assume that the two events were anything but coincidentally related.

They were sitting in their garden, only a low gate dividing

them from the Heath, when Finkler first brought up the invitation. It was that or help Tyler plant. Their garden had long been designated an area of non-relaxation on account of Tyler always being busy in it and Finkler having an allergic reaction to lawns, flowers and the idea of taking things easy. 'That's called a lounger – lounge!' Tyler used to order him. But she had discovered what he had always known – that his body wasn't built for lounging in a lounger. 'I'll lounge long enough in due course,' had been his answer. So either he didn't venture out into the garden at all, or he paced around its perimeter like a private detective looking for a corpse in the bushes, pausing to discuss what was on his mind, and that – at least the part he could relate to Tyler – was invariably work. The moment he dried up or slowed down he knew Tyler would recruit him to hold a bamboo stake for her, or to put his finger on a knot of green string. Not onerous tasks in themselves, but they made Finkler feel his life was ebbing away into manure and mulch.

'I've landed *Desert Island Discs*,' he told her from the garden's furthest extremity, his hands behind him holding on to a down-pipe for safety.

Tyler was on her hands and knees, coaxing life out of the stony soil. Absorbed in dirt. She didn't look up. 'Landed? How do you mean landed? I didn't know you were fishing for it.'

'I wasn't. They fished for me.'

'Then tell them to throw you back.'

'Why would I do that?'

'Why wouldn't you? What do you want with *Desert Island Discs*? For a start you go to pieces in a garden never mind a desert island. And you've never owned a disc. You don't know any music.'

'I do.'

'Name some music that you like.'

'Ah, *like* – that's not the same as know.'

'Pedantic sod!' she said. 'It's not enough you're a liar. You have to be a pedant as well. I recommend you don't do the programme. It will do you no favours. People can tell when you're making it up. You shout.'

Finkler might have been fished for, but he did not rise to his wife's bait. 'I won't be lying. Not every one of my records has to be music.'

'So what are you going to choose – Bertrand Russell reading his memoirs? I can't wait.'

She stood up and wiped her hands on the gardener's apron he had bought her years ago. She was wearing earrings he had bought her, too. And the gold Rolex he had given her on their tenth wedding anniversary. Tyler gardened fully made-up and in her jewellery. She could have gone from spreading fertiliser to dining at the Ritz without needing to do anything but peel off her gloves and run her fingers through her hair. The sight of his wife rising from the compost like a beau-monde Venus was the reason Finkler couldn't keep out of the garden no matter how much he feared it. It was a mystery to him why he bothered to have mistresses when he found his wife so much more desirable than any of them.

Was he a bad man or just a foolish one? He didn't feel bad to himself. As a husband he believed himself to be essentially good and loyal. It just wasn't written in a man's nature to be monogamous, that was all. And he owed something to his nature even when his nature was at odds with his desire, which was to stay home and cherish his wife.

It was his nature – all nature, the rule of nature – that was the bastard, not him.

'Well, to begin with,' he said, feeling sentimental, 'I thought of the music we had at our wedding . . .'

She walked over to the tap to turn on the hose. 'Mendelssohn's "Wedding March"? Not exactly original. And I'd prefer, if you don't mind, that you kept our wedding out of it, since it's the last thing you'll be thinking about on your desert island. If Mendelssohn is the best you can come up with, my advice is to tell them you're too busy. Unless he wrote an "Adultery March".'

'Too busy for *Desert Island Discs*? No one's too busy for *Desert Island Discs*. It's one of those offers you have to grab – it's a career thing.'

'You have a career. Grab the end of the hose for me instead.'

Finkler was not able to determine where the end of the hose was and began to stalk his garden like a private detective again, staring into bushes and scratching his head.

'It's the bit with the water coming out, you imbecile. How many years have you lived here? – and you still don't know where your own hosepipe is. Ha!' She laughed at her joke. He didn't.

'You can't be seen not to be asked to do *Desert Island Discs*,' he continued, finding the hose at last and then wondering what he was meant to do with it.

'You've been asked. They've asked you. Why can't you be seen to refuse? I'd have thought that would do your career no end of good. Prove you're not pushy. Give it here.'

'Not pushy?'

'Not eager. Not desperate.'

'You said pushy.'

'And?'

'Not a pushy Jew, you mean?'

'Oh, for God's sake. That's not at all what I meant and you know it. Pushy Jew is your own projection. If that's how you fear people see you that's your problem, not mine. I think you're just pushy full stop. Anyway, I'm the Jew in this relationship, remember.'

'That's nonsense and you know it.'

'Recite the Amidah, then. Tell me one of the Eighteen Blessings . . .'

Finkler looked away.

Once upon a time she might have thought about spraying him with water, knowing that he would spray her back and they would have a hose fight in the garden, ending in laughter or even lovemaking on the grass and bugger the neighbours. But they were past that . . .

. . . assuming it had ever happened. She tried to picture him chasing her and catching her, pressing his mouth to hers, and was alarmed to realise she was unable to.

He canvassed his friends. Not for their opinion as to whether he should do it or not. He knew he had to do it. But for music to lie on a desert island to. Libor suggested Schubert's Impromptus. And some fiddle concertos. Treslove wrote him down the names of the great death arias in Italian opera. 'How many do you need?' he asked. 'Six?'

'One's fine. They want variety.'

'I've given you six to be on the safe side. They're all very different. Sometimes it's the woman who's dying, sometimes it's the man. And I've even thrown in one in which they die together. Make a great end to the programme.'

And to my career, Finkler thought.

At last, though not without canvassing Alfredo as well, Finkler trusted his own instincts for populism and chose Bob Dylan, Queen, Pink Floyd, Felix Mendelssohn (going for Libor's suggestion of the Violin Concerto rather than the 'Wedding March'), Girls Aloud, a tranche of obvious Elgar, Bertrand Russell reading from his memoirs, and Bruce Springsteen, whom he referred to on the show as the Boss. For his book he picked the Dialogues of Plato but also wondered if they would bend the rules this once and let him take along the complete *Harry Potter* as well.

'As light relief from all that seriousness?' the presenter asked.

'No, that's the Plato,' Finkler said. Joking, of course, but also meaning it for those who wanted him to mean it.

To prove to his wife that she was not the only Jew in their

marriage he made much of going to the synagogue every morning with his father and listening to him saying prayers for his parents, great searing lamentations that moved and, yes, marked him deeply. *Yisgadal viyiskadash* . . . the ancient language of the Hebrew tolling for the dead. *May His great Name grow exalted and sanctified.* A prayer which he in turn said when he was orphaned. The rationalist philosopher acknowledging God in the face of truths that reason could never hope to penetrate. You could hear, he thought, a pin drop in the studio. His Jewishness had always been immeasurably important to him, he confided, a matter of daily solace and inspiration, but he couldn't stay silent about the dispossession of the Palestinians. 'In the matter of Palestine,' he went on, with a falter in his voice, 'I am profoundly ashamed.'

'Profoundly self-important you mean,' Tyler said when she heard the programme. 'How could you?'

'How couldn't I?'

'Because that wasn't what the programme was about, that's how you couldn't. Because no one was asking.'

'Tyler . . .'

'I know – your conscience made you. A convenient entity your conscience. There when you need it, not when you don't. Well, I'm ashamed of your public display of shame and I'm not even Jewish.'

'That's precisely why,' Finkler said.

Finkler was disappointed that none of his wittily glossed selections made *Pick of the Week* but was flattered to receive a letter, a fortnight after transmission, from a number of well-known theatrical and academic Jews inviting him to join a group which had been no more than an idea without direction so far but which they now intended to reform and name in honour of his courage in speaking out – Ashamed Jews.

Finkler was moved. Praise from his peers affected him almost as deeply as the prayers he had never said for his

136

grandfather. He scanned the list. Most of the professors he knew already and didn't care about, but the actors represented a new scaling of the heights of fame. Though he had never been much of a theatregoer and turned his nose up at most of Tyler's let's-go-and-see-a-play suggestions, he viewed being written to by actors – even actors he didn't think very highly of qua actors – in a different light. There was a celebrity chef on the list too, and a couple of stellar stand-up comedians.

'Jesus!' Finkler said when he got the letter.

Tyler was in the garden, lounging this time. A coffee cup in her hand, the papers open. She had been sleeping though it was only late morning. Finkler had not noticed that she tired more quickly than she used to.

'Jesus!' he repeated, so that she should hear him.

She didn't stir. 'Someone suing you for breach of promise, dearest?'

'Not everyone, it seems, was ashamed of me,' he said, naming the most eminent signatories to the letter. Slowly. One by one.

'And?'

She took as long over the one word as her husband had taken over the dozen names.

He flared his nostrils at her. 'What do you mean "and"?'

She sat up and looked at him. 'Samuel, there is not a person whose name you have just read out for whom you have the slightest regard. You abominate academics. You don't like actors – you particularly don't like *those* actors – you have no time for celebrity chefs and you can't abide stand-up comedians, especially *those* stand-up comedians. Not funny, you say about them. Seriously *not funny*. Why would I – no, why would *you* care what any of them think?'

'My judgement of them as performers is hardly pertinent in this instance, Tyler.'

'So what is? Your judgement of them as political analysts? Historians? Theologians? Moral philosophers? I don't recall your ever saying to me that though they were shit as comedians you thought them profound as thinkers. Every time you've worked with actors you've pronounced them to be cretins, incapable of putting a single sentence together or expressing half a thought. And certainly unable to understand yours. What's changed, Samuel?'

'It's pleasing to receive support.'

'From anywhere? From anyone?'

'I wouldn't call these people *anyone*.'

'No, in your own words *less than anyone*. Except they're someone now they're praising you.'

He knew he could not read her the whole letter, could not tell her that his 'courage' had inspired or at least revitalised a movement – small now, but capable of growing to who could say what size – could not say that it was nice to be appreciated, Tyler, so fuck you.

Yet still he could not leave her presence.

So he kept it brief. 'Praise is different when it's your own who are praising you.'

She closed her eyes. She could read his mind without having to keep them open.

'Jesus fucking Christ, Shmuelly,' she said. 'Your *own*! Have you forgotten that you don't like Jews? You shun the company of Jews. You have publicly proclaimed yourself disgusted by Jews because they throw their weight around and then tell you they believe in a compassionate God. And now because a few mediocre half-household-name Jews have decided to come out and agree with you, you're mad for them. Was that all it ever needed? Would you have been the goodest of all good Jewish boys if only the other Jewish boys had loved you earlier? I don't get it. It makes no sense. Becoming an enthusiastic Jew again in order to turn on Judaism.'

'It's not Judaism I'm turning on.'

'Well, it's sure as hell not Christianity. *Ashamed Jews?* It would be more honourable of you to kick around with David

Irving or join the BNP. Remember what it is you really want, Samuel . . . Sam! And what you really want isn't the attention of Jews. There aren't enough of them.'

He didn't listen to her. He went upstairs to his desk, his ears ringing, and wrote a letter of appreciation to Ashamed Jews – a letter in appreciation of their appreciation. He was honoured to join them.

But might he make a suggestion? In the age of sound bites, which, like it or not, this assuredly was, one simple, easy to remember acronym could do the work of a thousand manifestos. Well, an acronym – or something much like an acronym – lay concealed in the very name the group had already given itself. Instead of 'Ashamed Jews', what about 'ASHamed Jews', which might or might not, depending on how others felt, be shortened now or in the future to ASH, the peculiar felicity of which, in the circumstances, he was sure it wasn't necessary for him to point out?

Within a week he received an enthusiastic response on notepaper headed 'ASHamed Jews'.

He felt a deep sense of pride, mitigated, of course, by sadness on behalf of those whose suffering had made ASHamed Jews necessary.

Tyler was cruelly wrong about him. He didn't want what she accused him of wanting. His hunger for acclaim – or even for approval – was not that voracious. As God was his witness, he felt approved of enough. This wasn't about acceptance. It was about the truth. Someone had to speak it. And now others were ready to speak it with him. And in his name.

Had Ronit Kravitz not been the daughter of an Israyeli general he'd have rung her to propose a weekend of making ASHamed Jew whoopee in Eastbourne.

Tyler did, as it turned out, watch a second of her husband's television programmes in Treslove's Hampstead apartment that wasn't in Hampstead. And, at decent intervals, further series after that. She saw it as a consolation for her husband doing so much television. The thing she and Julian had going never blossomed into an affair. Neither was looking for an affair – or at least Tyler wasn't and Treslove had grown wary of looking for anything – but they found a way of showing kindnesses to each other over and above the conventions of an afternoon adultery fuelled by anger and envy.

Her growing tired was not lost on Treslove.

'You look pale,' he told her once, smothering her face with kisses.

She submitted to them, laughing. Her quiet, not her raucous laugh.

'And you are subdued somehow,' he said, kissing her again.

'I'm sorry,' she said. 'I didn't come round to depress you.'

'You don't depress me. Your pallor becomes you. I like a woman to look tragic.'

'God – tragic now. Is it as bad as that?'

It was as bad as that, yes.

Treslove would have said *Come and die at my place* but he knew he couldn't. A woman must die in her own home and in her own husband's arms, no matter that her lover would mop her brow with more consideration than the husband ever could.

'I do love you, you know,' he told her on what they both in their hearts suspected would be their last tryst. He had told her he loved her the first time they slept together, watching Sam on the box. But this time he meant it. Not that he didn't mean it then. But this time he meant it differently. This time he meant it for her.

'Don't be silly,' she told him.

'I do.'

'You don't.'

'I truly do.'

'You truly don't, but I am touched by your wanting to. You have been lovely to me. I am under no illusions, Julian. I get men. I know the bizarre way masculine friendship works. I have never fooled myself that I am any different to other wives in this position – a means for you two to work out your rivalry. I told you that at the beginning. But I've been happy to take advantage of that for my own purposes. And I thank you for having made me feel it was me you wanted.'

'It was you I wanted.'

'I believe it was. But not as much as you wanted Samuel.'

Treslove was horrified. '*I*, want Sam?'

'Oh, not in the wanting to fuck him sense. *I've* never loved him in the wanting to fuck him sense. I doubt anybody has. He's not a fuckable man. Not that that's ever stopped him . . . or them. But he has something, my husband, not a glow exactly, but some air of secrecy that you want to penetrate, a kind of fast-track competence or know-how that you would like to have rub off on you. He is one of those Jews to whom, in an another age, even the most avidly Jew-hating emperor or sultan would have given high office. He appears connected, he knows how to get on, and you feel that if you are close to him he will get on for the both of you. But I don't have to tell you. You feel it. I know you feel it.'

'Well, I didn't know I felt it.'

'Trust me, you feel it. And that's where I come in. I'm the bit that rubs off on you. Through me you connect to him.'

'Tyler –'

'It's all right. I don't mind being the stolen stardust that sprinkles you with second-hand importance. I get my revenge on him and at the same time get to feel more cared for by you.'

She kissed him. A thank-you kiss.

The kiss, Treslove thought, that a woman gives a man who doesn't shake her to her soul. For that was what his 'caring' for her denoted – that he was kind but not challenging, not a man of influence, not someone who gave her access to the fast track. Yes, she came round to his house, slid with angular infidelity into his bed and fucked him, but without ever truly noticing he was there. Even this kiss somehow glanced by him, as though she were really kissing a man standing in the room behind.

Was it true, what she had said? That sleeping with Sam's wife gave him temporary honorary entry to Sam's success? If it was true, why then didn't he feel more successful? He liked the idea of Sam being an unfuckable man, but what was that information worth if he was an unfuckable man himself. Poor Tyler, fucking two unfuckable men. No wonder she looked ill.

But poor me as well, Treslove thought.

A means to work out their rivalry, she had called herself. *Their* rivalry – implying that there was something in this for Sam too. Did that mean he knew? Was it possible that when she got home Tyler would tell her husband what an unfuckable man his friend was? And would Sam get off on that? Would they get off on it together?

Did Finklers do that?

For the first time, Treslove broke the rule all adulterers must obey or perish, and pictured them in bed together. Tyler, fresh from Treslove, turning to her husband smiling, facing him as she had never once faced Treslove, holding his penis in front of her like a bridal bouquet, not a problem to be solved behind her back like Treslove's. Looking at it even, perhaps giving it name, confronting it head-on, admiring it, as she had never once confronted and admired his.

'In the meantime,' she said, looking at her watch, though she didn't mean 'this minute', 'he's got himself a new craze.'

Did Treslove care? 'What?' he wondered.

She waved the subject away as though, now he asked, she wished she hadn't brought it up, or as though she felt he would never understand the ins and outs of it.

'Oh, this Israel business. Sorry, Palestine, as he insists on calling it.'

'I know. I've heard him.'

'You heard him on *Desert Island Discs*?'

'Missed it,' Treslove lied. He hadn't *missed* it. He had gone to great lengths not to hear it or to be in contact with anyone who had. Watching Finkler on television while sleeping with his wife was one thing, but *Desert Island Discs* to which the whole country tuned in . . .

'Wise move. I wish I'd missed it. In fact I'd have come round here *in order* to miss it but he wanted me to listen to it with him. Which should have made me suspicious. How come no Ronit . . . ?'

Again Treslove found himself thinking of Tyler and Sam in bed together, face to face, listening to *Desert Island Discs*, Tyler admiring Sam's penis, crooning over it while on the radio the man himself did his Palestine thing.

He said nothing.

'Anyway, that was where he came out with it.'

'Came out with what?'

'His confession of shame.'

'Shame about Ronit?'

'Shame about Israel, you fool.'

'Oh, that. I've heard him on the subject with Libor. It's nothing new.'

'It's new to announce it to the country. Do you know how many people listen to that programme?'

Treslove had a fair idea but didn't want to get into a discussion about numbers. Mention of millions hurt Treslove's ear. 'So does he regret it now?'

'Regret it! He's like the cat that got the cream. He has a

whole new bunch of friends. The ASHamed Jews. They're a bit like the Lost Boys. It's all down to careless mothering if you ask me.'

Treslove laughed. Partly in appreciation of Tyler's joke, partly to dispel the idea of Finkler having new friends. 'Does he know you call them that?'

'The Lost Boys?'

'No, the ASHamed Jews.'

'Oh, they're not my invention. They call themselves that. They're a movement, inspired, would you believe, by my hubby. They write letters to the papers.'

'As ASHamed Jews?'

'As ASHamed Jews.'

'That's a bit disempowering, isn't it?'

'How do you mean?'

'Well, to make your shame your platform. Reminds me of the Ellen Jamesians.'

'Haven't heard of them. Are they anti-Zionists too? Don't tell Sam. If they're anti-Zionist *and* women he'll join in a shot.'

'They're the deranged feminists in *The World According to Garp*. John Irving — no? Garrulous American novelist. Wrestler. Writes a bit like one. I made one of my first radio programmes about the Ellen Jamesians. They cut out their tongues in solidarity with a young woman who was raped and mutilated. Something of a self-defeating action, since they couldn't thereafter effectively voice their anger. A good anti-feminist joke, I always thought, not that I'm, you know —'

'Well. I doubt there'll be any tongue cutting with this lot. They're a gobby bunch, used to the limelight and the sound of their own voices. Sam's on the phone to them every minute God sends. And then there are the meetings.'

'They have meetings?'

'Not public ones, as far as I know. Not yet, anyway. But they meet at one another's houses. Sounds disgusting to me.

Like group confessionals. Forgive me, Father, for I have sinned. Sam's their father confessor. "I forgive you, my child. Say three *I am ashamed*s and don't go to Eilat for your holidays." I won't allow them in my house.'

'And is that all they stand for – being ashamed of being Jewish?'

'Whoa!' She laid a hand on his arm. 'You're not allowed to say that. It's not Jews they're ashamed of being. It's Israel. Palestine. Whatever.'

'So are they Israelis?'

'You know Sam is not an Israeli. He won't even go there.'

'I meant the others.'

'I don't know about all of them, but they're actors and comedians and those I've heard of certainly aren't Israelis.'

'So how can they be ashamed? How can you be ashamed of a country that's not yours?' Treslove truly was puzzled.

'It's because they're Jewish.'

'But you said they're not ashamed of being Jewish.'

'Exactly. But they're ashamed *as* Jews.'

'Ashamed *as* Jews of a country of which they are not citizens . . . ?'

Tyler laid a hand on his arm again. 'Look,' she said, 'what do we know? I think you've got to be one to get it.'

'Be one what? One of the ASHamed?'

'A Jew. You've got to be a Jew to get why you're ashamed of being a Jew.'

'I always forget that you're not.'

'Well, I'm not. Except by adoption and hard work.'

'But at least that way you're not ashamed.'

'Indeed I'm not. If anything I'm rather proud. Though not of my husband. Of him I'm ashamed.'

'So you're both ashamed.'

'Yes, but of different things. He's ashamed because he's a Jew, I'm ashamed because he's not.'

'And the kids?'

Tyler became abrupt. 'They're at university, Julian, remember. Which means they're old enough to make up their own minds . . . but I haven't brought them up Jewish only to be ashamed.' She laughed at her own words. 'Listen to me – *brought them up Jewish.*'

Treslove wanted to tell her he loved her again.

'And?' he asked.

'And what?'

'And what are they?'

'One is, one isn't, one's not sure.'

'You have three?'

She pretended to hit him, but with little force. 'You're the one who should be ashamed,' she said.

'Oh, I am, don't worry. I am ashamed of most things though none of them have anything to do with Jews. Unless I should be ashamed of *us.*'

She exchanged a long look with him, a look that spoke of the past, not the future. 'Don't you get sick of us?' she said, as though wanting to change the subject. 'I don't mean us us, I mean Jews. Don't you get sick of our, their, self-preoccupation?'

'I never get sick of you.'

'Stop it. Answer me – don't you wish they'd shut up about themselves?'

'ASHamed Jews?'

'All Jews. Endlessly falling out in public about how Jewish to be, whether they are or they aren't, whether they're practising or they're not, whether to wear fringes or eat bacon, whether they feel safe here or precarious, whether the world hates them or it doesn't, the fucking Holocaust, fucking Palestine . . .'

'No. Can't say I notice. Sam, maybe, yes. I always feel when he talks about Palestine that he's paying his parents back for something. It reminds me of swearing for the first time when you're a kid – daring God to strike you down. And wanting to show you belong to the kids who already do swear.

But I don't understand the politics. Only that if anyone's going to be ashamed then maybe we all should be.'

'Exactly. The arrogance of them – ASHamed Jews for God's sake, as though the world waits upon the findings of their consciences. That's what shames me –'

'As a Jewess.'

'I've warned you about that word.'

'I know,' said Treslove, 'but I get hot saying it.'

'Well, you mustn't.'

'My Jewess,' he said, 'my unashamed Jewess that isn't,' and took her to him and held her. She felt smaller in his arms than when he'd first tried to hold her a year ago or more. There was less spring in her flesh, he thought. And her clothes were less sharp. Literally sharp. He bled when he first held her. There was anger in her still, but no fight. That she would consent to enter his arms at all, let alone be still in them, proved her alteration. The less of her there was, the more of her was his.

'I meant it,' he said, 'I truly do love you.'

'And I meant it when I thanked you for your kindness.'

For a moment it seemed to Treslove that they were the outsiders, just the two of them in the darkness, excluded from the pack of others. Today he didn't want her to go home, back to Sam's bed, back to Sam's penis. Was Sam now ashamed of his penis, too? Treslove wondered.

He had flaunted his circumcision at school. 'Women love it,' he'd told Treslove in the shower room.

'Liar.'

'I'm not. It's true.'

'How do you know?'

'I've read. It gives them greater satisfaction. With one of these beauties you can go for ever.'

Treslove read up about it himself. 'You don't get the pleasure I get,' he told his friend. 'You've lost the most sensitive part.'

'It might be sensitive but it's horrible. No woman will want to touch yours. So what's the sensitivity worth? Unless you want to spend the rest of your life being sensitive with yourself.'

'You'll never experience what I experience.'

'With that thing you'll never experience anything.'

'We'll see.'

'We'll see.'

And now? Did Finkler's Jewish shame extend to his Jewish dick?

Or was his dick the one part of him to enjoy exclusion from the slur? Could an ASHamed Jew go on giving women greater satisfaction than an unashamed Gentile, Palestine or no Palestine?

That's if there'd ever been a grain of truth in any of it. You never knew with Jews what was a joke and what wasn't, and Finkler wasn't even a Jew who joked much. Treslove longed for Tyler to tell him. Solve the mystery once and for all. Did women have a preference? She was in the best position to make the comparison. Yes or no? Could her Shmuelly go for ever? Was her willingness to look at her husband's penis but not her lover's attributable to the foreskin and the foreskin alone? Was Treslove uncut too ugly to look at? Had the Jews got that one right at least?

It would explain, wouldn't it, why she fiddled with him the way she did, behind her back. Was she unconsciously trying to screw off his prepuce?

He didn't ask her. Didn't have the courage. And in all likelihood didn't want to hear the answer. Besides, Tyler wasn't well enough to be questioned.

You take your opportunity when you have it. Treslove was never given another.

'So where is she?' Libor asked, opening the door to Treslove. Normally he would have buzzed his friend in, but this time he came down in the lift. He wanted a private introduction to the mystery mugger who could smell a man's religion on him.

Treslove showed Libor the palms of his hands. Empty. Then pointed to his heart. 'In here,' he said.

Libor pointed to his friend's head. 'You sure she's not in there?'

'I can always leave.'

'And get attacked again? Don't leave. Come and meet the other guests. And by the way, we're having a *Seder*.'

'What's a *Seder*?'

'A Passover service.'

'I'll come back.'

'Don't be silly. You'll enjoy it. Everyone enjoys a *Seder*. There's even singing.'

'I'll come back.'

'You'll come up. It's an interesting gathering. Old, but interesting. And God is meant to be present. Or at least his Angel. We pour a glass of wine for him.'

'Is that why you're dressed formally? To greet the Angel?'

Libor was wearing a grey suit with a grey stripe in it and a grey lawyer's tie. The overall greyness made his face all but disappear. Treslove pretended to look down into his jacket to see where he had gone.

Libor nodded. 'You aren't surprised?'

'By your suit? Yes. Particularly by the fact that your trousers reach your shoes.'

'I'm getting shorter, that's all that means. Thank you for noticing. But I meant aren't you surprised by our having a *Seder* in September?'

'Why? When should you be having a *Seder*?'

Libor looked at him sideways, as if to say, *So much for your being Jewish.* 'March, April – about the time you have Easter. It's a moon thing.'

'So why are you having it early? For me?'

'We're not having it early, we're having it late. I have a dying great-great-great-somebody or other. Hard to credit, I know. She must be a hundred and forty. She's Malkie's side of the family. She was indisposed for this year's *Seder* and doubts she'll survive to see another. So we're making her one last one before she goes.'

Treslove touched Libor's grey sleeve. The idea of one last anything always upset him. 'And you can do that?'

'By a rabbi, maybe not. But by me it's immaterial. You have one when you feel like one. It might be my last as well.'

Treslove ignored that. 'Will I follow it?'

'Some of it. We're doing the speeded-up version. Quick, while there's life left.'

So as the old lady nodded through the last *Seder* of her life, Treslove, bowing to the assembled guests but being quiet about it, took a chair at his first.

He knew the story. Who doesn't know the story? Treslove knew it because he had sung in Handel's *Israel in Egypt* at school, an unnecessarily lavish production which Finkler's father had helped to fund by paying for the costumes and presenting every member of the cast with a strip of his miracle pills, no matter that the costumes were bed sheets sewn together by Finkler's mother and the pills gave everyone diarrhoea. Whatever Treslove sang, stayed in his mind ... The new pharaoh who knew not Joseph and set over Israel taskmasters to afflict them with burthens, the children of Israel sighing by reason of their bondage – he had loved 'sighing' over that bondage in the choir – Moses and Aaron turning the waters into blood, causing frogs to infest the pharaoh's bedchamber and blotches and blains to break forth on man

and beast, and a thick darkness to cover the land, 'even darkness which might be felt'. In the choir they had closed their
eyes and stretched out their hands, as though to feel the darkness. It was a darkness that Treslove could still close his eyes
and touch. Small wonder, he thought, that Egypt was glad to
see the Israelites depart, 'for the fear of them fell upon
them' . . . Job done, in his view.

But then there was Part the Second which consisted mainly
of the children of Israel telling God what He had done for
them, and how like unto Him there was no other.

'Is that why your God abandoned you,' he remembered
saying to Finkler after the concert, 'because you bored the
living fucking daylights out of him?'

'Our God has not abandoned us,' Finkler had replied in
anger. 'And don't you blaspheme.'

Those were the days!

Watching people around him reading from right to left he
recalled Finkler's schoolyard boast. 'We can read from both
ends of a book,' he had told Treslove, who couldn't begin to
imagine how it was possible to do such a thing or what
powers of secret knowledge and necromancy were necessary
to achieve it. And not just any old book, but books written
in a script so ancient it should have been scratched with a
sharp stone in rock not written back to front on paper. No
wonder Finkler didn't dream – there was no room in his
head for dreams.

Libor had quietly deposited Treslove more or less in the
middle of a long table that sat about twenty people, all with
their heads in books, reading from right to left. He was
between an old lady and a young – young by the standards of
the gathering, that was. Allowing for the wrinkles on the older
lady and the somewhat too much flesh on the younger,
Treslove took them to be closely related. Something about
the way they bent forward over the table, like birds. He assumed
that they were grandmother and granddaughter or maybe

maybe divided by one generation more than that, but he didn't want to scrutinise their features too closely while they were engrossed in the story of Jewish deliverance. One thing he could not take his eyes off, though, was the book from which the older lady read. It appeared to be a children's picture book with pop-ups and pull-outs. Fascinated, he watched her make a nursery game of reading, turning a wheel that on one page denoted the ceaseless tortures imposed on the Israelites as they laboured regardless of the hour, now under a burning sun, now under an icy scimitar-scooped moon – and on the opposite page showed the frogs and the boils and the darkness so thick you could feel it.

When it came to the crossing of the Red Sea the old lady pulled a tab, and lo! where the Israelites had crossed in safety the waters overwhelmed their enemies, and 'there was not one of them left'. She pulled the tab again and again, drowning the Egyptians over and over.

Talk about disproportionality, Treslove thought, remembering something he had read of Finkler's recently about Jews taking two eyes for every one. But when he next looked, the old lady was irritably tugging at another tab and making a little boy in a skullcap disappear beneath the table and come up with a piece of matzo. This, too, she caused to happen again and again. So it was repetition for the fun of it, not the vengeance.

He looked around him, struck by how different Libor's table was from how he remembered it in Malkie's day, or even the last time he was here with Finkler. So many Finklers today – though no Sam Finkler – so much food he didn't recognise, and so many elderly people at a form of prayer that was not always to be distinguished from chatter or sleep.

The next thing he knew he was being asked, as the youngest manchild present – 'Me?' he said in astonishment – whether he would like to recite the Four Questions.

'I would if I could,' he told them. 'In fact, there are many more than four questions I would like to ask. But I cannot read Hebrew.'

'Wrong order,' the old lady said, not taking her eyes from her book. 'We've gone past the Four Questions. We never do things in the right order in this family. Everything's upside down. Who is he anyway? Another of our Bernice's?'

'Mother, Bernice died thirty years ago,' someone at the other end of the table said.

'Then he shouldn't be here,' the old lady said.

Treslove wondered what he'd started.

The granddaughter, as he supposed, or was it the great-granddaughter laid a gentle hand on his. 'Take no notice,' she whispered. 'She's always like this at a *Seder*. She loves it but it makes her angry. I think it's the plagues. She feels a little guilty for them. But you don't have to read Hebrew. You can ask the Four Questions in English.'

'But I can't read right to left,' Treslove whispered back.

'In English you don't need to.'

She opened the Haggadah at the relevant page and pointed.

Treslove looked across at Libor who nodded and said, 'So ask the questions.' He had screwed his face up to resemble an old pantomime Israelite. 'You're the Jew boy, ask the questions' was the message Treslove read in it.

And Treslove, much embarrassed, but with a beating heart, did as he was told.

Why is this night different from all other nights?
   Why on this night must we eat bitter herbs?
   Why on this night do we dip our food twice?
   On all other nights we may eat either sitting or leaning, but why on this night must we all lean?

He found it difficult to listen to the answers. He had been made too self-conscious by his reading. How did he know how to ask Jewish questions in a room of Jews he had never before met? Were the questions meant to be rhetorical? Were they a joke? Should he have asked them as Jack Benny or Shelley Berman might have asked them, with the *bitter herbs* comically inflected? Or hyperbolically to denote the extremity of Jewish grief? The Jews were a hyperbolic people. Had he been hyperbolical enough?

Biiii . . . ttaah – what if he should have delivered it like that, with shuddery theatricality, in the manner of Donald Wolfit playing Hamlet's father's ghost?

'That's not the way you say them,' the old lady had shouted before he'd even finished asking the first question. But apart from calls of 'Shush, Mother' no one had taken any notice of her. But then no one had applauded him either.

If the answers to his questions amounted to anything it was that this story had to be told and retold – 'The more one speaks about the departure from Egypt the better,' he read. Which wasn't, if he understood the matter correctly, remotely Finkler's position. 'Oh, here we go, Holocaust, Holocaust,' he heard Finkler saying. So would he say the same about Passover? 'Oh, here we go, Exodus, Exodus . . .'

Treslove liked the idea of telling and retelling. It suited his obsessive personality. Further proof, if further proof were needed . . .

The service – if that was the word for something quite so shapeless and intermittent – continued at a leisurely pace. Some groups pointed passages out to one another, as though losing one's place and having it found for one again was part of the joy of it all, others fell into what Treslove took to be extraneous conversation, individuals nodded off or left the table to visit one of Libor's many lavatories, some not returning until the Jews were well out of Egypt, while one or two just stared into space, though whether they were remembering their people's departure from Egypt five thousand years before or were looking into their own departure tomorrow, Treslove was unable to tell.

'There aren't enough children here,' an old man sitting opposite him said. He had outworn skin and a great cowl of boastful black hair underneath which he glowered at the entire table as though everybody there had wronged him at one time or another.

Treslove looked about. 'I think there are *no* children here,' he replied.

The old man stared at him in fury. 'That's what I said. Why don't you listen to what I'm saying? There are no children here.'

The table came together again for the Passover meal, which seemed to mark the end of all liturgy. Treslove ate what was given him, not expecting to enjoy it. Bitter herbs plastered between two slices of matzo – 'To remind us of the bitter times we went through,' a person who had changed places with the woman who had helped him with the Four Questions said. 'And are still going through, if you ask me,' said someone else; an explanation contradicted by a third party who said, 'Rubbish, it represents the cement with which we built the pyramids with our bare hands' – followed by egg in salt water ('It symbolises our tears, the tears we spilt'), then chicken soup with kneidlach, then more chicken and potatoes which as far as Treslove could tell symbolised nothing. He was pleased about that. Food that symbolised nothing was easier to digest.

Libor came over to see how he was getting on. 'You like the chicken?' he asked.

'I like everything, Libor. You cook it yourself?'

'I have a team of women. The chicken symbolises the pleasure Jewish men take in having a team of women to cook it for them.'

But if Treslove thought the ceremony had concluded with the meal, he was mistaken. No sooner were the plates cleared away than it began again, with thanks for God's enduring loving kindness, songs which everyone knew and quibbles which no one attended to and fine points of learned exposition culled from the Jewish sages. Treslove marvelled. Rabbi Yehoshua had said this. Hillel had done that. Of Rabbi Eliezer a certain story was told . . . It wasn't just a historical event that was being remembered, it was the stored intelligence of the people.

His people . . .

He introduced himself, when it seemed appropriate, to the woman he took to be the old lady's great-granddaughter. She had taken up her place again after visiting people at the furthest reaches of the room. She had the look of a weary traveller returned from an arduous journey. 'Julian,' he told her, lingering on the first syllable.

'Hephzibah,' she said, giving him a plump and many-silver-ringed hand. 'Hephzibah Weizenbaum.'

Saying her name seemed to tire her too.

Treslove smiled and repeated it. *Hephzibah Weizenbaum* – getting his tongue knotted on the 'ph' which she pronounced somewhere between an 'h' and an 'f', but which he, for some reason – a Finkler thing? – couldn't. 'Hepzibah,' he said. 'Hepzibah, Heffzibah, I can't say it, but such a beautiful name.'

She was amused by him. 'Thank you,' she said, moving her hands more than he thought was necessary, 'however you want to say it.'

Her rings confounded him. They appeared to have been bought at a Hell's Angels' shop. But he knew where her clothes came from. Hampstead Bazaar. There was a Hampstead Bazaar near his apartment which he sometimes peered into on his way home, wondering why no woman he had ever proposed marriage to ever looked like the multilaterally swathed models in the window. Hampstead Bazaar designed clothes for women who had something to hide, whereas all Treslove's women had been skin and bones, the only thing they had to hide being Treslove. What would have happened, he mused, had his taste in women been different? Would a woman with a fuller figure have stayed longer in his company?

Might he have found happiness with her? Might she have anchored him?

Hephzibah Weizenbaum was tented and suggested the Middle East. There was an Arab shop on Oxford Street which sprayed perfume into the traffic. Treslove, on his way to nowhere in particular, sometimes stopped and breathed it in. Hephzibah Weizenbaum smelt like that — of car fumes, and crowds of tourists, and the Euphrates where it all began.

She smiled, not guessing what he was thinking. The smile enveloped him, like the warm waters of a pool buoying up a swimmer. He felt he floated in her eyes, which were more purple than black. He tapped the back of her hand, not thinking what he was doing. With her free hand she tapped his. The silver rings stung him in a way he found arousing.

'So,' he said.

'So,' she replied.

She had a warm voice, like melted chocolate. She was probably full of chocolate, Treslove thought. Normally fastidious about fat, he decided it looked good on her, swathed out of sight as it was.

She had a strong face, broad cheekbones — more Mongolian than Middle Eastern — and a full, vivacious mouth. Mocking, but not mocking him, and not mocking the ceremony. Just mocking.

Was he in love with her?

He thought he was, though he was not sure he would know how to love a woman who looked so healthy.

'This is your first one, then,' she said.

Treslove was astonished. How could she have known she was his first healthy woman?

She saw his confusion. 'Your first Passover,' she said.

He smiled, relieved. 'Yes, but I hope not my last,' he said.

'I'll remember to invite you to mine, then,' she said, bunching up her eyes at him.

'I'd like that,' Treslove answered. He hoped the reason she

157

knew it was his first Passover was his ignorance of the ritual, not his alien appearance.

'Libor has spoken of you many times,' she said. 'You and your friend.'

'Sam.'

'Yes, Sam. Julian and Sam, I feel I know you both well. I am Libor's great-great-niece by marriage, that's to say on Malkie's side, unless I am his great-great-great cousin.'

'Is everyone here the great-great-great cousin of the person sitting next to them?' he asked.

'Unless they are more closely related, yes,' she said.

He nodded in the direction of the old lady. 'She your . . . ?'

'She's my something. Just don't ask me to say precisely what. All Jews are at furthest remove one another's great-great-great cousins. We don't do six degrees of separation. We do three.'

'One big happy family?'

'I don't know about the happy. But family, yes. It can be a pain.'

'It wouldn't be a pain if you had never known an extended family.'

'Didn't you?'

'A mother and a father – that was it.'

He suddenly sounded orphaned to himself and hoped the spectacle of his loneliness wouldn't make her cry. Or not too much.

'What I sometimes wouldn't give to have had a mother and a father and that's it,' Hephzibah surprised him by saying. 'Though God knows I miss them.'

'They aren't here?'

'Passed away. So I turn myself into a sort of universal daughter.'

(*And mother?* Treslove wondered.)

'You have siblings?'

'Not exactly. So I turn myself into a sort of universal sister too. I have aunts, I have uncles, I have cousins, I have cousins of cousins . . . I spend a month's salary on birthday cards. And don't remember half their names.'

'And children of your own?' Treslove made it sound casual, like a question about the weather. *You finding it cold today?*

She smiled. 'Not yet. No hurry.'

Treslove, who had not been good with babies, saw the babies they were going to have, for this time it would be different. Jacob, Esther, Ruth, Moishe, Isaac, Rachel, Abraham, Leah, Leopold, Lazarus, Miriam . . . He began to run out of names. Samuel – no, not Samuel – Esau, Eliezer, Bathsheba, Enoch, Jezebel, Tabitha, Tamar, Judith . . .

Hudith.

'You?' she asked.

'Siblings? No.'

'Children?'

'Two. Sons. Both grown up. But I wasn't strictly instrumental in their rearing. I hardly know them really.'

He didn't want Hephzibah – Heppzibah . . . Heffzibah – Weizenbaum to feel threatened or excluded by his children. There were more children in him, he wanted her to understand.

'You and their mother divorced, then?'

'Mothers. Yes. Well, not divorced exactly. We only ever lived together. Separately, of course. And not for long.'

He didn't want her to feel threatened or excluded by the mothers of his children either. But nor did he want her to think he was a fly-by-night. He did something with his shoulders which he hoped she would interpret as emotional pain, but not too much.

'If you don't want to talk about it –' she said.

'No, no. It's just that this seems such a big family, and I haven't made much of a job of family –' *yet*, he thought about adding, but heard how wrong it might sound to her.

'Don't idealise us,' she warned, waving her ringed hands at him.

Us.

He melted into the word.

'Why not?'

'For all the usual reasons. And don't marvel at our warmth.'

Our.

Treslove looked at her evenly, though he felt the floor was swaying. 'Then I won't,' he said, warmly. 'But I do wonder, since you say Libor has mentioned me many times, why he has never introduced us. Has he been keeping you under wraps?'

Not tactful – *wraps*.

Had he not already been flushed from reading the Four Questions, he would have flushed now. But not only on account of his lack of tact. On account of his lack of reserve. 'Where have you been all my life?' his expression said.

She put her lips together and shrugged. A gesture Treslove thought she should forgo, given what it did to the flesh under her chin. He would find a nice way of telling her that when they were married.

Then she laughed, as though it had taken her a minute to hear what he had asked. 'It would need some wrap,' she said, pulling her shawl or tabard or whatever it was around her.

He was unable to hide his embarrassment. 'I'm sorry,' he said.

'Don't be.'

He met her eyes and searched for a question the answer to which would bring their faces closer together. 'Hepzibah,' he said, 'Heffzibah –' but his uncertainty around her name left him floundering for the question.

It brought her face closer to his anyway. 'Listen,' she said, 'if I'm too much of a mouthful for you –'

'You aren't.'

'But if I am . . .'

This time he showed her his teeth. 'Believe me, you aren't.'

'But *if* I am, my friends call me Juno.'

160

Treslove held on to the undercarriage of his chair. 'Juno? Juno!'

She wasn't sure why he was quite so astonished. She made a downward gesture with her hands, showing herself to him. Her bulk. She was under no illusions about her size. 'The war goddess,' she said, laughing.

He laughed back. Or he tried to laugh back. Jovially, like the war god.

'Though the real reason,' she quickly added, 'is, I'm afraid, more prosaic. I played Juno in *Juno and the Paycock* at school.'

'Juno? D'Jew say Juno?'

She looked at him in perplexity.

Well, that was something, Treslove thought. They don't all play word games. Not that for her he wouldn't have set himself the task of mastering every trick of verbal funsterism in the Finkler book of high-semantic footling. Words had numeric significance for Finklers, he'd read that somewhere. And even the name of God was a pun on something else. No doubt Juno, if he only knew how to numeralise and decode it, spelt out Treslove's Hour Has Come.

Why is this night different from all other nights?

The question answered itself.

Juno. Juno, by Jesus!

PART TWO

SIX

I

Every other Wednesday, festivals and High Holy Days permitting, Finkler met with fellow ASHamed Jews at the Groucho Club in Soho. Not all of them dreamed of punching their fathers in the stomach. Some still felt a tender attachment to the faith in which they'd been nurtured – hence their having to make their excuses when an ASHamed Jew night clashed with what they were still Jewish enough to call *Yom Tov:* Rosh Hashanah, Yom Kippur, Succot, Simchat Torah, Shavuot, Purim, Pesach, Hanukkah. 'And Uncle Tom Cobley and all,' as Finkler said.

In the case of such ASHamed Jews as these it wasn't the J word but the Z word of which they were ashamed. For which reason there was always a degree of fretting at the edges of the movement in the matter of what they called themselves. Wouldn't it more accurately describe the origin and nature of their shame if they changed their name to ASHamed Zionists?

On grounds of euphony, Finkler didn't think so. And on grounds of logic he didn't think so at all. 'Call yourselves ASHamed Zionists,' he said, 'and you at once preclude someone like me who was never a Zionist in the first place. What is more you open the group to a non-Jewish membership, allowing that there are many people out there who are, in their humanity, ashamed of Zionism. Whereas we are ashamed in our humanity *as* Jews. Which is the point of us, I think.'

It struck one or two of the members that there was racism implicit in this, as though a higher value was to be placed on Jewish shame than on any other sort, but Finkler quietened these rumblings by making the point that while they didn't have a monopoly on shame, and were surely open to the idea of making common cause with others who were as ashamed as they were – he, personally, welcomed a degree of ecumenicism in this – only Jews could be *Jewishly* ashamed. That is to say, only they could express, from the inside, the emotion of betrayal.

This did lead briefly to a discussion as to whether Betrayed Jews wouldn't, in that case, be the best name for them of the lot. But again Finkler won the day, arguing that betrayal was too petulant a word to nail their colours to, implying as it did that they were against Zionism only because it had excluded or jilted them in some way, and not because it was a crime against humanity.

If one or two ASHamed Jews thought Finkler was having it both ways on this – making a virtue of personal hurt and then decrying it – they kept the thought to themselves. Perhaps because for them too their shame both was and was not an accident of biography, both was and was not a murmuring of their hearts, both was and was not public property, its justice susceptible now to reason, now to poetry.

It was settled, at least temporarily, in this manner: those ASHamed Jews who were only partially ashamed – that's to say who were ashamed, qua Jews, of Zionism but not, qua Jews, of being Jewish – were permitted to put their mortification into abeyance on Rosh Hashanah, Yom Kippur and Hanukkah, etc., and would resume it again when the calendar turned secular.

As for the others, they were free to be whatever sorts of Jews they wanted. The group was nothing if not heterogeneous. It included Jews like Finkler, whose shame comprehended the whole Jew caboodle and who didn't give a hoot about a

High Holy Day, and Jews who knew nothing of any of it, who had been brought up as Marxists and atheists, or whose parents had changed their names and gone to live in rural Berkshire where they kept horses, and who only assumed the mantle of Jewishness so they could throw it off.

The logic that made it impossible for those who had never been Zionists to call themselves ASHamed Zionists did not extend to Jews who had never been Jews. To be an ASHamed Jew did not require that you had been knowingly Jewish all your life. Indeed, one among them only found out he was Jewish at all in the course of making a television programme in which he was confronted on camera with *who he really was*. In the final frame of the film he was disclosed weeping before a memorial in Auschwitz to dead ancestors who until that moment he had never known he'd had. 'It could explain where I get my comic genius from,' he told an interviewer for a newspaper, though by then he had renegotiated his new allegiance. Born a Jew on Monday, he had signed up to be an ASHamed Jew by Wednesday and was seen chanting 'We are all Hezbollah' outside the Israeli Embassy on the following Saturday.

It had been Finkler who suggested the Groucho Club as a venue for their meetings when ASHamed Jews co-opted him to their cause. Until then, the embryo ashamed had met at one another's houses in Belsize Park and Primrose Hill, but Finkler argued that that domesticated their struggle and made it inward-looking. To those who shrank from discussing matters of such urgency in a place of alcohol and laughter (and what is more was named after a Jew who joked about being Jewish) he urged the virtues of publicity. It made no sense at all to be ashamed of being an ASHamed Jew. The whole point of their shame was that it was out there for all to see.

It was Tyler's view that, for her husband, being an ASHamed Jew was continuous with being at the reflective end of show business. She had accompanied him to the Groucho Club on earlier non-ASHamed Jew business and seen the way he behaved – the ostentation with which he distributed alms to the educated dossers and *Big Issue* sellers who congregated ón the street outside, the flourish with which he inscribed his signature in the members' book, the small talk he made with the staff who rewarded him by being on mellifluous terms with his name, the pleasure he took in mixing with film directors and fellow media-academics at the bar. Now throw in his being a big shot with the ASHamed Jews and Tyler knew exactly how his triumph felt to him – the immodest delight he took in seeing his influence extend far beyond philosophy.

After Tyler's death – though he might have been expected, as a man no longer judged ironically by his wife, to have seized the opportunity to be more riotously self-satisfied still – he, if anything, toned his behaviour down. He owed her memory that, he thought. His seemliness a sort of epitaph to her.

That she would have preferred it had he given up being ASHamed altogether, he knew. But that far he couldn't go. The movement needed him. The Palestinians needed him. The Groucho needed him.

It wasn't all smooth sailing. On quiet nights a corner table in the restaurant gave them just the right degree of being 'out there' that they needed, but when the club was busy other guests could overhear their conversation and sometimes assumed they were free to join in. This was tolerable so long as uninvited interventions were sympathetic and not over-boisterous, but disagreements could get out of hand, as when a party of music-industry diners wearing red string Kabbalah bracelets got wind of what ASHamed Jews were about and tried to have them ejected from the club as anti-Semites. An ill-tempered altercation followed in the course of which the comedian Ivo Cohen ended up on the floor for the second time as an ASHamed Jew (the other coming at a demonstration in Trafalgar Square, on that occasion with a group calling themselves Christians for Israel).

'A fine example of Jewish spirituality, this is!' he huffed, tucking in his shirt, echoing his 'A fine example of Christian spirituality, this is!' with which he'd challenged his assailants in Trafalgar Square. He was a short round man who didn't have far to fall. And as his stage act belonged to the genre known as Marxist slapstick (Karl, not Groucho), which necessitated his falling over a great deal, no one took the incident too seriously. But the club wasn't prepared to allow an event of this sort to occur again and insisted that all further meetings of ASHamed Jews take place either somewhere else or in a private room on the second floor.

Though he had no desire to upset Kabbalists, whose teaching had a flakily practical side of which he approved, and who numbered among their seekers after truth Madonna and David Beckham – both of whom, he suspected, were readers of his books and would have liked to meet him – Finkler felt he couldn't let the occasion go without berating them for a scurrilousness that did the Jewish mysticism of which they claimed to be serious students no credit. As for charging ASHamed Jews with anti-Semitism, 'The imputation,' he told them, closing his face, 'leaves us stone cold.'

The quotation was from someone else. Finkler couldn't remember who. Doubtless some anti-Semite. Not that it mattered. It's not who says it, or what it means, but how you say it, and in what company.

Pleased with the reception from his fellow-ASHamees, Finkler repeated the formulation – 'The imputation that we are self-hating Jews leaves us stone cold' – in a rough draft of a letter that was ultimately published in the *Guardian* and signed by the twenty most eminent of the ASHamed along with '65 others'. 'Far from hating our Jewishness,' the letter went on, 'it is we who continue the great Jewish traditions of justice and compassion.'

One member of the group recognised the quotation and wanted it removed. Another feared that the phrase 'we are self-hating Jews' would be taken out of context and used against them, in the way that theatres extracted a phrase like 'wonderful drama' from the sentence 'A wonderful drama this is not'. A third asked why he and several other less prominent ASHamees were not named as signatories to the letter but had to suffer ignominious inclusion among the '65 others'. And a fourth questioned the efficacy of writing letters to the *Guardian* at all.

'Gaza burns and we quibble over efficacy!' Finkler remonstrated.

A sentiment which could have been said to meet with universal approval had Finkler only approved it himself. In fact, he wished he hadn't said it. Gaza had galvanised the movement as it had galvanised the country but for his part, perhaps because he liked to lead events not follow them, Finkler could have looked the other way as far as Gaza was concerned. Gaza didn't do it for him. The philosopher in him recoiled from all the talk of massacre and slaughter on the streets. You keep the big unequivocal words for the big unequivocal occasions, Finkler thought. And there was an illogicality in charging the country he didn't choose to name with wanton and unprovoked violence while at the same time complaining its bombardment of Gaza had been disproportionate. Disproportionate to what? Disproportionate to the provocation. In which case the operation had not been unprovoked.

Logically, too, disproportion was a dog's dinner of a concept. How do you measure? Do you trade rocket for rocket, life for life? Are you, once provocation is conceded, not permitted to mete out retribution that will put paid to it?

He was thinking beyond the specifics. The Israyelis were out of control. He didn't doubt that. But what is true in the individual instance has to be true in the general. And what his fellow ASHamees were saying in this instance could easily be shown to be nonsense when applied elsewhere. He did what was required of him; he drafted letters and stood on platforms, but his heart wasn't quite in it. The frightening part was wondering if he might just start forgetting what he was ASHamed *of*. Was there such a thing as a Gaza-induced Alzheimer's?

Prior to Gaza – and Gaza, he hoped, was his dirty little secret – the ASHamed Jews had pronounced themselves largely satisfied with his de facto leadership. He was seen to have given the fledgling movement a populist intellectualism which fully justified their original wooing of him.

Shortly after the Kabbalah fracas it was agreed with the club that they could start with dinner in the restaurant, in the course of which they would lower their voices and keep the conversation uncontroversial, and then move up to a private room on the second floor where they could talk without fear of being overheard or interrupted. Not even a drinks waiter would disturb them, if that was how they wanted it. This gave a clandestine and even dangerous savour to their deliberations.

It was here, about two years into his association with the group, that Finkler felt, for the first time since he'd joined – since, not to beat about the bush, he'd as good as fathered it – that there was growing opposition to his influence. He wasn't sure what caused it. Envy, presumably. Even the best causes are susceptible to envy. He had written too many of the group's letters. He had put himself forward for too many editions of *Newsnight* and the *Today* programme. He had taken away something of the group shame and appropriated it to himself. Sam Finkler – the ASHamed Jew.

'They'll soon realise their mistake,' Tyler had prophesied. 'With a greedy bastard like you around they'll soon discover how hard it is to get their own share of shame.'

But you can detect envy, Finkler believed, in the way

people look at you when they think you're not looking at them, and in the way they stop being able to listen to you, as though every word you utter is a trial for them, and this was a less personally based, more ideological, dissatisfaction, which caused people to rub their faces and screw up their eyes. Was Gaza the cause? Did they know him to be wobbling? He didn't believe he had been rumbled. His equivocations confused himself, never mind them. He had even lent his name to the disproportion argument in a much noticed article that went out under the heading 'How Many Eyes, How Many Teeth?'

Eventually it became clear to him that Gaza wasn't the problem, the problem was 'The Boycott'.

'The Boycott' was a shorthand term for the Comprehensive Academic and Cultural Boycott of Israeli Universities and Institutions. There were other boycotts on the table but the Comprehensive Academic and Cultural Boycott was the talk of the hour, the boycott that trumped all other boycotts, mainly for the reason that its chief sponsors were academics or otherwise cultured persons themselves and could imagine no greater deprivation than being denied access to academic conferences or having your latest paper refused by a learned magazine.

Finkler had poured scorn on the idea, firstly because he thought it feeble – 'What will we have next,' he asked, 'the Philatelic Association of Great Britain banning the licking of stamps in Israel?' – and secondly because it closed down conversation where conversation was most likely to bear fruit. 'I am in principle against anything which denies dialogue or trade,' he had said, 'but to bar communication between intellectuals, who are always our best hope of peace, is particularly self-defeating and inane. It declares, inter alia, that we have a) made up our minds about what we think, b) closed our minds to what others think, and c) chosen to go on hearing nothing with which we happen to disagree.'

'What else *is* there to hear?' Merton Kugle wanted to know. Merton Kugle was the group's prime boycotter. Already he was boycotting Israel in a private capacity, going through every item on his supermarket shelves to ascertain its origin and complaining to the manager when he found a tin or packet that was suspect. In pursuit of 'racist merchandise' – usually, in his experience, concealed on the lowest shelves in the darkest recesses of the shop – Merton Kugle had ruined his spine and all but worn out his eyes.

In Finkler's view, Kugle was one of the walking dead. But more than that, his putrefaction was infectious. The moment Kugle spoke, Finkler wanted to curl up in a corner and die.

'There is always more to hear, Merton,' Finkler said, holding on to the table to stay upright. 'Just as there is always more to say.'

'Well, some of us don't have the time to sit here and hear you say it,' Kugle said. 'So far you've asked us to oppose a consumer boycott of all Israeli goods and produce, a boycott on tourism to Israel, except where it might be of incidental benefit to the Palestinians, a boycott of Israeli athletes and sportsmen –'

'There aren't any,' Finkler said.

'– a boycott of all produce grown in the Occupied Territories, a suspension of EU trade with Israel –'

'What about where it might be of incidental benefit to Palestinians?'

'– divestment from Israeli companies, divestment from companies which invest in Israel or otherwise sponsor the illegal state, and now –'

Finkler looked around the room to gauge what support Kugle could command. As always he was disappointed to see so few of the illustrious actors and comedians – Ivo Cohen was not illustrious – so few of the living legends of the culture – Merton Kugle was not living – whose commitment to ASHamed Jews was what had originally attracted him to the group. He enjoyed being the star of the show, right enough, but he would have preferred the show in which he starred to have been a trifle starrier. First among equals was how he had envisaged his role, but where were his equals? Every now and then a letter or a text would be read out from one of the greats, presently touring in Australia or South America, wishing the group well in its indispensable work, and occasionally a DVD would show up in which the eminent musician or playwright would address the ASHamed Jews as though they were the Nobel Prize Committee whose faith in him he deeply appreciated and was only sorry he was unable to receive the award in person. Otherwise, only academics with nowhere else to go attended regularly, and writers like Kugle who hadn't written anything anyone wanted to publish, and a number of the free-floating opinionated who called themselves analysts and spokespersons, and the odd self-appointed director of the Institute of Nothing in Particular, and a couple of semi-secular rabbis with worried eyes.

If Finkler had gone into adult education, these were the sorts of people with whom he would have spent his evenings.

And they dared to be having second thoughts about him! Well, he had news for them: he was having second thoughts about *them*.

There were moments when he wondered what he'd let himself in for here. If I don't particularly want to be with Jews, where's the sense, he asked himself, in being with *these* Jews, solely because they don't particularly want to be with Jews either?

He could see that Reuben Tuckman was trying to say something. Tuckman was a Liberal rabbi who wore expensive summer suits in all seasons and suffered from a soft stuttering lisp – unless it was an affectation, which would not have surprised Finkler – that caused his eyes to close when he spoke. This gave his already raffish face a sleepy sensuousness which accorded ill, Finkler wanted to tell him, with the sanctity of his office. Tuckman, a man on semi-permanent sabbatical, had recently enjoyed notoriety for mounting a lonely vigil outside the Wigmore Hall where a little-known ensemble from Haifa was due to play. In fact, the ensemble had cancelled because of ill heath but Tuckman had kept up his protest anyway, as much to shame the concert hall (and as much, Finkler thought, to show off his new Brioni linen suit in Marylebone) as to dissuade the public from buying tickets. 'I love m-music as much as anyone,' he told a reporter, 'but I cannot allow my thoul to thoar on the back of innothent blood.'

Rather than be sidetracked into the turgid shallows of Tuckman's conversation, Finkler returned to Kugle.

'I want to ask you something, Merton,' he said. 'Are we not family?'

'You and me?'

'Don't look so worried. Not you and me in particular. All of us. We've had this argument a thousand times, but what are we ashamed of if not our own? We wouldn't call ourselves ASHamed Jews if the object of our criticism was Burma or Uzbekistan. We're ashamed of our family, are we not?'

Merton Kugle could not give his assent to this. Where was the catch? The other ASHamed Jews looked wary also.

Reuben Tuckman had put his hands together horizontally, as though praying Buddhistically. 'Th-Tham,' he said, making a peace offering of Finkler's name.

But Finkler couldn't wait. 'So if we're family, what's with the boycott? Whoever boycotted his own family?'

He had stolen the line shamelessly from Libor. But that's what friends were for. To give you things.

He was pleased to remember Libor, a Jew he liked.

'Dad, how do you ever know you're with the right woman?'

'How do *I* ever know or how does *one* ever know?'

'How do *I* ever know?'

It relieved Treslove to hear Rodolfo express any sort of interest in women, let alone wonder how he would know when he'd found the right one.

'Your heart tells you,' Treslove said, laying a hand on his.

'Forgive my French, but that's bollocks, Dad,' Alfredo butted in.

They weren't in France, they were in Italy, on the Ligurian Riviera, eating pesto by a hotel pool and looking at women. The holiday which both Finkler and Libor had suggested he take he was finally taking, only in the company of his sons, which no one had suggested. It was entirely his own idea.

A five-day excursion, arranged very hurriedly, Dad paying, in the course of which they would eat well, enjoy some late autumn sunshine, get to know one another at last, and Treslove would attempt to clear his head of some of the nonsense that had been filling it.

'So why is it bollocks?' Treslove asked.

'Well look at that one. Don't tell me that whoever you're with you're not going to want a piece of that.'

'Her,' Treslove said.

'Yes, her.'

'No, *her*.'

Alfredo stared at him.

'You called her *that*. A piece of that. You should say a piece of her.'

'Christ, Dad. I thought we were meant to be on holiday. *Her*, then. But take my point. Look at her figure. Perfect. Long legs, lean stomach, small breasts. You take a woman like that away with you and you think you'll never look at another woman again. But now you see that – *her*. Voluptuous figure, big tits, creamy thighs, and you wonder what you ever saw in the skinny one.'

'You're nothing if not a philosopher,' Treslove said. 'Have you been dipping into Uncle Sam's book on Descartes and Dating again?'

'Well, you never did any better,' Rodolfo chipped in. 'Mum says you were never with any woman for more than a fortnight.'

'Well that's only what your mum says.'

'Mine says the same,' Alfredo said.

'They have always thought alike on many matters,' Treslove said, ordering another bottle of Montalcino.

He wanted to spoil the boys. Give them what they'd missed. And spoil himself too. Clear his head. That was the phrase he kept using. Clear his head.

He lay in a deckchair and read – hiding his book when he thought someone might be looking – while his sons swam and talked to women. It was pleasant. Not the view – the view down into the Ligurian Sea was spectacular. What was pleasant – no more than pleasant, but pleasant was enough – was the being here with his sons. Should he leave it at this? he wondered. Accept the role of paterfamilias, take his sons away twice a year, and forget the rest. He would be fifty soon. Time to settle. Nothing else had to happen. Who he was, he was. Julian Treslove. Bachelor of this parish. Gentile. Enough.

Enough already.

In the middle of the afternoon Rodolfo came to sit by him. Treslove hid his book.

'So?' Rodolfo asked.

'So, what?'

'So what's the answer to my question? How do you settle? How can you be sure? And if you aren't sure, isn't the decent thing to do nothing? Don't worry, I'm not asking your advice or anything. I just want to talk about it. I want to know I'm not abnormal.'

Treslove wondered how to bring up the sandwich shop in which Rodolfo wore an apron to mix ingredients. Not a leather or a PVC apron. A floral apron.

For the holiday he wore a black velvet ribbon in his ponytail.

'Has it occurred to you that you might be gay?' he said at last.

Rodolfo got up out of his deckchair. 'Are you mad?' he said.

'I'm just asking.'

'Why are you asking?'

'Well, in fact I'm not asking anything. You're the one who's asking what's normal. Everything is normal is my answer to that, or nothing is normal. Why do you care?'

'Why do you think I'm gay?'

'I don't think you're gay. And even if you were –'

'I'm not. OK?'

'OK.'

Rodolfo returned to his deckchair.

'I like *her*,' he said after a decent interval, nodding at the figure of a young woman climbing out of the pool. So did Treslove. What woman doesn't look good coming up out of a pool? But over and above that – woman rising from the amniotic slime – she had the famished look that excited him. A far cry from . . . well, from what was waiting for him at home.

The bottom half of the woman's bikini hung loose and wet on her. It was impossible not to imagine sliding a hand inside, palm flat, fingers pointing downwards, the tickle of the fur. Presumably Rodolfo, now he wasn't gay, was imagining that very thing.

Unless he was just faking it for his father.

'Go get her, son,' Treslove enjoyed saying.

That evening there was dancing on the hotel terrace. Both Alfredo and Rodolfo had found women. Treslove watched them contentedly. That's all as it should be then, he thought. Successful fathering was not as hard as people made out.

After the dancing Alfredo brought his woman to meet his father.

'Hannah, my dad; Dad, Hannah.'

'I'm pleased to meet you,' Treslove said, getting up and bowing. To his daughters-in-law, presumably, a man had to be ultra-courteous.

'You've got something in common,' Alfredo said behind his sunglasses, laughing his empty restaurant pianist's laugh.

'What's that?'

'You're both Jewish.'

'So what was that about?' Treslove asked before the three of them retired. The women had gone. Treslove didn't ask his sons if they were intending to go after them.

This generation was easier about women than his had been. They didn't go running. If the women left, they left. In Treslove's day a woman leaving was catastrophic to your self-esteem. It presaged the end of the universe.

'It was about fun, Dad.'

'You know what I'm talking about. What was that about my being Jewish?'

'Aren't you?'

'Would it matter to you if I were?'

'There you go, answering a question with a question. That in itself makes you Jewish, doesn't it?'

'I'll ask you again. Would it matter to you if I were?'

'Are you asking if we're anti-Semites?' Rodolfo said.

'And would it matter to you if we were?' Alfredo added.

'Well I'm definitely no anti-Semite,' Rodolfo said. 'You, Alf?'

'Nope. You, Dad?'

'Everyone's an anti-Semite to a degree. Look at your Uncle Sam, and he's Jewish.'

'Yes, but you?'

'What's this about? What's been said to you?'

'Who by? You mean our mums?'

'You tell me. What's the joke?'

'I ran into Uncle Sam a few weeks ago. He said you'd been the victim of an anti-Semitic attack. He said a few other things as well, but let's just stick with the anti-Semitic part. I asked how you could be the victim of an anti-Semitic attack if you weren't a Semite. He said he'd asked you the same question, and your answer was that you were.'

'I think that's one of my friend Finkler's famous simplifications.'

'Maybe, but *are* you?'

He looked from Alfredo to Rodolfo and back again, wondering if he'd ever seen them before, and if so where. 'It doesn't mean that *you* are,' he said, 'if that's what's concerning you. You can continue being whatever you want to be. Not that I know what that is. Your mothers never told me.'

'Maybe you should have asked them,' Rodolfo said. 'Maybe they would have appreciated your taking a hand in our religious education.'

He snorted before he'd finished.

'Let's not get into that,' Alfredo said. 'You say that just because *you* are it doesn't mean that *we* are. But it does, doesn't it, a bit?'

'Depends which bit you're referring to,' Rodolfo said, still snorting.

'You can't be a bit Jewish,' Treslove said.

'Why not? You can be a quarter Indian or one tenth Chinese. Why can't you be part Jewish? In fact, it would make us half and half, wouldn't it? Which is considerably more than a bit. I'd call that a lot. I have to say I quite fancy the idea, what about you, Ralph?'

Rodolfo went into an imitation of Alec Guinness being Fagin. 'I don't mind if I do, my dears,' he said, rubbing his hands.

The two boys laughed.

'Meet one of the half-chosen,' Alfredo said, extending his hand to his brother.

'And allow me to introduce you to the other half,' Rodolfo said.

No, never seen them in my life before, Treslove thought. And wasn't sure he wanted to again.

My sons the goyim.

3

Out of the blue, Libor received a letter from a woman he hadn't seen in more than fifty years. She wanted to know if he was still writing his column.

He wrote back to her saying how nice it was to hear from her after all this time but he'd stopped writing his column in 1979.

He wondered how she'd found his address. He'd moved several times since he'd known her. She must have put herself to some trouble to find where he lived now.

He didn't tell her his wife had died. He couldn't be sure she even knew he'd been married. And you don't go mentioning to women you haven't seen in fifty years, and who have put themselves to trouble to find your address, that you're a widower.

Hope life has been kind to you, he wrote. *It has to me.*

After he sent the letter he worried that the melancholy tone would give her a clue. *It has to me* – there was a dying fall in that. It invited the question, *And does it go on being kind to you?* On top of which it somehow painted him as frail: a man in need of kindness.

Only afterwards did it occur to him that he hadn't asked the reason for her enquiry. *Are you still writing your column?* Why did she want to know?

That was rude of me, he wrote on the back of a postcard. *Did you enquire about my column with a purpose?*

After he posted the postcard — it was a Rembrandt self-portrait, the artist as an old man — he feared she would think he had chosen it to solicit her pity. So he sent her another one of King Arthur in full regalia and in the bloom of youth. No message. Just his signature. She would understand.

Oh, and nothing meant by it, his phone number.

That was how he came to be sitting in the bar of the University Women's Club in Mayfair, clinking glasses of house champagne with the only woman other than Malkie he had ever lost his heart to. A little. Emmy Oppenstein. He had thought she'd said Oppenheimer when they first met in 1950 or thereabouts. That wasn't the reason he had fallen for her, but without doubt it added to her attractiveness. Libor was no snob but he was a child of the Austro-Hungarian Empire and names and titles mattered to him. But by the time he'd realised his mistake they had slept together and he was interested in her for herself.

Or at least he thinks he was.

He sees nothing in her face that he remembers and of course nothing in her figure. A woman in her eighties does not have a figure. He intended no unkindness by that. To himself he said he meant no more than that at eighty a woman is entitled at last to be free of being ogled for her shape.

He could see that she had been beautiful in a Slav way, with wide apart ice-grey eyes and cheekbones on which an unwary man might cut himself going for a kiss. But it wasn't a beauty he remembered. Would it be the same sitting with Malkie, he wondered, had he left her fifty years ago and were she living still? Had Malkie retained her beauty for him because she'd retained it for a fact, for everyone who saw her, or had he kept her beauty alive in his eyes by feasting on it every day? And if so, did that make her beauty illusory?

Emmy Oppenstein was out of the question for him. He saw that at once. He hadn't gone to meet her with the intention of courting her again, he absolutely had not. But had he, *had* he, he would have been disappointed. As he hadn't, he was not disappointed, how could he be, but *had* he . . .

Not disappointed because she had worn badly. For most decidedly she had not; she was, if anything, remarkable for her age – alert, elegant, well dressed in a fluffy woven suit, which Malkie had taught him to recognise as Chanel, and even wore high heels. For her age a woman couldn't have looked better. But *for her age* . . . Libor wasn't looking for a woman to replace Malkie, but had he been looking for a woman to replace Malkie the brutal truth was that this woman was, well, too old.

Libor was not blind to the cruel absurdity of such thoughts. He was an elfin man with no hair, his trousers didn't always reach his shoes, his ties had lain in drawers for half a century and had lost their colour, he was liver-spotted from head to foot – who the hell was he to find any woman too old? What is more, where he had shrunk, she must have grown taller, because he had no memory of ever lying with a woman this size. A thought which he could see, as she surveyed him, mirrored hers exactly. No doubt about it: if she was out of the question for him, he was still more out of the question for her.

And all this Libor had decided in the moment of their shaking hands.

She was, or she had been, a school governor, a justice of the peace, the chair of an eminent Jewish charity, the mother of five children, and a bereavement counsellor. Libor noticed that she left the bereavement counselling to the end. Was that because she knew of Malkie and of her death? Was that why she had written to him? Did she want to help him through?

'You must be wondering –' she began.

'I *am* wondering but I am also marvelling,' Libor said. 'You look so wonderfully well.'

She smiled at him. 'Life has been kind to me,' she said, 'as you wrote that it had been to you.'

She touched his hand. Rock steady hers, as quivery as a jellyfish his. Her nails had been freshly painted. She wore, as far as he could tell, at least three engagement rings. But one might have been her mother's and another her grandmother's. And then again they might have been all hers.

He enjoyed a retrospective pride in his own manliness for having slept with a woman as impressive as she was. He wished he could remember her but he couldn't. Time and Malkie, maybe just Malkie, had wiped out all erotic memories.

So did that mean he hadn't slept with her at all? Libor feared losing the life he had lived. He forgot things – places he had visited, people he had known, thoughts that were once important to him. So would he soon lose Malkie? And would it then be as though she too had never existed erotically (*eloticshrly*) for him? As though she had never existed at all in fact.

He told Emmy about Malkie, as he imagined to keep her alive a little longer.

'I'm sorry,' she said when he had finished. 'I had heard something.'

'Would you drink to her with me?' he said. 'You can't drink to her memory because you didn't know her, but you can drink to my memory of her.'

'To your memory of her,' she said.

'And you?'

She lowered her gaze. 'Yes, the same.'

'Then I drink to you and your memories,' Libor said.

And so they sat and sipped champagne together companionably, both bereft, while single university ladies, some probably older than Malkie was when she died, drifted by them lost in thought, or slowly climbed the stairs to their bedrooms for an afternoon sleep in their London club.

Be a good place to die if you were a single woman, Libor thought. Or a single man.

'I'm flattered,' he said after a while, 'that you knew I had a column, even if you hadn't noticed I'd stopped writing it a century ago.'

'It's hard to keep up,' she said, unembarrassed.

Had she ever been embarrassed? Libor wondered. Had she been embarrassed when he'd undressed her, that's if he ever had? More likely, looking at her now, that she'd undressed him.

'I'll tell you why I contacted you,' she continued. 'I've been writing to all my friends who have a public voice.'

Libor dismissed the idea of his having a public voice, but that only seemed to make her impatient. She shifted in her chair. Gracefully. And shook her hair. Grey, but not an elderly grey. Grey as though it were a colour of her choosing.

'To what end?' he asked. He recognised the public woman, the charity chief, used to commandeering the airwaves of men's attention for causes she cared about.

And then she told him, without tears, without false sentiment, that her twenty-two-year-old grandson had been stabbed in the face and blinded by an Algerian man who had shouted 'God is great' in Arabic, and 'Death to all Jews'.

'I'm very sorry,' Libor said. 'Did this happen in Algeria?'

'It happened here, Libor.'

'In London?'

'Yes, in London.'

He didn't know what further questions to ask. Had the Algerian been arrested? Did he offer any explanation for what he'd done? How did he know the boy was Jewish? Did it happen in an area known to be dangerous?

But what was the point of any of them? Libor had been lucky in love but in politics he was from a part of the world that expected nothing good of anybody. Jew-hating was back – of course Jew-hating was back. Soon it would be full-blown

Fascism, Nazism, Stalinism. These things didn't go away. There was nowhere for them to go to. They were indestructible, non-biodegradable. They waited in the great rubbish tip that was the human heart.

It wasn't even the Algerian's fault in the end. He just did what history had told him to do. God is great . . . kill all Jews. It was hard to take offence – unless, of course, the blinded boy was your child or grandson.

'I'm unable to find anything to say that isn't banal,' he told her. 'It's terrible.'

'Libor,' she said, touching his hand again, 'it will be more terrible still, unless people speak up. People in your profession for a start.'

He wanted to laugh. '*People in my profession?* People in my profession interview famous film stars. And I'm not even in my profession any more.'

'You don't write at all now?'

'Not a word, except for the odd poem to Malkie.'

'But you must know people still, in journalism, in the film industry.'

He wondered what the film industry had to do with anything. Was she hoping he knew someone who would make a film about the attack upon her grandson?

But she had another reason for her specificity, for seeking out a journalist of Libor's sort, with Libor's connections. She named a film director of whom Libor had assuredly heard but had never met – not his sort of film director, not Hollywood, not show business – whose recent comments, she believed, were nothing short of scandalous. Libor must have read them.

He hadn't. He wasn't up with the gossip.

'It's not gossip,' she explained. 'He has said he understands why some people might want to blind my grandson.'

'Because they're deranged?'

'No. Because of Israel. Because of Gaza, he says he understands why people hate Jews and want to kill them.'

For the first time, her hand began to shake.

'Well, I can see why one might want to trace cause and effect,' Libor said.

'Cause and effect! Where's the cause in the sentence "The Jews are a murderous people who deserve all they get"? In the Jews or in the author of the sentence? I can tell you the effect, but where's the cause, Libor?'

'Ah, Emmy, now you are turning logician on me.'

'Libor, listen to me.' She bent her ice-grey eyes upon him. 'Everything has a cause, I know that. But he says he *understands*. What does *understand* mean here? Is he simply saying he can see why people are driven to do appalling and terrible things? Or is he saying something else? Is he saying that there is a justice in it, that my grandson's blindness is justified by Gaza? Or that Gaza vindicates in advance whatever crimes are committed in its name? Can no wickedness now be done to any Jew of any age living anywhere that doesn't have Gaza as its reasoning? This isn't tracing an effect back to its cause, Libor, this is applauding the effect. I *understand* why people hate Jews today, he says, this man of culture. From which it must follow that I *understand* whatever actions they take in expression of their hatred. Dear God, will we now *understand* the Shoah as justified by German abhorrence of the Jews? Or worse, as retrospective justice for what the Jews were *going* to do in Gaza? Where does it end, this *understanding*?'

Libor knew where it ended. Where it always ends.

He shook his head, as though to contradict his own bleak thoughts.

'So I ask you,' Emmy Oppenstein went on, 'as I am asking as many people in your profession as I know, to speak out against this man, whose sphere, like yours, is the imagination, but who abuses the sacred trust of the imagination.'

'You cannot tell the imagination where it can and cannot go, Emmy.'

'No. But you can insist that where it goes, it goes with generosity and fairness.'

'No, you can't, Emmy. Fairness is not a province of the imagin-ation. Fairness is the business of a tribunal, which is not the same animal.'

'I don't mean that sort of fairness, and you know it. I'm not talking balance. But what is the imagination for if not to grasp how the world feels to those who don't think what you think?'

'But isn't that the very understanding you cannot forgive in your film man?'

'No, Libor, it is not. His sympathy is the simple expression of political allegiance. He understands what his politics lead him to understand. He agrees – that's all. Poof!' She clicked her fingers. A thing worth no more of her time than that. 'Which means all he understands is himself, and his own propensity to hate.'

'Well, that's something.'

'It's nothing. It's less than nothing if you don't call that propensity what it is. People hate Jews because they hate Jews, Libor. They don't need an excuse. The trigger isn't the violence in Gaza. The trigger, in so far as they need a trigger – and many don't – is the violent, partial, inflammatory reporting of it. The trigger is the inciting word.'

He felt that she was blaming him. Not his profession – *him*.

'Every story is a distortion, Emmy. Will your way of telling it be any more impartial than his?'

'Yes,' she said, 'it will. I see villains on all sides. I see two people with competing claims, now justified, now not. I spread the wrong.'

A couple of women settled at a table opposite, both two decades younger than Emmy, Libor guessed. He thought in decades now – ten years his lowest unit of measurement. They smiled at him. He smiled back. They looked like vice chancellors. Something about the length of their skirts. Two vice chancellors meeting to discuss their respective universities. He could live here, if they'd have him, as a sort of mascot. He would promise not to make a nuisance of himelf, not to play his radio late at night and not to talk about Jews. Take tea and biscuits with lady professors and rectors. Discuss declining standards of written and spoken English. At least they'd know who Jane Russell was.

He changed his mind. They wouldn't. And anyway, they weren't Malkie.

Villains on all sides, yes. And the word. What had she just said about the word? Its power to incite. Well, that had never been a journey any of his words had been on. Excite, maybe. Incite, never. He lacked the seriousness.

'There is a big difference,' he reminded her, as though half ashamed of what he had done with his life, 'between writing about Anita Ekberg's chest and the rights and wrongs of Zionism.'

But that wasn't the category of nicety she had met him to discuss. 'I tell you where the big difference is, Libor. The big difference is between *understanding* – ha! – and acquittal. Only God can give absolution. You know that.'

He wanted to say he was sympathetic but couldn't help. Because he was in no position to help and because none of it mattered. For none of it did matter. But finding the right form of words for saying to Emmy Oppenstein that none of it mattered was beyond him.

'It's not Kristallnacht,' he thought.

But he couldn't say that.

He'd had his Kristallnacht. Malkie dying – without God's absolution of either of them, as far as he could see – what worse was there?

But he couldn't say that either.

'I'll speak to a few people I know,' was the best he could do.

But she knew he wouldn't.

In return – in return for nothing but an old affection – she gave him the number of a bereavement counsellor. He told her he didn't require a bereavement counsellor. She reached out and put a hand on each of his cheeks. This gesture meant that everyone needed a bereavement counsellor. Don't think of it as counselling or therapy. Think of it as conversation.

So what was this? Was this not conversation?

A different kind of conversation, Libor. And it wouldn't do, she explained, to be counselling him herself.

He was unable to decide whether he was disappointed that it wouldn't do for her to counsel him or not. To know that he would have had to locate the part of himself in which expectation resides. And he couldn't.

SEVEN

I

The agreement had been that Treslove would take his sons on holiday and then see.

Heads he'd resume his previous existence, forget all the rubbish, go out looking like Brad Pitt and return home, alone, at a reasonable hour in the evening to his Hampstead flat that wasn't in Hampstead.

Tails he'd move in with Hephzibah.

'I don't want to be making room and then have you changing your mind in a fortnight,' she told him. 'I'm not saying this is for life, God help us both, but if you're going to seriously disrupt me, disrupt me because you want to, not because you're at a loose end.'

He had told her about the mugging, but she did not set much store by it. 'That's what I mean by being at a loose end,' she said. 'You go wandering around with your head in the clouds, get your phone snatched like just about everyone else at sometime or another, and think God's called you. You aren't busy enough. There's been too little going on in your head and, from the sound of it, your heart.'

'Libor's been talking.'

'Nothing to do with Libor. I can see it for myself. I saw it when I first clapped eyes on you. You were waiting for the roof to fall in.'

He went to kiss her. 'And it did,' he said with exaggerated courtliness.

She pushed him away. 'I'm the roof now!'

He thought his heart would break with love for her. She was so Jewish. *I'm the roof now!* And he'd thought Tyler was the business. Well, when had poor Tyler ever done what Hephzibah had just done with language? *I'm the roof now!*

That was what it was to be a Jewess. Never mind the moist dark womanly mysteriousness. A Jewess was a woman who made even punctuation funny.

He couldn't work out how she had done it. Was it hyperbole or was it understatement? Was it self-mockery or mockery of him? He decided it was tone. Finklers did tone. As with music, they might not have invented it, but they had mastered its range. They revealed depths in it which the inventors of tone, like the great composers themselves – for neither Verdi nor Puccini was a Finkler, Treslove knew that – could never have dreamed were there. They were interpreters of genius. They showed what could be done with sound.

I'm the roof now! God, she was wonderful!

For his part he'd been ready to jump right in. Then and there. Marry me. I'll do whatever has to be done. I'll study. I'll be circumcised. Just marry me and make Finkler jokes.

She was what he'd been promised. And the fact that she didn't look anything like the woman he thought he'd been promised – the fact that she made fools of all his expectations – only proved that something far more powerful than his inclination was in operation. Far more powerful than his dreaming inclination, even, for she was decidedly not the schoolgirl bending to fasten her shoelace in his dreams. Hephzibah could not have bent that far down. When she tied her laces she put her foot up on a stool. She was not his kind of woman. She came from somewhere other than his wanting. Ergo – she was a gift.

It was she who was not sure. 'I, you see,' she explained, 'have not been waiting for the roof to fall in.'

He tried to emulate her joke. 'I'm not the roof!'

She didn't notice.

He threw in everything he had – a shrug, a 'so', a 'now' and an extra exclamation mark. '*So, I'm not the roof now!!*'

Still she didn't laugh. He couldn't tell if she was annoyed with him for trying. Or maybe it was just that Finkler jokes didn't work in the negative. It sounded funny enough to him. *So, I'm not the roof now!!* But it could have been that Finklers only permitted other Finklers to tell Finkler jokes.

She'd had two husbands and wasn't looking for a third. Wasn't, in fact, looking for anything.

Treslove didn't believe that. Who isn't looking? Stop looking and you stop being alive.

But what she was most not sure of was him. How sure, or how reliable in his sureness, *he* was.

'I'm sure,' he said.

'You've slept with me once and you're sure?'

'It's not about sleeping.'

'It will be about sleeping if you meet someone you want to sleep with more.'

He thought about Kimberley and was glad he'd managed to squeeze her in in time. A last indulgence before life turned serious. Though she hadn't been about sleeping either.

But he did as he was told. He went to Liguria with his two goyische sons and came back ready to move in.

'My *feygelah*,' he said, taking her in his arms.

She laughed one of her big laughs. '*Feygelah*, me? Do you know what *feygelah* means?'

'Sure. Little bird. Also homosexual, but I wouldn't be calling you a homosexual. I bought a Yiddish dictionary.'

'Call me something else.'

He'd come prepared. When he was certain his sons weren't looking he had studied the Yiddish dictionary by the swimming pool in Portofino. His aim had been a hundred Yiddish words to woo her with.

'My *neshomeleh*,' he said. 'It means my little darling. It comes from neshomeh, meaning soul.'

'Thank you,' she said. 'I fear you're going to teach me how to be Jewish.'

'I will if you like, *bubeleh*.'

She had an apartment opposite Lord's. From her terrace you could watch the cricket. He was marginally disappointed. He hadn't moved in to watch cricket. He was sorry she didn't have a terrace that overlooked the Wailing Wall.

There was another problem he had to negotiate. She had once worked for the BBC. Not any longer, and it had been television rather than radio, which diluted her offence a little, but she retained a number of her BBC friendships.

'I'll go out when they come,' he told her.

'You'll stay here,' she said. 'You say you want to be a Jew – well, the first thing you need to know is that Jewish men don't go out without their wives or girlfriends. Unless they're having an affair. Other than another woman's flat there's nowhere for Jewish men to go. They don't do pubs, they hate being seen uncompanioned at the theatre, and they can't eat on their own. Jewish men must have someone to talk to while they eat. They can't do only one thing at a time with their mouths. You'll learn. And you'll learn to like my friends. They're lovely.'

'*Nishtogedacht*,' Treslove replied.

The good news was that she had left the BBC to set up a museum of Anglo-Jewish culture – 'what we have achieved, not what we have undergone; our triumphs not our tribulations' – on Abbey Road where the Beatles had made some of their most famous records and pilgrims still turned up by the busload to cavort on the famous zebra crossing. Now they would have a museum of Anglo-Jewish culture to visit when they'd finished paying homage to the Beatles.

It wasn't so far-fetched. The Beatles had a Jew as their manager in their breakthrough years. Brian Epstein. The fans knew how well he had guided them and that his suicide might have been prompted by his unrequited love for John Lennon, a non-Jew and therefore forbidden fruit. So there was a tragic Jewish element to the Beatles story. This wasn't the prime motivation for building a museum of Anglo-Jewish culture on Abbey Road, but it was a practical consideration.

And yes, the Brian Epstein story would figure. A whole room was being given over to the contribution made by Jews to the British entertainment industry. Frankie Vaughan, Alma Cogan, Lew Grade, Mike and Bernie Winters, Joan Collins (only on her father's side, but a half is better than nothing), Brian Epstein and even Amy Winehouse.

Hephzibah had been headhunted by the eccentric Anglo-Jewish philanthropist who was himself a music producer and whose brainchild the museum was. She was the best person for the job, in his view and in the view of his foundation. The only person for the job. And Hephzibah, for her part, relished the challenge.

'Considering that he believes the BBC is biased in its reporting of the Middle East, it's something of a surprise he chose me,' she told Treslove.

'He knows you're not like the rest of them,' Treslove said.

'Not like the rest of them in what sense?'

'In the sense of being biased in their reporting of the Middle East.'

'Is that what you think?'

'About you? Yes.'

'I mean about the rest of them?'

'Being biased against what your Uncle Libor calls Isrrrae? Of course.'

'Have you always thought that?' She didn't want him changing his politics just for her. He would only end up resenting her for that.

'No, but that's only because I didn't think about it at all. Now I do, I remember what anti-Semites they all were there, especially the Jews.'

For a moment he wondered if that was the reason he had fared so badly at the BBC himself – anti-Semitism.

'Then you must have known very different Jews at the Beeb to those I knew,' she told him.

'The Jews I knew pretended they weren't Jewish. That was why they went to the BBC – to get a new identity. It was the next best thing to joining the Roman Catholic Church.'

'Bollocks,' she said. 'I didn't go there to get a new identity.'

'Because you're the exception, as I have said. The ones I met couldn't wait to put their Jewish history behind them. They dressed like debutantes, spoke like minor royalty, took the *Guardian*, and shrank from you in horror if you so much as mentioned Isrrrae. Anyone would have thought the Gestapo was listening in. And all I was trying to do was ask them out an date.'

'Why would you have said the word Isrrrae – and can we stop pronouncing it like that – if you only wanted to ask them out on a date?'

'Small talk.'

'Maybe they thought you couldn't see them without thinking of Jewish history, have you put your mind to that?'

'And why would that have been a problem for them?'

'Because Jews don't want to go around with nothing but their history on their faces, Julian.'

'They should be proud.'

'It's not for you to say what they should be. But anyway, I have to say I never came across anything of the sort you're describing. I would have opposed it if I had. Jew isn't the only word in my vocabulary, but I am not prepared to have my Jewishness monkeyed about with. I can take care of myself.'

'I don't doubt it.'

'That, though, doesn't mean I don't allow other Jews to be as lukewarm about their Jewishness as they like. OK?'

'OK.'

She kissed him. Yes, OK.

But he returned to the subject later. 'You should ask Libor what he thinks,' he said. 'Libor's World Service experiences were very similar to mine.'

'Oh, Libor's an old Czech reactionary.'

She had, in fact, already asked Libor, not about Jewish anti-Semitism at the BBC but about Treslove. Was he for real? Was he fucking with her mind? Had he really been the victim of an anti-Semitic attack? Could Libor vouch for him at any level?

Yes, no, who could say and absolutely, Libor replied. He had known Treslove since he was a schoolboy. He was deeply fond of him. Would he make a good husband . . .

'I'm not looking for a husband.'

. . . only time would tell. But he hoped they would be very happy. With one reservation.

She looked alarmed.

'I lose a friend.'

'How do you lose him? He'll be living closer to you if anything. And you can come here for your supper.'

'Yes, but he won't be free to come out whenever I call him. And I'm too old to be making long-range appointments. I take it a day at a time now.'

'Oh, Libor, nonsense.'

But it did strike her that he wasn't in the pink.

'In the pink? He's nearly ninety and he's recently lost his wife. It's a miracle he can still breathe.'

Turning over in bed, Treslove surveyed the miracle that had transformed his life. He had never shared a mattress with anyone her size before. Some of the women he had slept with had been so narrow he hadn't always known they were there when he woke. He had to search the bedclothes for them. And as often as not they were gone. Hopped it. Slipped away in the early morning without a sound, as slithery as rats. When

Hephzibah so much as stirred Treslove's half of the bed rolled like the Atlantic. He had to hang on to the mattress. This didn't disturb his sleep. On the contrary he slept the sleep of his life, confident in the knowledge that she was by his side – let her toss as tumultuously as she liked – and was not going anywhere.

He now understood what Kimberley was for. She had been given him to soften him up. To wean him off aetiolated women. She was a halfway house to Hephzibah – his Juno.

She was not mountainous, his Juno. He wasn't sure it was fair even to call her plump. She was simply made of some other material than he was accustomed to women being made of. He remembered the woman coming out of the pool in Liguria, the bottom half of her bikini wet and loose, her skin the same, at one and the same time spare and floppy, as though the small amount of flesh she did have was still too big for her bones. Hephzibah occupied her frame, that was how he saw it. She was physically in harmony with herself. She filled herself out. Without her clothes she was not bulky as he'd feared, there were no rolls of plumpness or flaps of excess flesh. If anything she was taut and strong, only her neck a trifle too thick. Consequently she was better to look at out of her clothes than in them. He had dreaded what those purple and maroon Hampstead Bazaar cloaks and shawls would conceal, and lo, when she removed them she was beautiful! Hunoesque.

The big surprise was the lightness of her skin. Light in colour, he meant, not light in weight. Every time he met a Finkler they changed the rules to which Finklers were meant to adhere. Sam Finkler hadn't been dark and beetling, he'd been red and spidery. Libor was a dandy not a scholar. And here was Hephzibah whose name evoked belly dancers and bazaars and the perfume they sprayed outside the Arab shop on Oxford Street, but whose looks once you peeled her clothes off her were . . . he thought Polish or Ukrainian at first, but the longer he feasted on her nakedness, the more he thought Scandinavian, Baltic maybe. She could have been the figurehead of an Estonian fishing boat – the *Lembitu*, the *Veljo* – that plied the Gulf of Riga for herring. He had done a module on Norse sagas at university. Now he knew why. To prepare him for his own Brunhild. As his friendships with Finkler and Libor were to prepare him for his Brunhild being Jewish.

There were no accidents. Everything had a meaning.

It was like a religious conversion. He would wake to the sight of Hephzibah heaving towards him and experience an unfathomable joy, as though the universe and his consciousness of it had miraculously joined up, and there was nothing inharmonious in himself or in anything outside him. It wasn't just Hephzibah he loved, it was the whole world.

God, being Jewish had stuff going for it!

He gave up working as a double at her request. It demeaned him to be playing someone else, she thought. Now he had found her it was time he played himself.

Thanks to provident parents and a couple of good divorces she was not short of money. She was sufficiently not short, at least, for him to be able to take time to think about what he was going to do. What about getting back into arts administration? Hephzibah's suggestion. Every town in England, every village in England, now had a literary festival; they must be crying out for people with his knowledge and experience. Perhaps he could even start one of his own on Abbey Road, close to the recording studios and the museum. Between the Beatles and the Jews, a St John's Wood Festival of the Written and Performing Arts. Perhaps featuring a permanently sited Centre of BBC Atrocities? His suggestion. Hephzibah thought not.

He wasn't sold on the festival idea, anyway. He remembered the woman who kept her Birkenstocks on during lovemaking. No, he was done with the arts.

He wondered about training to be a rabbi.

'There could be obstacles to that,' she told him.

He was disappointed. 'What about a lay rabbi?'

She wasn't sure whether Judaism recognised a laity in the way that Anglicanism did. Perhaps Liberal Judaism had something of the laity in it, but she was pretty sure he would still have to submit himself to strict Judaic criteria. And there was something called Reconstructionism, but she thought that was American, and she didn't want to go and live in America with him.

In fact she didn't want him to be a rabbi full stop.

'You can want a break from Jewishry,' she said.

He said he hoped that wasn't why she'd chosen him.

She said it wasn't, but she'd had two Jewish husbands, and while she wasn't for a moment suggesting that she and he were looking to get spliced, she was relieved not to be living with a third Jewish man in any capacity. Not a Jewish man in the usually accepted sense of the term, at any rate, she added hurriedly.

Then she had a bright idea. What about assisting her in setting up the museum? In just how professional a capacity she couldn't be certain until she'd discussed it with the philanthropist and his board, but she would appreciate his help in whatever form it came, if only while he looked about him.

He was elated. He didn't wait for her to discuss him with the board. He gave himself a job description. Assistant Curator of the Museum of Anglo-Jewish Culture.

It was what he had been waiting for all his life.

2

What Finkler hadn't been waiting for all his life was a dressing-down from an ASHamed Jewish comedian.

Least of all when that comedian was Ivo Cohen who thought it was funny to fall over.

On his own initiative, Finkler had begun to refer to ASHamed Jews as ASH, the acronym he had suggested on the day he agreed to join the group. 'We in ASH,' he said in a newspaper interview about his work with ASHamed Jews, and he had repeated the phrase on an early-morning radio show.

'Firstly there already is an ASH,' Ivo Cohen said. 'It's an anti-smoking charity with which, as a thirty-a-day man, I would rather not be confused. Secondly, it sounds like we've been burnt alive.'

'And thirdly,' Merton Kugle interposed, 'it too closely resembles AISH.'

AISH was an educational and dating organisation for young Orthodox Jews, one of whose aims was to promote travel to Israel.

'Not much chance we'd be confused with that,' Finkler said.

'All we're asking,' Merton Kugle said, 'is that you don't change our name without discussing it with us first. It isn't your movement.'

The unresolved boycott issue still rankled with Kugle who had now taken to stealing Israeli produce from his supermarket and getting himself arrested.

Merton Kugle, burnt-out match of a man, according to Finkler, a dead-faced blogger whom nobody read, an activist who activated nothing, a no one – a *nebbish*, a *nishtikeit*, a *nebechel*: sometimes, even for Finkler, only Yiddish would do – a *gornisht* who belonged to every anti-Zionist group that existed, along with several that did not, no matter that some were sponsored by far-out Muslims who believed that Kugle, as a Jew, dreamed of world conspiracy, and others expressed the views of ultra-Orthodox Jews with whom Kugle would not in any other circumstances have shared a biscuit; so long as the phrase anti-Zionist was in the large or in the small print, Kugle signed up.

'I am a Jew by virtue of the fact that I am not a Zionist,' he had recently written in a soul-searching blog.

How can you be anything, Finkler wanted to know, by virtue of what you're not? Am I a Jew by virtue of not being a Blackfoot Indian?

Looking around the room, Finkler met the blinking red-lidded gaze of the oral-sociologist and socio-psychologist Leonie Leapmann. Finkler had known Leonie Leapmann at Oxford when she was a literary theorist, famous for her short skirts. She had a forest of flaming red hair in those days, far more livid than his pale orange, which she would arrange around herself when she sat, her naked legs drawn up to her chin, like a cat clothed only in its fur. Now her hair was cropped and the fires had all but gone out of it. The tiny skirts had gone too, in favour of ethnic leggings of all sorts, on this occasion a set of Hare Krishna jodhpurs with dropped crotch. It was a look Finkler couldn't read. Why would a woman want to wear a garment that made her resemble an overgrown baby that had filled its pants? It affected all his dealings with her, as though whenever she spoke there was a smell in the room from which he had to avert his nose.

'Oh please, not this again,' she pleaded.

Finkler averted his nose.

Leonie Leapmann had always just come back from, or was always just about to go to, the Occupied Territories where she had many close personal friends of all persuasions, including Jews who were as ashamed as she was. On Leonie people could reach out and touch the conflict. In the orbs of her strained, red-lidded eyes they could see the suffering as in a goldfish bowl.

It was like watching a film in 3D.

'Not *what* again, Leonie?' Lonnie Eysenbach enquired with offensively studied politeness.

Lonnie was a presenter of children's television programmes and a writer of school geography books from which he famously omitted Israel. He had a hungry horse's face and yellow horse's teeth which his producers were growing extremely anxious about. He was scaring the children.

Lonnie and Leonie, both fractious and inflammable, had once been lovers and carried the embers of a simmering resentment along to every meeting.

'I have friends out there, of both persuasions, who are close to suicidal or homicidal despair,' Leonie said – which, to Finkler's sense, though he wasn't going to make an issue of it, amounted almost to a threat of violence against his person – 'and here we are still discussing who we are and what to call ourselves.'

'Excuse me,' Kugle said, 'I am not aware that I have been discussing what to call ourselves. I am a democrat. I bow to the majority decision. It's Sam with his ASH –'

'We can call ourselves the Horsemen of the Fucking Apocalypse for all I care,' Leonie shouted.

'Horsemen of the Fucking Apocalypse is good,' Lonnie said. 'Though shouldn't it be Horsemen and Horsewomen.'

'Fuck you!' Leonie told him.

Averting his nose, Finkler sighed a sigh deep enough to shake the foundations of the Groucho club. What was the point of this rehearsal of first principles every time they met? But it pained him to agree with Kugle about anything. If day followed night to Kugle, then Finkler prayed for night never to end. 'I bow to no one in my Jewish shame,' he said. 'But isn't it important that we make a distinction here?'

Kugle groaned.

'You have something more to say?' Finkler snapped.

Kugle shook his head. 'Just clearing my throat.'

'Oh, for God's sake,' cried Leonie Leapmann.

'You don't believe in God,' Lonnie Eysenbach reminded her.

'Let me see if I can help here.' The speaker was Tamara Krausz, academically the best known of the ASHamed Jews, a woman whose quiet authority commanded respect not only in England but in America and the Middle East, wherever anti-Zionists – Finkler would not have gone so far as to say wherever anti-Semites – were gathered.

Even Finkler wilted a little in her presence.

'Don't we have to show,' she continued – though her continuance was never in doubt, for who would dare interrupt her? – 'that to be a Jew is a wonderful and various thing, and that it carries no more of a compulsion to defend Israel against all criticism than it does to live in constant fear. We are not, are we, a victim people? As that brave Israeli philosopher' – a nod here to Finkler – 'Avital Avi said recently in a heart-warming speech in Tel Aviv which I had the honour to hear from the platform, it is we who are keeping the Holocaust alive today, we who continue where the Kapos left off. Yes, of course it demeans the dead to forget them, but to disinter them in order to justify carnage demeans them more.'

Her voice was silvery and controlled, a reproach in particular, Finkler thought, to Leonie Leapmann whose diction lolled and wavered. In her clothes, too, she put Leonie to shame. Leonie dressed like a native of no place one could quite put a name to – the People's Republic of Ethnigrad was Finkler's best shot – whereas Tamara never appeared in public looking anything other than an executive of a fashion consultancy, at once businesslike and softly feminine.

Finkler, waiting, eyed her up. In shape she reminded him of his late wife, but she was at once more steely and more fragile. She clawed the air, he noticed, when she spoke, making fists at random, as though to crush the life out of any idea that wasn't hers. He imagined her screaming in his arms, he didn't know why. Just something to do with the way she was put together and the atmosphere of psychic disintegration she gave off. In fact, psychic disintegration was precisely how she understood the history of modern Israyel. Sent mad in the Holocaust, not least by their own impotence and passivity, Jews were spilling what was left of their brains over the Palestinians and calling it self-defence. Finkler didn't share this theory of madness begetting madness, but he was saving up the occasion when he would tell her so, in the hope of getting her to scream in his arms.

While in Palestine, Tamara reported — it was as though she was telling the group about her holidays: indeed, Finkler wondered how long it would be before the snaps came out — she had met with a number of representatives of Hamas to express her concern in the matter of its recent forced Islamisation programme, which included accosting unsuitably dressed women on the beach, harassing shopkeepers who openly sold Western-style lingerie, segregating the sexes in schools, and generally imposing more and more restrictions on the human rights of women. That this would impact nega- tively on the support Hamas could count on from otherwise sympathetic groups in Europe and America she did not scru- ple to warn them. Entranced, Finkler imagined the leadership of Hamas quaking before Tamara's exquisitely outraged femi- nism. Did they, too, imagine her screaming in their arms?

'Not good,' he said.

'No,' she agreed, 'not good at all. And especially not good as we can expect pro-Zionists to pounce on this as evidence of Hamas's intrinsic extremism and intolerance. Whereas . . .'

Tamara Krausz breathed deeply. Finkler breathed with her.

'Whereas . . .' he said.

'Whereas the truth of it is that what is being enacted here is the direct consequence of the illegal occupation. You cannot isolate a people, cut them off from their natural connection to the country, degrade and starve them, and not expect extrem- ism to follow.'

'You certainly cannot,' Leonie said.

'No,' Tamara said quickly, before Leonie could say anything

else. 'Avital, with whom I discussed this, even went so far as to suggest it was a dark fulfilment of deliberate Israeli policy. Drive Gaza further and further into itself until the West would be begging Israel to reconquer it.'

'Sheesh,' Finkler said.

'I know,' she said, meeting his eyes.

'How is Avital?' he asked suddenly.

Tamara Krausz opened her face to him. Finkler felt he'd been handed a flower. 'He isn't well,' she said. 'Not that he'd admit it. He's tireless.'

'Yes, isn't he,' Finkler replied. 'And Navah?'

'Well, thank God. Well. She's his right hand.'

'Is she ever.' Finkler smiled, handing her a flower in return.

The knowledge that this moment of insider intimacy between them was driving the others crazy filled him with a quiet satisfaction. He could hear Kugle's heart shrivel.

Only poker gave him comparable pleasure.

3

Libor went to see the bereavement counsellor Emmy had recommended. A dark, towering woman big enough to dandle him on her knee. She could have been the ventriloquist, he her dummy.

'Jean Norman,' she said, extending an arm long enough to go around his back and work his levers.

Jean Norman. Such a plain name for such an exotic personage, he thought it must have been assumed to calm the bereaved. Real name Adelgonda Remedios Arancibia.

He did it as a favour to Emmy. For himself he wouldn't have bothered. What did he hope to be counselled into feeling? Cheerful about his prospects?

He felt bad that he had not been able to answer Emmy's appeal for support. Finkler was the most eminent public figure he knew now and Finkler was hardly going to speak out against the film director who understood why people wanted to kill Jews. For all Libor knew to the contrary the two were bosom friends.

So going to the bereavement counsellor was the second-best thing he could do for Emmy.

Jean Norman. Real name Adelaïda Inessa Ulyana Miroshnichenkop.

She lived in Maida Vale, not all that far from where Treslove lived, though Treslove had called it Hampstead, or rather from where Treslove *had* lived before he moved in with Libor's great-great niece. He would have preferred it had she worked out of a clinic or a hospital, but she saw him in the front room of her house.

She was, she explained, retired. But still counselled . . .

Libor thought she was going to say for a hobby or to keep her hand in, but she left the sentence to dangle like a person on the end of a rope . . .

The house was large but the room she invited Libor into was diminutive, almost like a room in a doll's house. There were prints on the walls of rural scenes. Shepherds and shepherdesses. And a collection of porcelain thimbles on the mantelpiece. She was too tall for the room, Libor thought. She had to fold herself almost into three in order to fit into her chair. Her height made Libor feel foolish. Even with both of them sitting down he had to look up at her.

She had a fine Roman nose with open dark nostrils into which Libor had no choice but to stare. Despite her foreignness there was an air of the Women's Institute about her, that look of shy strait-laced provincial glamour which proved such a success when women of this sort took their clothes off for a charity calendar. She would have long pendulous breasts and a deep dark open Sicilian navel, Libor guessed.

He wondered if her ability to make him imagine her without clothes, though she was covered from her neck to her

ankles and never made a movement that was remotely sugges-
tive, was part of her bereavement counselling technique.

They talked briefly about Emmy. Emmy had told her who
Libor was. She remembered his articles and even described
one or two of them correctly. There were famous photographs. She remembered some of those too. Libor laughing
with Garbo. Libor lying on a bed with Jane Russell, Libor
looking the less masculine of the two. Libor dancing with
Marilyn Monroe, cheek to cheek in an impossible parody of
romance, given all the disparities.

'You should have seen me dance with my wife,' Libor said.

He said it as a favour to her, just as coming to see her was
a favour to Emmy. He assumed this was his role. To do favours
and be bereaved.

He was relieved she didn't say anything inane about the
death of loved ones – he hated the expression loved ones;
there weren't loved ones, there was only loved Malkie – or
cycles of emotion or pathways for grief.

Nor, for which he was no less grateful, did she treat him to
any sideways glances of compassion. She did not sorrow for
him. She left him to sorrow for himself.

As the time wore on he found it increasingly difficult to
concentrate on anything she was saying. Jean Norman. Real
name Fruzsina Orsolya Fonnyasztó.

He continued to look up into her nostrils where it was
soothingly dark and quiet.

As for what he said to her, he had no idea. He mouthed his
feelings. He play-acted at grief. He spoke the words which he
imagined the bereaved spoke at such a time. Even made the
accompanying gestures. Had he stayed there long enough he
believed he'd have begun to wring his hands and tear his hair.

His self-consciousness surprised and appalled him. What
need was there for this? Why did he not simply speak his
heart?

Because the heart did not speak, that was why. Because

language presupposes artificiality. Because in the end there was nothing, absolutely nothing, to be said.

Did she know that, Jean Norman? Real name Maarit Tuulikki Jääskeläinen. Was it part of her professional knowledge that the bereaved sat in front of her, looked up into her nostrils and lied?

He should have howled like an animal. That at least would have been a genuine expression of how he felt. Except that it wasn't. There was no genuine expression of how he felt.

She had a question for him before he left. She became, in the asking of it, more animated than in the whole time he had been with her. Clearly this was the real, in fact the only, reason he was here. What she was about to ask him she had wanted to ask him from the moment he walked in the room. No, from the moment she knew he was coming to see her.

'About Marilyn,' she said.

'Marilyn Monroe? What about her?'

'You knew her well?'

'Yes.'

She blew out her cheeks and patted her chest. 'So tell me . . .'

'Yes?'

'Did she take her own life, or was she murdered?'

4

Treslove and Hephzibah are singing love duets in the bath.

Finkler is losing money at poker.

Libor is sinking fast.

Finkler is losing money at poker but his books are selling well and at least he hasn't made a pass at Tamara Krausz.

Libor is sinking fast because he has lost Malkie. Emmy has been ringing him with news of her grandson. He will not get his sight back. There has been another attack on two Jewish boys wearing fringes, Emmy also tells him. And headstones in a Jewish cemetery in north London have been defaced. Swastikas. What does she want him to do? Start a vigilante group? Mount a guard on every Jewish burial place in London?

Libor is at pains not to confuse his feelings about Jews being attacked again in public places with his feelings for Malkie.

Treslove and Hephzibah are singing 'O soave fanciulla', 'Parigi o cara', 'E il sol dell'anima', 'Là ci darem la mano', and so on.

Whatever aria he knows she knows. How astonishing is that? he asks himself.

Everything they sing is either a hello or a goodbye. That's opera for you. Treslove sings them all as goodbyes. Hephzibah as hellos. So even when they differ they are complementary and he is the beneficiary.

Her voice is strong, more suited to Wagner. But they won't be singing any Wagner, not even *Tristan und Isolde*. 'My rule of thumb is that if there's an "und" anywhere I won't be singing it,' she tells him.

He's beginning to understand Finkler culture. It's like Libor and Marlene Dietrich, assuming Libor had told the truth about Marlene Dietrich. There are some things you don't do. Very well, Treslove won't do them either. Show him a German and he'll kick the living shit out of the *mamzer*.

Mamzer is Yiddish for bastard. Treslove can't stop using the word.

Even of himself. Am I a lucky *mamzer* or what am I? he asks.

In celebration of being such a lucky *mamzer*, Treslove invites Finkler and Libor to a dinner party. Come and toast my new life. He thought of asking his sons but changed his mind. He doesn't like his sons. He doesn't like Finkler either, come to that, but Finkler is an old friend. He chose him. He didn't choose his sons.

Finkler whistled through his teeth when he walked out of the lift straight on to Hephzibah's terrace.

'You've landed on your feet,' he whispered to Treslove.

Crude *mamzer*, Treslove thought. 'Have I?' he asked, tersely. 'I wasn't aware I'd been *off* my feet.'

Finkler dug his ribs. 'Come on! Teasing.'

'Is that what you're doing? Well, glad you like it here, anyway. You can watch the cricket.'

'Can I?' Finkler liked cricket. Liking cricket made him, he thought, English.

'I meant *one* can. *One* can watch cricket from here.'

He had no intention of inviting Finkler over to watch cricket. Finkler enjoyed enough advantages already. Let him buy a ticket. Failing which, let him sit on his own terrace and watch the Heath. There was lots to see on the Heath, as Treslove remembered. Not that he remembered much of Hampstead now. He had been in St John's Wood three months and couldn't recall ever having lived anywhere else. Or *with* anyone else.

Hephzibah occluded his past.

He took Finkler into the kitchen to meet Hephzibah who was brewing at the stove. He had been waiting for this moment a long time.

'Sam, d'Jew know Jewno?' he said.

Not a flicker of understanding or recollection from Finkler.

Treslove thought about spelling it out to jog his memory, though he believed it unlikely that Finkler ever forgot anything he himself had said. Finkler never went anywhere without a notebook in which he wrote down whatever he heard that interested him, mostly his own observations. 'Waste not, want not,' he once told Treslove, opening his notebook. Which Treslove took to mean that Finkler routinely recycled himself, knowing he could get a whole book out of a mumbled aside. So Treslove's money was on Finkler remembering his D'Jew know Jewno jest but not wanting to allow Treslove a jest in return.

But by now the two had already shaken hands anyway, Hephzibah wiping hers on her cook's apron.

'Sam.'

'Hephzibah.'

'My delight is in you,' Finkler said.

Hephzibah inclined her head graciously.

Treslove's face was a question mark.

'That's what Hephzibah means in Hebrew,' Finkler told him. 'My delight is in you.'

'I know that,' Treslove said, miffed.

The bastard had got him again. You never knew from which direction it would come. You prepared yourself for a Finkler joke and they bamboozled you with Finkler scholarship. You could never steal a march on them. They always had something you didn't, some verbal or theological reserve they could draw on, that would leave you stumped for a response. The *mamzers*.

'I must go on with what I'm doing,' Hephzibah said, 'or you won't eat tonight.'

'My delight is in your cooking,' Treslove said, to no one's interest.

In fact, in Treslove's eyes Hephzibah didn't so much cook as lash out at her ingredients, goading and infuriating them into taste. No matter what she was preparing she always had at least five pans on the go, each of them big enough to boil a cat in. Steam rose from four of them. Burning oil from the fifth. Every window was open. An extractor fan sucked noisily at whatever it could find. Treslove had suggested closing the windows when the fan was on, or turning the fan off when the windows were open. They countermanded each other's function, he explained scientifically, the fan sucking in half the

212

fumes of St John's Wood. But Hephzibah ignored him, banging her cupboard doors open and closed, using every spoon and every casserole she owned, breathing in the flames and the smoke. The sweat poured down her brow and stained her clothes. Every couple of minutes she would pause to wipe her eyes. Then on she'd go, like Vulcan stoking the fires of Etna. And at the end of it, there was an omelette and chives for Treslove's supper.

Though he complained of the illogic of her methods, Treslove loved to watch her. A Jewish woman in her Jewish kitchen! His own mother had prepared five-course meals in an egg pan. The three of them would sit and wait for the food to cool and then eat in silence. As for the washing up, there wasn't any. Just the egg pan and the three plates.

Finkler breathed in the odours of Hephzibah's devastated kitchen – had the Cossacks been through they'd have left it tidier – and said, 'Ahhhh! My favourite.'

'You don't even know what I'm preparing,' Hephzibah laughed.

'Still my favourite,' Finkler said.

'Name an ingredient.'

'*Trayf.*'

Treslove knew what *trayf* meant. *Trayf* was whatever wasn't kosher.

'Not in this kitchen,' Hephzibah said with mock offence. 'My Julian won't eat *trayf.*'

My Julian. Music to Treslove's ears. Schubert, played by Horowitz. Bruch played by Heifetz.

Hey, Sam – D'Jew know Jewno?

Finkler made a noise like a gargle from far back in his throat. 'You've koshered the old boy now?'

'He's koshered himself.'

It disconcerted Treslove – her Julian or not – to watch the two Finklers go on eyeing each other up and verbally trying each other out. He felt like piggy in the middle. Hephzibah was his woman, his beloved, his Juno, but Finkler appeared to believe he had an older claim. It was as though they spoke a secret language. The secret language of the Jews.

I must learn it, Treslove thought. I must crack their code before I'm through.

But at the same time he felt pride in Hephzibah that she could do what he could not. In twenty seconds she had reached deeper into Finkler's soul than he ever had. He even appeared relaxed in her company.

When Libor arrived, Treslove truly felt outnumbered. Hephzibah exerted an unexpected influence on his two guests – she dissolved their Jewish differences.

'Nu?' Libor asked of Finkler.

Treslove wasn't sure if that was the way to report it. Do you ask 'Nu' *of*? Or do you just ask, transitively? *'Nu?' he asked*. And is it even a question in the accepted sense? *'Nu,' he said*. Would that have been better? *Nu*, meaning how are things with you, but also I know how things are with you.

So much to master.

But the surprise was that Finkler answered in kind. When there had been no Hephzibah he had castigated Libor for his Jewish barbarisms, but today he twinkled like a rabbi. '*A halber emes izt a gantser lign,*' he said.

'A half truth is a whole lie,' Hephzibah whispered to Treslove.

'I know,' he lied.

'So who's been telling you half-truths?' Libor asked.

'Who hasn't?' Finkler replied. But that was as far as he was prepared to go.

Nu, then, wasn't searching. You didn't have to answer. It permitted prevarications in the name of our common imperfect humanity.

Got it, Treslove thought.

At dinner, though, Libor went for Finkler as in the old days. 'Not your Jewish anti-Semite friends?'

'Not my Jewish anti-Semite friends what?'

Normally, Treslove noted, Finkler denied his Jewish friends were anti-Semites.

'Telling you lies?'

'They're fallible like the rest of us,' he said.

'You're sick of them already? That's good.'

'What's good,' Finkler said, 'is this . . .' He reached for more of everything. Herrings in red wine, herrings in white wine, herrings in cream, sour cream, vinegar, herrings curled around an olive with toothpicks through them, herrings chopped in what was said to be a new way, and of course chopped still in the old – herrings brought in fresh from the North Sea on the trawler of which Hephzibah was the figurehead, one breast bared – and then the pickled meat, the pastrami, the smoked salmon, the egg and onion, the chopped liver, the cheese that had no taste; the blintzes, the tsimmes, the cholent. Only the cholent – the meat and bean and barley shtetl stew, or Czech stew as Hephzibah called it in honour of Libor who loved coming over to eat it – was hot. All those roaring flames, all those fuming pans, and yet everything that came to the table, barring the cholent, was cold.

Treslove marvelled. There was no getting to the bottom of the miracles his wife performed, allowing that she wasn't yet his wife.

'I knew it,' Finkler said when he got to the cholent. 'Helzel! I knew I could smell helzel.'

Treslove knew it, too, but only because Hephzibah had told him. Helzel was stuffed chicken neck. In her opinion, no cholent could call itself a cholent without helzel. Finkler clearly thought the same.

'You've used oregano in the stuffing,' he said, licking his lips. 'Brilliant touch. My mother never thought of oregano.'

Mine neither, Treslove mused.

'Is it a Sephardic version?' Finkler wondered.

'It's *my* version,' Hephzibah laughed.

Finkler looked at Treslove. 'You're a lucky man,' he said. A lucky *mamzer*.

Treslove smiled in agreement, savouring the helzel. Stuffed chicken neck, for Christ's sake! The entire history of a people in a single neck of chicken.

And Finkler the philosopher and ASHamed Jew, licking his chops over it as though he'd never left Kamenetz Podolsky.

After the cholent, the towelling down.

Hephzibah kept an elegant table, had Treslove polish the glasses and the silverware hours before anyone arrived, but in the matter of napery they might as well have been in a transport cafe. In front of every guest was a stainless-steel dispenser of paper napkins. The first time Treslove ever set the table for the two of them he folded napkins as his mother had taught him, in the shape of sailing ships, one per person. Hephzibah commended his dexterity, unfurling the little ship and laying it daintily on her lap, but when he next went to fold the napkins he found the serviette dispensers in their place. 'I am not encouraging gluttony,' Hephzibah explained, 'but I don't want whoever sits at my table to feel they must hold back.'

Hephzibah herself would get through a dozen napkins, more after cholent. Treslove's mother had brought him up not to leave a mark on a napkin if possible, so that it could be folded back into a sailing ship and used again. Now, following Hephzibah's example, he used a fresh one for every finger.

Everything was different. Before Hephzibah he had eaten only with his mouth. Now he ate with his whole person. And it took many paper napkins to keep his whole person clean.

'So this museum . . .' Finkler said, when the table was cleared.

Hephzibah inclined her head in his direction.

'. . . don't we have enough of them already?'

'Museums in general, you mean?'

'Jewish museums. Everywhere you go now, every town,

every shtetl, you find a Holocaust museum. Do we need a Holocaust museum in Stevenage or Letchworth?'

'I'd be surprised if you'd find a Holocaust museum in Letchworth. But this isn't a Holocaust museum anyway. It's a museum of Anglo-Jewish culture.'

Finkler laughed. 'Is there any? Will it mention our being thrown out in 1290?'

'Of course. And of our being welcomed back in in 1655.'

Finkler shrugged, as though to an audience who already believed what he believed. 'Same old, same old,' he said. 'You'll get to the Holocaust in the end, if only under the heading "British Attitudes To". You'll stick up photographs of the gas ovens, you mark my word. Jewish museums always do. What I want to know, if we must have suffering, is why we can't at least change the track from time to time. What about a Museum of the Russian Pogrom? Or a Museum of the Babylonian Exile? Or, in your case, since you already have the site, a Museum of All the Nasty Things the English Have Ever Done to Us?'

'The brief is not to bring up English nastiness,' Hephzibah said.

'I'm glad of it.'

'Nor,' Treslove chimed in, 'is it to bring up anybody else's. Our museum won't so much as mention the Holocaust.'

Finkler stared at him. *Our! Who asked you?* his expression said.

Libor stirred in his chair. In an inconsequent but oracular voice, he said, 'The grandson of a friend of mine has just been blinded.'

Finkler wasn't sure what to do with his face. Was this some sort of a wind-up? *So?* was what he wanted to ask. *So how does that bear upon our conversation?*

'Oh, Libor, who?' Hephzibah asked.

'You don't know the grandson, you don't know the grandmother.'

'Well, what happened?'

So Libor told them, leaving out the information that in another age he and Emmy had been lovers.

'And this,' Finkler said, 'you adduce as reason for there to be a Holocaust museum in every parish in the country.'

'I notice you say *parish*,' Treslove said. 'Your satire acknowledges an incongruity that is only to be explained by Christianity's inhospitability to Jews.'

'Oh, for fuck's sake, Julian. My satire, as you call it, acknowledges no such thing. I see Libor is upset. I mean no disrespect to his feelings. But the actions of one deranged person don't justify us wringing our hands and claiming the Nazis are back.'

'No, and nor do I claim any such thing,' Libor said in return.

Hephzibah left the table and went over to him. She stood behind his chair and put her hands on his cheeks as though he were her little boy. Her rings were bigger than his ears. Libor leaned back into her. Hephzibah put her lips to his bald head. Treslove feared the old man was going to cry. But that might only have been because he feared *he* was going to cry.

'I'm all right,' Libor said. 'I am as much upset by my own impotence as by what's happened to my friend's grandson whom I have never met and didn't know existed two months ago.'

'Well, there's nothing you can do,' Hephzibah said.

'I know that. But it isn't only the doing nothing that's upsetting, it's the feeling nothing.'

'I wonder whether we feel nothing,' Finkler said, 'precisely because we rehearse our feelings on the subject too freely and too often.'

'Crying Wolfowitz, you mean?' Hephzibah said with a wild laugh.

God, I love her, Treslove thought.

'You think we don't?' Finkler persisted.

'I think we can't.'

'You don't believe that too many false alarms result in no one taking any notice?'

'When is an alarm a false alarm?' Hephzibah persisted.

Treslove saw Finkler wondering whether to say *When our friend Julian raises it*. What he said instead was: 'It seems to me we create a climate of unnecessary anxiety, a) by picturing ourselves forever as the victim of events, and b) by failing to understand why people might occasionally feel they have good reason to dislike us.'

'And blind our children,' Hephzibah said. Her hands were still on Libor's face.

Libor put his hands up to hers, as though to deafen himself. 'As in *anti-Semitism is perfectly comprehensible to me*,' he said, in imitation of the empathetic film director.

'And so around it comes,' Hephzibah said.

Finkler shook his head as though there was nothing to be done with any of them. 'So your Museum of Anglo-Jewish Culture is a museum of the Holocaust after all,' he said.

The *yutz*, Treslove thought. The *groisser putz*. The *shtick drek*.

Finkler and Libor sat and drank whisky while Treslove and Hephzibah washed up. Hephzibah normally left the dishes until the next day. Piled up in the sink so that it was near impossible to fill a kettle. And what the sink couldn't take would stay on the kitchen table. Pans and crockery sufficient for a hundred guests. Treslove liked that about her. She didn't believe they had to clean up after every excess. There wasn't a price to pay for pleasure.

She didn't leave the dishes so that *he* should do them either. She just left them. It seemed fatalistic to him. A carelessness acquired courtesy of the Cossacks. Since you don't know where you're going to be tomorrow, or indeed whether you're going to be alive or dead, why worry over dishes?

But tonight she led him by the elbow into the kitchen. And neither Finkler nor Libor offered to get up and help out. It was as if each couple was giving the other space.

'Our friend appears very happy,' Libor said.

Finkler agreed. 'He does. There's a shine on him.'

'And my niece, too. I think she's good for him. It would seem that what he needed was a mother.'

'Always did,' Finkler said. 'Always did.'

EIGHT

I

Finkler was looking forward to a few hands of online poker before bed, so he was disappointed, when he arrived home, to find a message on his answerphone from his daughter Blaise. Immanuel, the younger of his two sons, had been involved in an anti-Semitic incident. Absolutely nothing to worry about. He was perfectly OK. But Blaise wanted her father to hear it from her first, rather than from some other, possibly mischievous, source.

Over a crackling line, Finkler could not make out all the details. As he pressed the replay button it occurred to him that the message could easily be a wind-up – Julian, Libor and Hephzibah, who were still drinking when he left, teaching him a little moral lesson. See how you feel when it happens to you, Mr ASHamed Jew Philosopher. But the voice was definitely Blaise's. And though she said there was absolutely nothing to worry about, there obviously was, otherwise why would she have rung?

He rang back but Blaise wasn't answering. She often didn't. Immanuel's line was permanently engaged. Maybe the bastards had stolen his phone. He tried his other son, Jerome, but he was at a redder, more robust university than Blaise and Immanuel and was inclined to be scathing about their doings. 'Anti-Semites massing outside Balliol? I don't think so, Dad.'

As it was too late to call his driver, and he was too drunk to drive himself, Finkler rang a limo firm he sometimes used. Oxford, he told the operator. Right away.

He had to ask for the radio to be turned down and then turned off altogether. This so incensed the driver, who claimed he needed it on for traffic alerts, that Finkler feared he was going to be involved in an anti-Semitic incident himself. Traffic alerts! At midnight! Once they were out of London, on quieter roads, it occurred to Finkler that the real reason the driver needed the radio on was to keep him awake. 'Maybe we should have it on after all,' he said.

He fell prey to all manner of irrational anxiety. He had unnecessarily annoyed the person taking him to see his son. He had, for all he knew, annoyed his son, too, in any one of the thousands of ways that a father annoys his children. Had his son got into a fight with anti-Semites on his father's behalf? Shamed or not shamed, Finkler was an eminent English Jew. You couldn't expect racist thugs to grasp the fine distinctions of Jewish anti-Zionism. *Ha, so you're Sam Finkler's son are you, you little kike? Then here's a bloody nose.*

Unless it was worse than a bloody nose.

He curled up in the corner of the Mercedes and began to cry. What would Tyler say? He felt he had let her down. She had made him promise to make the children his first priority. 'Not your fucking career, not your Jewish mistresses with fat tits, not those weirdos you hang around with at the Groucho – your sons and daughter. Your sons and daughter, Shmuelly – promise!'

He'd promised and he meant it. At the funeral he'd put his arms around the boys and they had stood together a long time looking into Tyler's grave, three lost men. Blaise had held herself apart from them. She was with her mother. Against all men, lost or not. The three of them had stayed with him a week, and then gone back to their universities. He wrote to them, he rang them, he invited them to launches and screenings. Some weekends he drove to Oxford, on others to Nottingham, booking himself into the best hotel he could find and treating them to slap-up dinners. He believed he had done well, morally, on those occasions, not to take a woman with him. Especially when he stayed at Raymond Blanc's Manoir Aux Quat'Saisons in Oxfordshire, a hugger-mugger hotel-restaurant which cried out for a mistress. But a promise is a promise. He was putting his children first.

He liked his children. They reminded him, in their different ways, of his poor wife – sharp, edgy, scratchy boys, a scathing girl. None had chosen to study philosophy. He was glad of that. Blaise was a lawyer. Immanuel, more unsteady, had changed from architecture to languages and looked set to change again. Jerome was an engineer. 'I'm proud of you,' Finkler told him. 'A nice non-Jewish occupation.'

'How do you know I won't be going over to Israel to build walls when I'm qualified?' the boy said. But his father looked so alarmed he had to explain he was only joking.

Both the boys had girlfriends to whom, he believed, they were fastidiously faithful. Blaise was wilder and uncommitted. Like her mother. Jerome wasn't sure he had found Miss Right yet. Immanuel thought he might have. Already, he wanted children of his own. Finkler imagined him wheeling his family around the Ashmolean, bending over their prams, explaining this and that, adoring their little bodies. The new man. He had never quite managed to be that sort of a father himself. There were too many things he had found interesting apart from his children, apart from his wife, too, come to that. But he was trying to make amends now.

What if it was all a bit late? What if his neglect had contributed in some ways to this attack? Had he left his children vulnerable, unable to take care of themselves, insufficiently aware of danger?

And then there'd been the conversation earlier in the evening. He had listened unsympathetically to the story of a boy blinded for no other reason than that he was a Jew. Was that chancing providence? Finkler didn't believe in the validity of such a thought, but he had it nonetheless. Had he dared the Jewish God to do His worst? And had the Jewish God decided, for the first time in however many thousands of years, to buckle up and meet the challenge? A terrible thought occurred to him: had Immanuel been blinded?

And a more terrible thought still: was it his doing?

Finkler the rationalist and gambler made a compact through his tears. If Immanuel had suffered any serious harm he would tell the ASHamed Jews where to shove it. And if he hadn't suffered any serious harm . . . ?

Finkler didn't know.

It made no sense to implicate ASHamed Jews in this. They were not to blame for anything. They just *were*. As anti-Semites just *were*. But you can't play fast and loose with primal passions. He wasn't sure, though, as he crouched in the corner of the car, willing the miles to fly by, whether it was any longer defensible even to use the word Jew in a public place. After everything that had happened, wasn't it a word for private consumption only? Out there in the raging public world it was as a goad to every sort of violence and extremism.

It was a password to madness. Jew. One little word with no hiding place for reason in it. Say 'Jew' and it was like throwing a bomb.

Had Immanuel been boasting of his Jewishness? And if he had, why had he? To pay him, Finkler, back? To express his disappointment in him? *My father might be ashamed to be a Jew but I as sure as fuck am not.* Whereupon *whack!*

It all came back to *him*. Whichever way he looked at it, he was to blame. Bad husband, bad father, bad example, bad Jew – in which case, bad philosopher as well.

But this was no better than superstition, was it? He was a prin-cipled amoralist. What you did you did, and there was no retributive force out there holding you to account. Yes, there was material cause and effect. You drove badly, you had a crash. But there was no moral cause and effect. Your son did not get blinded by an anti-Semite because you took mistresses, or because you did not take the threat of anti-Semitism as seriously as some of your more hysterical fellow Jews believed you should.

Or did he?

This was not the first time, Finkler remembered, that mistresses had destabilised the workings of his highly rational mind. Take a mistress and you have a car crash. Finkler did not of course believe that. Except in the material cause-and-effect sense. Take a mistress and have her give you a blow job while you're driving down the M40 and your car might well spin out of control. That's not morality, it's concentration. So why, when he was out driving with a mistress, did he feel a little less safe than when he was out driving with his wife? Men and women were not fashioned, he believed, to live monogamously. It was no crime against nature to sleep with more than one woman. It was a crime against aesthetics, maybe, to be out on the town with Ronit Kravitz's vertiginous décolletage when he had an elegant wife waiting for him at home, but no payment was ever exacted by God or society for a crime against aesthetics. So whence his apprehension?

Yet apprehensive he always was, whenever he committed one of those sexual crimes which in his eyes were no crime. The car would crash. The hotel would burn down. And yes – for it was as primitive as this – his dick would fall off.

He could explain it. Terror pre-dated reason. Even in a scientific age men retained some of that prehistoric ignorance of which irrational fear was the child. That Finkler understood the causes and consequences of events made not a jot of difference. The sun might still not rise one morning because of something he had done or some ritual he had left unobserved. He was afraid, as a man born half a million years before him would have been afraid, that he had disobeyed the ordinances of the gods and they had visited their vengeance on his son.

* * *

He arrived at Immanuel's lodgings sometime after one o'clock in the morning. There was no one in. He tried the phone again but the line was still engaged. Blaise, too, was not answering. He directed the driver to the Cowley Road where Blaise lived. The lights were on in her front room. Finkler knocked, needlessly, at her window. Someone he didn't recognise drew the curtains back, then Blaise showed her face. She appeared astonished to see him.

'This wasn't necessary,' she said, letting him in. 'I said he's OK.'

'Is he here?'

'Yes, he's lying down on my bed.'

'Is he all right?'

'I've said. He's fine.'

'Let me see him.'

He found his son sitting up on Blaise's bed reading a celebrity magazine and drinking rum and Coke. He had a plaster on his cheek and his arm was in a home-made sling. Otherwise he looked perfectly well.

'Oops,' he said.

'What do you mean, "oops"?'

'Oops as in oops-a-daisy. It's what you used to say when one of us fell over.'

'So you fell over, did you?'

'I did, eventually, yes.'

'What do you mean, "eventually"?'

'Dad, are you going to keep asking me what I mean?'

'Tell me what happened.'

'There's a prior question, Dad.'

'What's that?'

'How are you, Immanuel?'

'I'm sorry. How are you, Immanuel?'

'I'm reasonably OK, thank you, Dad. As you can see. There was a kerfuffle, that was what happened. Outside the Union. There'd been a debate – *This house believes that Israel has forfeited its right to exist*, or something along those lines. I was surprised, actually, that you hadn't been invited to speak.'

So was Finkler, now that he'd come to hear of it.

'And . . .'

'And you know what these things are like. Tempers got a little frayed. Words were exchanged, and the next thing fists were flying.'

'Are you hurt?'

Immanuel shrugged. 'My arm hurts, but I doubt it's broken.'

'You haven't been to the hospital?'

'No need.'

'Have you spoken to the police?'

'The police have spoken to me.'

'Have they charged anyone?'

'Yes. Me.'

'You!'

'Well, they're thinking about it, anyway. Depends on the other guys.'

'Why would they think of charging you? Has the world gone mad?'

At that moment Blaise came into the room with coffee for them all. Finkler looked at her in wild alarm.

'I was there,' she said. 'Your mad son started it.'

'How do you mean "started it"?'

'This is not an oral examination, Dad,' Immanuel said from the bed. He had gone back to reading his magazine. Let his father and his sister sort it out. Her fault for calling him in the first place.

'Blaise, you told me there'd been an anti-Semitic incident. How do you *start* with anti-Semites? Do you jump up and down and say "I'm a Jew, come and get me"?'

'He didn't have a go at anti-Semites. You have it the wrong way round.'

'What are you saying, the wrong way round?'

'They were Jews.'

'Who were Jews?'

'The people he picked a fight with.'

'Immanuel picked a fight with Jews?'

'They were Zionists. The real meshuggeners with black hats and fringes. Like settlers.'

'Settlers? In Oxford?'

'Settler types.'

'And he picked a fight with them? What did he say?'

'Nothing much. He accused them of stealing someone else's country . . .'

She paused.

'And?'

'And practising apartheid . . .'

'And?'

'And slaughtering women and children.'

'And?'

'There is no and. That's all.'

'That's all? That's all he said? Immanuel, you said all this?'

Immanuel looked up. He reminded Finkler of his late wife, challenging him. He had that same expression of ironic unillusionedness that comes with knowing a person too well. 'Yes, that's what I said. It's true, isn't it? You've said as much yourself.'

'Not specifically, to a person, Immanuel. It's one thing to iterate a general political truth, it's another thing to pick a fight with a person in the street.'

'Well, I'm not a philosopher, Dad. I don't iterate general political truths. I just told them all what I thought of them and their shitty little country and called one of them, who came up to me, a racist.'

'A racist? What had he said to you?'

'Nothing. It wasn't about him. I was talking about his country.'

'Was he an Israeli?'

'How do I know? He wore a black hat. He was there to oppose the motion.'

'Did that make him a racist?'

'Well, what would you call it?'

'I can think of other words.'

'I can think of other words, too. But we weren't playing Scrabble.'

'And then what happened?'

'And then I knocked his hat off.'

'You knocked a Jew's hat off.'

'Is that so terrible?'

'Jesus Christ, of course it's so terrible. You don't do that to anyone, least of all a Jew.'

'Least of all a Jew! What? Are we a protected species now or something? These are people who bulldoze Palestinian villages. What's a hat?'

'Did you hurt him?'

'Not enough.'

'This is a racist assault, Immanuel.'

'Dad, how can it be a racist assault when they're the racists?'

'I'm not even going to answer that.'

'Do I look like a racist? Look at me.'

'You look like a fucking little anti-Semite.'

'How can I be an anti-Semite? I'm a Jew.'

Finkler looked at Blaise. 'How long has this shit been going on?' he asked.

'How long has he been a fucking little anti-Semite? It comes and goes, depending on what he's been reading.'

'Are you telling me this is my fault? He won't have got any of this racist/apartheid crap from me. I don't go there.'

Blaise met his stare evenly. In her eyes, too, he saw his avenging wife.

'No, I'm not telling you that. I doubt he reads a word you write, actually. But there are plenty of other people he can read.'

'I also have a mind of my own,' Immanuel said.

'I doubt that,' Finkler said. 'I doubt you can call what you've got a mind at all.'

Had he known how to do such a thing, and had he not made a solemn promise to Tyler, he would have pulled his son off the bed and broken his other arm.

2

As Assistant Curator of the Museum of Anglo-Jewish Culture, Julian Treslove did not exactly have too much on his plate. It would be different when it was up and running, Hephzibah assured him, but in these early stages it was all about architects and electricians. The best Treslove could do for the museum, and for her, was ruminate. Think of who and what else they should be honouring. A suggestion which she no sooner made than she regretted. It wasn't fair to him. Jews might have been possessed of a crowded almanac of Jewish event, a Jewish Who's Who extending back to the first man and woman, but Treslove couldn't be expected to know in every instance Who Was and Who Was Not, Who Had Changed His Name, Who Had Married In or Out. What is more he would have no instinct for it. Some things you cannot acquire. You have to be born and brought up a Jew to see the hand of Jews in everything. That or be born and brought up a Nazi.

The museum was housed in a high-Victorian Gothic mansion built on the design of a Rhineland fortress. It had pointed gables, mock castellations, fantasy chimneys and even a rampart you couldn't get out on to. To the side was a pretty garden in which Hephzibah imagined they would one day serve teas.

'Jewish teas?' Libor had asked.

'What's a Jewish tea?' Treslove wondered.

'It's like an English tea only there's twice as much of it.'

'Libor!' Hephzibah scolded him.

But the idea of serving specifically Jewish afternoon teas appealed to Treslove who had learned to call cakes *kuchen*, and crêpes stuffed with cream or jam *blintzes*.

'Let me write the menu,' he said. And Hephzibah agreed he could.

His only worry was that the location of the museum would prohibit the sort of passing trade you needed for a successful tea garden, or for a museum, come to that. It was only a short walk from the Beatles' old studios but it wasn't a walk you would naturally take. Parking would not be easy. There were yellow lines everywhere, and because of the slight incline in the road on which the Rhineland fortress had been built buses laboured at that very spot, distracting motorists who might have been searching for the museum. Plus there were over-hanging trees.

'People just won't see it,' he warned Hephzibah. 'Or they'll crash looking.'

'Well, that's helpful,' she said. 'What would you like me to do, have the road flattened?'

Treslove saw himself standing outside in his curator's uniform, waving down the traffic.

He had another worry which he chose not to express. Vandalism. It was licensed hereabouts. Just about everyone who visited the Abbey Road Studios wrote messages on the outside walls. Mostly these were good-natured – *So-and-So loves so-and-so, We all live in a yellow submarine, Rest in peace, John!* – but one day when Treslove was passing he noticed a new aerosoled graffito in Arabic script. Perhaps it too was a message of love – *Imagine there's no countries, it isn't hard to do* – but what if it was a message of hate – *Imagine there's no Israel, imagine there's no Jew . . . ?*

That he had no reason to suppose any such thing, he knew. Which was partly why he kept his suspicions to himself. But the Arab script looked angry. It was like a scribble over everything else that had been written on the walls, a refutation of the spirit of the place.

Or did he imagine that, too?

Though he was sensitive to condescension, Hephzibah's suggestion that the best thing he could do for her right now was ruminate suited him just fine. There was much to think about and he was happy to think about it in a semi-professional capacity. Sometimes he thought about it at home, in an office Hephzibah had made for him from a room where she stored the Hampstead Bazaar shawls she had essentially finished with but didn't quite want to throw away. (Treslove was pleased to observe that when it came to a choice between him and the shawls, the shawls lost.) At other times he thought about what there was to think about in the as-yet-unfinished museum library – the advantage of that being the access he had to Jewish books. The disadvantage being the hammering of carpenters and the suspect graffiti he had to read on the way.

In the end he stayed in the shawl room. Or sat and read on the terrace with its view of Lord's. And to the left, a few buildings along, a view of a synagogue, or at least a view of its courtyard. He had hoped he would see bearded Jews singing and dancing here, carrying their children on their shoulders, ceremonially cutting their hair in the way he'd seen in a television documentary, or arriving solemnly for a festival, their prayer shawls under their arms, their eyes turned towards God. But it seemed not to be that sort of synagogue. Either he looked at the wrong times, or the only person using the synagogue was a burly Jew (he looked like Topol, that's how Treslove knew he was a Jew) who came and went on a big black motorbike. Treslove didn't know if he was the caretaker – he had too much swagger for a caretaker – or the rabbi – but he didn't look much like a rabbi either. It wasn't just the motorbike that counted against the rabbi proposition, it was the fact that he wore a PLO scarf which he would wind around his face, like a warrior going into battle, before putting on his helmet and roaring off on his bike.

Day after day, Treslove sat on the terrace and looked out for the Jew on the motorbike. This became so obvious that day after day the Jew on the motorbike looked out for Treslove. He glowered up, Treslove glowered down. Why was he wearing a PLO scarf, Treslove wanted to know. And not just wearing it but swathing himself in it as though it and it alone defined his identity. In a synagogue!

Treslove accepted that under Libor's tutelage he had grown obsessive about the PLO scarf. It frightened him. Whatever its innocent origins as a headdress ideally suited to a cruel climate – Abraham and Moses, presumably, would have worn something like – it had taken on a huge symbolic significance, no matter that the PLO was now, as Libor explained to him, the least of Isrrrae's worries. To wear it was to make an aggressive statement, regardless of the rights and wrongs of the situation. Fine, if you were a Palestinian, Libor always said; a Palestinian had a right under all the laws of grievance to his aggression. But on an Englishman it only ever denoted that greed for someone else's cause, wedded to a nostalgia for simplicities that never were, that was bound to make a refugee from the horrors of leftism shudder. So Treslove, who was a refugee only from Hampstead, shuddered along with him.

But this ageing biker who couldn't wait to muffle himself in a PLO scarf was not just one more English ghoul feeding on the corpses of the oppressed, he was a Jew, and what is more he was a Jew who seemed to have made his home in a Jewish house of prayer! Explain that, Libor. But Libor couldn't. 'We have become a sick people,' was all he said.

In the end Treslove had no choice but to ask Hephzibah, whom he had wanted to spare.

'Oh, I make a point of never looking there,' she told him when he at last mentioned what he'd been watching for the last however many weeks.

She made the place sound like Sodom, which one cast an eye over at one's peril.

'Why?' he asked. 'What else goes on there?'

'Oh, I doubt anything goes on. But they do parade their humanity a bit.'

'Well, I'm all for humanity,' Treslove was quick to make clear.

'I know you are, darling. But the humanity they parade is largely on behalf of whoever isn't us. By *us*, I mean . . .'

Treslove waved away her awkwardness. 'I know who you mean. But couldn't they do that without going so far as to wear that scarf? Can't you want better of your own without actually cheering on your enemy? By *your*, I mean . . .'

She kissed the back of his head. Meaning, he had a lot to learn.

So he sat at home and tried to learn it. He felt that Hephzibah preferred it that way, not having him under her feet in the museum. And he preferred it that way too, guarding the apartment while she was out, being a proud Jewish husband, breathing in the smell of her, waiting for her to come home, sighing a bit with the excess weight she carried, her silver rings jingling like a belly dancer's on her fingers.

He liked the hopeful way she would call his name the moment she let herself in. 'Julian! Hello!' It made him feel wanted. When the others used to call his name it was in the hope that he was out.

It was a relief to hear her. It meant he could call it a day with his education. He wished he had done a module or two in Jewish Studies at university. Perhaps one on the Talmud, and one on the Kabbalah. And maybe another on why a Jew would wear a PLO scarf. Starting from scratch was not easy. Libor had suggested he learn Hebrew and was even able to recommend a teacher, a remarkable person almost ten years older than he was and with whom he sometimes enjoyed a leisurely lemon tea at Reuben's restaurant on Baker Street.

'By leisurely I mean it takes him three hours to drink it through a straw,' Libor explained. 'He taught me the little Hebrew I know in Prague before the Nazis turned up. You'll have to go to him, and you might not be able to understand much of what he's telling you, his accent is still pretty thick, he came from Ostrava originally – he certainly won't be able to hear you, by the way, so there's no point in your asking him anything – and you'll have to put up with the odd neck spasm – his, I mean, not yours – and he'll cough over you a lot, and maybe even shed a tear or two, remembering his wife and children, but he speaks a beautiful classical pre-Israeli Hebrew.'

But Treslove considered Hebrew, even if he could find someone to teach him who was still alive, to be beyond him. It was more history he wanted. In the history of ideas sense. And the knack of thinking Jewishly. For this Hephzibah recommended Moses Maimonides' *The Guide for the Perplexed*. She hadn't read it herself, but she knew it to be a highly regarded text of the twelfth century, and since Treslove owned himself to be perplexed and in need of a guide, she didn't see how he could do any better.

'You're sure you don't just want me out of your hair?' he checked, once he'd seen the contents page and the size of the print. It looked like one of those books which you started as a child and finished in an old persons' home lying in a bed next to Libor's Hebrew teacher.

'Look, as far as I'm concerned you're perfect as you are,' she told him. 'I love you perplexed. This is what you keep saying you want.'

'You sure you love me perplexed?'

'I adore you perplexed.'

'What about uncircumcised?'

It was a subject to which he frequently returned.

'How often must I tell you,' Hephzibah told him. 'All that's immaterial to me.'

'All *that*?'

'Immaterial.'

'Well, it isn't exactly immaterial to me, Hep.'

He offered to talk to someone. It was never too late. She wouldn't hear of it. 'It would be barbaric,' she said.

'And if we have a son?'

'We aren't planning to have a son.'

'But if we do?'

'That would be different.'

'Ah, so what would be good for him, would not be good for me. Already, there are competing criteria of maleness in this house.'

'What's maleness got to do with it?'

'That's my question.'

'Well, go and get yourself an answer from some higher authority. Read Moses Maimonides.'

He dreaded getting so far with Maimonides and then suddenly hitting that blank wall of incomprehension that awaited him at about the same point, even at about the same page, in every work of philosophy he had ever tried to read. It was so lovely, bathing in the lucidities of a thinker's preliminary thoughts, and then so disheartening when the light faded, the water turned brackish, and he found himself drowning in mangrove and sudd. But this didn't happen with Maimonides. With Maimonides he was drowning by the end of the first sentence.

'Some have been of opinion,' Maimonides began, 'that by the Hebrew *zelem*, the shape and figure of a thing is to be understood, and this explanation led men to believe in the corporeality [of the Divine Being]: for they thought that the words "Let us make man in our *zelem*" (Gen. i. 26), implied that God had the form of a human being, i.e., that He had figure and shape, and that, consequently, He was corporeal.'

Of themselves, Treslove believed he might have made some headway with these refined distinctions relating to the appearance, or not, of the divine, but first he had to ascertain the exact status of the word *zelem* and at that point he was among the mystics and the dreamers. OK, literally the word meant what Maimonides said it meant, an image or a likeness, but it had a strange disquieting sound to Treslove's ear, almost like a magic incantation, and when he tried to track down those with whose 'opinion' Maimonides was arguing – for one needed to know the extent of one's perplexity in order to be guided out of it – he found himself in a world where commentary was piled upon commentary, striations of reference and disagreement as old as the universe itself – until there was no knowing who was arguing with whom, or why. If man was indeed made in the *zelem* of God, then God must have been incomprehensible to Himself.

This religion is too old for me, Treslove thought. He felt like a child lost in a dark forest of decrepit lucubrations.

Hephzibah noticed that a mood of despondency had fallen on him. She put it down at first to his not having enough to do. 'Another few months and we'll be up and running,' she said.

What exactly Treslove's responsibilities were going to be when the museum was up and running had never properly been discussed. Sometimes Treslove imagined he would be a sort of Anglo-Jewish culture maître d', welcoming people to the museum, showing them the way to the exhibits, explaining what they were looking at – the Anglo as well as the Jewish – exhibiting in himself that spirit of free unschismatic enquiry and cross-cultural interchange the museum existed to foster. And it was possible that Hephzibah had not progressed beyond that idea herself.

The question of what precisely Treslove was for – whether in the professional, the religious or indeed the marital sense – remained to be addressed.

'Everything all right between you?' Libor had asked his great-great-niece early on.

'Perfect,' she had told him. 'I believe he loves me.'

'And you?'

'The same. He needs a bit of looking after, but then so do I.'

'I'm very fond of you both,' he said. 'I want you to be happy.'

'We should be half as happy as you and Aunt Malkie were,' Hephzibah said.

Libor patted her hand and then fell vacant.

Hephzibah was worried about him. But as Treslove noticed the day she helped him with the Four Questions, worrying over men came naturally to her. It was another of those Finkler traits that he admired. Finkler women knew that men were fragile. Just Finkler men or all men? He wasn't sure. But he was the beneficiary of her concern either way. Seeing him in low spirits, she would gather him into her arms, graze him accidentally with her rings – it hurt, but what the hell! – and hide him away in her shawls. The symbolism wasn't lost on him. When his actual mother had found him downcast she would peck him on the cheek and give him an orange. It wasn't love he'd lacked, it was envelopment. Wrapped around in Hephzibah he knew true peace. It was better there – inside her in the non-erotic sense, though it wasn't without its eroticism – than anywhere he'd ever been before.

'You're not having second thoughts?' she asked, seeing him slumped in an armchair looking heavenwards.

'About us, absolutely not.'

'About what then?'

'Yours is a tough religion,' he said.

'Tough? It's you that's always saying how full of love we are.'

'Intellectually tough. You keep going off into metaphysics.'

'I do?'

'Not you specifically, your faith. It does my head in, as one of my sons says, just don't ask me which.'

'That's because you insist on understanding it. You should try just living it.'

'But I don't know what parts to live.'

'Maimonides not helping?'

He pulled a weary face. 'I guess no one ever promised that the process of being unperplexed would be easy.'

But secretly he wondered if the task was beyond him. He felt sorry for Hephzibah. Had he passed himself off as something he could never be? He was in danger of reverting to type and picturing only one end to this – Hephzibah dying in his arms while he told her how much he adored her. Verdi and Puccini played in his head, even as he ploughed on with Moses Maimonides. *The Guide for the Perplexed* became a romantic opera for him, ending the way all the operas he loved ended, with Treslove onstage alone, sobbing. Only this time as a Jew.

That's if he ever made it as a Jew.

He stumbled blindly from one chapter to another. 'Of the divine Names composed of Four', 'Twelve and Forty-two Letters', 'Seven Methods by which the Philosophers sought to Prove the Eternity of the Universe', 'Examination of a passage from Pirke di-Rabbi Eliezer in reference to Creation'.

And then he got on to circumcision and found himself galvanised into thought.

'As regards circumcision,' Maimonides had written, 'I think that one of its objects is to limit sexual intercourse.'

He read it again.

'As regards circumcision, I think that one of its objects is to limit sexual intercourse.'

And then again.

But we don't have to follow him through every reading.

As a matter of course he read every sentence of Maimonides a minimum of three times, but that was to seek clarity. Here was no obfuscation in need of conscientious penetration. Circumcision, Moses Maimonides argued, 'counteracts excesssive

239

lust', 'weakens the power of sexual excitement' and 'sometimes lessens the natural enjoyment'.

Such a claim merited reading and rereading simply for itself. And indeed for himself, if he was ever to get to the bottom of who Finklers were and what they really wanted.

Among the many thoughts that crowded into Treslove's mind was this one: did it mean he'd been having a better time than Finkler – Sam Finkler himself – all along? At school Finkler had boasted of his circumcision. 'With one of these beauties you can go for ever,' he had said. And Treslove had countered with what he'd read, and with what made perfect sense to him, that Finkler had lost the most feeling part of himself. A verdict in which Moses Maimonides unequivocally concurred. Not only had Finkler lost the most feeling part of himself, it had been taken from him precisely in order that he should not feel what Treslove felt.

A great sadness, on behalf of Tyler, suddenly welled up in him. He had enjoyed her more than Finkler had. No question of it. He had the wherewithal to enjoy her more with.

But did it follow from that that she had enjoyed him more than she had enjoyed Finkler? He had not thought so at the time. 'No woman will want to touch yours,' Finkler had warned him at school, and Tyler's apparent reluctance to look at him seemed to bear that out. But was it a reluctance or was it a kind of holy dread? Did she fear to look upon what gave her so much pleasure? Had he been a godhead to her?

For what gave him more pleasure must surely have given her more pleasure too. A man made reluctant by his circumcision would logically communicate that reluctance to his partner. The 'weakened power of sexual excitement' had to work both ways. What counteracted 'excessive lust' in the one had to counteract 'excessive lust' in the other, else there was no point in it. Why maim the man to limit sexual intercourse if the woman went on demanding it as fervently as ever?

Indeed, Maimonides said as much. 'It is hard for a woman, with whom an uncircumcised had sexual intercourse, to separate from him.' Women had not found it hard to separate from Treslove, but that could have been attributable to other causes. And initially he had always done reasonably well – 'If you think I'm going to let you fuck me on our first date you've got another think coming,' they had said to him, letting him fuck them on their first date – which suggested it was what they later discovered about him as a person that was the problem, not the prepuce.

He felt possessed of a thrilling power he had never known was his. He was the *uncircumcised*. From whom women found it hard to separate.

Physically hard to separate, did Maimonides mean, in that the uncircumcised somehow knotted inside the woman like a dog? Or emotionally, in that the uncircumcised's untiring lustfulness besotted her?

Both, he decided.

He was the *uncircumcised*, and he had spoken. Both.

In retrospect, he fell in love with Tyler all over again, knowing now that she must have loved him more than she could ever admit. And had been afraid to look upon that which made her wanton.

Poor Tyler. Besotted with him. Or at least besotted with his dick.

And poor him for missing out on that exquisite knowledge at the time.

If only he'd known.

If only he'd known, what then? He wasn't sure. Just if only he'd known.

But it wasn't all regret. He was also excited by this discovery of his own erotic power. Lucky Hephzibah at least.

Unless his untiring lustfulness both wearied and disgusted her. And as a matter of ethno-religious principle she would have preferred him snipped.

He rang Finkler.

'You ever read Moses Maimonides?' he asked.

'Is that the purpose of your call?'

'That and to enquire how you are.'

'I've been better, thank you.'

'And Moses Maimonides?'

'I guess he's been better too. But have I read him? Of course. I count him as among my inspirations.'

'I didn't think you found Jewish thought inspiring.'

'Then you think wrong. He teaches how to make abstruse thought available to the intelligent layman. He is all along saying more than he appears to say. We plough the same furrow, he and I.'

Oh yeah, Treslove thought – *Guide for the Perplexed* and *John Duns Scotus and Self-Esteem: a Manual for the Menstruating*.

But what he said was, 'So what do you reckon to what he says about circumcision?'

Finkler laughed. 'Why don't you just come right out with it, Julian? Hephzibah wants you to have it done – yes? Well, I wouldn't stand in her way. But between ourselves – ha! – I think you might be a wee bit old. As I recall, Maimonides warns against it past the eighth day. So that's you out. Just.'

'No, Hephzibah does not want me to have it done. She loves me as I am. Why would she not? Maimonides says circumcision limits sexual intercourse. I impose no limits myself.'

'I am pleased to hear it. But is this about you or Moses Maimonides?'

'It's not about me. I simply wonder what you, as a philosopher who ploughs the same furrow, think about Maimonides' theory.'

'That circumcision is to put a brake on sex? Well, it

certainly exists to make us afraid, and making us afraid of sex is part of it.'

'You always told me Jews enjoyed sex inordinately.'

'Did I? That must have been a long time ago. But if you're asking me whether circumcision as a means of inhibiting the sexual impulse is specifically Jewish, I would say not. Anthropologically speaking, it isn't primarily about sex anyway, except in so far as all initiation ceremonies are about sex. It's about cutting the apron strings. What *is* Jewish is interpreting the circumcision rite in the way Maimonides does. It's he – the medieval Jewish philosopher – who would wish us to be more restrained and imagines circumcision as the instrument. But I have to tell you it has never worked on me.'

'Never?'

'Not ever that I recall. And I think I would recall it. But I do know someone who believes himself to have been cheated of pleasure, and is in the process of having the operation reversed.'

'You can have it reversed?'

'Some people think so. Read Alvin Poliakov's blog. You can find it at something like www.ifnotnowwhen.com. Alternatively I can fix you up with an introduction. He's perfectly affable, wants to talk about nothing else, and might even show you his dick if you ask him nicely. Apparently it's progressing. He's halfway to not being a Jew any more.'

'He's one of your ASHamed Jews, presumably.'

'Sure is. You don't get more ashamed than that.'

'You're not ashamed of yours, then?'

'You think I should be?'

'Just asking. You carried it with pride at school.'

'I was probably trying to rile you. I just carry it, Julian. I am a widower. Being circumcised or not does not figure high among my concerns right now.'

'I'm sorry.'

'Don't be. I'm pleased for you that your life is dickcentric at the moment.'

'I'm only speaking philosophically, Sam.'

'I know you are, Julian. I expect nothing less of you.'

Treslove remembered one more question before he rang off. 'As a matter of interest,' he asked, 'are your boys circumcised?'

'Ask them,' Finkler said, putting down the phone.

He had more conversational joy with Libor.

Libor's fears that he would see less of Treslove now that he was no longer single had been unfounded. Any change was in Libor himself. He ventured out less. But he would still occasionally take a taxi to Hephzibah's apartment in the afternoon when Hephzibah was at the museum and the two of them would sit at the kitchen table together drinking white tea.

They both liked it that the ghost of Hephzibah boiling up a witches' coven of cauldrons in which to cook a single egg inhabited the space. They breathed her in and smiled at each other with the knowledge of her, incorrigible wifelovers that they were.

Libor was now walking with a stick. 'It's come to this,' he said.

'It suits you,' Treslove said. 'It suggests old Bohemia. You should get one with a blade in the handle.'

'To protect myself against the anti-Semites?'

'Why you? I'm the one who gets attacked.'

'Then you get a stick with a blade in it.'

'Speaking of which,' Treslove said, 'where do you stand on circumcision?'

'Uncomfortably,' Libor said.

'Has it been a problem to you?'

'It would have been a problem to me had it been a problem to Malkie. But she never said anything. Should she have?'

'It hasn't stopped you enjoying sex?'

'I think what you carry around would have stopped me enjoying sex. Don't get me wrong – on you I'm sure it looks wonderful, but on me it wouldn't have looked so good. Aesthetically I have nothing to complain about. I look the way I'm supposed to look. Or I did. It is aesthetics we're talking?'

'No, not really. I've been reading that circumcision reduces sexual excitation. I'm canvassing opinion.'

'Well, it will certainly reduce yours if you decide to have it done at your age. As for me, I have never known any different. And I've never thought to complain. To be candid with you, I wouldn't have wanted to be any more sexually excited than I've been. It's been plenty, thank you. In fact, more than enough. Does that answer your question?'

'Yes, I suppose it does.'

'You only suppose it does?' He saw Treslove looking at him narrowly. 'I know what you're thinking,' he said.

'What am I thinking?'

'You're thinking I protest too loudly. Had I not been circumcised, you're thinking, I wouldn't have found it so easy to resist Marlene Dietrich. You're too polite to say so but you're wondering whether it was only God's covenant with Abraham that kept me away from the Hun.'

'Well, you have always claimed you were the most faithful of husbands, despite facing temptations most men can't begin to comprehend . . .'

'And you're asking if it was having a desensitised penis that kept me faithful?'

'I would never put it so grossly, Libor.'

'Except that you just have.'

'Forgive me.'

Libor sat back in his chair and rubbed his head. A melancholy smile from somewhere very far away lit up his face. An old smile.

'This is my own fault,' he said. 'Perhaps I've been too

anxious to promote a particular view of myself, and perhaps you've been too ready to believe it. I ask this one favour of you: in the report you give of me when I am gone, speak of me as a loving husband but don't make me too chaste. Allow me at least one errant little fuck.'

'Regarding that errant little fuck,' he said before he left. He wanted Treslove to understand that he'd been thinking and worrying about what he'd said.

'Yes?'

'It's for Malkie, too, I ask it.'

Treslove blushed. 'Are you telling me that Malkie . . . ?'

'No, not that I would ever know or want to know. I mean it's her reputation, too, I ask you to protect. A woman shouldn't be married to a totally faithful man all her life.'

'Why not?'

'It demeans her.'

Treslove blushed again, this time for himself. 'I don't understand that, Libor,' he said.

Libor kissed his cheek and said no more.

But Treslove read his silence. 'You don't understand because you're not one of us,' he read.

4

As a rule, Hephzibah took a shower the moment she returned home from the museum. It was still something of a building site over there and she was unable to relax until she had washed the dust and the grime from her. She would shout to Treslove to let him know she was home, and either he would pour a glass of wine for them both – she liked the gesture of his pouring for her but she rarely touched a drop – or, if he was more Priapus than Bacchus that evening, he would join her in the shower.

It wasn't always what she wanted. A shower was a private place to Hephzibah, not least as she took up most of the available room in it. But she was careful not to rebuff Treslove's ardour, and was sometimes grateful for the massage he would give her when it became plain that she was looking for nothing else.

'Oh, that's good,' she would say, and he enjoyed feeling her back relax under his fingers in the hot spray.

There was something about the way she pronounced the word 'good', in reference to whatever he was doing to her – whether in the phrase 'Oh, that's good', or 'Oh, that's so good', or 'That's good of you' or 'You're very good to do that' – that made Treslove feel he had found his niche as a man.

As a man?

Well, he knew that she was always just a fraction away from saying, as he was just a fraction away from hearing, 'Who's a good boy?' A rhetorical question beloved of dogs and children. He made no bones about this to himself. She ran the show, and he was happy with the arrangement. But it wasn't only the mother or the dog walker that he looked up to in her. It was – not to allow this to become too fanciful – the creative Jewish force: if you like, the Creator herself. *And God called the dry land Earth; and the gathering together of the waters called he Seas: and God saw that it was good.*

Good in that sense was what Treslove heard when Hephzibah praised his efforts. *Good* meaning more than good – *good* meaning congruent, perfected, harmonious.

Good as an expression of the absolute rightness of the universe.

He had been a man of misadventures and now he was a man of congeniality. Everything fitted. He was a good man in a good world. With a good woman.

What was good about her kept changing the longer he was with her. He had thought of it as a Finkler thing at first. A matter of fecundity, though not in the offspring sense. A fecundity of affection and loyalty, a fecundity of friends and family, a fecundity of past and future. Alone, Treslove felt himself spinning pointlessly around the universe like a fragment of a forgotten planet. Hephzibah was his firmament. His Finkler firmament. He had a place in her. He felt populous in her orbit.

Whether this was, after all, a Finkler thing he didn't know. Drop the Finkler, then. What she was to him was *humanly* important, whatever that meant. And he idolised her for it. The sun did not shine out of her, the sun *was* her.

So go tell him he wasn't Jewish.

And then one evening she came home, sat down at the kitchen table, not only asked him for a drink but drank it, and burst into tears.

He went to put his arms around her but she gestured him away.

'My God,' he said, 'what is it?'

She covered her face and shook, though whether it was with grief or laughter he couldn't tell.

'Hep, what is it?'

When she showed him her face he still couldn't tell if something too terrible to express had happened, or something laughable beyond words.

She collected herself, requested another glass of wine – the wine really did disturb him: two glasses of wine was for Hephzibah a year's ration – and told him.

'You know the oak doors that have just been fitted? Perhaps you don't. They're the external doors to the side entrance. To where your tea rooms will eventually be. I showed you photographs of the brass handles which we've had made to resemble shofars – rams' horns – remember? Right, well, don't get a shock, but they've been defaced. It must have happened while I was inside with the architect late this afternoon because they were fine when I popped out for lunch, but when I left the building tonight, there it was, or rather there *they* were. I mean, for fuck's sake, Julian, why would anyone do that? Why?'

Swastikas, Treslove thought. He had read about the swastikas reappearing everywhere. He had told Finkler about them and Finkler had said ring me back when they're killing Jews in the streets again. Fucking swastikas!

'So what were they?' he asked. 'Painted on?'

He dreaded hearing blood. Blood and faeces were favourite. Blood and faeces and sperm. Hephzibah had already received a couple of letters written in blood and shit.

'I haven't finished telling you.'

'Then tell me.'

'It was bacon.'

'It was what?'

'It was bacon. They — I'm assuming *they* — had wrapped rashers of bacon around the handles. Two or three packets of them   so no expense spared.'

She seemed about to cry again.

He went over to her, determinedly this time. 'That's terrible,' he said. 'How vile!'

She shook behind her hands.

He put his arms around her. 'Christ,' he said, 'who are these people? It makes you want to kill them.'

It was then he realised she was laughing.

'It's only bacon,' she said.

'Only bacon?'

'I'm not saying it's nice. You're right, it's vile. The desire to do it is vile. But it's such a feeble gesture. What do they think we're going to do? Pack up and go home? Scrap the plans because of a few rashers of bacon? Sell the site? Leave the country? It's too absurd. You have to see the funny side.'

Treslove tried. 'I suppose you do,' he said. 'Yes, you're quite right. It's laughable.' And he tried a laugh as well.

Hephzibah dried her tears. 'On the other hand,' she said, 'it makes you wonder what's going on out there. You read things like this happening in Berlin in the twenties and you think why didn't they read the signs and get out.'

'Perhaps because they never really believed them,' Treslove said. 'Perhaps because they tried to see the funny side.'

He had turned solemn again.

Hephzibah sighed. 'In St John's Wood,' she said, 'of all places.'

'Nowhere's safe now,' Treslove said, remembering what had been done to him, virtually on the doorstep of the BBC.

You Ju.

They both fell silent, each picturing the hordes of anti-Semites marauding through the West End of London.

Then Hephzibah began to laugh. She saw the rashers of bacon wrapped painstakingly around the ram-horn handles. And the plugs of meat and fat, which she hadn't got round to telling him about, stuffed into the keyholes of the doors. She imagined the vandals going into Marks & Spencer and buying what they needed, paying at the till, perhaps using a reward card, and then, like vigilantes, vigilantes armed with bacon, the greatest defilement they could conceive, descending on the Museum of Anglo-Jewish Culture, which didn't have signs up yet, and so which strictly couldn't even be said to exist.

'It isn't just their overestimation of our horror of the pig,' she said, wiping her eyes. 'I'm sure, for example, they don't know how much I love a bacon sandwich, but it isn't only that, it's their exaggeration of our presence. They find us before we find ourselves. Nowhere is safe from them because they think nowhere is safe from us.'

Treslove couldn't keep up with the fluctuations of her feelings. She wasn't, he realised, going from fear to amusement and back again, she was experiencing both emotions simultaneously. It wasn't even a matter of reconciling opposites because they were not opposites for her. Each partook of the other.

He didn't know how to do what she did. He didn't possess the emotional flexibility. And wasn't sure he wanted to. Wasn't there an irresponsibility in it? It was as though he were to laugh at the moment Violetta dies in Alfredo's arms. A thought he found unthinkable even as he tried to think it.

Not for the first time in recent days, Treslove felt he'd failed a test.

NINE

I

Libor's mind was turning fetid. That was his own verdict.

In the first months following Malkie's death he had found the melancholy of his mornings unbearable. He woke hoping to discover her. He imagined he saw the sheets stir on her side of the bed. He spoke to her. He opened her wardrobe doors and imagined helping her to choose clothes. If he put an outfit together in his mind, perhaps she would emerge in it.

Everything he remembered was painful by virtue of its sweetness. But now the pain was of another kind. So many bad things had happened to them, between them, as a consequence of them. He had angered her parents. He had robbed her of a musical career. They had failed to have a child, no unbearable loss for either of them, but there'd been a miscarriage which upset them precisely because it didn't. She hadn't travelled to Hollywood with him, not liking aeroplanes or caring to make new acquaintances. The only company she wanted, she told him, was his. Only he interested her. But now he came to think of it, hadn't that been awful for her, and an intolerable burden on him? He had been lonely without her. He was subjected to temptations he would have overcome with less ado had she been with him. And he dared never fail her, whether as an indefatigable companion who came home from his travels with wonderful stories to tell, as a man who would return her love and show her it had not been wasted, or as a husband bound at every turn to justify her complete confidence in him.

None of these thoughts turned him against her. But they changed the atmosphere around the memory of her, as though a golden halo had – no, not slipped but darkened. This might be for the best, he thought. Nature's way of helping him through. But what if he didn't want to be helped through? Who was nature to decide!

And worst of all were the black events he kept recalling, which had spoilt their life together whether they'd known it at the time or not. There was a Yiddish phrase his parents had used and which he thought meant 'long ago'. *Ale shvartse yom* – all the black years. All those black years were now *their* black years – his and Malkie's. The events that marred them were the anti-myths of their romance, peopled by monsters, proving that they had not lived in paradise together at all, but – through no fault of their own – in a place that was more like hell.

Malkie's parents, the guttural Hofmannsthals, had been property-owning German Jews. For Libor – whose politics were hopelessly, Czechoslovakianly confused – this made them on two accounts the worst kind of Jews of all. They had been so disappointed in her choice of husband they had all but disowned her, treating Libor as though he were dirt beneath their feet, refusing to attend their wedding, demanding he stay away from every family function, including funerals. 'What do they think I'm going to do, dance on their graves?' he asked her.

They were right to worry. He would have.

And what was his sin? Being too poor for her. Being a journalist. Being a Sevcik, not a Hofmannsthal, being a Czech Jew, not a German Jew.

They couldn't entirely disown her. They had to will their property to someone. They left her a small block of flats in Willesden. Willesden! Anyone would have thought from their exclusivism, Libor thought, that they were aristocracy, and all they were were fucking landlords of some run-down flats in Willesden.

'It's a good job I'm Jewish,' he told Malkie, 'otherwise your lot would have turned me Fascist.'

'They might have liked you more had you not been Jewish,' Malkie said, meaning had he only been a musician or had property of his own.

'So what did Horowitz have? A dacha in Kiev?'

'He had fame, darling.'

'I have fame.'

'Wrong sort. And you didn't have any sort when I married you.'

But if he despised her German parents and their property he despised even more their tenants on account of whom he and Malkie, as property owners themselves now, had no choice but to soil their souls with commerce. Here was every sort of mean, malingering, whining and thieving human nature. These tenants, to whom he would not in any other circumstance have given shelter, not so much as a cardboard box, knew the letter of every law that might indulge them while breaking every other law there was. They fouled the space they inhabited while they lived there, then stole from it with a minute pettiness – every switch and bulb, every latch and handle, every thread from every carpet – when they left.

Get rid of the whole block was his advice, it isn't worth the vexation. But she felt it tied her to her parents. They had made their lives again in London, and to have sold Willesden would have been to wipe their history out a second time. 'A dirty money-grubbing Jew,' the tenants called her when she did not flinch before their menace. And they were right in that she'd been grubbed and dirtied by her contact with them.

Human vermin, Libor thought, lover of the English though he was. Except that vermin probably honoured their habitations more. Now, in his imagination he conflated these tenant troubles with Malkie's illness, though she had long before done what Libor had suggested and sold them off. How dared

they call a woman in her frail health such names! How horrible for her that at such a time she had to encounter the human
animal at its most repugnant. All the black years. Yes, they'd
been happy together. They'd loved each other. But if they
thought they'd escaped contamination they'd fooled themselves. It was as though black spiders crawled across the belly
of his beautiful beloved Malkie as she slept in the filthy earth.

He called up Emmy and asked her to have breakfast with
him. She was surprised by the request. Why breakfast? In the
morning, he explained, I am at my blackest. And the advantage to me in that? she wondered. None, he said. It's for me.
She laughed.

They met at the Ritz. He had dressed up for her. David
Niven as he lived and breathed. But with the sad defeated
Prague Spring smile of Alexander Dubček.

'You aren't wooing me here again?' she asked.

There was no reason not to. She was an elegant woman
with good legs and Libor had no vows or memories to protect.
The past was infested with black spiders. But he was curious
about her use of the words 'here' and 'again'.

'This was where you brought me last time.'

'For breakfast?'

'Well, for bed and breakfast. I see you have forgotten.'

He apologised. He was about to say it had escaped his
memory, but the expression sounded wrong for the occasion,
as though his memory was a captor of good times. An idea
which she could construe as insulting, if he had allowed this
good time to get away.

'Gone,' he said, touching his head. 'Like just about everything else.'

Had he really brought her here for bed and breakfast? How
could he have afforded the Ritz all those years ago in his
impoverished pre-Malkie days? Unless it was not as long ago
as that, in which case . . . In which case it were better all
memory of it had gone.

Yet how could it have gone?

She gave him time to think what he was thinking – it wasn't hard to tell what he was thinking – then enquired as to the progress of his bereavement counselling.

Bereavement counselling? Then he remembered. 'Gone,' he said, touching his head again.

'I've asked you here,' he said, not giving her time, 'one, because I'm lonely and wanted the company of a beautiful woman, and two, in order to say that I can't do anything.'

She didn't understand.

'I can't do anything about your grandson. Or about that anti-Semite film director. Or whatever else. I can't do anything about any of it.'

She smiled him an understanding smile, putting the fingers of her well-looked-after hands together. Her rings flashed fire under the chandeliers. Ah well. 'If you can't, you can't,' she said.

'Can't and won't,' he said.

She started back as though he'd made to hit her.

A Russian couple at the next table turned to stare at them. 'Won't?'

Libor stared back at the Russians. Clinking oligarch and pale-painted prostitute. But when had Russians ever been anything else?

You don't sit next to a citizen of Prague if you are a Russian and you know what's good for you, Libor thought.

'Won't because there is no point,' he said, turning back to Emmy. 'This is how things are.. And maybe how things should be.'

He was surprised himself by what he said, heard his words as though someone else were speaking them, but still he knew what this other person meant. He meant that as long as there were Jews like Malkie's parents in the world, there would be people to hate them.

Emmy Oppenstein shook her head as though she wanted to rid Libor from it.

'I'll go,' she said. 'I don't know what you want to punish me for – I assure you there isn't anything either of us has done that warrants it – but I understand why it is necessary for you to do so. I hated everyone when Theo died.'

She rose to leave but Libor stayed her. 'Just listen to me for five more minutes,' he said. 'I don't hate you.'

He wondered if the Russians thought he too was an oligarch squabbling with his prostitute, never mind that both of them were in their eighties. What else could the Russian imagination conceive?

Emmy sat down. Libor admired her movements. When she rose from the table it was as a chief justice taking leave of the court. Now she was returned to deliver judgement.

But he admired in a part of his brain that wasn't working properly.

He leaned forward and took her hands. 'I have discovered in myself a profound necessity,' he said, 'to think ill of my fellow Jews.'

He waited.

She said nothing.

He would have liked to see fear or hatred in her eyes, but he saw only a patient curiosity. Maybe not even curiosity. Maybe only patience.

'I don't *wish* ill on them, you understand,' he went on, 'I only *think* ill of them. Which makes it difficult for me to care what happens to them. It's been going on too long. What's that phrase you read sometimes in the papers – compassion fatigue, is it?'

She blinked her eyes at him.

'Except that it never was compassion that I felt. Compassion comes from another place. You can't feel compassionate towards yourself or towards your own. It's more fiercely protective than that. When a Jew was attacked, I was attacked. *These are the generations of Adam* . . . We go back to the same father. I *was* my brother's keeper. But it's too long ago now. Too long ago for us, and too long ago for those who aren't us. There has to be a statute of limitation. That's enough now with the Jew business. Let's not hear from any of you on the subject again, especially from you Jews yourselves. Have a bit of decency. Accept that when your time is up, your time is up.'

He waited, as though to hear her make a speech of acceptance. *Yes, Libor, my time is up.*

She let him wait. And then, in a lowered voice – the Russians, Libor, the Russians are listening – she said, 'But what you're describing is not what you call "thinking ill". I feared you were going to say we get what we deserve. That it is my grandson's fault that he is blinded. The logic of our film director friend. A Jew dispossesses an Arab in Palestine, another Jew must be blinded in London. What the Jewish people sow, the Jewish people will reap. I don't think I hear you saying that.'

Now her hands were holding his.

'My dear wife's parents,' he said, 'who must have had something good in their souls or they would not have produced her, were contemptible people. I can tell you what made them contemptible, I can imagine circumstances way back – let's say hundreds, let's say thousands of years ago – that would have made them something else. But I can't go on making these allowances. I can't go on telling myself that that American swindler who has just been put in jail to serve a hundred life sentences is only coincidentally Jewish, or that bad-faced business Jew we see on television who brags about his money and the ruthlessness of his pursuit of it – I can't convince me, let alone others, that it is only by chance that such men resemble every archetype of Jewish evil that Christian or Muslim history has thrown up. When Jews of this sort enjoy the eminence they do, how can we expect to be left to live in peace? If we are back in the medieval world it is because the medieval Jew himself is back. Did he even go away, Emmy? Or did he survive the rubble of the destruction and the entombments like a cockroach?'

She tightened her hold on his fingers, as though to squeeze this upsetting ugliness out of him.

'I will tell you something,' she said. 'What you see is not what non-Jews see. Not the fair-minded ones and most of them are that. The bad-faced business Jew you refer to, assuming I know who you mean – and it doesn't matter because, yes, of course I know the type – is not the hate figure to Gentiles that he is to you. Some like him, some admire him, some don't bother their heads about him one way or another. You might be surprised to learn how few people see the archetypal Jew every time they see him. Or even know that he's a Jew. Or care. You are the anti-Semite, not they. You're the one who sees the Jew in the Jew. And cannot bear to look. This is about you, Libor.'

He did her the justice of thinking about her words.

'I would not be so quick to see the Jew in the Jew,' he said at last, 'if the Jew in the Jew were not so quick to show himself. Must he talk about his wealth? Must he smoke his cigar? Must he be photographed stepping into his Rolls?'

'We are not the only people to smoke cigars.'

'No, but we are the very people who should not.'

'Ah,' she said.

The sound carried so much force of revelation that Libor thought he heard the Russian and his trollop echo it. As though even they could see him now for what he was.

'*Ah* what?' he said. As much to them as to her.

'Ah, you have given the game away. It is you who say the Jew must live his life differently to others. It is you who would segregate us in your head. We have as much right to our cigars as anyone. You have the Yellow Star mentality, Libor.'

He smiled at her. 'I have lived in England a long time,' he said.

'So have I.'

He allowed her that, before saying, 'You aren't, I hope, accusing me of merely expressing hatred of myself. I have a clever friend of whom that is true. And I am nothing like him. It doesn't pain me that Jews are lording it for a brief period in the Middle East. I am not one of those who is comfortable only when Jews are scattered and under someone else's heel. Which they will be again, anyway, soon enough. This is not about Israel.'

He did not, with Emmy, treble the *r*s or lose the *l*. There was no necessity.

'I know that,' she said.

'I cheer Israel,' he went on. 'It's one of the best things we've done these last two thousand years, or it would have been had Zionism remembered its secular credentials and kept the rabbis away.'

'Then go there. But you won't escape cigar-smoking Jews in Tel Aviv.'

'I wouldn't mind them in Tel Aviv. Tel Aviv is where they should be doing it. But as I have said, this is not about Israel. None of it is about Israel. Not even what most of its critics say about Israel is about Israel.'

'No. So why do you bring it up?'

'Because I am not like my clever friend, the rabid anti-Zionist. I want to think ill of Jews my way, and for my own reasons.'

'Well, you are looking backwards, Libor. I must look forwards. I have grandchildren to be concerned for.'

'Then send them to Sunday school, or a madrasa. I will have no more Jews.'

She shook her head and rose to leave. This time he didn't stop her.

It crossed his mind to ask her to go upstairs with him. It seemed a shame to waste the Ritz.

But it was too late for all that.

On a night he lost in excess of two thousand pounds playing online poker, Finkler went to find himself a prostitute. Perhaps Libor, sitting next to one, had transmitted the thought to him by magic. They were close, no matter that they disagreed about everything.

Finkler was not in need of sex, he was in need of something to do. The only arguments against going with prostitutes that had ever carried any weight with him, as a rational amoralist, were cost and the clap. A man is free to do as he wishes with his body, but you don't impoverish or infect your family in the process. However, when you've lost two thousand pounds playing poker, three hundred more for an hour with a decent-looking prostitute is hardly going to make much difference, philosophically speaking. And as for the clap – there was no one left he could infect.

There was another calculation he had to make. People knew his face. It was unlikely the prostitute would. Prostitutes are working at the time documentaries go out on television. But other men looking for prostitutes might recognise him, and he knew he could not count on any solidarity of the fallen. In minutes he would be up on someone's Facebook as having been seen prowling around Shepherd Market, never mind that the person who had seen him was out prowling himself.

He could have gone to the bar of one of the obvious Park Lane hotels, where the pickup was more discreet, but it was the prowling he liked. Prowling mimicked the fruitless search for the hidden face or memory which was all the pursuit of sexual happiness amounted to. Prowling was romance skinned to the bone. You could prowl and then go home empty-handed and still tell yourself you'd had a good night. A *better* night in Finkler's case, since he couldn't remember ever having found a prostitute he'd liked; but then what he liked was the hidden face or memory whose function was to stay forever hidden. In fact, he wouldn't have said no to a nice Jewish girl with Manawatu Gorge breasts, rather than another of those slender ice-pick Polacks, but he probably wouldn't have said yes to her either.

Which made it safe for him, he thought, to prowl the streets. A man as visibly lukewarm in his desires as he was ran only a minimal risk of being suspected of looking for sex.

So he almost jumped out of his skin when he heard his name called.

'Sam! Uncle Sam!'

The wise thing would have been to ignore the call and keep on walking. But he knew he had jerked his head at the sound of his name, and to have gone on walking then would have been to invite suspicion. He turned round and saw Alfredo standing outside the Market Tavern, at the edge of a crowd of drinkers, sucking on a bottle of Corona.

'Hey, Alfredo.'

'Hey, Uncle Sam. You off somewhere special?'

'Depends what you call special.' Finkler looked at his watch. 'I have to meet my producer any minute. Already a bit late.'

'This another telly series?'

'Well, early stages of.'

'What's this one?'

Finkler let his hands make circles of profound vagueness in the air.

'Oh, Spinoza, Hobbes, free speech, CCTV cameras, all that.'

Alfredo took off his sunglasses, put them back again, and rubbed his neck. Finkler could smell drink on his breath. Was he too out looking for a prostitute? Finkler wondered. And was he drinking to get his courage up?

If so he'd overdone it. No prostitute would go near this amount of courage.

'Do you know what I think about all this surveillance shit, Uncle Sam?' Alfredo said.

Finkler hated it when Alfredo Uncled him. The sarcastic little shit. He looked at his watch. 'Tell me.'

'I think it's a blast. I hope we're being looked at by a camera now. I hope we all are.'

'Why's that, Alfredo?'

'Because we're such lying, cheating, thieving bastards.'

'That's a very bitter analysis. Has someone just done any one of those things to you?'

'Yes, my father.'

'Your father? What's your father done?'

'What hasn't my father done, you mean.'

Finkler wondered if Alfredo was going to fall over, so unsteady was he.

'I thought you were getting on with your father. Didn't you go on holiday with him recently?'

'That was ages ago. And haven't heard a word from him since, though now I hear he's moved in with a woman.'

'Hephzibah, yes. I'm surprised he hasn't told you. No doubt he means to. Is your point that more cameras in the street would have caught him moving in?'

'My point, Uncle Sam, my point, as you call it, is that my father, as you call him, invites friendship one minute and doesn't speak to you the next.'

Finkler thought about saying he knew what Alfredo meant, but suddenly didn't relish the role of playing proxy father. Let Julian sort his kids out himself. 'Julian's got a lot going on in his head at the moment,' he said.

'And a lot in his pants, too, from what I hear.'

'I must go,' Finkler said.

'Me too,' Alfredo said. He nodded, as though to say *coming, coming*, in the direction of a group of young men, a couple of whom, Finkler thought, were wearing Palestinian scarves, though it was hard to tell these days, given that many fashion scarves looked the same and were worn similarly.

He wondered if there'd been a demo earlier that day in

Trafalgar Square. If so, he wondered why he hadn't been invited to address it.

'Then I'll see you when I see you,' he said. 'Where are you playing at the moment?'

'Here, there and everywhere.' He took Finkler's hand and drew him close. 'Uncle Sam, tell me – you're his friend – what's all this Jew shit?'

Slurred, Jew shit came out sounding more like Jesuit, a word which Alfredo would not have known even when sober. The other thing he seemed not to know, or to have forgotten, was that Finkler was Jew shit himself.

'Why don't you ask him?'

'No, but listen – I mean altogether. I've been reading that none of it happened, you understand what I'm saying . . .'

'None of what, Alfredo?'

'That shit. Camps and all that. One big lie.'

'And where have you been reading that?'

'Books, you know. And friends have been telling me. There's this Jewish boogie-woogie drummer I've been play-ing with.' Alfredo played air drums with a pair of imaginary sticks, in case Finkler didn't know what a drummer did. 'It's all bullshit, he says. So why would he say that if it isn't the truth? He was like a soldier in the Israeli army or some shit and now he plays the skins like Gene Krupa. He says it's all bullshit and lies so that we'll look the other way.'

'Look the other way from what?'

'Whatever they're doing there. Concentration camps and shit.'

'Concentration camps? Where are there concentration camps?'

'Wherever, whatever. Nazis, fucking gas chambers, except that none of it happened, right?'

'Happened where?'

'Israel, Germany, I don't fucking know. But it's all –'

'I really must,' Finkler said, freeing himself, 'Or I'll be late

264

for my producer. But listen, don't believe everything people tell you.'

'What do you believe, Uncle Sam?'

'Me? I believe in believing nothing.'

Alfredo made to kiss him. 'That's two of us. I believe in believing nothing either. It's all bullshit. Like that fucking hepcat says.'

He beat the air again with his sticks.

Finkler took a taxi home.

3

Strange, how well you can come to feel you know a person, Treslove thought, from a name, a word, and a few photographs of his penis.

But then Treslove could afford to be generous: he had what Alvin Poliakov, epispasmist, had wanted all his life – a foreskin.

Epispasmos, Treslove learned from Alvin Poliakov's blog, is foreskin restoration. Except, as Alvin Poliakov explains, you cannot restore a foreskin. Once it's gone, it's gone. But it is not beyond the ingenuity of man to conjure up a faux foreskin in its place. This, Alvin Poliakov sits in front of a camera every day to prove.

For interest's sake, and by way of a break from Maimonides, and what with Hephzibah being out often at the moment, attending to problems with the museum, Treslove watches him.

Alvin Poliakov, son of a depressed Hebrew teacher, bachelor, bodybuilder, one-time radio engineer and inventor, founder member of ASHamed Jews, begins his morning by tugging at the loose skin on his penis, easing a little more skin up the shaft. He does this for two hours, breaks for mid-morning tea and a chocolate digestive biscuit, and then begins again. It is a slow, slow process. In the afternoon he takes measurements, collates the morning's data and writes his blog.

'I speak,' he confides to his readers, 'for the millions of mutilated Jews the world over, who feel what I have felt all my life. But not only for Jews, because there are millions of Gentiles out there who have been circumcised under the erroneous medical assumption that you are better without a foreskin than with.'

He doesn't say, *the Jews misleading the world again*, but only an uncomplaining fool, happy to be unforeskinned, could miss the implication.

Alvin Poliakov writes the way cinema newsreel announcers of the 1940s spoke, as though mistrustful of the technology and so shouting to be heard.

'Ever since the dawn of civilisation,' he says, 'men have sought to restore what was stolen from them, in violation of their human rights, before they were old enough to have a say in the matter. What has driven them to do this is a sense of incompletion, a consciousness of something as disabling as amputation.'

He cites the anguish of Jews in classical Greek and Roman society, longing to assimilate and strut their stuff but unable to go to the baths and show other men their penises, for fear of encountering mockery. (How many Jewish men actually wanted to do this? Treslove wonders.) This has led many desperate Jews to seek a remedy in surgery, often with tragic consequences. (Treslove shudders.) The only proven method of restoring an at best passable simulacrum of a foreskin is the one the blogger himself practises.

Behold.

Do not hope for too much. But do not settle for too little. This is Alvin Poliakov's philosophy.

As for the methodology --

Procure a good supply of sticky paper, surgical adhesive, office tape (Treslove finds himself thinking about the

Sellotape with which Josephine, the mother of one of his children, he was not sure he could remember which, repaired her boots), suspender straps, elastic bands, weights and one strong wooden chair.

Every morning Alvin Poliakov photographs his penis from various angles with a view to posting the photographs on the Web later in the afternoon, along with diagrammatic details of the procedures he has followed in the course of the day – the construction of cardboard collars, the application of tape, the lubrication of sore skin, the hours spent slumped forward on his wooden chair coaxing the skin downward, ever downward, and the system of weights he has devised using copper jewellery, keys from a children's xylophone, and a pair of small brass candlesticks, which, he earnestly explains, can be bought cheaply from any good market or shop selling Indian knick-knacks.

Like a monk of self-denial he sits, shaven-headed, pumped-up and muscled, with his head between his knees, a snake charmer who knows the snake will not show himself for years, that's if he shows himself at all. There is no lubricity in the procedure. Whatever sex there once was in Alvin Poliakov's head has long since vanished in the service of the tapes, the adhesives, the collars and the weights. It was because he felt cheated of pleasure that Alvin Poliakov embarked on this course, but pleasure is not the issue any longer. Jews are the issue.

As an accompaniment to the photographs and the diagrams, Alvin Poliakov appends a daily portion of tirade against the Jewish religion in whose anti-service, so to speak, he now expends his energies. The crime of sexual mutilation, he argues, is just one more of the countless offences against humanity to be laid at the gates of the Jews. Every day he publishes the name of another Jewish child, just come into the world, whose integrity has been compromised and whose rights to a full complement of sexual activities have been tragically curtailed.

Where these names come from, Treslove cannot imagine. Have they been lifted from the births and deaths pages of Jewish news-papers? It is impossible to imagine that the guilty parents would have given them to him. In which case isn't Alvin Poliakov himself guilty of stealing from the child what the child is too young to give freely?

Or has he just made them up?

Imperturbable, for he cannot hear Treslove's objections and would not heed them if he could, Alvin Poliakov, breathing like an athlete, coaxes the skin of his penis into a foreskin. Every evening he believes he can see one coming, but every morning it is as though he must start again. Except for those nights when he attends meetings of ASHamed Jews, he does not leave the house. An elderly sister does the shopping for him. She has recently converted to Catholicism. It is not clear whether she is aware of how her brother passes his days, but he is not a man to keep his causes to himself. And she must wonder what he is doing on his wooden chair, tugging at his penis. Though it is possible she misinterprets.

He listens to the radio, noting how rarely the sufferings of mutilated Jews, or Gentiles mutilated as proxy Jews, are referred to. That the BBC has a pro-Jewish bias he does not have the slightest doubt. Why else is there so little heard from those whose lives have been destroyed by Zionists and circumcision?

He wrote an afternoon play about one such life himself. But the BBC, though it thanked him for it, has not put it on. Censorship.

This barbarous ritual, Alvin Poliakov maintains, is analogous to cutting off young men's hair before enrolling them in the army, and serves an identical function. It is to destroy individuality and subjugate every man to the tyranny of the group, whether religious or military. There is irrefutably, therefore, in Alvin Poliakov's view, a direct link between the Jewish ritual of circumcision and Zionist slaughter. The helpless Jewish baby and the unarmed Palestinian become one in the innocent blood that Jews do not scruple to take from both.

While he is sitting with his head between his knees, Alvin Poliakov thinks up dedications to the victims of Zionist brutality. He likes to post a new dedication whenever he can, above the latest photograph of his brutalised penis, thereby hammering home the connection. On the day Treslove decides he won't continue any longer with the blog, the dedication above Alvin Poliakov's penis, from which weights of assorted sizes and materials hang, reads: *To the mutilated of Shatila, Nebateya, Sabra, Gaza. Your struggle is my struggle.*

'Put it this way,' Treslove said, describing the blog to Hephzibah who had declined his offer to email her the link, 'if you were a Palestinian –'

'Absolutely. With friends like him . . .'

'But not just that. It's the appropriation–'

'Absolutely.'

'And in such a trivial cause.'

'Not trivial to him, though, clearly.'

'No, but all other questions aside, aren't Muslims circumcised anyway?'

'As far as I know they are,' she said, turning away, not wishing to encourage him in this new interest.

'So . . . ?'

'Yes, precisely,' she said.

'And yet this Alvin Poliakov receives commendations at least purporting to be from Palestinians.'

'How do you know?'

'He posts them.'

'Darling, you mustn't believe everything you read on the internet. But even if they're genuine it's understandable. We all turn a blind eye to one issue for the sake of another. And these are desperate people.'

'Isn't everybody?'

She told him to close his eyes. Then she kissed them.

'*You* aren't.'

He thought about it. No, he wasn't desperate. But he was agitated.

'This is weird stuff,' he said. 'It makes me feel unsafe.'

'*You* unsafe?'

'Everybody unsafe. What if ideas are like germs? What if we are all being infected? This Alvin Poliakov – hasn't he been infected somewhere along the line?'

'Take no notice,' she said. She was beginning to prepare supper, getting pans out. 'The man's a meshuggener.'

'How can you take no notice? The work of a meshuggener or not, this stuff circulates. It comes from somewhere. It goes somewhere. Opinion doesn't evaporate. It stays in the universe.'

'I don't think that's true. We don't as a society believe today what we believed yesterday. We have abolished slavery. We have given votes to women. We don't bait bears in the public streets.'

'And Jews?'

'Oh, darling, Jews!'

With which she kissed his eyes closed again.

4

She liked him. She definitely liked him. He was a change for her. He seemed without ambition, a lack she had not encountered in her husbands. He listened to her when she talked, which the others hadn't. And he appeared to want to be with her, keeping her in bed in the morning, not for sex – not *only* for sex – and following her around the apartment when she was in, which could have been irritating yet wasn't.

270

But there was a tendency to sudden gloom in him which worried her. And more than that a hunger for gloom, as though there wasn't enough to satisfy him in his own person and he had come to suck out hers. Was that, at bottom, all that his Jewish thing was really about, she wondered, a search for some identity that came with more inwrought despondency than he could manufacture out of his own gene pool? Did he want the whole fucking Jewish catastrophe?

He wasn't the first, of course. You could divide the world into those who wanted to kill Jews and those who wanted to be Jews. The bad times were simply those in which the former outnumbered the latter.

But it was a bloody cheek. Jews proper had to suffer for their suffering; and here was Julian Treslove who thought he could just nip on the roundabout whenever the fancy took him and feel immediately sick.

And she wasn't even sure he liked Jews as much as he claimed to. She didn't doubt his affection for her. He slept inside her skin and kissed her with gratitude the minute he awoke. But she couldn't be the all-in-all Jewess to him he wanted. For a start she wasn't, at least in her own view, anything like Jewish enough. She didn't open her eyes to the world and say Hello, here comes another Jewish day, which she had a feeling was what Julian wanted her to say and hoped he would soon start saying on his own behalf. Hello, here comes another Jewish day, except that . . .

The 'except that' was half the stuff she tried on his insistence to initiate him into. 'I want the ritual,' he had told her, 'I want the family, I want the day-to-day tick-tock of the Jewish clock,' but he was no sooner given it than he backed away. She had taken him to synagogue – not, of course, the synagogue next door where they prayed in PLO scarves – and he hadn't liked it. 'All they do is thank God for creating them,' he complained. 'But what's the point of being created if all you do with your life is thank God for it?'

She had taken him to Jewish weddings and engagements and bar mitzvahs but he hadn't liked those either. 'Not serious enough,' was his complaint.

'You want them to be thanking God more?'

'Maybe.'

'You are hard to please, Julian.'

'That's because I'm Jewish,' he said.

And though he raved like a madman about Jewish family and Jewish warmth, the moment she introduced him to her family, he fell silent in their company – Libor excepted – and behaved as though he hated them, which he assured her he didn't, and generally embarrassed her by his lack of – well, warmth.

'I'm shy,' he said. 'I am abashed by the vitality.'

'I thought you liked the vitality.'

'I love the vitality. I just can't do it. I'm too *nebbishy*.'

She kissed him. She was always kissing him. 'A *nebbish* doesn't know he's a *nebbish*,' she said. 'You aren't a *nebbish*.'

He kissed her back. 'See how subtle that is,' he said. ' "A *nebbish* doesn't know he's a *nebbish*." It's too sophisticated for me. You're all too quick on your feet.'

'Have to be,' she said. 'You never know when you might be packing your bags.'

'I'll carry them. That's my role. I'm the *schlepper*. Or doesn't a *schlepper* know he's *schlepper*?'

'Oh, a *schlepper* knows he's a *schlepper* all right. Unlike a *nebbish*, a *schlepper* is defined by his knowledge of himself.'

He kissed her again. These Finklers! Here he was, as good as married to one. Almost one himself. In his heart one, certainly. Only in his practice deficient. And yet there still seemed so far to go.

'Don't ever leave me,' he said. He wanted to add, 'Don't go first. Promise me you won't go first.' But he remembered that those had been Malkie's words to Libor, and to have reproduced them would have struck him as sacrilege.

'I'm not going anywhere,' she said. 'Unless they make me.'

'In which event,' he told her, 'I'll be your *schlepper*.'

He had not yet introduced her to his sons. Why was that? His explanation to her, since she'd with good reason asked for one, was that he didn't much care for them.

'So?'

'So why would I want them to come into contact with you for whom I do much care?'

'Julian, that is a nonsense in more ways than I have sufficient breath in my body to tell you. Perhaps if you met them with me you would like them more.'

'They are a part of my life I want to be done with.'

'You told me you were done with them before you'd even met them.'

'That's true. And that's the part of my life I want to be done with – being done with people.'

'And how does not introducing them to me ensure that?'

'It wouldn't work out. You wouldn't like them. And then I'd have to be done with them again.'

'Are you sure you don't think it's they who wouldn't like me?'

He shrugged. 'They might not. Who cares? It's a matter of profound indifference to me.'

She wondered if that were true.

She couldn't tell if he wanted a child by her. He'd raised the matter in the course of one of his interminable circumcision conversations – was he beautiful enough for her, was there too much of him, was he too sensitive, what would they do if they had a son, would he be like his father or like Moses? – but it had all been highly hypothetical and more about him than a child. She wasn't thinking children herself. 'No hurry,' she'd told him. Which was a nice way of saying 'no interest'. But would he see that as a failure between them? By his own account he was the worst father in history. He told her that

273

again and again in a way that made her wonder if he wanted to prove he could do better.

She asked him.

'What, be a Jewish father this time? I don't think so. Unless you . . .'

'No, no, absolutely not. It was you I was . . .'

As for the Jew thing in general, it had struck her as amusing to begin with but now concerned her. Had he come to suck that out of her along with her gloom? It worried her that he confused the two.

'Jews can be joyous, you know,' she told him.

'How can I forget that when I met you at a Pesach dinner?'

'Well that wasn't joyous in the way I mean. Remembering when we were slaves in Egypt. Maybe I've used the wrong word. I mean boisterous, vulgar, earthy.'

As she said it she realised she had been less any of those things since she had met him. He constrained her. He wanted her to be a certain kind of woman and she didn't want to let him down. But on some nights she would have preferred watching a soap opera on television to discussing circumcision or Moses Maimonides. It was a strain being a representative of your people to a man who had decided to idealise them. It wasn't only him she didn't want to let down; it was Judaism, all five thousand troubled years of it.

'Then let's do something boisterous,' he said. 'There's a klezmer band with Jewish dancing on at the Jewish Cultural Centre down the road. Why don't we go there?'

'I think I'd rather have your baby,' she said.

'Would you?'

'Joking.'

She could hear his mind whirring. How does telling someone you would like to have his baby constitute a joke for Jews?

But the other side of all this was that she didn't want to worry him. The bacon smearers had been back. This time they had painted *Death to Jewishes* on the walls. *Jewishes* was Muslim hate talk. There were more and more reports of small children being abused as *Jewishes* in mixed schools. Hephzibah considered this a far more seriously menacing development than the swastikas with which white thugs defaced Jewish cemeteries. There was an idle half-heartedness in swastikas. It was more a memory of hate than hate itself. Whereas *Jewishes*! – the word had a terrible ring to it, to her. *Jewishes* were creeping things. They were made low and viscous by their faith. If you trod on them their *Jewishesness* would ooze out of them. It was an abuse that went far deeper than Yid or kike. It was directed not at individual Jews but at Jewish essence. And of course it came from a part of the world where the conflict was already soaked in blood, where hatreds were bitter and perhaps ineradicable.

Libor, too, had been telling her things she would rather not have known. Passing stories of violence and malice on to her as though that was the only way he could empty his own system of them. 'Do you know what the Swedish papers are saying?' he asked her. 'They are saying Israeli soldiers kill Palestinians in order to sell their organs on the international organ market. Remind you of anything?'

Hephzibah bit her lip. She had been through this already at work.

But Libor didn't have colleagues he could exchange fears with. 'It's the blood libel,' he told her, as though she needed telling.

'Yes, Libor,' she said.

'They've got us feasting on blood again,' he said. 'And they've got us making big money out of it. We could be back living in the Middle Ages. But then what else can you expect from Swedes who have never left the Middle Ages!'

She didn't want to hear but she heard it every day. The roll-call of Jewish crimes. And the roll-call of answering acts of violence.

Only the other day a security guard at a Jewish museum in Washington had been shot. This sent a little shock of fear through all those who ran Jewish public institutions. Emails of anxious solidarity began to be exchanged. They were fair game – that was the consensus. There was no stopping a lunatic striking anywhere, of course. But there was much in the currency of contemporary Israel-hating for lunatics to latch on to. There had been spillage, from regional conflict to religious hatred, there could be no doubt of that. Jews were again the problem. After a period of exceptional quiet, anti-Semitism was becoming again what it had always been – an escalator that never stopped, and which anyone could hop on at will.

In keeping this from Treslove, not mentioning the guard who had been shot, not telling him about the emails, not passing on what Libor told her – though it was not impossible Libor was telling him himself – Hephzibah recognised that she was protecting him as she would have protected a parent or a child. Though more a parent, in that she was being careful of Jewish susceptibilities. She would have done the same for her father had he been alive. 'Don't tell your father, it will kill him,' her mother would have said. Just as her father would have said, 'Don't tell your mother, it will kill her.'

That's what Jews did. They kept terrible news from one another. And now she was doing it with Treslove.

5

Finkler, who did not dream, had a dream.

People were punching his father in the stomach.

It had been friendly at first. His father was in the shop, entertaining customers. Go on, harder, harder. Do I feel anything? Not a tickle. And I had a cancer there two years ago. Impossible to believe, I know, but true. Ha ha!

But then the atmosphere had changed. His father wasn't

joking any more. And his customers weren't laughing with him. They had forced him to the floor of his shop where he lay among ripped cartons of sunglasses and punctured cases of deodorant spray. The shop always looked as though there had just been a delivery. Boxes remained unopened on the floor for weeks. Toothbrushes and babies' dummies and combs and home perms lay where they had fallen or simply been left where the suppliers had placed them. 'Who needs shelves when you've got a perfectly good floor?' the comedian-chemist would say while grubbing about on his hands and knees, wiping whatever it was that a customer had asked for on his lab coat. It was his theatre, not a pharmacy. He performed there. But this time the chaos was not of his own making. Those people not punching him were pulling things from the shelves. Not looting them, just throwing them about as though they were not worth stealing.

They had knocked his fedora off too, though in real life he never wore it in the shop. His fedora was for going to the synagogue in.

Finkler, concealed in a corner of his dream, waited for his father to call for help.

Samuel, Samuel, *gvald*!

He was curious about himself, curious to see what he would do. But no cry for help came.

It was when the kicking started that Finkler woke.

He hadn't even been in bed. He had fallen asleep in front of his computer.

He was anxious about the following day. He had a speaking engagement with Tamara Krausz and two others in a hall in Holborn. The usual subject. Two against, two for. Normally he did these in his sleep. But his sleep was not a good place for him at the moment. He knew what he would say at the public meeting. And there was little to fear from those who opposed him. Or from the audience. Audiences were hungry to hear what Finkler told them, whatever the subject, on account of his being on television, but in the matter of Palestine they were as empty buckets. That didn't mean they hadn't made their minds up. They had. But they sought Finkler's confirmation. A thinking Jew attacking Jews was a prize. People paid to hear that. So nothing to agitate him there. It was Tamara Krausz who made him jumpy.

He didn't trust himself with her. He didn't mean romantically. She was more Treslove's kind of woman than she was his. He remembered his friend running off a list of all the fraught women he had fallen for. They sounded like the string section of a women's orchestra, or rather a women's orchestra that had nothing but a string section in it. His nerves vibrated just listening to Treslove's descriptions. 'Not for me,' he'd said, sucking his teeth. Now here he was allowing Tamara Krausz to run her bow across his spinal cord.

He wondered if there was any way he could ask her to leave him alone. She would deny, of course, that she had done anything to him. He was flattering himself if he supposed she as much as noticed him as a man outside his professional capacity as fellow ASHamee. She had made no play for him. If he imagined her screaming in his arms, the drama was entirely of his own making.

True, as far as it went, but the screaming he anticipated was not to be confused with the sounds a vain man fancies he can coax out of a sexually frustrated woman. The screams he heard in advance of Tamara Krausz's actually screaming them were ideological. Zionism was her demon lover, not Finkler. She could not, in her fascinated, never quite sufficiently reciprocated hatred of Zionism, think about anything else. Which is how things are when you're in love.

Finkler's fault, if Tamara had only to say 'West Bank' or 'Gaza' to set his nerves on edge. Finkler's fault, if the word 'occupation' or 'trauma' on Tamara Krausz's inappositely submissive lips – moist like a harlot's in the middle of her small, anxious face – inflamed him almost to madness. He knew what would happen if by some mischance or mutual misunderstanding they ended up in bed together and she screamed the dialectic of her anti-Zionism in his ear – he would come into her six or seven times and then kill her. Slice off her tongue and then slit through her throat.

Which might have been the very thing she was referring to when she spoke of the breakdown of the Jewish mind, the Final Solution causing Jews to go demented and seek final solutions of their own, the violence begot of violence. Indeed, Finkler would have done no more than illustrate her thesis.

Was this not the very thing she sought? Kill me, you demented Jew bastard, and prove me right.

The strange thing about all this was that she had not yet, either in his hearing, or in any article of hers that he had read, said a word with which he disagreed. She was more sold on psychic disintegration than he was, and more trusting of Israel's enemies – Finkler felt able to inveigh against the Jewish state without having to make friends with Arabs: as a philosopher he found human nature flawed on both sides of every divide – but otherwise their diagnoses concurred at every point. It was the way she put it that irked and excited him. It was the rise and fall of her voice. And it was her methodology, which was to quote whoever said something that supported her, and then to ignore them when they said something different.

Again as a philosopher, Finkler was bound to condemn such a practice. It was the totality of a person's thought one should adduce in argument, not stray bullets of opinion that just happened to suit yours. This made him wary of her personally, as well. You might inadvertently whisper something to her about one subject which she would quote against you on another. I can think only of you, I can hear only you, I can see only you, he might say to her in the dead of night, and she would bring it up at an ASHamed Jews meeting as proof that his concentration had begun to wander and that he was no longer single-minded in his commitment to the group.

It felt like spite. As though she had got wind of something the Jewish people had said about her – in the dorm after lights out – and was now hell-bent, by fair means or foul, on paying them back.

He put on a black suit and a red tie. Normally he spoke from platforms in an open-necked shirt. On this occasion he wanted to be formidable in appearance as well as content. Or maybe he was concerned to protect his throat, confusing his with hers.

They took their places next to each other on the platform. He was surprised to note how little of her there was below the desk; how short her legs were, and how small her feet. As he inspected her legs he was aware of her inspecting his. How long they are, she must have thought, and how big his feet. She made him feel ungainly. He hoped he made her feel insubstantial.

At the other end of the table were two establishment Jews. Men on the boards of charities and synagogues, watchdogs of the community, custodians of the Jewish family and the good name of Israel, and therefore Finkler's natural enemies. They didn't mix, the watchmen Jews and the insurrectionary Jews of questions and ideas. One of them reminded Finkler of his father when he was out of the shop, praying or talking to other Jews who shared his communal concerns. He had that same look of worldly acumen combined with an untried innocence that comes with believing that God still took a particular interest in the Jewish people. Now protecting them as He protected no one else, now punishing them more ferociously than He punished any other of His creatures. The communal solipsism of the Jews. They blink with the ongoing wonder of it all, such men, while driving a hard bargain.

Tamara Krausz leaned into him. 'I see they've dug out the

most hysterical ones they could find,' she whispered. Her contempt was like fine oil sliding into his ear.

'Hysterical' was an ASHamed Jew word. Whoever did not admit to shame had capitulated to hysteria. The charge went all the way back to the medieval superstition of the effeminised Jew, the Jew who nursed a strange and secret wound and bled as women bleed. The new hysterical Jew was as a woman in that he was in a state of unmanly terror. Wherever he looked he saw only anti-Semites before whom he quaked in his soul.

'They've dug out the most *what* they could find?' Finkler asked.

He'd heard but he wanted to hear again.

'The most hysterical.'

'Ah, hysterical . . . Are they hysterical?'

He felt that all the strings in his body had shrunk, so that if he twitched a shoulder blade his fingers would retract and tighten into a fist.

She didn't have time to answer. The debate was under way.

Finkler and Tamara Krausz won it, of course. Finkler argued that you couldn't wax lyrical about one people's desire for nationhood and at the same time deny it to another. Judaism is essentially an ethical religion, he said. Which made it fundamentally contradictory at heart, *pace* Kierkegaard, because it is impossible to be ethical *and* religious. Zionism had been Judaism's great opportunity to escape its religiosity. To seek from others what they wanted for themselves, and to give back in the same spirit. But with military victory, Jewish ethics succumbed once more to the irrational triumphalism of religion. Only a return to ethics could save the Jews now.

Tamara saw it somewhat differently. For her, the Zionist ideal was criminal from its inception. To prove this she quoted people who mainly believed the opposite. The victims of that criminality were not only the Palestinians, but Jews themselves.

Jews everywhere. Even in this room. She spoke coldly, as though defending a client she didn't quite believe in, until she came to the question of 'what the West calls terrorism'. Then, as Finkler sitting next to her noticed, her body began to heat up. Her lips grew swollen, as though from a demon lover's kisses. There is a kind of eroticism in violence, she told the enthralled assembly. You can gather those you kill to your heart. As you can gather those who kill you. But because the Jews had loved the Germans too much, and gone passively to their deaths, they had resolved against Eros, emptied their hearts of love, and now killed with a coldness that chilled the blood.

Finkler didn't know whether this was poetry, psychology, politics or piffle. But all the talk of killing discountenanced him. Had she somehow guessed what he wanted to do to her?

The community Jews were no match for her. Which wasn't saying much. They'd have been no match for a clown like Kugle. Had they been the only speakers they'd still have contrived to lose the debate. They confounded themselves. Finkler sighed as they went through routines that had been tired when he first heard them from his father thirty or more years before – how tiny Israel was, how long-standing were Jewish claims to the land, how few of the Palestinians were truly indigenous, how Israel had offered the world but every effort at peacemaking had been rebuffed by the Arabs, how much more necessary than ever a secure Israel was in a world in which anti-Semitism was on the increase . . .

Why didn't they hire him to write their scripts? He could have won it for them. You win by understanding something of what the other side thinks, and they understood nothing.

He meant win in every sense. Win the argument and win the Kingdom of God.

It was his oldest argument with his father: that Jews, for whom the stranger was supposed to be remembered and given water, for whom doing unto others as they would have done unto them was the virtue to end virtues, had turned into a people with ears only for themselves. He couldn't bear his father's clowning in the shop, but at least there he was a democrat and humanitarian; whereas dressed in his black coat and his fedora, talking politics on the way home from synagogue, he closed his face as resolutely as he closed his mind.

'They fought and lost,' his father used to say. 'They would have thrown us into the sea but they fought and lost.'

'That is no reason for us not to imagine what it is like to lose,' the young Finkler argued. 'The prophets didn't say we had to show compassion only to the deserving.'

'They get what they deserve. We give them what they deserve.'

And so Finkler had thrown his skullcap away and shortened his name from Samuel to Sam.

'Same old, same old,' he muttered to Tamara.

'As I said – hysterical,' she answered in an undertone.

Finkler's fingers retracted so far he could feel his fists retreating into his sleeves.

It was only when there were questions from the floor that the evening became lively. People on both sides of the debate shouted and told stories of a personal nature which they mistook for proof of whatever it was they believed. A Gentile woman with a sorrowing face stood and in the manner of a confessional told how she had been brought up to be in awe of what Professor Finkler – he wasn't a professor but he let it go – had called the sublime Jewish ethic – he had said no such thing but he let that go as well – but since then she had been to the Holy Land and discovered an apartheid country ruled by racist supremacists. She had a question for the gentlemen on the platform who complained that Israel was uniquely singled out for censure: what other country defines itself and those it permits to enter it on racial grounds? Is the reason you are uniquely singled out for censure, that you are uniquely racist?

'She is a lesson to us,' Tamara Krausz said to Finkler in her silken undertone. It was like listening to a woman you didn't want to love removing her slip for you, Finkler thought.

'How so?' he asked.

'She speaks from the bruised heart.'

Was it that that made Finkler not wait for the gentlemen to whom the question had been put to answer it? Or was it his certain know-ledge that they would answer it as ineffectually as they had answered everything else? Finkler himself didn't know. But what he said he too said from a bruised heart. The mystery was: whose bruised heart was it?

6

What Finkler said was this:

How dare you?

For a moment he said nothing else. It isn't easy to let a phrase hang in silence at the noisy end of a public meeting when everyone is eager to be heard. But Finkler, one time exhibitionistic Oxford don, now experienced media philosopher, was not without some mastery of the tricks of eloquence. As one-time beloved husband of Tyler, now grieving widower, as one-time proud father, now not, as potential murderer of Tamara Krausz, he was possessed of some of the tricks of gravity, too.

'How dare you? was unexpected of him politically, unexpected as a response to the careworn woman who had once been a celebrant of Jewish ethics and spoke now from the soul of suffering humanity, and unexpected by the violence of its tone. A single pistol shot would not have carried more threat.

He allowed the report of it to go on reverberating through the hall – a tenth of a second, a half a second, a second and a quarter, a lifetime – and then, in a voice no less shocking for the calm pedagogic reasonableness in which he had cocooned it, he said:

'How dare you, a non Jew – and I have to say it impresses me not at all that you grew up in awe of Jewish ethics, if anything your telling me so chills me – how dare you even think you can tell Jews what sort of country they may live in, when it is you, a European Gentile, who made a separate country for Jews a necessity?

'By what twisted sophistication of argument do you harry people with violence off your land and then think yourself entitled to make high-minded stipulations as to where they may go now you are rid of them and how they may provide for their future welfare? I am an Englishman who loves England, but do you suppose that it too is not a racist country? Do you know of any country whose recent history is not blackened by prejudice and hate against somebody? So what empowers racists in their own right to sniff out racism in others? Only from a world from which Jews believe they have nothing to fear will they consent to learn lessons in humanity. Until then, the Jewish state's offer of safety to Jews the world over – yes, Jews first – while it might not be equitable cannot sanely be construed as racist. I can understand why a Palestinian might say it feels racist to him, though he too inherits a history of disdain for people of other persuasions to himself, but not you, madam, since you present yourself as a bleeding-heart, conscience-pricked respresentative of the very Gentile world from which Jews, through no fault of their own, have been fleeing for centuries . . .'

He looked around him. There was no wall of applause. What did he expect? Some people enthusiastically clapped. Rather more booed. Had he not carried the authority he did, there would, he presumed – he bloody well hoped – have been cries of 'Shame!' A demagogue likes to hear cries of 'Shame!' But mainly what he saw was humanity trapped in conviction, like rats in rat traps.

Those who saw as he saw, saw what he saw. Those who didn't, didn't. And the didn't had it.

Fuck it, he thought. It was at that moment the sum total of his philosophy. *Fuck it.*

He turned his head to Tamara Krausz. 'So what do you think?' he enquired.

She had a strange smile on her face, as though everything he had just said he had said at her bidding.

'Hysterical,' she told him.

'You wouldn't care to lie in my arms and scream that, would you?' he asked, in his most inviting manner.

TEN

I

In time, Treslove came to believe he could very easily have reason to suspect Finkler of setting his sights on Hephzibah. If this was a rather roundabout way of putting it, that was because Treslove's suspicions were themselves rather roundabout.

In fact, he had no reason to believe that Finkler had set his sights on Hephzibah but he chose to suspect him anyway. Nothing he had seen, nothing that either Finkler or Hephzibah had said, just a feeling. And in jealousy a feeling is a reason.

He accepted that such a feeling might simply be the child of his devotion. When you love a woman deeply you are bound to imagine that every other man must love her deeply too. But it wasn't every other man he had reason to believe had set his sights on Hephzibah. Just Finkler.

Without doubt, Finkler had changed. He was less cocksure, somehow. He held his head differently. When he came round to dinner with Libor he was quiet and unwilling to be drawn on Isrrrae. It was Hephzibah's understanding, and Hephzibah was professionally in the know, that he had fallen out with his fellow exponents of Jewish ASHamedness in the matter of the proposed academic boycott. Though how serious was the falling-out she couldn't say.

'That would be because he doesn't want to lose an all-expenses-paid lecture tour of Jerusalem, Tel Aviv and Eilat,' Treslove guessed.

'Julian!' Hephzibah said.

(See!)

'Julian what?'

'Do you know that for a certainty?'

Treslove conceded that he didn't. But he knew his friend.

'Well, I wonder sometimes if you do,' Hephzibah said.

(See!!)

With Treslove, too, Finkler was less combative, as though sensitive to the changes wrought in him by Hephzibah's influence. But did that mean he saw Treslove differently or simply wanted some of what Treslove had found for himself?

Yet Hephzibah was surely not Finkler's type, particularly if Tyler was anything to go by. Treslove knew that Finkler had always taken mistresses. Jewish ones, too, Tyler had told him. But he was unable to picture them. The deep dark separation of Ronit Kravitz's breasts, for example, would have come as a surprise to him had he seen them. When he put his mind to Finkler's mistresses he imagined them as Jewish versions of Tyler whom he had always taken for a Jewess anyway. Razor-blade women with narrow jaws, more likely to favour sharply tailored trouser suits than shawls and cloaks. Women who hit the ground running, in creases and stilettos, not women who floated slowly down in acres of material. So no one remotely resembling Hephzibah. Which could mean one of two things: either Finkler was after Hephzibah only in order to get back at Treslove for something or other, or he had fallen for her as a woman entirely beyond his experience and preference, and in that case was likely to be dangerously smitten. Just as Treslove himself had been. Just as Treslove himself still was. The sixty-four-thousand-dollar question was what Hephzibah felt. Was she smitten too?

He brought the matter up with her in bed at the end of a couple of unusually taciturn days between them. What he didn't know was that she was keeping information about the second attack on the museum from him.

'Should we have Sam over for dinner one night soon?' he said. 'With Libor? I think he's lonely.'

'Libor? Of course he's lonely.'

'No, Sam.'

Hephzibah sipped her tea. 'If you like.'

'Well, only if *you* like.'

'Yes, I like.'

'Him or the idea of dinner?'

'Explain that.'

'Do you like the idea generally of having somebody round for dinner and that somebody might as well be Sam, or do you especially like the idea of its being Sam?'

She put her tea down and rolled over to his side of the bed. He loved the billowing undulations of the mattress when Hephzibah moved in his direction. Everything was momentous with her. From the start the earth had moved for him in her company, the oceans had heaved, the skies had gathered and gone black. Making love to her was like surviving an electrical storm. And some nights he wouldn't have minded had he not survived. But the mornings too were heavy with promise. Something would be said. Something would happen. No day went by without her being an event.

So different from the mothers of his sons, whose pregnancies he had failed to notice.

But then they had left him by the time they discovered they were pregnant.

But then he should have noticed that they'd left him.

'What's this about?' Hephzibah asked, coming at last to rest in the small corner of the bed that belonged to him.

'*This?* Nothing. I just wondered if you liked the idea of dinner.'

'With Sam?'

'Ah, so you do like the idea of Sam? That's to say of dinner with Sam?'

'Julian, what's this about?'

'I'm wondering if you're having an affair with him.'

'With *Sam?*'

'Or at least thinking about having an affair with him.'

'With *Sam*?'

'There you are, you see, you can't stop saying his name.'

'Julian, why would I be having or thinking of having an affair with anybody? I'm having an affair with you.'

'That doesn't stop people.'

'Wouldn't it stop you?'

'Me, yes. But I'm not like other people.'

'That's true,' she said, 'but then neither am I. You should believe that.'

'Then I do.'

She made him look at her. 'I have no interest in Sam Finkler,' she said. 'I don't find him interesting or attractive. He is the kind of Jewish man I have been avoiding all my life.'

'What kind is that?'

'Arrogant, heartless, self-centred, ambitious, and convinced his intelligence makes him irresistible.'

'That sounds like a description, from your own account, of the two men you married.'

'Exactly. In between marrying them I was avoiding them. And since marrying them I *have* avoided them.'

'But you only avoid what you fear, surely. Do you fear Sam?'

She laughed loudly. Too loudly?

'Well, he would no doubt love the idea that I do, but I don't. It's a strange question, though. Could it be that it's you who fears Sam?'

'Me? Why would I fear Sam?'

'For the same reason that I do.'

'But you said you don't.'

'And you aren't sure you believe me. Did you have a thing together at school?'

'Me and Sam? Christ, no.'

'Don't be so horrified. Boys do that, don't they?'

'Not any boys I knew.'

'Then maybe you should have. I think it's good to get all that out of the way early. Both my husbands had things at school.'

'With each other?'

'No, you fool. They didn't know each other. With other boys.'

'Yes and you weren't happy being married to them.'

'But not for that reason. I was waiting all along for you.'

'The goy?'

She wrapped a grand arm around him and gathered him into her bosom. 'As a goy – I have to tell you – you're a bit of a disappointment. Most goys I know don't spend their time reading Moses Maimonides and memorising Yiddish endearments.'

He let himself be storm-tossed, riding her billowing sea. When she held him like this he could see nothing, but the colour of his blindness was the colour of waves breaking.

'*Neshomeleh*,' he said, into her flesh.

But he couldn't leave it at that. The next day, over his five-pan omelette, he said, 'Is there a special bond?'

'Between?'

'Jews.'

'Depends on the Jews.'

'Is it like being gay? Is there a Jewdar that enables you to pick one another out?'

'Again, depends. I rarely think someone is Jewish when they're not, but I quite often don't know I'm talking to a Jew when I am.'

'And what is it you look for?'

'I'm not looking for anything.'

'What is that you recognise, then?'

'Can't explain. It's not one thing, it's a collection of things. Features, facial expression, a way of talking, a way of moving.'

'So you're making racial calculations?'

'I wouldn't call them racial, no.'

'Religious?'

'No, definitely not religious.'

'Then what?'

She didn't know what.

'But you make a connection.'

'Again, depends.'

'And with Sam?'

'What about with Sam?'

'Do you make the connection?'

She sighed.

She sighed the next time Treslove brought it up as well. And the time after that. She thought she'd put his suspicions to bed. But that wasn't the only reason she sighed the third time. Strangely enough, Sam had called in to see her that afternoon at the museum. This was not something he had ever done before. Nor was it a visit she could explain. It was as though, when she saw him, he had materialised out of Treslove's conversation, or even out of Treslove's will.

He must have been surprised himself, so open-mouthed was her welcome.

'To what do I owe this?' she asked, giving him her hand.

She knew the answer. She owed it to her lover's fears.

'Oh, I was driving past and I just thought I would call in,' he said. 'See how it's going. Is Julian here?'

'No. He's stopped coming in. There's not a lot he can do here while we're still in this state.'

He looked about. At the finished cabinets, at the murals, at the banks of computers and headphones. On a far wall he thought he caught sight of a photograph of Sir Isaiah Berlin and Frankie Vaughan. Not together.

'It's looking pretty well advanced to me,' he said.

'Yes, but nothing's connected.'

'So I can't trace my genealogy yet?'

'I didn't know you wanted to.'

He shrugged his shoulders. Who could say what he

wanted? 'Any chance of a guided tour,' he asked, 'or are you too busy?'

She looked at her watch. 'I can give you ten minutes,' she said. 'But only if you promise to be less ironical about us than you were the last time we talked. This is not, I remind you, a Holocaust memorial museum.'

He smiled at her. He was not, she thought, so unattractive.

'Oh, I wouldn't mind if it were,' he said.

2

When Treslove told Hephzibah he thought Finkler was looking lonely he omitted to mention where the thought came from. Other, that is, than from his own fear of being lonely. It came from a text Alfredo had sent him. *saw your freaky telly friend out looking for tarts surprised you weren't with him*

Treslove texted back *how do you tell when a man's out looking for tarts?*

It took Alfredo a couple of days to work up a reply. *his tongues hanging out*

Treslove texted back *you are no son of mine*, but decided against sending it. He didn't want to give Alfredo a free shot at him for his paternal negligence.

As for Finkler, leaving Hephzibah out of it, he was sorry for him if Alfredo's low supposition happened to be true, and sorrier still if it wasn't but Finkler just looked like a man with no home to go to and no wife to care for.

It was a terrible thing to lose the woman you loved.

3

'You're probably imagining it,' Libor said.

Treslove had taken him out for a salt-beef sandwich in the

reopened Nosh Bar on Windmill Street. Years before, Libor had brought Treslove and Finkler here. Part of his introducing the young men to the hidden delights of the city Libor had come to love above all others. Then, a salt-beef sandwich in Soho was to Treslove as a descent into the underworld of cosmopolitan debauchery. He felt as though he were living through the last days of the Roman Empire, no matter that the Romans would not have known of salt-beef sandwiches. Now Treslove wondered if he was living through the last days of himself.

Libor, too, it seemed to him. The old man painstakingly separated the beef from the rye bread because the latter did not digest easily, and then he didn't touch the beef. He had asked for no mustard. He wanted no pickled cucumber.

He no longer ate his food, he merely pulled it apart.

In the past he would have looked out of the window and enjoyed the parade of dissolutes. Today he stared as through shuttered eyes. I have done him no favours bringing him here, Treslove thought.

But then the outing hadn't been planned as a favour to Libor. It was a necessity to Treslove.

'Why would I imagine it?' he asked. 'I'm happy. I'm in love. I believe I am loved. Where would I conjure up this dread from?'

'The usual place,' Libor said.

'That's too Czech for me, Libor. Where's the usual place?'

'The place everything we fear comes from. The place where we store our longing for the end of things.'

'That's more Czech still. I have no longing for the end of things.'

Libor smiled at him and laid an old unsteady hand on his. But for the old and the unsteady the gesture reminded Treslove of Hephzibah. Why did everybody pat him?

'My friend, all the years I've known you you've been longing for the end of things. You've lived in preparation, on the edge of tears, all your life. Malkie noticed that about you. She wasn't sure she should even play Schubert when you were listening. He doesn't need any encouragement, that one, she said.'

'Encouragement to do what?'

'To throw yourself into the flames. Isn't that what being with my niece and reading Moses Maimonides is about?'

'I don't think of Hephzibah as fire.'

'Don't you? Then what are you so anxious about? I think you're getting what you went in there to get. The whole Jewish *gesheft*. You think it's a short cut to catastrophe. And I'm not going to say you're wrong.'

He wanted to say that's crap, Libor. But you don't ask an elderly man out for salt-beef sandwiches he is unable to digest and tell him that what he's saying is crap. 'I don't recognise what you're describing,' he said instead.

Libor shrugged. If you don't you don't. He didn't have the strength to argue. But he could see Treslove needed more. 'The fall, the flood, Sodom and Gomorrah, the Last Judgement, Masada, Auschwitz – see a Jew and you think of Armageddon,' he said. 'We tell good creation stories but we do destruction even better. We're at the beginning and the end of everything. And everyone's after a piece of the action. Those who can't wait to pitchfork us into the flames, want to go down screaming by our side. It's one or the other. Temperamentally, you were always going to choose the other.'

'You sound like your great-great-niece.'

'Not surprising. We're family, you know.'

'But isn't all this a bit solipsistic, Libor, as Sam would say? By your account there's no escaping the Jews for anyone.'

Libor pushed his plate aside. 'There's no escaping the Jews for anyone,' he said.

Treslove stared out of the window. On the opposite side of the narrow street, an ill-favoured, fat girl in a short skirt was trying to persuade men to come into a club only a desperate or a deranged person would enter. She saw him looking at her and beckoned him over. Bring your friend, her gesture implied. Bring your salt-beef sandwich. He lowered his eyes.

'And you think,' he said, picking up Libor's thread, 'that I am imagining Hephzibah and Sam in order to hasten my end?'

Libor waved his hands in front of his face. 'I didn't quite say that. But people who expect the worst will always see the worst.'

'I haven't *seen* anything.'

'Exactly.'

Treslove put his elbows on the table. 'Libor, since you tell me Hephzibah is your family, what's your view? Do you think she would do this?'

'With Sam?'

'With anybody?'

'Well, her being my family doesn't make her different from any other woman. Though I have never gone along with the view that women are by nature inconstant. My own experience has been very different. Malkie never played me false.'

'Can you be sure?'

'Of course I can't be sure. But if she allowed me to believe she had never played me false, then she never played me false. You don't judge fidelity by every act; it's the desire to say you're faithful and the desire to be believed.'

'That can't be true, Libor. Outside Prague.'

'We didn't live in Prague. What I'm saying is that an indiscretion needn't matter. It's the overall intention of fidelity that counts.'

'So Hephzibah might mean to be faithful to me but still happen to be fucking Sam.'

'I hope she isn't.'

'*I* hope she isn't.'

'And I doubt she is. The question is, why don't you doubt she is, if you have seen nothing to make you suppose otherwise.'

Treslove thought about it.

'I need to order another sandwich,' he said, as though truthful reflection were dependent on it.

'Have mine,' Libor said.

Treslove shook his head and thought of Tyler. 'Have mine,' Finkler had said, if not in so many words. 'Have mine, I am otherwise engaged.'

He had never told Libor of his evenings with Tyler, watching Finkler's documentaries. He had never told anybody. They were not his alone to tell. They were poor Tyler's too. And in a sense they were Finkler's also. But he wished he could mention the affair, if it ever really was an affair, to Libor now. It would help to explain something, though he wasn't sure what. But how would he know what if he didn't hear himself put the question into words. Libor was old. Who would he tell? The secret that would otherwise go to the grave with Treslove, would surely go to the grave much sooner with Libor.

So on an impulse, he told.

Libor listened quietly. When it was over, to Treslove's astonishment, he cried. Not copious tears, just a tear or two in the corner of an old man's rheumy eye.

'I'm sorry,' Treslove said.

'You should be.'

Treslove didn't know what to say. He hadn't expected a response of this sort. Libor was a man of the world. Just squeeze me in a little fuck when you come to make a report of my life, he had told Treslove. Men and women did these things. *An indiscretion needn't matter* – Libor's own words.

'I shouldn't have told you,' Treslove said. 'It was wrong of me.'

Libor looked into his hands. 'Yes, it was wrong of you to tell me,' he said, as though not talking to Treslove at all. 'Probably more wrong of you to tell me than to do it. I don't want the burden of the knowledge. I would prefer to remember Tyler differently. And you. Sam it doesn't really matter about. He can look after himself. Though I would rather have not known about the falsity of your friendship. You make the world a sadder place, Julian, and it is already sad enough, believe me. Why did you tell me? It was unkind of you.'

'I don't know. And I say again I'm truly sorry. I don't know what made me do this.'

'You do. One always does know why one tells. Is it because you are proud of it as an escapade?'

'An escapade? God, no.'

'A conquest, then?'

'A conquest? God, no.'

'So you are proud of it as something. Are you proud of it because you got one over on Sam?'

Treslove knew he had a duty to think about his answer. Saying *God, no* all the time would not suffice.

'Not got one *over*, Libor. I hope not that. More having got *into* his world. Their world.'

'From which you'd felt excluded?'

He had a duty to think about that, too. 'Yes.'

'Because they were a glamorously successful pair?'

'I suppose so, yes.'

'But Sam was your friend. You'd grown up with him. You continued to see him. He didn't inhabit a universe that was beyond yours.'

'I'd grown up with him but he'd always been different to me. A mystery in some way.'

'Because he was clever? Because he was famous? Because he was a Jew?'

Treslove's salt-beef sandwich arrived, dripping in mustard the way he'd learned to like it. Accompanied by not one but two pickled cucumbers chopped into fine slices.

'That's a tough one to answer,' he said. 'But yes, all right, all of those.'

'So when you lay in the arms of his wife you were, for a moment, as clever as he was, as famous as he was, as Jewish as he was.'

Treslove didn't say that he had never lain in Tyler's arms, and that she had never lain in his. He didn't want Libor to know that she had turned her back to him.

'I guess.'

'Any one more than the others?'

Treslove sighed. A sigh from deep in the bowels of his guilt and of his fears. 'I can't say,' he said.

'Then let me say for you. It was the Jew part that mattered to you most.'

Treslove leaned across the table to halt him. 'Before you go on,' he said, 'you do know that Tyler wasn't Jewish. I'd thought she was, but it turned out that she wasn't.'

'You sound disappointed.'

'I was, a little.'

'All the more, then, I say it was the Jew. And I know that it was the Jew because of what you are afraid of in Sam and Hephzibah now.'

Treslove looked at him, an old man with no digestion system left, telling riddles. 'Don't follow,' he said.

'You suspect Sam and Hephzibah of what? Having sex together. And on what evidence? None, except that you suppose that is what they will do because they share something that excludes you. They are Jews, you are not, therefore they are fucking.'

'Oh, come on, Libor.'

'Please yourself. But you have no better explanation for your suspicions. You won't be the first Gentile to ascribe lasciviousness to Jews. We had horns once, and a tail, like goats or like the devil. We bred like vermin. We polluted Christian women. The Nazis —'

'Libor, stop — this is foolish and insulting.'

The old man sat back in his chair and rubbed his head.

Once upon a time he had a wife who rubbed it for him, laughing as she polished, like a housewife delighting in her chores. But that was long ago.

Insulting? He shrugged.

'I am deeply ashamed,' Treslove said. 'For telling you what I told you.'

'You are deeply ashamed? Then that's something else you two share.'

'Show me mercy,' Treslove begged.

'Julian, you started this,' Libor said. 'You invited me out to discuss your fear that Sam and Hephzibah are fucking. I ask you what your suspicions are built on. You tell me an indefinable dread. I'm your friend – so I'm doing my best to define it for you. You attribute strange and secret sexual powers to them, that's why you are afraid. You think they can't stop themselves because they are driven by an ungovernable sexual urge, Jew to Jew, and you think they won't stop themselves because they are unscrupulous, Jew to Gentile. Julian, you're an anti-Semite.'

'Me?'

'Don't sound so astonished. You're not alone. We're all anti-Semites. We have no choice. You. Me. Everyone.'

He had not eaten a bite of food.

4

They went to the theatre together – Hephzibah, Treslove and Finkler. It was Treslove's birthday and Hephzibah had suggested an outing instead of a party, since every day was a party for them. They had asked Libor along but he didn't fancy the sound of the play.

None of them fancied the sound of the play. But as Finkler said, if you don't go to the theatre whenever you don't like the sound of a play, when do you ever go to the theatre?

Besides, it was only on for a week, a piece of agitprop that people were writing angry or enthusiastic letters to the papers about. London was buzzing with it.

'Are you sure it won't spoil your birthday?' Hephzibah asked, having second thoughts.

'I'm not a child,' Treslove told her. He didn't add that everything was spoiling his birthday so why pick on this.

It was called *Sons of Abraham* and charted the agonies of the Chosen People from ancient times up until the present when they decided to visit their agonies on someone else. The final scene was a well-staged tableau of destruction, all smoke and rattling metal sheets and Wagnerian music, to which the Chosen People danced like slow-motion devils, baying and hallooing, bathing their hands and feet in the blood that oozed like ketchup from the corpses of their victims, a fair number of whom were children.

Finkler, sitting on the other side of Hephzibah from Treslove, was surprised to discover from the programme notes that Tamara Krausz had neither written it nor assisted in its production. Watching it made him feel she was in the theatre somewhere. Not quite next to him. Hephzibah was next to him. But nearby. He could smell the harlot allure of her vindictive intelligence, laying out her daughters of Hebron beauty for her father's enemies to feast and avenge themselves upon.

In the final seconds of the drama an aerial shot of a mass grave at Auschwitz was projected on to a gauze curtain, before dissolving into a photograph of the rubble of Gaza.

Pure Tamara.

It received a standing ovation. Neither Hephzibah nor Treslove rose from their seats. Finkler laughed loudly, turning round so that people could observe him. Treslove was surprised by this reaction. Not just by the judgement it implied but by the antic nature of it. Had Finkler flipped his lid?

A number of ASHamed Jews were in the audience but

Finkler thought their response to seeing him there was decidedly cold. Only Merton Kugle made an approach.

'Well?' he asked.

'Superb,' Finkler said. 'Simply superb.'

'So why were you laughing?'

'Wasn't laughter, Merton. Those were the contortions of grief.'

Kugle nodded and went out into the street.

Finkler wondered if he'd popped into a supermarket on his way to the theatre and had tins of proscribed Israeli sturgeon in his pockets.

People left the theatre quietly, deep in thought. That deep in thought that is available only to those who already know what they think. They were mainly from the caring and the performing professions, Finkler reckoned. He believed he recognised a number of them from demos in Trafalgar Square. They had the air of seasoned marchers. *End the massacre! Stop Israeli genocide!* At another time he'd have shaken hands with them, in sombre festivity, like survivors of an air raid.

He suggested a birthday drink for Treslove at the bar in the crypt of the theatre. It reminded them all of their student days. Rare ales on tap. Houmous and tabbouleh with pitta bread to eat. Old couches draped with black curtains to talk things over on. Finkler bought the drinks, clinked his glass with Treslove and Hephzibah and then fell quiet. For ten minutes they didn't speak. Treslove wondered whether the silence denoted suppressed eroticism on the part of the other two. It surprised him greatly that Finkler had accepted their invitation — that's to say Hephzibah's invitation — to accompany them to the play. He must have known they would react differently to it from him and perhaps even end up having a row. So there was an underlying motive to his acceptance. Out of the side of his head, Treslove kept an eye on their mutual glances and hand movements. He saw nothing.

In the end it was another person who broke what Treslove took to be their ideological deadlock.

'Hey! Surprised to see you here.'

Treslove heard the voice before he saw the person.

'Abe!'

Hephzibah, getting caught up in the couch drapes, rose in a tangle of shawls. 'Julian, Sam, this is Abe – my ex.'

Which one of us, Treslove speculated, does Abe think she's with now – Julian or Sam?

Abe shook hands and joined them. A roguish and yet somehow angelically handsome man with a crinkled halo of black hair shot with white, like gleams of light, a hawkish nose and eyes close together. He has a face that bores, Treslove thought, meaning a face that stabs and pierces not a face that wearies. A prophet's or philosopher's face – which thought pleased him in that it would be Finkler who should be jealous, therefore, not him.

Hephzibah had of course told him about her two husbands, Abe and Ben, but he had to rack his brains to remember which was the lawyer and which the actor. Given where they were, how he looked and the black T-shirt he was wearing, he calculated that Abe must be the actor.

'Abe's a lawyer,' Hephzibah said. She was flushed, even flustered, Treslove thought, with the attentions of so many men. Her past, her present, her future . . .

'So why did you say you were surprised to see Hep here?' Treslove asked, staking a claim which a more confident man would have considered already staked.

Abe glowed like the embers of a fire that had only just gone out. 'Not her kind of play,' he said.

'Do I have a kind of play?' Hephzibah enquired. Skittish, Treslove reckoned, noticing everything.

'Well, not this kind.'

'You've heard about my museum?'

'I have.'

'Then it shouldn't surprise you that I have to keep my ear to the ground.'

'Though not necessarily that low to it,' Finkler said.

Treslove was astonished. 'You're telling me you didn't like it?'

Hephzibah too. 'That's interesting,' she said.

So was that what he was doing, Treslove wondered, *interesting* Hephzibah?

Finkler turned to Abe. 'Julian and I went to school together,' he said. 'He thinks he knows what I like.'

Treslove stood up for himself. 'You're an ASHamed Jew. You're the Sam the Man of ASHamed Jews. You had to like it. It was written for you. Could have been written *by* you. I've heard you speak it.'

'Not *those* words have you ever heard me speak. I don't do Nazi analogies. The Nazis were the Nazis. Anyway, did you hear me say I didn't like it? I loved it. I only wished there'd been more singing and dancing. It lacked a show-stopper like "Springtime for Hitler", that's my only complaint. I couldn't tap my feet. Put it this way, did you see anyone going out humming the Wagner?'

'So let me get this straight,' Treslove said. 'This is a taste issue for you, is it?'

'Isn't it for you?'

'Not in the musical sense, no.'

Finkler put an arm around his shoulder. 'Do you know,' he said, 'I think I'd like to leave this conversation to the rest of you. I'll get more birthday drinks. Abe?'

Abe didn't drink. Or at least he didn't drink tonight. In a manner of speaking, he told them, he was working.

'Aren't you always,' Hephzibah said, exercising the privilege of an ex.

'Doing what?' Treslove asked.

'Well, essentially just watching the play and gauging responses to it. One of the co-writers is a client.'

'And you're here to see if he has a case for claiming damages from the Jewish people?' Hephzibah continued, squeezing his arm. Treslove felt that he had seen into their marriage and wished he hadn't.

On two glasses of wine, more than her year's allowance, Hephzibah had, in his view, exceeded her yearly allowance of skittishness also.

'Well, if you're here to gauge responses I'm happy to give you mine,' he said, but he was out of time with the conversation and wasn't heard.

'Abe always did know how to screw the last penny out of a defendant,' Hephzibah told him.

'That's not quite the way of it,' Abe said.

'What, the Jewish people are suing him?'

'No, not the Jews. And it's not about money either. He's just been sacked by his university department. He's a marine biologist when he's not writing plays. He was sacked when he was underwater. I'm trying to get him his job back.'

'Sacked for writing this play?'

'Not exactly. For saying that Auschwitz was more a holiday camp than a hell for most of the Jews in there.'

'And where there's no hell, there's no devil – is that the idea?'

'Well I can't speak for his theology. What he argues, and claims he can prove beyond doubt, is that there were casinos and spas and prostitutes laid on. He has photographs of Jews lying on their backs in swimming pools being fed iced strawberries by camp hostesses.'

Hephzibah guffawed. 'Then by the terms of his own play,' she said, 'Gaza must be a holiday camp too. He can't have it both ways. No point calling out the Jews as Nazis if the Nazis turn out to have been fun-loving philanthropists.'

'Maybe Sam was right in that case and what we've just watched was a light romantic comedy,' Treslove said, but he was out of time again.

'I think that's being a bit literalist about the way analogy is meant to work,' Abe said, replying to Hephzibah not Treslove.

But he looked at Treslove, man to man, husband to husband. Such literalists, wives!

'So as a Jew, what do *you* think?' Treslove asked, raising his tempo.

'Well as a lawyer —'

'No, as a Jew what do you think?'

'About the play? Or about my client?'

'About the lot. The play, your client, the Auschwitz lido.'

Abe showed him the palms of his hands. 'As a Jew I believe that every argument has a counter-argument,' he said.

'That's why we make such good lawyers,' Hephzibah laughed, squeezing both men's arms.

These people don't know how to stand up for themselves, Treslove thought. These people have had their chips.

He went to the bathroom. Bathrooms always made him angry. They were places that returned him to himself. Illusionless, he looked in the mirror. They've ceded their sense of outrage, he said to his reflection, washing his hands.

When he returned he saw that Sam had joined the party again. Sam, Hephzibah, Abe. A cosy coterie of Finklers. Or maybe it's just me who's had his chips, Treslove thought.

ELEVEN

I

Walking to the museum a week later, Hephzibah thought I am at the end of my tether with the lot of them.

She didn't know if Finkler was chasing her. But Abe, her ex, definitely was. He rang her two or three times after their chance meeting at *Sons of Abraham*. No dice, she told him, I'm happy.

He replied that he could see she was happy, which was no more than she deserved, but wanted to know what her being happy had to do with meeting him for a drink.

'I don't drink.'

'You were drinking the other night.'

'That was a special occasion. I'd just been accused of infanticide. When you're accused of infanticide you drink.'

'I'll accuse you of infanticide.'

'Don't joke about it.'

'All right, you don't drink. But you do talk.'

'We're talking.'

'I'd like to hear about the museum.'

'It's a museum. I'll send you a prospectus.'

'Is it a Holocaust museum?'

Christ, another one, she thought.

One in, one out. Finkler had stopped being ironical about the museum. He hadn't paid another surprise visit to her there but he somehow or other contrived to be around her more, showed up where he was not expected, and even when he wasn't in evidence in person somehow succeeded in making his presence felt, popping up on television or in some third party's conversation, as when Abe, trying to prise her out, said how pleased he was to meet Sam Finkler at the theatre as he had always admired him. Though she was by no means a sexually vain woman – she was too reliant on shawls for sexual vanity – she didn't quite believe in Finkler's latest expressions of curiosity about her work. Curiosity did not come naturally to him. But at least the jeering had been replaced by civility. As for what that civility denoted she couldn't judge it clearly because Treslove's apprehensions clouded her view.

So she was at the end of her tether with herself as well. Yet again seeing the world as the man she loved saw it.

But perhaps all these irritations were a smokescreen for some other anger or sadness altogether. Julian worried her. He was beginning to look like a man who didn't know what to do with himself next. Libor too. She had barely seen him in weeks and when she did he didn't make her laugh. Libor without jokes was not Libor.

And the information that poured into her office – continuing accusations of apartheid and ethnic cleansing, news of world charities and human rights organisations citing war crimes and advocating boycotts, an incessant buzzing of rumour and reproach in the ears of Jews, a demoralisation that was no less effective for being random (she hoped to God that it was random) – only added fuel to her disquiet. Hephzibah was not a fervent Zionist. She had never been a land-centred Jew. St John's Wood was fine for her as a place to be Jewish in. She only wished she could find a reference in the Bible to God's covenant with English Jews, promising them St John's Wood High Street. But Zionism's achievements could not go unnoticed in a museum of Anglo-Jewish culture, given the contribution to Zionism English Jews had made, even a museum situated a step from the zebra crossing made famous by the Beatles. The question she had to wrestle with was how far Zionism's failures had to be noticed as well.

There had been a lull in odious incident. No bacon had been smeared on the door handles for weeks, no defacements vowing revenge and death. (Revenge, in St John's Wood!) Things had fallen quiet in the Middle East, at least as far as the British media were concerned, so the rage that clung on to the coat-tails of news report had temporarily abated. Yes, *Sons of Abraham* had reinvigorated some of it among the broadsheet-reading, theatregoing classes where, it seemed to her, it lay smouldering all the time now, like a fire that wouldn't go out, but at least Jews weren't for the moment the only topic of educated conversation. The trouble was that the calm felt more sinister than the storm. What would it take, what action against Gaza or Lebanon or even Iran, what act of belligerence or retaliation, what event in Wall Street, what incidence of Jewish influence of the wrong sort round the corner in Downing Street, for it all to start up again, next time with more violence than the last, the more virulent for its slumbers?

She herself hadn't slept easily in an age, and that wasn't simply down to having Treslove in her bed. She didn't walk to work in easy spirits. She didn't meet her friends in easy spirits. An anxiety had settled like a fine dust on everything she did, and on everyone she knew — on all the Jews at least. They too were looking askance — not over their shoulders exactly, but into a brittly uncertain future which bore fearful resemblances to an only too certain past.

Paranoia, was it? she asked herself. The question itself had become monotonous to her. It was the natural one to ask as she walked to work in the wintry sunshine, skirting an empty Lord's, wishing she could be a man who forgot himself in sport, full of dread as to what she would find when she arrived at the museum. *Am I becoming paranoid?* The rhythm of the wondering affected her pace. She had begun to walk in time to it.

The thought that the museum was a target frightened her.

But she was frightened of her fear no less. Jews were supposed to have put all this behind them. 'Never again' and all that. Well, it was hard to picture herself as a deportee in a thin floral dress, carrying a little suitcase, her eyes hollow with terror, as she strolled through leafy St John's Wood with her jewellery clinking and a bag costing fifteen hundred pounds under her arm. But the hollow-eyed woman in the floral dress – wouldn't she have once found her fate hard to picture too?

So was it paranoia? She didn't know. No one knew. There were people who claimed that the paranoid create the thing they fear. But how could that be? How does being afraid of hate manufacture it? Were there Nazis out there who didn't know they were Nazis until a Jew showed his alarm? Did the smell of Jewish apprehension send them out to the costumiers in search of a brown shirt and jackboots?

The old *foetor Judaicus*. She had always taken the imagined smell to be sulphurous, an accompaniment to the tail and horns, conclusive proof that the Jew was friendly with the devil and that his natural habitat was hell. A cabinet in her museum would mention the *foetor Judaicus* along with other Christian superstitions about Jews, now long consigned to the dustbin of medieval hatred, a reminder of how far Jews in this country had travelled.

Or had they?

But what if the *foetor Judaicus* was not hellish in origin at all? What if the smell that medieval Christians sniffed on the horned and hairy bodies of Jews was simply the smell of fear?

If so – if there are people who will murder you because they are aroused by the odour of your fear – is the concept of anti-Semitism itself an aphrodisiac, an erotic spur to loathing?

Could be. She loathed the word herself. *Anti-Semitism*. It had a medicinal, antiseptic ring to it. It was something you kept locked away in your bathroom cabinet. She had long ago made a vow never to open the cupboard. If you can help it, don't see the thing; if you can avoid it, don't use the word. Anti-Semite, anti-Semite, anti-Semite — its unmusicality pained her ear, its triteness degraded her.

If there was one thing she couldn't forgive the anti-Semites for, it was making her call them anti-Semites.

A couple of Muslim men, perhaps stopping for a talk on their way to the Regent's Park Mosque, looked at her in a way she found uncomfortable. Or was she looking at them in a way they found uncomfortable? She paused to root through her handbag for her keys. The men moved on. Across the road a boy of about nineteen was talking into his mobile phone. He held it suspiciously she thought, cradling it, as though only pretending to talk. Had he been using it as a camera?

Or a detonator?

2

Treslove tried to fix a time to see Finkler. There were things to talk about. Libor for one. Where was he? How was he?

And the play. All very well for Finkler to clown about it, but something needed to be said. Perhaps an answering play to be written. *Sons of Ishmael*, or *Jesus's Children*. Treslove would have been prepared to have a go himself, but he wasn't a writer. Nor do I know much about the subject, he told Hephzibah, though that, as they agreed, hadn't stopped the authors of *Sons of Abraham*. Finkler, on the other hand, was a one-man word factory. And appeared to have become more fluid in his politics. More fluid in something, anyway.

'Don't count on it,' Hephzibah said, which Treslove interpreted in a dozen ways, all of them upsetting to his peace of mind.

Hephzibah was, of course, another reason to see Finkler, face to face.

It wasn't his intention to bring the subject of her up. But

Finkler might. And whether he did or he didn't, the odd phrase or look would surely betray something.

And then there was the matter of the prostitutes. He had no intention of prying or giving advice. He had no advice to give. But he was supposed to be Finkler's friend. And if Finkler was in distress, well . . .

He got him on the phone. 'Come out and play,' he said.

But Finkler wasn't in the mood. 'I have of late,' he said, 'lost all my mirth.'

They had worked out a standard answer to that in school. 'I'll find it for you.'

'Nice of you, but I doubt you'll know where to look. I'll take a raincheck if that's all right.'

He didn't say he had prostitutes to visit. Or online poker to play. Or that what he had in fact lost of late was his money. Nor did he say, *And give my love to Hep.* Was that significant?

Alfredo's prostitute text continued to cause Treslove unease. About Alfredo not least. Why the malice? Why the mischief? Or was he trying to tell his father that he was reduced to going out looking for prostitutes himself thanks to his deprived upbringing? You were such a shit dad that I must seek the consolation of whores.

Treslove wished the pox on him. Then immediately unwished it. All this being a Jew when he might have done better being a father.

He did not understand why anyone would seek the consolation of whores. He did not, himself, do unassociated desire. And he had no reason to think Finkler did. So either he was so far from himself that there was no knowing what he would do, including make a move on Hephzibah, or he had already made a move on Hephzibah, been rejected and turned to prostitutes as Treslove turned to opera.

Unless he had made a move on Hephzibah, been accepted and turned to prostitutes either a) to assuage his guilt, or b) to express the superabundance of his satisfaction. That one

Treslove did understand: that you might go with a second woman as a delirious after-effect of having just been with the first.

But not a prostitute. Not after Hephzibah!

Treslove didn't want to be feeling any of this. Either about his friend who in all likelihood was simply in the deep dejection of widowerhood still. Or about Hephzibah who was worried sick about the imminent opening of the museum, and wouldn't have thanked Treslove for saddling her with the extraneous perturbations of adultery. Or about himself. He wanted to be happy. Or, if he was happy, he wanted to be happier. Sane. Or, if he was sane, saner.

He didn't quite believe his own suspicions. Jealousy wasn't in his nature. That wasn't self-flattery. He tried to work up a passion over Finkler and Abe and anyone else Hephzibah might be seeing at the museum, the architect, the works foreman, the electrician, the person employed to wipe the bacon fat off door handles, the person doing the smearing even, but he couldn't find any lasting rage or sorrow. What Treslove did was exclusion, not jealousy. And though they were related, they were not the same. Jealousy would have made him angry with Hephzibah, it might even have aroused him; but all he felt was lonely and rejected.

It was like being a child among adults; not unloved but unlistened to. At best humoured. He wasn't the real McCoy, that was what it came to. Not only wasn't he a Jew, he was a jest to Jews.

The real McGoy.

Hephzibah's mysteriously extended family was a case in point. Every time she took him round to meet the second half-cousin of an aunt-in-law three times removed, always surrounded by nephews and nieces and the children of nephews and nieces who looked just like the last lot but weren't, they pounced on Treslove, as though he had just been found wandering naked and without language in the Mata Atlântica, in order to be the first to explain to him the complexities of family relations in the civilised world, information for which he would certainly have been grateful had it not been delivered to him as though any kinship system beyond being the only child of divorced drug-taking parents was bound to be outside the comprehension of a Gentile.

It was in the same spirit, too, that they fed him, pushing food on him as though he hadn't had a square meal since being abandoned to savages twenty years before and neither knew the names of any foodstuff that wasn't grass nor was prepared for any taste that wasn't coconut. 'Be careful, that's hot!' they would shout when he spooned horseradish on to a slice of tongue, though he reckoned the mashed banana and strained peach with which one of the babies was covering his face would have been far hotter. Followed by, 'You might not like that, it's tongue, not everybody can cope with tongue.'

Not everybody? Did they become *everybody* the minute they clapped eyes on him?

No harm was meant, he knew. Quite the opposite. And Hephzibah found it all very funny, going over to him while it was happening and running her hands through his hair. But it wore him down. It wouldn't stop. There was never a time when they opened the door to him and said *Julian, how nice to see you, come in, we have nothing in the way of food or other secrets of our culture to test you with today and are no more conscious of your being a Gentile than you are of our being Jews.*

He was always a curiosity to them. Always a bit of a barbarian who had to be placated with beads and mirrors. He charged himself with ingratitude and humourlessness. Each time he fell into a pet he promised he would learn to do better. But he never did. They wouldn't let him. Wouldn't let him in.

And then when they did . . .

3

The face-painting incident.

Once, in his student days, Treslove met a very beautiful hippy girl, a true wispy child of nature and marijuana, dressed in a big girl's version of a little girl's nightgown. The occasion was a gestalt nostalgia party in East Sussex. They were being their parents as they imagined their parents had been. But they were doing it for real as well, in the sense that they had an ecological agenda.

Though Treslove was doing a module in Pollution and Conservation he didn't exactly have an ecological agenda himself. But he was happy that other people did. It made for a good party.

It was an early summer's evening, and gentleness was in the air. Everyone sat on cushions on the floor and told everyone else what they thought of them. Only rarely did anyone express anything other than deep affection. There were candles in the garden, music played, people kissed, cut out shapes from coloured paper which they hung from trees, and painted one another's faces.

Treslove had little aptitude for art of any sort, but for face-painting he had no aptitude whatsoever. The beautiful hippy girl floated across to where he was sitting on a garden bench, smoking dope. Through her little girl's dress he could see her big girl's breasts. 'Peace,' he said, offering her the spliff.

She was carrying paints. 'Paint me,' she said.

'I can't,' he told her. 'I have no aptitude.'

'We can all paint,' she said, kneeling in front of him, offering her face. 'Just let the colours flow.'

'Colours don't flow with me,' he explained. 'And I can never think of a subject.'

'Paint the me you see,' she told him, closing her eyes and pulling back her hair.

315

So Treslove painted a clown. Not an elegant or tragic clown. Not a Pierrot or Pirouette, but an Auguste with an absurd red nose, and big splotches of white outlined with black around the mouth and above the eyes, and crimson patches on the cheeks. A drooling, dribbling splosher of a clown.

She cried when she saw what he had done to her. The host of the party asked him to leave. Everyone was looking. Including Finkler who was down from Oxford for the weekend and whom Treslove had taken to the party. Finkler had his arms around a girl whose face he had exquisitely painted with floating shapes, in the manner of Chagall.

'What have I done?' Treslove wanted to know.

'You've made a fool of me,' the girl said.

Treslove would not have made a fool of her for the world. In point of fact he had fallen in love with her while he painted her. It was just that a red nose and big white mouth and crimson patches on the cheeks were all that he could think of painting.

'You have humiliated me,' the girl cried, sobbing into a tissue. The tears mingling with the face paint made her look even more ridiculous than Treslove had made her look. She was beside herself with distress.

Treslove looked over to Finkler for support. Finkler shook his head as over someone to whom he had shown infinite patience in the past but could forgive no more. He enfolded his girl in his arms so that she should not have to see what his friend had done.

'Leave,' the host said.

Treslove was a long time recovering from this incident. It marked him, in his own eyes, as a man who didn't know how to relate to people, especially women. Thereafter, he hesitated when he was invited to a party. And started, in the way that some people start from spiders, whenever he saw a box of children's paints or people painting one another's faces at a fete.

That the girl he had painted as a clown might have been the Judith who avenged herself on him outside the window of J. P. Guivier had of course crossed his mind. Everything crossed Treslove's mind. But for it to have been her, she must have changed considerably over the years both in physique and in temper.

Was it likely, either, that she would nurse her grievance, not only for more than a quarter of a century but to the extent of deliberately tracing Treslove's whereabouts and tracking him through the streets of London? No. But then again trauma is incalculable in its effects. Could he, with a box of paints, have made an insanely unforgiving brute out of that sweet-natured girl?

Such questions were purely academic now that he had become a Finkler. What had been, had been. Indeed, he remembered the face-painting incident only when Hephzibah took him to a family birthday party at which the paints came out. Though children did not normally take much account of Treslove whom they managed not to see, this little girl – he was not sure of her relation to Hephzibah, so assumed a great-great-niece: it was either that or great-great-aunt – this little girl for some unaccountable reason did.

'Are you Hephzibah's husband?' she asked him.

'In a manner of speaking,' he replied.

'In a manner of speaking yes or no?'

Treslove was uncomfortable talking to children, not knowing whether he should address them as very young versions of himself, or very old versions of himself. Since she was a Finkler and therefore, he assumed, preternaturally smart, he opted for the very old version of himself. 'In a manner of speaking both,' he said. 'In the eyes of God, if not in the eyes of society, I am her husband.'

'My daddy says there is no God,' the little girl said.

This took Treslove to the limits of what he knew about speaking to children. 'Well,' he said, 'there you are then.'

'You're funny,' the little girl told him. There was a precocity about her he couldn't fathom. She appeared almost to be flirting with him. An impression augmented by how grown-up her clothes were. He had noticed this before about Finkler children. Their mothers dressed them in the height of adult fashion, as though no opportunity to find a husband was to be forgone.

'Funny in what way?'

'Different funny.'

'I see,' he said. By different did she mean not Finkler? Was it evident to a child?

It was at this point that Hephzibah came over carrying paints. 'You two seem to be hitting it off,' she said.

'She knows I'm not *unserer*,' Treslove said under his breath. 'She's picked me for *anderer*. It's uncanny.'

Unserer, as Hephzibah's family used the word, meant Jewish. One of us. *Anderer* was one of them. The enemy. The alien. Julian Treslove.

'That's nonsense,' Hephzibah said, under her breath.

'Why are you whispering?' the little girl asked. 'My daddy says it's rude to whisper.'

Rude to whisper, Treslove thought, but not rude to be a fucking atheist at seven.

'I know what,' Hephzibah said, 'why don't you ask Julian nicely and he'll paint your face for you?'

'Julian Nicely, will you paint my face for me?' the little girl said, much amused by her own joke.

'No,' Treslove said.

The little girl's mouth fell open.

'Julian!' Hephzibah said.

'I can't.'

'Why can't you?'

'I can't, leave it at that.'

'Is this because you think she knows you're not *unserer*?'

'Don't be ridiculous. I just don't paint faces.'

318

'Paint hers for me. Look, she's upset.'

'I'm sorry if you're upset,' he said to the little girl. 'But you might as well get used to the idea that we don't always get what we want.'

'Julian!' Hephzibah said again. 'It's only face-painting. She isn't asking you to buy her a house.'

'*She*,' Treslove said, 'isn't asking for anything. It's you.'

'So *I* am to be taught a lesson in what not to expect from life?'

'I'm not teaching anyone anything. I just don't do face-paints.'

'Even though two young women are deeply upset by your refusal?'

'Don't be cute, Hep.'

'And don't you be objectionable. Just paint her fucking face.'

'No. How many more times must I say it? No. Face-painting is not my scene. OK?'

Whereupon, in what Hephzibah was to describe to herself as a most unmanly fit of petulance, he swept out of the room and indeed out of the house. When Hephzibah returned several hours later she found him in their bed, his face turned to the wall.

Hephzibah was not a woman who allowed silences to build up. 'So what was that about?' she asked.

'You know what it was about. I don't do face-painting.'

Hephzibah assumed this was code for *I don't do your family*.

'Fine,' she said. 'Then would you please stop this fantasy about how wonderful you find us?'

Treslove assumed *us* was code for Finklers.

He didn't promise he would stop. But nor did he tell her she was wrong in her assumption.

It was all too much for him – children, parties, face paints, families, Finklers.

He had bitten off more than he could chew.

4

And yet he was more them than they were, felt more for them and what they stood for than they, as far as he could see, were capable of feeling for themselves. He wouldn't have gone so far as to say they needed him, but they did, didn't they? They *needed* him.

He had left the theatre seething with rage. On behalf of Hephzibah. On behalf of Libor. On behalf of Finkler, whatever Finkler felt or pretended to feel about the poison play. Why, he was even prepared to feel rage on behalf of Abe, whose client called the Holocaust a holiday and wondered why he'd lost his job while he was snorkelling in the Med.

Someone had to feel what he felt because on behalf of themselves what did they feel? Not enough. Hephzibah he knew was angry and disconsolate but preferred to look somewhere else. Finkler thought it was a joke. Libor had turned his head away from everything and everyone. Leaving only him, Julian Treslove, son of a melancholy and friendless cigar seller who played the fiddle where no one could hear him; Julian Treslove, ex of the BBC, ex arts administrator, one-time lover of a host of hopeless unfleshly girls who wore too many bras, father of a sandwich-making in-denial homosexual and a Jew-hating opportunist piano player; Julian Treslove, Finklerphile and would-be Finkler except that the Finklers in their ethno-religious separatism or whatever one was meant to call it just didn't fucking want to know.

Hard to go on feeling outrage for people who behaved to you exactly as they were accused of behaving to everyone else precisely because of which accusations you were outraged for them. Hard, but not impossible. Treslove saw where this was taking him and refused to go there. A principle of truth – political truth and art truth – stood beyond such personal betrayals and disappointments. *Sons of Abraham*, like much else of its kind, was a travesty of dramatic thought because it lacked imagination of otherness, because it accorded to its own self-righteousness a supremacy of truth, because it mistook propaganda for art, because it was rabble-rousing, and Treslove owed it to himself, never mind his inadequately affronted friends, not to be rabble-roused. He wished he had an arts programme to produce again. He would have enjoyed giving *Sons* – as it was no doubt called within the fraternity – the once over at three o'clock in the morning.

Treslove's bit for honour and veracity.

'But are you saying Zionism is exempt from criticism? Are you denying what we have seen with our own eyes on television?' the BBC bosses would have asked him at programme review, as though he, Julian Treslove, son of a melancholy and friendless cigar seller etc., had suddenly become Zionism's spokesman, or truth was to be apprehended in ten seconds flat on *Newsnight*, or humanity was incapable of addressing one wrong without instigating another.

He knew what he thought. He thought there would be no settling this until there'd been another Holocaust. He could see because he was outside it. He could afford to see what they – his friends, the woman he loved – dared not. The Jews would not be allowed to prosper except as they had always prospered, at the margins, in the concert halls and at the banks. *End of.* As his sons said. Anything else would not be tolerated. A brave rearguard action in the face of insuperable odds was one thing. Anything resembling victory and peace was another. It could not be borne, whether by Muslims for whom Jews were a sort of erroneous and lily-livered brother, always to be kept in their place, or by Christians to whom they were anathema, or by themselves to whom they were an embarrassment.

That was the total of Treslove's findings after a year of

being an adopted Finkler in his own eyes if in no one else's – they didn't have a chance in hell.

Just as he didn't.

So that, at least, was something they were in together. Schtuck.

'In schtuck' was a favourite expression of his father's, a man who got by essentially without expression. Remembering it recently, Treslove thought the word must have been Yiddish and his father's using it the proof that something Jewish was trying to force its way out of him. Schtuck – it looked Yiddish, it sounded Yiddish, and it meant something – a sort of sticky mess – that only Yiddish could adequately express; but he didn't find the word in any of the museum's Yiddish dictionaries. The evidence of his Jewish antecedence proved as recalcitrant as ever. But in this at least he was a Jew – he was in deep schtuck.

5

The worst times, Libor remembered, were the mornings. For her and for him, but it was her he was thinking about.

There was never making any peace with it; neither had what could be called religious faith, both rejected false consolation, but there would be an hour there when the lights were dim and he would lie by her side, stroking her hair or holding her hand, not knowing if she was awake or asleep – but he was thinking about her, not him – an hour when, awake or asleep, she appeared to have accepted what she had no choice but to accept, and the idea of returning to earth, or even to nothing, caught the quiet of assent.

She could smile at him in the night when the pain was eased. She could look deep into his eyes, beckon him to her and whisper what he thought would be a fond memory into his ear, but which turned out to be a raucous allusion, an obscenity even. She wanted him to laugh, because they had laughed so often together. He had made her laugh at the beginning. Laughter had been his most precious gift to her. His ability to make her laugh was the reason – one of the reasons – she had chosen him above Horowitz. Laughter had never been at war with the softer emotions in her. She could roar and be gentle in the same breath. And now she wanted laughter to be her final gift to him.

In the stealthy alternations of rudery and sweetness, somewhere between waking and sleep, light and darkness, they found – she found, she found – a modus mortis.

It was bearable, then. Not a peace or a resignation, but an engagement of the fact of death with the fact of life. Though she was dying they were still living, together. He would turn the lights out and return to her side and listen to her going off and know that she was living with dying.

But in the morning the horror of it returned. Not only the horror of the pain and what she knew she must have looked like, but the horror of the knowledge.

If Libor could only have spared her that knowledge! He would have died for her to spare her that knowledge, only that would have been to burden her with another, and she assured him, greater loss. He could not bear, when morning broke, her waking up to what she had perhaps forgotten all about while she slept. He imagined the finest division of time, the millionth of a millionth of a second of pure mental excruciation in which the terrible incontrovertibility of her finished life returned to her. No laughter or consoling obscenities in the first minutes of the morning. No companionable sorrowing together either. She lay there on her own, not wanting to hear from him, unavailable to him, staring up at the ceiling – as though that was the route out she would finally take – seeing the ice-cold certainty of her soon becoming nothing.

The morning was always waiting for her. No matter where they had got to the night before, no matter what quiet almost bearable illusion of living with her dying he believed her to have attained, the morning always dashed it.

So the morning was always waiting for Libor too. The morning waiting for her to wake. And now the morning waiting for himself to wake.

He wished he'd been a believer. He wished they both had, though perhaps one of them might have taken the other along. But belief had its underbelly of doubting, too. How could it be otherwise? You would see the meaning in the night, see God's face even, if you were lucky – the *shechina*: he had always loved that concept, or the sound of it at least, God's refulgence – but the next day, or the next, it would be gone. Faith wasn't a mystery to him; the mystery to him was holding on to faith.

He kissed her eyes at night and tried to fall asleep himself in hope. But things didn't get better; they got worse, precisely because every careful crafting of feeling better, of assent, submission, accommodation – he didn't have the word – survived no more than a single night. Nothing was ever settled. Nothing ever sealed. The day began again as though the horror had that very moment been borne in on her for the first time.

And on him.

6

Tyler's life was over much more quickly. A brisk woman in all her dealings, including her adulteries, she dealt in a businesslike manner with death. She arranged what needed arranging, left instructions, demanded certain promises of Finkler, took as unemotional a farewell of her children as she could bear to take, shook hands with Finkler as over a deal that had not worked out wonderfully but had not worked out too badly either, all things considered, and died.

'Is this all I get?' Finkler wanted to shake her and say.

But over time he discovered there were things she had wanted to say to him, matter she had wanted to bring up, but had not, either for fear of upsetting him or for fear of upsetting herself. Not tender things or sentimental matter – though he continued to find letters he had written to her and photographs of them both and of the family which she had bundled prettily and tied with ribbons and kept in places he presumed to be sacred – but issues of a practical and even argumentative nature, souvenirs of their disagreements, such as the documents relating to her conversion to Judaism, and a number of articles he had written which she had, unknown to him, annotated and filed, and a tape of the broadcast of *Desert Island Discs* in which he had announced his shame to the world and for which she had never, and never would for all eternity, she had vowed, forgive him.

In a box marked 'To Be Opened By My Husband When I Have Gone', which at first he thought she might have prepared prior to going in a more mundane sense – had she ever *seriously* thought of leaving him? he wondered – he found photographs of him as a nice Jewish boy being bar mitzvahed, and photographs of him as a nice Jewish bridegroom being married to her, and photographs of him as a nice Jewish father at the bar mitzvahs of his sons (these in an envelope bearing a large ? as though to ask why, why, Shmuelly, did you consent to any of these ceremonials if you intended to shit on them?), together with a number of articles on the Jewish faith and on Zionism, some written by him, and heavily annotated again, some written by other journalists and scholars, and one short typewritten manuscript, expostulatory, overpunctuated, and tidied-up in a plastic folder, like homework, the author of which was none other than Tyler Finkler, his wife.

Finkler folded himself in two and wept when he found this.

She was too overwrought to be a good writer, Finkler had always thought. Finkler himself was no stylist, but he knew how to make a sentence trot along. A reviewer of one of

Finkler's first self-help books – Finkler wasn't sure whether he meant to be kind or unkind, so he took it for the former – described reading his prose as being like taking a train journey in the company of someone who might have been a genius, but then might just as easily have been a halfwit. Tyler's writing did not veer between these extremes. Reading her was like being on a train journey with an indubitably clever person who had given her life to composing messages on greetings cards. A criticism, as it happens, that had been levelled at Finkler's early bestseller *The Socratic Flirt: How to Reason Your Way into a Better Sex Life*.

Tyler had had a sudden insight into her husband, that was what made her put her thoughts on paper. He was too Jewish. He didn't suffer from an insufficiency of Jewish thought or temperament, but the opposite. They all did, these *Shande* Jews. (*Shande* Jews was her name for the ASHamed. *Shande* means shame as in disgrace, and that was what she thought about them. That they *brought* shame.) But he, the pompous prick, more than the others.

'The thing with my husband,' she wrote, as if to a divorce lawyer, though Finkler himself was the addressee, 'is that he thinks he has jumped the Jewish fence his father put around him, but he still sees everything from a WHOLLY Jewish point of view, including the Jews who disappoint him. Wherever he looks, in Jerusalem or Stamford Hill or Elstree, he sees Jews living no better than anybody else. And because they are not exceptionally good, it follows – to his extremist Jewish logic – that they are exceptionally bad! Just like the conventional Jews he scorns to spite his father, my husband adheres with arrogance to the principle that Jews either exist to be "a light unto the nations" (*Isaiah 42: 6*) or don't deserve to exist at all.'

Finkler cried a couple more times. Not because of what his wife had charged him with, but because of the childlike conscientiousness of her Bible citations. He could see her bent

326

over the page, concentrating. Perhaps reaching for a Bible to be sure she had cited Isaiah correctly. It made him think of her as a little girl at Sunday school, reading about the Jews with a pencil in her mouth, not knowing that one day she would marry and give her life to one, and become a Jew herself, though not in the eyes of Orthodox Jews like his father. And maybe not even in the eyes of Finkler either.

He had at no time been sympathetic to Tyler's Jewish aspirations. He didn't need to be married to a Jew. He was Jew enough – at least in his antecedence – for both of them. Fine, he'd said when she told him what she intended to do. He assumed she wanted a Jewish wedding. What woman didn't want a Jewish wedding? Fine.

So off she went to talk to the rabbis and when she told him she would take the Reform route he nodded without listening. She could have been describing a bus journey she was planning. It would take about a year, she said, perhaps more for her because she was starting from scratch. Fine, he said. Take as long as you like. It wasn't that this gave him time to be with his mistresses. He had not yet married Tyler – she wouldn't marry him until she was a Jew – and so mistresses were not yet in the picture. He was a scrupulous man. He would not have taken a mistress before he had a wife. Another woman yes, a mistress no. He was a philosopher; nomenclature mattered to him. So there was no motive for his indifference. He was unable to put his mind to Tyler getting a Jewish education for the pure and simple reason that he couldn't have cared less.

She went to classes once a week for fourteen months. There she learned Hebrew, he gathered, was told God knows what about the Bible, told what not to eat, told what not to wear, told what not to say, taught how to run a Jewish home and be a Jewish mother, paraded before a council of rabbis, submerged (at her own insistence) in water – and lo! he had a Jewish bride. He didn't listen when she came back each week and tried to interest him in what she'd learned. *His* life was more interesting. He nodded his head, waited for her to finish, then told her he'd been to see a publisher. He hadn't yet written a book, but he felt he needed a publisher. He was on the way. People were taking notice. She wanted a Moses to lead her into the Promised Land? He was that Moses. She should just follow him.

So little notice did he take of her studies that she might have been having an affair with one of the rabbis for all he knew. These things happened. Rabbis, too, were men of flesh and blood. And teaching was . . . well Finkler knew as well as anyone what teaching was.

He wouldn't begrudge her if she had. Now that she was dead he wanted her to have had a better life than he had given her. No husband is ever more magnanimous, he thought, than when he becomes a widower. There was an article in that.

It was in her conversion class, presumably, that she had been told about the Jewish aspiration to be 'a light unto the nations'. Had they – had the rabbi he wished to have been in love with her and who he hoped had secretly taken her to kosher restaurants to teach her how to eat lokshen pudding – had *he* shown her how to put a little bracket around the chapter and verse that she was citing?

Poor Tyler.

(Tyler Finkler 49: 3) The age at which she died and the number of children she had left motherless.

It broke his heart. But that didn't mean he cared to go on reading. The last thing he wanted to remember about his wife was her baby Hebrew education. He put her little essay back into its folder, blew it a kiss, and stored the box it came in at the bottom of her wardrobe, where she had kept her shoes.

Only on the night he returned from accompanying Hephzibah and Treslove to *Sons of Abraham* did the impulse to look at it again seize him. He couldn't have said why. Maybe he was lonely without her. Maybe he was desperate to hear her voice. Or maybe he just needed something, anything, to stop him going to his computer and playing poker.

Her argument was as he remembered but he felt more tenderly towards it now. It can take time for a husband to discover that his wife's words are worth attending to.

She had hit upon a paradox.

(Think of it – Tyler hitting on a paradox! The things of which a husband does not know his wife to be capable!)

Her paradox was this:

'The *Shande* Jews my husband spends his evenings with, (when he isn't spending them with his mistress), accuse Israelis and those they call 'Zionist fellow-travellers' of thinking they enjoy a *special* moral status which entitles them to treat everyone else like shit; but this accusation is itself founded on the assumption that Jews enjoy a special moral status and should know better. (Do you remember what you used to say to the kids, Shmuel, when they complained they were being told off for doing nothing different to what other kids did? "I judge you by a more exacting standard," you told them. Why? Why do you – *you* of all people – judge Jews by a more exacting standard?)'

Her own 'wise' husband had told her that the state of Israyel – a state he could not bear to name without putting in a derisive *y* – had been founded on an act of brutal expropriation. So what state wasn't? Tyler asked, mentioning the American Indian and the Australian Aborigine.

Finkler smiled. Fancy Tyler, in her jewellery and furs, caring about the Australian Aborigine.

She saw it this way . . .

The cheek of her! *She saw it this way*. Tyler Gallagher, the granddaughter of Irish tinkers, who won a prize at Sunday school when she was eight years old for a drawing of the baby Jesus holding out his podgy hands to take his Christmas presents from the Three Wise Men. Telling him how she saw it.

This, anyway, was the way it looked to her, whatever her husband thought.

'For pogrom after pogrom Jews bowed their heads and held on. God had picked them for His own. God would help them. The Holocaust – yes, yes, here we go, Shmuelly, Holocaust, Holocaust!! – the Holocaust changed all that FOREVER. Jews finally woke up to being on their own. They had to look out for themselves. And that meant having their own country. In fact they already had it, but let's not get into that, Mr Palestine. They had to have their own country and when you have your own country you become different from who you were *before* you had your own country. You become like everybody else! Only *you* and *your cronies* won't let them be like everybody else, because for you, Shmuel, they are still obliged to obey the God (in whom you don't believe!) and be an example to the world!

'Explain to your poor, uneducated, would-be Jewish wife why else you can't leave the Jews of the country I've even heard you call Canaan, you sick fucker, alone? Are you afraid that if you don't get in with your criticism early, worse will come from somewhere else? Is yours some perverted patriotism that burns up territory you're afraid of losing so that it won't fall into enemy hands??

'Answer me this: Why don't you mind your own fucking business, Shmuel? You won't be judged alongside Israyelis unless you choose to be. You have your country, they have theirs – a fact, to quote you on being married to me, that "invites neither exceptional sympathy nor exceptional censure". They are now just ordinary bastards, half right, half wrong, like the *rest* of us.

'Because even you, my false, beloved husband, are not ALL wrong.'

This time he didn't fold her little essay away but sat with it awhile in front of him. Poor Tyler. Which he knew very well was Finkler-speak for poor him. He missed her. They'd fought and fought but there had always been companionableness in it. He had never raised his hand to her, nor she to him. They had always talked everything through, the sound of each other's voice a daily source of unremarked pleasure to them both. He would have loved to hear her voice now. What he would have given to be able to go out into their now neglected garden with her and put his finger on the knot of green string she was always asking him to help her tie.

They had not been together long enough for it to be one of the great marital adventures, akin to that enjoyed by Libor and Malkie, but they'd been on an enjoyable trek together. And they'd brought up three smart children, no matter that some were smarter than others.

He sat and cried a little. Tears were good in that they were undiscriminating. He didn't have to know for whom or what he wept. He wept for everything.

He liked Tyler's point about his being a patriot, burning up what he was afraid of losing. He didn't know if it was true but he liked the idea. So was Tamara the same? Were all the ASHamed Jews killing the thing they loved for fear of its falling into the enemy's hands?

Tyler's was as good a guess as any. Something had to explain the queer, passionate hatred of these people. Self-hate certainly didn't get it. Self-haters would surely go about in surly isolation, but the ASHamed sought out one another's company, cheered one another on, expressed their feelings as a group activity, as soldiers might on the eve of battle. It could easily be, in that case, just as poor Tyler had described it, another version of the old beleaguered Jewish tribalism. The enemy remained who the enemy had always been. The *others*. This was just the latest tactic in the age-old war. To kill our own before the *others* could.

Certainly, Finkler never once came away from their meetings without feeling exactly as he had felt when accompanying his father to synagogue – that the world was too Jewish for him, too old, too communal in an anthropological, almost primal sense – too far back, too deep down, too long ago.

He was a thinker who didn't know what he thought, except that he had loved and failed and now missed his wife, and that he hadn't escaped what was oppressive about Judaism by joining a Jewish group that gathered to talk feverishly about the oppressiveness of being Jewish. Talking feverishly about being Jewish *was* being Jewish.

He stayed up late watching television, trying to stay away from his computer. Enough with the poker.

But poker served a purpose. T. S. Eliot told Auden that the reason he played patience night after night was that it was the nearest thing to being dead.

Patience, poker . . . What difference?

TWELVE

I

It was thought that Meyer Abramsky had been suffering from severe depression. He had seven children and his wife was heavy with his eighth. He had been told by the Israeli army to prepare to remove his family from the settlement he had helped to found, in accordance with God's promise, sixteen years before. He had travelled from Brooklyn with his young wife in order to keep his bargain with God. And they were doing this to him! Assistance would be given to rehouse him, and consideration would be shown to his wife's condition. But the settlement had to go. Thus spake Obama.

It was agreed that they would not go quietly, not any of them. To go quietly would be to accede to blasphemy. This was their land. They didn't have to share it, they didn't have to do deals to secure it, it was theirs. He could point to the verse in the Torah where it said so. There the promise, there the place. Why, if you looked closely and read as you were meant to read, Meyer Abramsky's house itself was mentioned. There. Right there where the page was worn thin with pointing.

After threatening to barricade his family in their house and shoot whoever tried to move them – never mind that they were fellow Jews; fellow Jews do not eject their own people from sacred land – Meyer Abramsky read about himself in the newspapers. There was talk of his succumbing to a 'siege mentality'. *Siege mentality!* What else did they expect? It wasn't only Meyer Abramsky who was under siege, it was the entire Jewish people.

He never did carry out his threat to shoot the Israeli soldiers who ejected him. Instead, he boarded a bus and shot an Arab family. A mother, a father, a baby. One, two, three bullets. One, two, three victims. Thus spake the Lord.

2

It was not known whether Libor read about the incident and was affected by it. It seemed unlikely. Libor had not read a newspaper for weeks.

Whether he bought a paper to read on the train to Eastbourne isn't known either. Had he done so he would certainly have seen photographs of Meyer Abramsky on the front pages. But by that time Libor had already made his decision. Why else would he have taken the train to Eastbourne?

He sat opposite Treslove's son Alfredo on the train without either knowing who the other was. Only later did this emerge, causing Treslove to unwind a chain of improbable causality at the end of which he found his guilt. Had Treslove been a better father and not fallen out with Alfredo he might have had him round to dinner at Hephzibah's where he would have met Libor, and had he met Libor he would have recognised him on the train and then . . .

So Treslove was to blame.

Alfredo was travelling to Eastbourne with his dinner jacket in his overnight bag. He would be playing 'Happy Birthday' and similar requests at the best hotel in Eastbourne that night.

He thought the old man sitting opposite him was yellow. He must have been about a hundred, he said. Alfredo didn't like old men much. These things probably start with fathers and Alfredo didn't like his father. In answer to the question of whether the old man sitting opposite him appeared anxious or depressed he repeated that he looked about a hundred – how else are you going to look at that age but anxious and depressed? He didn't talk to the old man other than to offer him a peppermint, which was refused, and to ask where he was going.

'Eastbourne,' the old man told him.

Yes, obviously Eastbourne, but where specifically? To stay with family? A hotel? (Alfredo hoped not the hotel he was playing at, which had an old enough clientele already.)

'Nowhere,' the old man told him.

Libor was more precise in his instructions to the taxi driver when he got to Eastbourne. 'Bitchy 'Ead,' he said.

'Do you mean Beachy Head?' the driver asked.

'What did I just say?' Libor answered. 'Bitchy 'Ead!'

Did he want to be dropped anywhere in particular? The pub, the lookout . . . ?

'Bitchy 'Ead.'

The driver who had a father of his own and knew that old men were made irritable by age explained that if he wanted him to wait he would. Otherwise he could ring for him to come back and collect him. 'Or there's a bus,' he said. 'A 12a.'

'Not necessary,' Libor said.

'Well, if you do need me,' the driver insisted, handing him his card.

Libor put the card in his pocket without looking at it.

3

He drank a whisky in the slate-floored pub, sitting at a small round table looking out to sea. He thought it was the identical table to the one he and Malkie had sat at on the day they drove here long ago to test each other's courage, but he might have been wrong about that. It didn't matter. The view was the same, the coast swirling away to the west, flinty and ancient, the sea colourless but for the thin line of silver on the horizon.

He drank another whisky then left the pub and climbed slowly up the downlands, bent as the trees and shrubs were bent. With no sun on them, the cliffs looked grimy, a mass of dirty chalk crumbling into the sea.

'You'd need some nerve to do this,' he remembered saying to Malkie.

Malkie had fallen silent, thinking about it. 'The dark would be best,' she had said at last, as they'd strolled back, arm in arm. 'I'd wait till it was dark and just keep on walking.'

He passed the little pile of stones, like something Jacob or Isaac might have built, with the plaque on which Psalm 93 was engraved. *Mightier than the thunder of many waters, mightier than the waves of the sea. The Lord on high is mighty.*

It seemed to him there were fewer of the randomly planted wooden crosses than he remembered. There should, surely, have been more. Unless, after a decent period of time, they were removed.

What was a decent period of time?

But again, tied to a scrap of wire fencing, there was a bunch of flowers. This one was from Marks & Spencer, with the price tag attached. £4.99. Don't splash out, he thought.

The place was not isolated. A bus had unloaded a party of pensioners. People walked their dogs and flew kites. Peered over. Shuddered. A hiking couple said hello to him. But it was very quiet, the wind blowing voices off the edge. He heard a sheep. 'Baaa.' Unless it was a seagull. And remembered home.

There was no evidence to support Malkie's fanciful conviction that it would take her beloved husband an unconscionable time to reach the bottom. Despite her believing she had married an exceptional man, he didn't fly or float. He went straight down like anybody else.

Treslove learned that Alfredo had been sitting opposite Libor on the Eastbourne train from Alfredo's mother. Alfredo had seen Libor's photograph on the South East television news – veteran journalist plunges to his death in Beachy Head's third suicide in a month – and realised it was the hundred-year-old man he had talked to on the train. This he mentioned to his mother, and this his mother took the trouble to communicate to Treslove when she herself read the dead man's name in the paper and recognised him as a friend of the father of her son.

'Strange coincidence,' she said in the same BBC voice with which she used to unpack rafts of ideas and unpick Treslove's sanity.

'Strange how?'

'Alfredo and your friend on the same train.'

'That's a coincidence. What makes it strange?'

'Two people from your past coming together.'

'Libor isn't from my past.'

'Everybody's from your past, Julian. That's where you put people.'

'Fuck you,' Treslove told her, ringing off.

He didn't hear of Libor's death this way. Had he done so he didn't know what violence he might have committed on Alfredo and Josephine. He didn't want them in the same breath or sentence as poor Libor, he didn't wish to think of them as having even shared existence with him. The fool of a boy should have seen something was wrong, should have engaged the old man in conversation, should have told someone. This wasn't any old train. You were meant to scrutinise people travelling alone to Eastbourne because there was just about only one reason why a single person would choose to go there.

He felt the same about the taxi driver. Who takes a lonely old man to a noted suicide spot in the late afternoon and leaves him? In fact, the driver thought this very thing about an hour after dropping Libor off and notified the police, but by then it was too late. This, as much as anything else, distressed Treslove – that his friend's last hour on earth had been spent staring at that cretin Alfredo in his pork-pie hat and discussing the weather with a numbskull Eastbourne taxi driver.

But he couldn't go on blaming other people. It was his fault in more ways than he could number. He had neglected Libor in recent months, thinking only about himself. And when he had spent time with him it was only to talk sexual jealousy. You don't talk sexual jealousy – you don't, if you have a grain of tact or discretion in your body, talk sexual anything to an old man who has recently lost the woman he had been in love with all his life. That was gross. And it was grosser still – worse than gross: it was brutal – to burden Libor with the knowledge of his affair with Tyler. That was a secret Treslove should have taken to the grave, as he supposed Tyler had. And Libor himself.

It wasn't out of the question that this uncalled-for confession was among the reasons Libor had ended his life – so that he didn't have to bear his friend's turpitude any longer. Treslove had seen Libor's face blacken when he'd bragged – let's call a spade a spade, it *was* bragging – about those stolen afternoons with Finkler's wife; he had seen the lights go out in the old man's eyes. It seemed to be a villainy too far for Libor. Treslove had blemished, discredited, defiled, the story of the three men's long-standing friendship, turned the trust between them, whatever their differences, into a fiction, a delusion, a lie.

Falsities spill over. Perhaps it wasn't only the romance of their friendship that Treslove had defiled; perhaps it was the idea of romance altogether. Once one cherished illusion goes, what's to stop the next? Had Treslove and Tyler's iniquity poisoned everything?

No, that in itself could not have not killed Libor. But who was to say it hadn't weakened his resolve to stay alive?

Treslove would have admitted all this to Hephzibah, begged for absolution in her arms, but to have done that he would have had to tell her, too, about Tyler, and that was something he couldn't do.

She was in a bad way herself. Though it was Libor who had brought Treslove and Hephzibah together, Treslove in his turn had made Libor more important to her than he had previously been. There had always been a fondness between them, but great-great-nieces are rarely intimate with their great-great-uncles. In her time with Treslove, though, this old, somewhat formal affection had blossomed into love, to the point where she was unable to remember not having him there, close to her, reminding her of Aunt Malkie, and making her love for Julian almost a family affair. She, too, castigated herself for allowing other concerns to consume her attention. She should have been keeping an eye on Libor.

But these other concerns would not let her alone. The murder of that Arab family on a bus was an unbearable event. She didn't know anyone who wasn't horrified. Horrified on behalf of the Arabs. Horrified *for* them. But, yes, horrified as well in anticipation of the consequences. Jews were being depicted everywhere as bloodthirsty monsters, however the history of Zionism was explained – whether bloodthirsty in their seizure of someone else's country from the start, or bloodthirsty as a consequence of events which bit by bit had made them strangers to compassion – yet no Jew was cheering the death of this Arab family, not in the streets nor in the quiet of their homes, no Jewish women gathered by the wells and ululated their jubilation, no Jewish men went to the synagogue to dance their thanks to the Almighty. Thou shalt not kill. They could say what they liked, the libellers and hate-mongers, stigmatising Jews as racists and supremacists, thou shalt not kill was emblazoned on the hearts of Jews.

And Jewish soldiers?

Well, Meyer Abramsky was no Jewish soldier. He vexed her moral sense in no way at all. It was only a pity he had been stoned to death. She would have liked to see him tried and found a thousand times guilty by Jews. *He is not one of ours.*

And then stoned to death by those whose moral character he had fouled.

A monument would eventually be erected in his name, of course. The settlers had to have their heroes. Who were these people? Where had they suddenly appeared from? They were alien to her education and upbringing. They had nothing to do with any Jewishness she recognised. They were the children of a universal unreason, of the same extraction as suicide bombers and all the other End of Time death cultists and apocalyptics, not the children of Abraham whose name they defamed. But try telling that to those who had taken to the streets and squares of London again, ready at a moment's notice with their chants and placards as though they woke to speak violence against the one country in the world of which the majority of the population was Jewish and were disappointed when a fresh day brought no justification for it.

It had started again, anyway. Her emails streamed reported menace and invective. A brick was thrown through a window of the museum. An Orthodox man in his sixties was beaten up at a bus stop in Temple Fortune. Graffiti began to appear again on synagogue walls, the Star of David crossed with the swastika. The internet bubbled and boiled with madness. She couldn't bear to open a newspaper.

Was it something or was it nothing?

Meanwhile there had to be a coroner's inquest into Libor's death. And more searching questions to be answered in their hearts by those who had loved him.

She knew what she thought. She thought Libor had gone for a walk at dusk — without doubt a lonely, melancholy walk, but just a walk — and had fallen. People do fall. Not everything is deliberated upon.

Libor fell.

5

'The hardest part,' Finkler told Treslove, 'is not to be defined by one's enemies. Just because I am no longer an ASHamed Jew does not mean I have relinquished my prerogative to be ashamed.'

'Why bring being ashamed into it at all?'

'You sound like my poor wife.'

'Do I?' Treslove, head down, blushed.

Finkler, thankfully, did not notice. '"What's it to you?" she used to ask me. "How does it reflect on you?" But it does. It reflects on me because I expect better.'

'Isn't that grandiosity?'

'Ha! My wife again. You didn't discuss me with her, did you? That's a rhetorical question. No, I don't think it's grandiosity to take what that lunatic Abramsky did personally. If any man's death diminishes me, because I am of mankind, then any man's act of murder does the same.'

'Then be diminished as a member of mankind. The grandiosity is to feel diminished as a Jew.'

Finkler clapped an arm around his friend's shoulder. 'I'll be paid out as a Jew,' he said, 'whatever you think.'

He smiled weakly, seeing Treslove in a *yarmulke*. The two men had walked aside, leaving Libor's family to be at his graveside with him, alone. The service had concluded, but Hephzibah and a number of others had wanted time to reflect away from the attentions of gravediggers and rabbis. When they had gone, Treslove and Finkler would have their hour.

They would rather not have talked about Abramsky. About Abramsky there was nothing civilised to say. But they held back from discussing Libor because they were afraid of their feelings. Treslove, especially, was unable to look at the ground in which Libor – still warm, was how he imagined him, still aggrieved and hurt – had been laid. Next to his mound of earth was Malkie's grave. The thought of them lying side by side, silent for all eternity, no laughter, no obscenities, no music, was more than he could bear.

Would he and Hephzibah . . . ? Would he be allowed to lie in a Jewish cemetery at all? They had already asked. All depended. If she wanted to be buried where her parents were buried, in a cemetery administered by the Orthodox, Treslove would probably be refused the right to be buried next to her. If, however . . . So many complications when you took up with a Jew, as Tyler had discovered. It was a shame she wasn't still here to ask. 'In the matter of sleeping-over rights, Tyler . . . ?'

Libor and Malkie had wanted to be buried in the same grave, one above the other, but there had been objections to that, as there were objections to everything, in death as in life, though no one was sure whether on religious grounds or simply because the earth was too stony to take a grave deep enough for two. And anyway, Malkie had joked, they would only end up fighting over who was to be on top. So they lay democratically, side by side, in their decorous Queen-size bed.

Hephzibah signalled that she and the family were leaving. She looked rather wonderful, Treslove thought, in veiled, shawled black, like a Victorian widow. A majestic relict. Treslove motioned that they would stay a little. The two men took each other's arms. Treslove was grateful for the support. He thought his legs would give way beneath him. He was not framed for cemeteries. They spoke too vividly to him of the end of love.

Had he looked around he would have been struck by the lack of statuary eloquence. A Jewish cemetery is a blank, mute place. As though by the time one reaches here there is nothing further to be said. But he kept his eyes to the ground, hoping to see nothing.

The two men stood silently together, like headstones themselves. 'To what base uses we may return,' Finkler said after a while.

'I'm sorry,' Treslove said, 'I can't play. Not today.'

'Fair enough. It wasn't my intention to be flippant.'

'I know,' Treslove said. 'I wouldn't accuse you of that. I don't doubt you loved him as much as I did.'

Silence again between them. Then, 'So what could we have done differently?' Finkler asked.

Treslove was surprised. That category of question normally belonged to him.

'Watched over him.'

'Would he have let us?'

'Had we done it as it should have been done he wouldn't have noticed.'

'Strange,' Finkler mused, not meaning to disagree, 'but I felt he left us.'

'Well, he's done that all right.'

'I mean earlier.'

'How much earlier?'

'When Malkie died. Didn't you think that when Malkie died he stopped?'

Treslove thought about it. 'No, that's not how I felt it,' he said. For Treslove a woman's death was a beginning. He was a man made to mourn. He had always imagined himself bent double, like the aged Thomas Hardy, revisiting the torn haunts of love. If anything, he had found Libor a touch vigorous after Malkie died. He would have cut a more distraught, tormented figure himself. 'To me,' he went on, 'it seemed that he left when I got together with Hephzibah.'

'Now who's being grandiose?' Finkler said. 'Do you think he thought his earthly task was done then, or what?'

If Finkler thought that was grandiose, what would he say if he ever found out that Treslove thought Libor had committed suicide because of what he knew about his and Tyler's adultery? Not that he ever would find that out. Supposing, of course, that he didn't already know.

'No, of course not that. But my new beginning, for what it is' – why did I say that, Treslove wondered, why the apology? – 'my new beginning with Hephzibah might have made him think there could be no new beginnings for him.'

'He should have palled out with me more in that case,' Finkler said. 'I'd have kept him company in no new beginnings.'

'Oh, come on.'

'*Oh, come on* nothing. We couldn't have competed with you. Yours was a beginning to end beginnings. You weren't a widower. You weren't even a divorcee. You started from scratch. New woman, new religion. Libor and I were dead men inhabiting a dead faith. You took both our souls on two counts. Good luck to you. We had no use for them. But you can't pretend the three of us were ever in anything together. We weren't the Three Musketeers. We died so that you could live, Julian. If that isn't too Christian a thought in such a place. You tell me.'

'What do I know, except that you ain't no dead man, Sam.'

Or was he? Sam the Dead Man. Treslove didn't dare raise his eyes from the earth to look at his friend. He hadn't seen him since they'd got here. He hadn't seen anything or anyone – except of course Hephzibah whom he couldn't miss.

'Well, of the two of us –' Finkler began, but he was unable to finish. A third person had arrived at the graveside. She stood quietly, anxious not to disturb their conversation. After a moment, she bent and took a handful of soil which she sprinkled like seeds on the mound of earth.

The men fell quiet, making her self-conscious. 'I'm sorry,' she said. 'I'll come back.'

'Please don't,' Finkler said. 'We're going in a minute ourselves.'

Before she rose, Treslove was able to get a look at her. An elderly woman, but not aged, elegant, her head covered with a light scarf, poised, not unaccustomed to Jewish cemeteries and funerals, he thought. This much Treslove had discovered: the Jewish faith frightened even Jews. Only a few were at home in all the ceremonials. This woman was not awed, even by death.

'Are you a relative?' Finkler asked. He wanted to tell her that the family had been and left, and that if she wanted to join them . . .

She stood, without difficulty, and shook her head. 'Just a long-time friend,' she said.

'Us too,' Treslove said.

'This is a very sad day,' the woman said.

She was dry-eyed. Dryer by far than Treslove. He couldn't have said how dry Finkler was.

'Heartbreaking,' he said. Finkler added his assent.

They found themselves walking away from the grave together. 'My name is Emmy Oppenstein,' the woman said.

The two men introduced themselves to her. There were no handshakes. Treslove liked that. The Jews were good at making one occasion not like another, he thought. The protocol alarmed him but he admired it. Good to divide this from that. Why is this night different from all other nights. Or *was* it good? They pursued difference to the grave.

'How long is it since either of you saw him?' Emmy Oppenstein enquired.

She wanted to know how he had been in the time before his death. She herself had not seen him for many months, but they had spoken on the phone a few times more recently than that.

'In the normal course of events you saw a lot of him, then?' Treslove asked. Annoyed for Malkie.

'No, not at all. In the normal course of events I saw him once every half century.'

'Ah.'

'I made contact with him again after all that time because I needed his help. I suppose I'm wanting to hear that I didn't put more pressure on him than he could bear.'

'Well, he never said anything,' Treslove told her. He wanted to add that Libor had never so much as mentioned her existence, but he couldn't be quite so cruel to a woman her age.

'And did you get his help?' Finkler asked.

She hesitated. 'I got his company,' she said. 'But his help, no, I don't think I can say he was able to give me that.'

'Not like him.'

'No, that was what I thought. Though of course after such a long time I was in no position to know what he was like. But it hurt him to refuse me, I thought. The strange thing was that it felt as though he wanted it to hurt him. And of course it saddens me deeply to think I was in some way the agency of his hurting himself.'

'We are all punishing ourselves with that sadness,' Finkler said.

'Are you? I'm sorry to hear that. But that's a natural thing for friends to feel. I hadn't been a friend for so long I have no right, and indeed *had* no right, to think of myself as one. But I needed a favour.'

She told them, in the end, what the favour was. Told them about the work she did, about what she feared, about the Jew-hatred which was beginning to infect the world she'd inhabited all her life, the world where people had once prided themselves on thinking before they rushed to judgement, and about her grandson, blinded by a person she didn't scruple to call a terrorist.

Both men were affected by the story. Libor was, too, she

said, but the last time she saw him he seemed to turn his back on it. That was the way of things, he had told her. That was what happened to Jews. Change your tune.

'Libor said that?' Treslove asked.

She nodded.

'Then he was in a worse way than I realised,' he said. The emotion which had been misting up his eyes ever since he had seen Libor's coffin lowered into the earth began to choke him.

Finkler, too, found it hard to find words. He remembered all the arguments he'd had with Libor on the subject. And it pleased him not at all that Libor had surrendered at the last. Some arguments you don't have in order that you will win.

Finkler and Emmy Oppenstein wished each other long life on parting. Hephzibah had told Treslove of this custom. At a funeral Jews wish one another long life. It is a vote for life's continuance in the face of death.

He turned to Emmy Oppenstein. 'I wish you long life,' he said, looking up.

6

Treslove, who has always dreamed, dreams that he is beckoned to a death chamber. The room is dark and smells. Not of death but food. The remains of lamb chops which have been left out too long. To be precise it is the sweet smell of lamb fat he can smell. Strange, because he recalls Libor saying that he could never bear to eat lamb as a consequence of adopting as a childhood pet a lamb which had nibbled grass in a field behind his house in Bohemia. 'Baaa,' the lamb had said to little Libor. And 'Baaa,' little Libor had said back. Once you've conversed with a lamb you can't eat it, Libor had explained. Same with any other animal.

In his dream, Treslove wonders what St Francis found to eat.

He doesn't doubt he has come to pay his last respects to Libor but dreads seeing him. He is afraid of the face of death.

To his horror, a weak voice calls him from the bed. 'Julian, Julian. A word . . . come.'

The voice is not Libor's. It is Finkler's. Faint, but decidedly Finkler's.

Treslove knows what he is going to hear. Finkler is playing their old clever-clogs schoolyard game. 'If thou didst ever hold me in thy heart,' he is going to say, 'absent thee from felicity awhile . . .'

And Treslove will say back, 'Felicity? Who's Felicity?'

He approaches the bed.

'Closer,' Finkler says. The voice strong suddenly.

Treslove does as he is told. When he is close enough to feel Finkler's breath, Finkler sits up and spits in his face, a violent stream of filth – phlegm, sour wine, lamb fat, vomit.

'That's for Tyler,' he says.

Treslove knows his way, by now, around his dreams. So he doesn't even bother to ask himself whether it was really a dream or just a vivid dread.

It was both.

Or whether the dread was half desire.

Aren't all dreads half desires?

He had begun to wake to the old sense of absurd loss again. Searching for the acute disappointment he felt and locating it in a sporting catastrophe: a tennis player he didn't care about losing to another tennis player he had never heard of; the English cricket team being defeated by an innings and several hundred runs on the Indian subcontinent; a football match, any football match, ending in a gross injustice; even a golfer losing his nerve on the final hole – golf a game he neither played nor followed.

It wasn't that sport allowed him to deflect his melancholy;

sport *spoke* for his melancholy. Its vanity of expectation was his vanity of expectation.

He had discerned something Jewish in this, an avid reaching after setback and frustration, like supporting Tottenham Hotspur as some of Hephzibah's Jewish friends did, but now he was not so sure.

He was seeing too many dawns. Dawns did not suit Treslove.

'What you'd prefer is a dawn that happens at about midday,' Hephzibah had joked when she first discovered his fear of them. She loved them herself and in their first months together would wake him to see. One of the advantages of her high-terraced apartment was that she could walk directly out of her bedroom and catch the wonderful panorama of a London dawn. It was a measure of how much he loved her that he would wake the moment she shook him and step out on to the terrace with her and gasp at the glory of it as he knew she wanted him to. The dawn was their element. Their creation. Treslove the new-born happy man and Jew. As long as the dawn broke all was well in their world. And not just their world. The whole world.

Well, the dawn still broke but their world was no longer well. He loved her no less. She had not disenchanted him. Nor he, he hoped, her. But Libor was dead. Finkler was dying in his dreams and, if appearances were anything to go by, putrefying in his life. And, he, Treslove, was no Jew. For which, perhaps, he should have been grateful. This was not a good time to be a Jew. Never had been, he knew that. Not even if you went back a thousand, two thousand years. But he had thought it would at least be a good time for *him* to be a Jew.

You can't, though, can you, have one happy Jew in an island of apprehensive or ashamed ones? Least of all when that Jew happens to be Gentile.

Now he was rising early not because Hephzibah woke him

to see the beauty of the daybreak but because he couldn't sleep. So these were reluctant, resented dawns. Hephzibah was right about their splendour. But not about their breaking. The verb was wrong. It suggested too sudden and purposeful a disclosure. From her terrace the great London dawn bled slowly into sight, a thin line of red blood leaking out between the rooftops, appearing at the windows of the buildings it had infiltrated, one at a time, as though in a soundless military coup. On some mornings it was as though a sea of blood rose from the city floor. Higher up, the sky would be mauled with rough blooms of deep blues and burgundies like bruising. Pummelled into light, the hostage day began.

Treslove, wrapped in a dressing gown, paced the terrace drinking tea that was too hot for him.

There was disgrace in it. He wasn't sure whose. Just the being part of nature, maybe. Just the not having got beyond its rising tide of blood after all these hundreds of thousands of years of trying. Or was it the city that was a disgrace? The illusion of civility it stood for? Its faceless indomitability, like the blank, mulish obstinacy of a child that wouldn't learn its lesson? Which one had swallowed up Libor as though he had never been, and would soon swallow up the rest of them? Who was to blame?

Alternatively, the disgrace was himself, Julian Treslove, who looked like everyone and everybody but was in fact no one and nobody. He sipped his tea, scalding his tongue. Such specificity as he sought – if someone as indeterminate as he was could ever be called specific – was unnecessary. The disgrace was universal. Just to be a human animal was to be a disgrace. Life was a disgrace, an absurd disgrace, to be exceeded in disgracefulness only by death.

Hephzibah heard him get up and go outside and didn't want to follow him. There was no longer any charm in sharing the dawn with him. You know when the person you're living with finds life disgraceful.

She would not have been human had she not asked herself whether it was her fault. Not so much what she had done as what she had failed to do. Treslove was another in a long line of men who needed saving. Were they the only men who came to her – the lost, the floundering, the dispossessed? Or was there no other sort?

Either way their demands wearied her. Who did they think she was – America? *Give me your tired, your poor . . . the wretched refuse of your teeming shore.* She looked strong and secure enough to house them, that was the problem. She looked capacious. She looked like safe harbour.

Well, Treslove, for one, had that wrong. She hadn't saved him. Perhaps he wasn't saveable.

Much of it was about Libor, she knew that. He had still not grasped it. For reasons she didn't understand, he appeared to blame himself. On top of which, quite simply, he missed Libor's company. Therefore she had no business barging in and asking, 'Anything I've done, honey?' The decent thing was to leave him alone for a while. She could use the privacy herself. She too was grieving. But still she wondered and was sorry.

On top of which, the museum . . .

She was growing increasingly anxious about the opening. Not because the building would still be unfinished – that didn't matter – but because the atmosphere was wrong. People wanted to hear less of Jews right now, not more. There are times when you open your doors, and there are times when you close them. Had there been only herself to consider, Hephzibah would have bricked the museum up.

All she could do was hope that the world would, on a whim, change its tune, that the ugly talk would somehow stop of its own accord, that a gust of fresh wind would blow clean away the deadly miasmas poisoning Jews and their endeavours.

So hope was what she did.

Head down, eyes lowered, fingers crossed.

Except that it wasn't in her nature to submit passively to events. She couldn't leave the matter where her masters, the philanthropic sponsors of the museum, wanted her to leave it. Again, she urged the badness of the timing. A postponement would be embarrassing, but not exactly unheard of. They could cite building delays. The economy. Somebody's ill health. *Her* ill health.

That would be no lie. She wasn't in good mental health. She was reading what it did her no good to read – the wild proliferation of conspiracy theory, Jews planning 9/11, Jews bringing down the banks, Jews poisoning the world with pornography, Jews harvesting body organs, Jews faking their own Holocaust.

Holocaust fucking Holocaust. She felt about the word Holocaust as she felt about the word anti-Semite – she cursed those who reduced her to wearing it out. But what to do? There was blackmail in the wind. Shut up about your fucking Holocaust, they were saying, or we will deny it ever happened. Which meant she couldn't shut up about it.

The Holocaust had become negotiable. She had recently run into her ex-husband – not Abe the attorney, but Ben the blasphemous, actor, raconteur and liar (funny how you no sooner ran into one unreliable ex-husband than you ran into another) – and had listened to him spin a hellish tale about his sleeping with a Holocaust denier and negotiating numbers in return for favours. He'd come down a million if she'd do this to him, but would want to put a million back in return for doing that to her.

'I felt like Whatshisname,' he told her.

'Give me a clue.'

'The one who had a list.'

'Ko-Ko?'

'Did I tell you I once played the Mikado, in Japan?'

'A thousand times.'

'Did I? I'm humiliated. But not him. The other list man.'

'Schindler?'

'Schindler, yes – only in my case I was saving those already exterminated.'

'That's foul, Ben,' she had said. 'That could be the foulest joke, no, those could be the foulest *two* jokes, I've ever heard.'

'Who's joking? That's the way of it out there now. The Holocaust has become a commodity you trade. There's a Spanish mayor who's cancelled his town's Holocaust Memorial Day because of Gaza, as though they're somehow connected.'

'I know. The implication being that the dead of Buchenwald only get to be memorialised if the living of Tel Aviv behave themselves. But I don't believe you.'

'What don't you believe?'

'That you slept with a Holocaust denier. Even you couldn't have done that.'

'I did it out of honourable motives. I hoped I might fuck her to death.'

'Why didn't you just strangle her without fucking her?'

'I'm Jewish.'

'It's allowed with Holocaust deniers. It's more than allowed, it's obligatory. The Eleventh Commandment – Thou shalt wring the necks of all deniers for denial is an abomination.'

'Probably is, but I also wanted to reform her. Like with hookers. You know me –'

'Still soft hearted –'

He'd have kissed her had she let him.

'Still soft-hearted,' he said.

'And did you?'

'Did I what?'

'Reform her.'

'No, but I got her up to 3 million.'

'What did you have to do for that?'

'Don't ask.'

She didn't tell her bosses the Ben story. You never knew what a Jew was or was not going to find funny.

As for the museum, it would open when they wanted it to open. You couldn't run scared. Not in the twenty-first century. Not in St John's Wood.

THIRTEEN

I

On mornings when the disgrace was too great to bear, and too insulting for poor Hephzibah to have to witness, Treslove put on a coat, left the apartment and walked through the park to Libor's place. He still called it Libor's place. There was no fancy in this. He didn't expect that he would see Libor at the window. But something of Libor remained harboured there, as he feared that something of his own disgrace still lingered on Hephzibah's terrace though in actual person he had left it.

At this time, Regent's Park was the property of joggers, dog owners and geese. The fowl all had their hour. In the early morning the geese were in possession, taking to the dry land with their beaks, pecking at the earth for what was theirs. Later on it would be the herons' turn, and then the swans' and then the ducks'. It would have been good, Treslove thought, had humans learned to apportion their lives similarly. Never mind fighting over land, simply parcel out the days. Muslims in the morning, Gentiles in the afternoon, Jews at night. Or some other ordering. It didn't matter who got when, only that they all got a part.

The park was the biggest outdoor space for thinking in London, bigger even than Hampstead where too many thinkers jostled with you for thought room. Some mornings Treslove believed he was the only person in the entire park thinking – simply thinking, not thinking while running, or thinking while walking a dog, but doing nothing but thinking. He would send his thoughts out at one end of the park and meet them again at the other, borne along by the otherwise unoccupied trees – as telegraph poles transmit the human voice. The same thoughts which he'd brought into the park waiting for him as he left it.

It was not purposeful thinking, it was just thinking. Reliving himself. Thinking meaning existing in his head.

And what then did these mornings of free, unimpeded thinking amount to?

Nothing.

Zero.

Gornisht.

He'd had a fancy when he'd first taken up with Hephzibah that they would walk together to the lake, sit on a bench for half an hour, watch the herons, talk about Jews and Nature – why the Bible was so light in natural description, why even Paradise was sketchy in the matter of vegetation etc. – and wait for Libor to join them. Whereupon, after much exchange of kisses, Hephzibah would leave to go to the museum and Libor and Treslove would stroll together arm in arm like a pair of elderly Austro-Hungarian gentlemen, swapping anecdotes in a Yiddish in which Treslove would by then have become wonderfully proficient. Later they would sit again on a bench by the lake and Libor would explain why Jews were so expert at living in the city. Treslove had lived in the metropolis all his life but did not 'exude' it as Libor did. As the geese were to Regent's Park lake, so was Libor to the streets around it. And yet he hadn't even been born here and mispronounced half the English words he used. Treslove not only wanted that skill explained, he wanted to be told how it could be acquired.

If this fancy was idle, only circumstance had made it so. Hephzibah being busy, Treslove being forgetful, the weather being inclement, and Libor being unwilling, unable and eventually vanishing from Treslove's life like an unheeded ghost. But he, Treslove, had wanted it intensely. It was to be a way of living. Not a path to a new way of living, though he saw himself emerging from it as a different person, but the new life itself. This is what it would consist of – the walks with Hephzibah and Libor in their demi-Eden, however unappreciated from the point of view of nature, a Jew on each arm and a Jew, of sorts, in the middle.

Well, the symmetry was broken now. But in truth it had only ever been Treslove's idea and no one else's. Only Treslove was looking for a way out or a way in. Libor had taken his. And Hephzibah had been happy where she was until Treslove had turned up to idealise her into misery.

So every walk in the park was now a memorial walk to the new life that had not materialised. Anyone observing him – though no one did observe him, because dog walkers care only for what's at the end of their leads and joggers care only for their heartbeat – would have taken him to be a man in mourning.

What they would not have known was how much and how many he was in mourning for.

What it was on this particular day that made him return to the park after he had completed his pilgrimage to Libor's – what made this day different from all other days – he couldn't have said. He had followed his usual course, rubbing at the itch of memory, coming out at the gate closest to Libor's apartment, where he would stand and look up for half an hour, identifying the windows with the rooms behind them, and the rooms with what he had done or seen in them: Malkie playing Schubert, the countless animated dinner parties, Libor's heavy furniture, Libor's initialled bedroom slippers, Libor and Finkler jousting over Isrrrae, seeing Hephzibah for the first time – 'Call me Juno if it would be easier for you'. He had only happy memories of Libor's apartment, no matter that he had shed many a tear there and been mugged a few hundred yards from it, for that, too, was a happy memory in that it had led more or less directly to Hephzibah.

What he would normally do then was walk briskly past the BBC, that rathole of a place of which he had not a single happy memory, linger a little outside the window of J. P. Guivier, breathe in the cigar smells that still clung to the brickwork of the street in which his father had had his shop, stop for coffee, indulge a little melancholy for the hell of it – too much time on his hands, that was the problem, too much waiting for whatever it was to happen – and eventually go home in a taxi. But today, the weather being more inviting than it had been for weeks, with great puffball clouds tumbling through the sky, he took twice the time to do all these things, decided he would have an expiatory lunch in the salt-beef bar where he had violated Libor's hearing, and then that he would return to the park and walk home slowly the way he had come. By mid-afternoon he was tired and surprised himself by snoozing on a bench like an old tramp. He woke with a neck ache, his chin bobbing on his chest. He had taken a circuitous route back, deliberately not hurrying, through a wilder stretch of park. He didn't normally like it here. It didn't feel like London, or it felt like the wrong London. It smelt of trouble, though all that ever happened was that Brazilian boys played thirty-a-side football against Polish boys and made a lot of noise.

It was noise that must have woken him. A crowd of school-children of all colours and sexes was shouting something he couldn't quite hear, but it wasn't a jumbled shout, it was the repetition of a phrase, the repetition itself being a sort of taunt. But who they were taunting he couldn't see either.

Nothing to do with him, and although he knew an adult no longer dared disperse a crowd of schoolchildren, no matter how great their mischief, because the chances were that at least one of them would be armed with a machete, he left the bench as though on business of his own – little as he knew of having business of his own – and tried to get a little closer to them.

Big mistake, he thought, even as he was making it.

In the middle of the circle of schoolchildren was a youth of about fifteen in a black suit, lanky, rather pretty in a Spanish and Portuguese way, with blue-black sidelocks, fringes spilling from his shirt, a boy's fedora on his head – no, not a boy's fedora, for there was nothing boyish about him, but a small man's fedora. That's what he was – a small Sephardic Jew. A holy man in all but age.

Revulsion swept through Treslove.

As, presumably, it had swept through the children. The phrase they were taunting him with was, 'It's a Jew!'

'It's a Jew!' they cried. 'It's a Jew!'

As though they had made a discovery. Look what's turned up, look what we've found, out of its natural habitat.

It.

The schoolchildren didn't look capable of a lynching. Not from the best of schools, Treslove calculated, but not from the worst of schools either. The boys didn't appear to be armed. The girls were not foul-mouthed. There was a limit to the menace. They wouldn't kill the boy. They would just prod him the way you might prod something foreign washed up on a beach. 'It's a Jew!'

The holy man in all but age – the holy boy – was distressed but not terrified. He, too, seemed to know they would not kill him. But this could not be allowed to continue, whatever he thought. Unsure how to proceed, Treslove looked around. A woman his age, walking a dog, caught his eye. This cannot be allowed to continue, her look said. Treslove nodded.

'Hey, what's going on?' the woman with the dog shouted.

'Hey!' Treslove shouted.

The schoolchildren weighed up the situation. Maybe it was the woman's dog that decided them. Maybe they just wanted to be shown a way out of this themselves.

'We're just messing about,' one of them said.

'Shoo!' the woman said, bringing her dog forward. It was only a terrier, with a bemused upper-class Bertie Wooster expression, but a dog's a dog.

'Shoo yourself,' one of the girls told her.

'Cunt!' shouted a boy, backing off.

'Hey!' Treslove shouted.

'We were only being friendly,' another girl said. She made it sound as though these two busybodies had gone and lost the Jew a whole new bunch of chums.

They broke up and withdrew, not all at once but a bit at a time, like the tide receding from the outlandish thing it had washed up. Left alone, the outlandish thing went on its way. He didn't thank the woman or Treslove or even the woman's dog. Probably against his religion, Treslove thought. But for a fleeting second Treslove caught his beautiful coal-black eye. The boy was not angry. Treslove wasn't even sure he'd been afraid. What Treslove saw in his face was accustomedness.

'You OK?' Treslove asked.

The boy shrugged. It was almost an insolent gesture. This is simply the way of it, the shrug said. Don't make a fuss. With maybe a touch of proud, God-protected, stand-offishness in it. He finds me an unclean thing, Treslove thought.

Treslove rolled his eyes at the woman. She did the same to him. Go figure these kids.

Treslove returned to the bench on which he'd been dozing earlier. He was, he discovered, shaking.

He couldn't get the phrase out of his head. *It's a Jew!*

But he was battling other phrases of his own. *Then why dress like that? Then why present yourself to them? And why couldn't you thank us? And why did you look at me as though to you I too am an 'it'?*

One of the girls had not run off with the others. She lingered, looking about her. Treslove had the dread thought that she was going to try to pick him up. Maybe offer him services for pocket money. He must have looked an easy touch, sitting on the bench, shaking.

She bent down, not looking at him, to take off her shoes. It was at that moment that he recognised her. She was the schoolgirl in his once recurring dream – once recurring before Hephzibah, that is – the schoolgirl who paused in her running to take off the shoes that impeded her – whether vulnerable or resolute in her pleated skirt, white blouse, blue jumper and artfully twisted tie, he had never been able to decide. The schoolgirl in a hurry of which he hadn't ever known if he would like to be the object.

'Why are you taking off your shoes?' he asked.

She surveyed him as though it would have been obvious to anyone but a moron why she was taking off her shoes: in order to scrape him off the bottoms.

'Freak!' she said, contorting her face at him, and then running off through the grass.

It's a freak.

Nothing personal, then. *It's a freak, it's a Jew.* Just whoever wasn't them.

Not worth anybody dying for.

Or was the opposite the truth: Not worth anybody living for?

3

It was early evening by the time he got back to the apartment. He'd needed a drink.

It was a good job that no fragile shiksa with a watery Ophelia expression had come into the bar in which he drank. He might have taken her back into the park and drowned them both.

The apartment was oddly quiet. No Hephzibah. He went looking for her. No Hephzibah in the kitchen, no Hephzibah sprawled out in the living room watching television and wondering where he'd been, no Hephzibah in the bedroom in an oriental housecoat and with a rose between her teeth, no Hephzibah in the bathroom. But he could smell her perfume. One of her wardrobe doors was open and there were shoes scattered on the floor. She had gone out.

Then, as though a stone had been thrown at his temples, he remembered. It was the museum night. The launch. The Grand Opening, as Hephzibah had refused to call it. Jesus Christ! They were meant to be there at five thirty, the doors opening for guests at six fifteen. Early had been Hephzibah's instruction. Early and brief. Get in, get out, attracting as little attention as possible. Even the invitations had been insignificant and posted late. Normally, as Treslove had observed to Hephzibah, Jews loved invitations. They were totemic, invariably embossed in gold Gothic lettering on thick slabs of card, over-enthusiastic in expression and sent out months in advance. Come to a party! Start thinking about a present! Start planning your wardrobe! Start losing weight! Hephzibah made sure her invitation was small and flimsy and crept into the world.

He had not promised her he would not be late. There was no need. He was never late. Most of the time he didn't leave the apartment. And he did not forget arrangements.

So why *was* he late, and why *had* he forgotten this arrangement?

He knew what Hephzibah would say. She would say he forgot because he wanted to forget. Not for her to reason why. Because he had fallen out of love with her, perhaps. Because he was irrationally jealous of his friend. Because he had begun to oppose the museum in his heart.

She had not left him a note. That, to Treslove, suggested a very high degree of anger and hurt. He had cut her out without a word; she would do the same.

He wondered if it was all over between them. Libor's

doing, if so. There are some events which make it impossible to go back to where you were. After Libor, who had brought them together, nothing. Not impossibly, that was his intention. Those whom I have joined together I will put asunder. Treslove sympathised with Libor's reasoning. Libor had discovered him to be a sneak and a fornicator and a braggart. He had fouled Finkler's nest and would foul Libor's via Hephzibah. What did he want with them, this cuckoo goy? Sucking at their tragedy because his own life was a farce. Go home, Julian. Go back to where you came from. Leave us in peace.

He sat on the edge of his bed, his head banging, agreeing with that judgement. His life *had* been a farce. Every element of it ludicrous. And yes, it was true, he had tried to nose his way into other people's tragedy and grandeur since he couldn't lay hands on any of his own. He had meant no harm or disrespect by it, quite the contrary; but it was theft all right.

'It's a Jew!' the schoolchildren had laughed, and Treslove had taken the taunt personally. It had been as a spear in his own side. But what, beyond the obligation as an adult to clip every one of the little *mamzers* round the ear, did any of it have to do with him? Why had he staggered from his park bench like a wounded beast, and gone looking for alcohol? To take away the pain of what?

Time for another goodbye, then. Why not? Goodbyes were what he had always been good at. What was one more?

He watched his life go in a variety of directions. It was like being drunk. Being drunk was like being drunk. Maybe he would lurch out of the door and never be seen again. Maybe he would pack a case and go back to his Hampstead flat which was not in Hampstead. Maybe he would throw on some clothes and dash over to the museum. 'Sorry, darling, am I in time for a last kosher canapé?'

One of those illusory fits of exhilaration to which purposeless men are susceptible seized him. The world was all before him, where to choose his place of rest. Lurching out of the door and vanishing was favourite. There was honour in it as well as wildness. Gifting Hephzibah his absence and gifting himself his liberty. Let's go, he thought. Let's be on our way. He would have punched the air had he been a man who punched the air.

But the sight of Hephzibah's shoes in a tangle touched him. He loved the woman. She had synced him up with the universe. She might not ever forgive him for what he'd done but he owed her, owed himself, owed them both, a second chance. He showered quickly, put on a black suit, and ran out.

The darkness shocked him. He checked his watch. Eight forty-five! How had that happened? It was just after seven when he got back from the park. Where had the time gone? Was it possible he had passed out on the bed, between imagining making a run for it, and remembering how much he loved her through her shoes? He must have. There was no other explanation. He had fallen asleep for the second time that day and not known it. He was not in charge of himself. Things happened to him. He was not the agent of his own life. He wasn't even living his own life.

It was only a ten-minute walk but it was fraught with dangers. The lamp posts were rearing up at him again. He imagined colliding with trees and pillar boxes. There was too much traffic on the road, all going too fast. Buses laboured up the incline. Behind them cars pulled out on nothing other than a hunch that it was safe for them to do so. Every bone in his body ached in anticipation of the impact.

He tried not to read the Arab graffiti on the walls of the Beatles' old recording studio.

It was about nine when he arrived at the museum. The lights were on in the building and a small number of people – perhaps a dozen – were congregated outside. Congregated was not, perhaps, the word. Congregation suggests intention and he wasn't sure there was any reason for these people to be there. He had half expected to see banners. *Death to Jewzs.* Cartoons of glutton-Yids devouring babies and Stars of David metamorphosing into swastikas. Such images were no longer even shocking. You could find them inside, or even on the covers of the most reputable publications. The streets had been full these last few weeks with stray demonstrators from Trafalgar Square and the Israeli Embassy, the human shrapnel of a deafening barrage of outrage, and Treslove would not have been surprised to see them here, hoping to get the attention of one or other of Hephzibah's important Jewish guests, an ambassador, an MP, a pillar of the community. *Stop the massacre. Condemn the carnage. Kill the Jewzs.* But everything appeared quiet and orderly. There wasn't even, as far as he could see, an ASHamed Jew come out to protest his hang-dog dissolidarity with his own people.

Finkler? Was Finkler in or out? Finkler hidden in the small crowd, biding his time, or in the building, Hephzibah's proxy escort since her real one had let her down?

It was a Finkler event. Sam had a more natural right to be inside than Treslove did.

He wasn't outside, anyway. These were just smokers, Treslove decided. Or people come out to get some air.

He walked around them to the entrance where a couple of security men asked to see his invitation. He didn't have it. There was no reason, he explained, for him to be carrying an invitation. He was not a guest. He was virtually the host.

Entrance was strictly by invitation only, they told him. No invitation, no party. He explained that it wasn't a party. It was a reception. See! – how would he know it was a reception and not a party if he was merely a stranger looking for trouble? He could tell them what was in every room. Go on, test me. Hephzibah Weizenbaum, the director of the museum, was his partner. Perhaps if someone could notify her he was here . . .

They shook their heads. He wondered if she'd warned

them not to let him in. Or maybe they smelt alcohol on his breath.

'Come on, guys,' he said, attempting to push past them, but non-aggressively, a sort of ironic sidle. The bigger of the two grabbed him by his arm.

'Hey!' Treslove said. 'That's assault.'

He turns in the hope of encountering a sympathetic face. Perhaps someone who recognises him and can vouch for the truth of what he's saying. But he finds himself looking into the wild eyes of the grizzled warrior Jew in the PLO scarf who parks his motorbike in the forecourt of the synagogue he can see from the terrace of Hephzibah's apartment. Ah, he thinks. Ah! He gets it. These people are not, after all, smokers or guests from the reception come out to take the air. They are holding a silent vigil. A woman is carrying a blown-up photo-graph of an Arab family. A mother, a father, a baby. Next to her, a man carries a candle. They themselves might be Arabs, but not all the party are. The grizzled biker in the PLO scarf, for example. He is not an Arab.

'So what's this?' Treslove asks.

They ignore him. No one wants trouble. The security man who grabbed Treslove's arm approaches him again. 'I'm going to have to ask you to move on, sir,' he says.

'Are you Jewish?' Treslove asks.

'Sir,' the security man says.

'I'm asking you a civil question,' Treslove says. 'Because if you're Jewish I want to know why you're allowing this demon-stration to go ahead. This is not an embassy. And if you're not Jewish I want to know what you're doing here at all.'

'It's not a demonstration,' the man holding the candle says. 'We're just here.'

'*You're just here.* I can see that,' Treslove says. 'But why are you just here? This is a Jewish museum. It's a place of study and reflection. It isn't the fucking West Bank. We're not at war here.'

Someone takes hold of him. He is not sure who. Perhaps two people take hold of him. They might be the security men, they might not. Treslove knows where this must end. He is not frightened. The Sephardic boy was not frightened, he will not be frightened. He sees the boy's weary, accustomed face. 'It's a Jew!' That's just the way of it. He sees the schoolgirl bending to tie her shoelace. 'Freak!'

He lashes out. He doesn't care who he hits. Or who hits him. He would like it to be, either way, the traitor in the PLO scarf. But if it isn't, it isn't. He has no desire, though, to hit an Arab. He hears shouting. He would like it if one of them pushed him up against a wall and said, 'You Ju!' It's heroic to die a Jew. If you have to die for something, let it be for being Jewish. 'You Ju,' and then the knife at your throat. That's what you call a serious death, not the shit Treslove's been doing all his life.

Something presses in his ribs but it's not a knife. It's a fist. He punches back. They are struggling now, Treslove and he is not sure who or how many. He hears a commotion, but it might be the commotion of his heart. He stumbles, losing his footing on the unlevel ground. Then he falls headlong. Headlights blind him. Suddenly his shoulder hurts. He closes his eyes.

When he opens them the Jew in the PLO scarf is bending over him. 'Are you all right?' he asks.

Treslove is surprised by the gentleness of his manner. He would have expected him to spit fire, like his motor bike.

'Do you know where you are?' His questions are almost doctorly. Is that what the madman is, Treslove wonders – an eminent Ju physician in a PLO scarf?

He stares up at him, wondering if he's been recognised as the glowerer from Hephzibah's terrace. Since this is Hephzibah's occasion the connection would not be difficult to make.

But if the biker does recognise him, he doesn't let on. 'Do you know your name?' he persists, still showing concern.

'Brad Pitt,' Treslove replies. 'What's yours?'

'Sydney.' His voice is cultivated and soothing. Patient. He takes off his scarf and makes a pillow of it for Treslove's head. 'You were lucky he had good brakes,' he says.

'Who?' Treslove asks, but doesn't hear the answer.

Rather than be beholden to Sydney, and whatever sickly cause of humane self-abnegation he serves by wreathing himself in the scarf of his people's enemies, Treslove wishes the brakes had not been so good.

Rather than be beholden to Treslove and the woman with the dog, had the young Sephardic Jew wished, likewise, to be left to his tormentors?

Funny thing, ingratitude, Treslove thinks, closing his eyes again. It's been a long day.

He is not badly hurt but the hospital keeps him in overnight. To be on the safe side. Hephzibah visits but he is sleeping. 'Don't wake him,' she says.

She believes he knows she's there but doesn't want to acknowledge her. She has become part of all that disgusts him. Like Libor, he wants out. She's wrong. But it doesn't matter. What she might be wrong about today she will be right about tomorrow.

EPILOGUE

Since Libor has no children, we will say Kaddish for him, Hephzibah and Finkler had agreed. As a non-Jew, Treslove was not permitted to recite the Jewish prayer for the dead and so had been excluded from their deliberations.

I am not a synagogue person, Hephzibah says. I cannot bear the business of who you can and who you cannot say Kaddish for, where and when you sit, let alone what is permitted to a woman and how that differs from one denomination of synagogue to another. Our religion does not exactly make it easy for you. So I will pray at home.

And she does.

For the dead and the dead to her.

For Libor she cries her eyes dry.

For Julian, because she cannot in her heart exclude Julian, she cries bitter tears that come from a part of her she doesn't recognise. She's cried for men she's loved before. But with them it was the finality of separation that pained her. With Julian it's different: was he ever there to feel separated from? Was she just an experiment for him? Was she just an experiment for her?

He'd told her she was his fate. Who wants to be somebody's fate?

It is less convenient for Samuel Finkler but perhaps more straightforward. He must go to his nearest synagogue and say the prayer he first heard on his own father's lips. *Yisgadal viyiskadash* . . . the ancient language of the Hebrews tolling for the dead. *May His great Name grow exalted and sanctified.* This he does three times a day. When the deceased is not a parent the obligation to say Kaddish ceases after thirty days rather than eleven months. But Finkler does not give up saying it after thirty days. No one can make him. He is not sure he will even give up saying it after eleven months, though he grasps the reasoning in favour of stopping: so that the souls of the unlamented dead might find their way at last to Paradise. But he doesn't think it will be his praying that prevents them getting there.

The beauty of the Kaddish, to his sense, is that it's non-specific. He can simultaneously mourn as many of the dead as he chooses.

Tyler at last, he doesn't know why. He thinks that Libor has somehow made that possible. Unloosed something.

Tyler whom he failed as a husband, Libor whom he failed as a friend.

Yisgadal viyiskadash . . . It's so all-embracing he might as well be mourning the Jewish people.

Not that he draws the line at Jews. Even Treslove gets a look in, a sideways glance of grief, though he is alive and well – as well as he ever can be – and presumably back working as a lookalike.

It's from Hephzibah, with whom he is in frequent contact, that Samuel Finkler takes his cue. Her sense of incompletion, of a thing not finished that might never have begun, becomes his sense. He never really knew Treslove either. And that too strikes him as a reason for lamentation.

There are no limits to Finkler's mourning.